KT-157-553

THE RAW SHARK TEXTS

THE RAW SHARK TEXTS

STEVEN HALL

CANONGATE

Edinburgh · New York · Melbourne

First published in Great Britain in 2007 by
Canongate Books Ltd, 14 High Street,
Edinburgh EH1 1TE

This paperback edition first published in 2007 by
Canongate Books

1

Copyright © Steven Hall, 2007
The moral right of the author has been asserted

British Library Cataloguing-in-Publication Data
A catalogue record for this book is available on
request from the British Library

.

ISBN 978 1 84767 024 3 (UK edition)
ISBN 978 1 84767 023 6 (Export edition)
UNSBN CF01 45712 092251 9 (Unspace edition)

Designed and typeset in Minion by Cluny Sheeler
Printed and bound in Great Britain by Clays Ltd, St Ives plc

www.canongate.net

X 000.000.027 4231

For Stanley Hall
1927-1998
A gentleman and a scholar

ONE

Some limited and waning memory of Herbert Ashe, an engineer of the southern railways, persists in the hotel at Adrogue, amongst the effusive honeysuckles and in the illusory depths of the mirrors.

Jorge Luis Borges

1

A Relic of Something Nine-tenths Collapsed

I was unconscious. I'd stopped breathing.

I don't know how long it lasted, but the engines and drivers that keep the human machine functioning at a mechanical level must have trip-switched, responding to the stillness with a general systems panic. *Autopilot failure – switch to emergency manual override.*

This is how my life started, my second life.

My eyes slammed themselves capital O open and my neck and shoulders arched back in a huge inward heave, a single world-swallowing lung gulp of air. Litres of dry oxygen and floor dust whistled in and snagged up my throat with knifey coughing spasms. I choked and spat through heaves and gasps and coughing coughing coughing heaves. Snot ropes unwound from my nose. My eyesight melted into hot blurs over my cheeks.

The shudder-hacking violence of no air then too much knocked me dizzy, sent the floor tilting away under my fingers. Static behind my eyes bacteria-swarmed dangerously towards another blackout and, snow-blind and shaking, I pushed my wet mouth down tight into the palms of my hands, trying to pull controlled, steady breaths through my fingers –

Slowly, slowly-slowly, the world began to reappear in sickly greens and thumping purples and after maybe a minute, it steadied itself into a shaky-solid kind of balance.

I wiped my hands on my jeans and gave in to a last scratchy cough before rubbing out the last of the tears.

Okay. Just breathe, we're okay.

I had no idea who or where I was.

This was no sudden revelation, no big shock. The thought had congealed itself under the gasping and the choking and even now, with my body coming back under control and the realisation fully formed, it didn't bring with it any big horror or fear. Against all that physical panic it was still a small secondary concern, a minor oddity at the corner of things. What mattered most to me – a million times more than anything – was air, breath, the easy lungfuls coming and going now. The beautiful, heavenly, angel-singing fact – I could breathe and that meant I would live. Pressing my forehead down into the wet carpet, I imagined breathing mile after mile of smooth blue savannah sky as the last of the shudders worked their way out of my body.

I counted to ten then I looked up from the floor. I propped up onto my elbows and when that seemed okay, all the way up onto my knees. I was kneeling at the foot of a double bed in a bedroom. A bedroom stocked with all the ordinary, usual things. There was a wardrobe in the corner. A bedside table with a collection of water glasses of varying ages and an alarm clock with red digital numbers – 4.34 p.m., a chest of drawers cluttered with deodorant cans and lids, a tub of multivitamins and the remains of a blue toilet roll, used right down to where the paper goes wrinkly, like bath fingers. All just normal bedroom things – but I didn't recognise any of them. None of it felt strange, but none of it was familiar either. It was all just there; unremarkable but alien *stuff*. The thought came that maybe I'd fallen and concussed myself, except nothing hurt. I felt around my skull to make sure, but no, nothing.

I climbed carefully up onto my feet but the new angle didn't do anything for my memory either. And that's when the first real stabs of worry started to land.

It isn't all coming back to me. I don't know any of this at all.

I felt that prickling horror, the one that comes when you realise the extent of something bad – if you're dangerously lost or you've made some terrible mistake – the reality of the situation creeping in through the back of your head like a pantomime Dracula.

I did not know who I was. I did not know where I was.

That simple.

That frightening.

I clamped my teeth together and turned around on the spot, three slow visual sweeps of the bedroom, my eyes touching and exploring every ordinary incidental thing and recognising absolutely none of them. I tried the same thing mentally – closing my eyes, searching around inside my head, feeling through the black for any familiar shape. But it was all just cobwebs and shadows; I couldn't find myself in there either.

I walked over to the bedroom window. The outside world was a long street and a facing row of terraced houses. There were regular lamp posts, irregular telegraph posts and the sounds of a distant busy road – constant car engine hum, truck bang-clatter and occasional bass box thump, but – I squashed my nose up against the glass and looked left and right – no people. It was a cloudy day, grey and edgeless. I felt edgeless too. I suddenly had an urge to rush out of the house shouting for help and running for as long as I could so someone would see me and acknowledge me as a real person and they'd call a doctor or somebody who could fit me back into my proper place, the way a clockmaker realigns all the tiny makings inside a broken watch. But I had an equally strong fear that if I did this, if I ran and shouted, no one would come, no one would see. I'd get to the end of this street only to find the traffic sounds were coming from an old tape player on the corner of an abandoned, litter-washed main road in an empty, deserted world.

No. Come on, that's not useful. I rubbed my palm heels against my eyes, pushed down the panic and tried to clear my head. Patting down my pockets I found a wallet. I fingered through cash, receipts, bus tickets and an empty book of stamps, then – a driver's licence.

I stared at the picture and the name on the card.

The man in the wardrobe mirror carefully touched his fingers over his thin cheeks, his nose, his mouth, his short crop of dirty brown hair. He was in his late twenties, tired, pale and a bit sickly looking. He frowned at me. I tried to read the history hidden inside the frown as he made it – *what kind of person wrinkles his forehead like that? what sort of life builds up a pattern of lines like those?* – but there was nothing to be seen that I could decode. The man was a stranger and his expressions were written in a language I couldn't begin to understand. We reached out to each other and our fingertips met, mine warm and oily, his cold and smooth and made only of coloured light bouncing off glass. I drew my hand back and called the reflection by his name. And he said the same thing back, but silently, just moving his lips:

Eric Sanderson.

Eric Sanderson. When I heard myself speak it, the name sounded solid and real and good and normal. It wasn't. It was a ruin of loose masonry, broken windows and flapping blue tarpaulin sheets. It was a derelict. A relic of something nine-tenths collapsed.

•

"I imagine you have a lot of questions, Eric."

I nodded.

"Yes." *Yes?* It was difficult to know what to say. It was difficult to say anything. Despite the fear and the memory blindness, my overwhelming feelings were of embarrassment; incapacity, the stupidity of myself and my situation. How could I sit here and ask this stranger to help me pick up the facts of my life? The shopping bags had burst and all my things were rolling out over a packed pavement with me scurrying after them, stooping and bumping and tripping: *Excuse me. I'm sorry. Excuse me. Could you just . . . Excuse me.*

It was one hour and five minutes after I'd opened my eyes on the bedroom floor.

"Yes," the doctor said. "I appreciate this isn't at all easy for you. It must be terribly unsettling. You *are* doing very well though and you should try to relax if you can."

We were sitting in a green leafy conservatory on big cushioned wicker chairs, a small wicker and glass coffee table with cups of tea between us and a small brown dog sleeping under one of the potted cheese plants by the door. All very informal, very laid back.

"Would you like a biscuit?" The doctor's big face tipped towards the plate of chocolate digestives.

"No." I said. "No thanks."

She nodded at this, took two for herself and placed them one on top of the other, chocolate side to chocolate side, and then dunked them into her tea, her heavy eyes coming back to me whenever this procedure allowed.

"Awful, I know," she said.

Dr Randle was more like an electrical storm or some complicated particle reaction than a person. A large clashing event of a woman whose frizzy hack job of white-brown hair hummed against a big noisy blouse which, in turn, strobed in protest against her tartan skirt. She had strontium grey eyes which crackled away to themselves behind baggy lids. She made the air feel doomy, faintly radioactive. You half expected your ears to pop.

I looked away as she finished her mouthful of biscuit.

I couldn't bring myself to start this conversation and she seemed almost as uncomfortable with the silence as I did. "Well. We should get the big things out of the way first and then we can go from there."

I nodded.

"Right then." She thunderclapped her hands. "What I believe you've been experiencing is memory loss caused by what we call a dissociative condition."

Having almost everything to ask often means there's nothing you *can* ask – no single question which, if asked before all the others, won't seem like a ridiculous place to start. And I felt ridiculous enough. And lost. And ashamed. So I just sat there.

"Dissociative," I said. "Okay."

"Yes. What this means is there is nothing physically wrong with you. Physically, there are no problems at all."

In setting it out like this of course, she was actually highlighting something else, the one thing she wasn't saying. It made me think of that old Peter Cook sketch: *I've got nothing at all against your right leg. The trouble is – neither have you.*

"You're telling me I'm crazy?"

Randle steepled her index fingers. "What you have is an injury. People suffer injuries of a million different kinds every day. It just that the injury you've suffered happens to be a . . . non-physical one."

She skirted around the word *mental.* Swerved around it, in fact.

"Okay," I said.

"The really good news is you *don't* have any kind of degenerative condition or sickness that could be causing permanent damage to your brain. You're fine physically and that means there's no reason why you can't make a complete recovery."

"So this is a temporary thing?"

The hard frozen *don't know* time I'd been living since I opened my eyes on the carpet seemed to split a little. A warm splash of relief hit me under the ribs.

"I believe so," the doctor smiled a reined-in smile. It reined in my relief too.

"But?"

"But we're probably looking towards the long term, I'm afraid."

"How long-term?"

She held up a gentle *put on the brakes* hand. "I think we might be getting ahead of ourselves. I'll answer all your questions as honestly as I can, but before we get too deep into this, there's something very important you need to hear. I think it's best if you hear it now, at the beginning."

I didn't say anything. I just sat squeezing my cold sweaty-wet hands together in my lap, waiting for whatever life I was about to be given.

"There was an accident, Eric. I'm sorry to tell you your partner was killed."

I just sat, blank.

"It happened in Greece. An accident at sea."

Blank.

"Does any of this sound familiar?"

Nothing.

"No."

All of it, everything, it suddenly made me feel very sick. Stupid, inhuman and sick. I rubbed the sides of my nose with my finger and thumb. I looked up. I looked away. The questions were hot and prickly as I asked them, two grabbed stupidly and randomly from thousands. "Who was she? What did she do?"

"Her name was Clio Aames and she was training to be a lawyer."

"Was it my fault? I mean – was there anything I could have done?"

"No, it was an accident. I doubt there was anything anyone could have done."

"Are there arrangements? Things I need to be doing now?" I came to these things as I said them. "Family? The funeral? Who's taking care of that?"

Dr Randle's heavy eyes pressed down on me from behind her cup. "Clio's memorial service has already happened. You organised a wake for her yourself."

I sat very still.

"Why don't I remember any of this?"

"We'll get to that."

"When?"

"Well, would you like to talk about it now?"

"No, I mean *when* did I organise it?"

"Clio died just over three years ago, Eric."

All the gathered, clutched-at and recently bolted-together facts of my life snapped, sheared and collapsed under my weight.

"I've been waking up without a thing in my head for three years?"

"No, no," Dr Randle came forward, big blotchy forearms on big tartan knees. "The condition you have, well, I'm afraid it's quite unusual."

•

When I left the bedroom I found myself on a small landing. I saw a second door but it was locked so I made my way downstairs.

The threadbare staircase led to a thin hallway with a front door at the far end. Next to the front door was a hallstand table and on the hallstand table was a big blue envelope, propped up and facing the stairs so I couldn't miss it. On the front of the envelope were big black felt-tip words: THIS IS ADDRESSED TO YOU, and underneath, OPEN NOW.

As I got nearer, I saw the envelope was only the most obvious of a cluster of objects arranged on the table. To the left was a telephone. A Post-it note stuck across the buttons had a biro arrow pointing at the receiver and the words: SPEED DIAL 1 – USE ME. To the right, a set of car keys; to the right of them, a Polaroid of an old yellow Jeep; and to the right of that, another Post-it, this one saying: DRIVE ME. A brown battered leather jacket hung from a hook on the stand.

I opened the envelope and found two sheets of paper – a typed letter and a hand-drawn map. This is what the letter said:

> Eric,
>
> First things first, stay calm.
>
> If you are reading this, I'm not around anymore. Take the phone and speed dial 1. Tell the woman who answers that you are Eric Sanderson. The woman is Dr Randle. She'll understand what has happened and you will be able to see her straight away. Take the car keys and drive the yellow Jeep to Dr Randle's house. If you haven't found it yet, there's a map in the envelope – it isn't too far and it's not hard to find.
>
> Dr Randle will be able to answer all your questions. It's very important that you go straight away. Do not pass go.

Do not explore. Do not collect two hundred pounds.

The house keys are hanging from a nail on the banister at the bottom of the stairs. Don't forget them.

With regret and also hope,

The First Eric Sanderson

I read through the letter a couple more times. *The First Eric Sanderson.* What did that make me?

I took the jacket from the stand and picked up the map. The door keys were hanging just where the letter said they'd be. I called the number.

"Randle," a voice said.

"Dr Randle?" I pushed the car keys into my pocket. "This is Eric Sanderson."

•

Dr Randle came back into the conservatory with more tea and biscuits and a box of tissues on a tray. The brown dog under the cheese plant lifted its head, sniffed in a sleepy, going-through-the-motions sort of a way, then closed its eyes again.

"Dissociative disorders," Randle descended slowly into her creaking wicker chair, "are quite uncommon. They sometimes occur in response to severe psychological trauma, blocking out memories which are too painful or difficult for the mind to deal with. A circuit breaker for the brain, you could say."

"But I don't feel like I've forgotten anything," I said, fumbling around again inside my head. "It's just, there's nothing there. I mean, I don't think I feel anything about that girl. I don't even –" I put my palms out in a gesture of emptiness and scale.

The Randle nebula shifted, strobed, stretched and rolled in on itself until a big meaty hand with a tissue in it was patting my knee.

"The first few hours are always difficult for you, Eric."

"What does that mean?"

"Well, as I said, your condition, I don't like to use the term unique, but it's quite distinctive in several –"

"How many times have we done this, Doctor?"

She didn't even stop to think about it.

"This will be your eleventh recurrence," she said.

•

"In the majority of cases, dissociative amnesias occur and resolve relatively quickly. Generally speaking, it's the trigger event, the traumatic incident causing the condition, which is forgotten. Sometimes, the memory loss can be –" Dr Randle made a vague circle with her hand "– more general, but not often. A single recurrence of any kind is very, very unusual."

"And eleven is off the charts."

"Yes. These things are rarely black and white, Eric, but even so, I have to tell you –" she cast around for the right words, and then gave up.

"I see," I said, scrunching the tissue.

Randle seemed to be thinking. The heaviness lifted for a few seconds as she turned her thoughts inwards. When she looked back over at me, her forehead knotted up.

"You haven't had any urge to pack up and leave, have you?"

"Leave?" I said. "And go where?"

"Anywhere. There's a very rare condition which we call fugue –"

"What?"

"It means 'flight'. People suffering from it do just that; they take off, run away. From their lives, from their identities, from everything." She made a vanished-in-a-puff-of-smoke gesture. "They just go. Before we go on, are you sure you haven't felt a desire to do anything like that?"

"I don't think so," I said, trying the idea for size. "No. I don't think

I want to go anywhere."

"Good. Can you give me a line from *Casablanca*?"

"Sorry?"

"A line from *Casablanca*."

I was in danger of being seriously left behind but I did what I was told.

"'Of all the gin joints in all the world, she has to walk into mine.'"

"Good," Randle nodded. "And who says that?"

"Bogart. Rick. The character or the actor?"

"It doesn't matter. Can you picture him saying it?"

"Yes."

"Is the film in colour or black and white?"

"It's black and white. He's sitting with a drink at –"

"And when was the last time you saw *Casablanca*?"

My mouth opened and an almost-sound happened in the back of my throat. But I didn't have an answer.

"You see? All that seems to be missing, Eric, is you. And that's a typically fugue-like state of affairs, I'm afraid." Randle thought for a minute. "The truth is, I'm reluctant to pin this down with a final diagnosis. So much about your case is unusual. For instance, your amnesia didn't even begin on the night of the accident. You appear to have shown no symptoms at all for almost twelve months."

"And how unusual is that?"

Dr Randle lifted her eyebrows.

"Right."

"When it finally happened, your memory loss related only to a single night – the night of the accident in Greece. You received three months of regular treatment for amnesia and you were even making some progress, but then you suffered your first recurrence."

"Which means?"

"You suddenly lost more memories." She left a break for me to take this in. "All the memories of your holiday in Greece had become patchy and there were little holes in memories from other parts of your life too, some of them quite unrelated."

Little holes. Little bits missing. Things nibbled away here and there.

"And the holes kept getting bigger?"

"I'm afraid so. With each recurrence, you remembered less."

I could feel the empty space inside me, in my skull, in my guts.

"And now here I am with nothing."

"I know it doesn't feel like it at the moment, Eric, but you have to keep focused on the fact that none of your memories are really lost. What you are suffering from – whatever the peculiarities of your case – is a purely psychological condition. It's a type of memory suppression, not actual damage. Everything is still in your head somewhere and, one way or another, it will start to come back from wherever you've hidden it. The trick will be in working out what's triggering the recurrences and finding a way to defuse it."

I nodded blankly.

"I think that's enough for today," Randle said. "It's a lot for you to take in all at once, isn't it? Perhaps you should go home now, try to get some rest. Shall we meet up again tomorrow evening?"

"Yes. Sure." They ached; my eyes ached. I started to push myself up on the wicker chair arms.

"Oh, before you go – one more thing."

I stopped.

"Okay," I said, for the hundred-thousandth time.

"In the past, you've written and left letters for yourself to be read after a recurrence. I must ask you – and this is very important now, Eric – under no circumstances write or read anything like this. It could be incredibly destabilising for you, possibly even leading to another –"

Something on my face gave me away. She stopped mid-sentence and chased my reaction.

"Has something like this happened already?"

"No." It was a knee-jerk, *things are complicated enough* thing to say, nothing to do with what would be the best or not the best thing to do. Was it even really a lie? I smoothed over the bumps deciding

I'd think about it later: "Well," I said. "There was a note by the front door telling me to phone you and how to get here, just that kind of thing."

Half true. Less than half true: *Good luck and sorry. The First Eric Sanderson.*

"Of course," she said. "You should leave that in place in case you ever need it again. But please – if you should come across anything else, bring it straight to me. *Don't* read it. I know what I'm asking you to do is difficult, but if I'm going to be able to help you, this is very, very important. Okay?"

"Yes," I said. "Sure," I said. "No problem."

2

Kitchen Archaeology and Second Post

*In the deep dark, in the thousand-fathom black waters
of ancestral memory and instinctive unconscious,
where old gods and primitive responses float invisible
and gigantic, something moves. The dust debris on
the ocean floor, sediment a million years still, lifts and
swirls in its wake*

s

H

u

c   o

he
it   m

p

lo   o
a
r
Aust   habilis

I woke in a jump of panic, flailing around inside my head, but I could still remember. The bedroom carpet, Randle, her wicker chairs, the yellow Jeep, the house. Just one evening of memories, but it was enough to know it hadn't happened again, I was still the same person I'd been the night before. I was lying on the sofa. I'd fallen asleep almost as soon as I'd got back from Dr Randle's and the TV was still on, all colourful, cheerful and breezy and not at all worse for wear after such a long shift. I sat up and rubbed my eyes. Breakfast television presenters with sculptured hair were talking to an American sitcom actor who'd just done the voice of an animated lion in a new film. I wondered how long a TV would carry on with this sort of thing if left on its own in an empty room and it bothered me that the answer was *probably forever*.

This wasn't my house. Being there, having made myself at home, it felt dangerously wrong. I was the tired burglar who'd stopped burgling for a quick forty winks and opened his eyes to see it was morning. I half expected the sound of the front door opening, for someone to walk in with bags of shopping or an overnight case, to stop in the doorway, look at me and scream. Only – it *was* my house. Eric's house. Remember it or not, I was home and even if I spent the next hundred years tensed up on the sofa listening for a key in the lock, nobody at all was going to come. I decided the only way to shake these feelings would be to explore, to get to know all the rooms and spaces and things on my own terms. I'd have to break the ice. Breakfast would be a good start. In spite of everything, I was starving.

The fridge was well stocked with all the makings of a full English. I clicked on the grill, found some plates, found the cutlery drawer on the third try. Then it hit me like a little void in the stomach:

I have a condition. A disorder.

What was that going to mean?

Randle said I didn't need to worry about work and that I had a 'quite sturdy' bank account. I'd found what was probably my PIN written on a little piece of paper in my wallet behind a video rental card, so there was no immediate crisis there. She also said I'd broken all contact with my family and friends not long before coming to her for treatment. Whatever the *First Eric Sanderson's* reasons for doing this, I made up my mind to undo it. I'd dig out his address book and make contact with my mum or my dad or whoever counted as important in my life.

I have a condition.

I peeled off a couple of rashers and slithered them over the chromy bars of the grill, saying it a couple more times to myself, trying to take it in. *I have a condition. I have a psychological disorder.* It was too big, too much for one person alone in an empty and unfamiliar house to deal with. I'd find an address book, contact numbers. I'd make contact with my old life by the end of the day. I leant back against the sink and watched the bacon start to cook.

I noticed little lived-in things. The limescale on the kettle, the half-used bottle of washing-up liquid. The couple of pieces of dried pasta in the gap between the fridge and the kitchen units. All the marks of use. Recent habitation. Signs of life. I was searching the cupboards for a tin of baked beans when I came across a packet of Penguin biscuits. There were two missing. I knelt there for a few minutes just looking at the packet sitting on top of tins of spaghetti hoops and chopped tomatoes, looking at the torn flappy plastic end. The me who had eaten those biscuits had been real and alive and here, living in this house. He'd been in this kitchen only yesterday, probably cooking just like I was today. The food he made was still working its way through my body. It all happened here in this room so recently and now he was gone. It's a stark thought that when we die most of us will leave behind uneaten biscuits, unused coffee, half toilet rolls, half cartons of milk in the fridge to go sour; that everyday functional things will outlive us and prove that we weren't ready to go; that we weren't smart or knowing or heroic; that we were just animals whose animal bodies stopped working without any sort of schedule or any consent from us.

Except.

Except nobody had died here yesterday.

There was no him or me. These were *my* biscuits that *I'd* been eating. There was only one Eric Sanderson and I was still standing there, in my house, in my kitchen, with my breakfast sizzling under the grill. I knew this to be the unarguable logic of the situation and I tried to bring myself back to it again and again, but the idea felt hollow and fragile and thinly spun out over a deep black space. I knew nothing about Eric Sanderson. How the hell could I claim to be him?

•

I ate my breakfast in front of the still-chattering TV and made a mental list of the things I wanted to find in the house. The list went like this:

- Address book to contact family/friends and tell them what had happened.
- Photographs/photograph album. I needed to see my past life. I needed to see a picture of me with the girl who died in Greece.
- I remembered there had been a locked door upstairs, next to the bedroom I'd woken up in. I'd find the key to the door and see what was so important that it had to be locked away *inside* the house.

I started off gently in the living room, picking things up, looking at them, trying to form some sort of connection; taking the time to read the title of every book in the bookcase, swapping a few around so the existing random order became my random order; going through the papers in the magazine rack; getting on my knees and looking at the wires coming out of the back of the TV and at the dust and chips on the skirting boards. Trying to get intimate, make the space familiar from every angle. Going through drawers and taking out the objects inside one by one.

After maybe two hours of exploring I still hadn't found any of the items on my list. No address book, no key, not a single photograph or photograph album. The more time passed and the more rooms I explored – the front room, the bedroom – the more I started to realise there were other things missing: I wasn't finding any letters or bank statements or bills, not even junk mail. Not a single thing with my name on it lying around or tucked away or lost under the sofa or bed or down the back of the chest of drawers. Nothing. And nothing that could be connected with Clio Aames. The gathering shock of all this, the level of sanitisation and control it implied, hit me pretty hard. I was frightened and I was hurt. What started as a careful, inquisitive, getting-to-know-you search began to derail itself, barrelling out of control into something hot and aggressive – a violent hunt for my own reference material. Soon, I was tipping out drawers, dissecting storage boxes and magazine stacks, raking out cupboards, gutting the wardrobe. I cried, red with tear-wet frustration, scrambling, searching, scattering. And when each anger charge inside me was drained and empty, I'd find myself coming to a stop in the debris I'd created and gulping over the fatter tears of *totally adrift* despair, or, as more time passed, falling into one of those periods of blank stillness that come from overspending on emotion. Still I didn't find anything. No photographs. No papers. No letters. Every accessible space in the house lay completely open and there was not a single solid trace of me or my past there at all.

All this only brought me full circle, of course. Now I knew where these things were being kept. I'd realised earlier I think but instead of stopping me, the realisation only drove me into the search harder, wanting to *prove* the cruelty of it all by laying the rest of the house bare. *And when there is absolutely nowhere else these things can be*, I'd been telling myself, pulling out boxes and folders and tipping them empty, *I will go upstairs and I will kick down that locked fucking door.*

But I didn't. When it came to it, after hours of tipping, sifting and scattering, the rage I had left wasn't fresh enough or hot enough. Now there was a smoky curl of caution where all that destructive fear and hurt had been. I stood on the landing with my hand palm-flat on the locked door and I let myself sink to my knees, all tired and used-up, my fingertips dragging down in squeals against the white gloss paint.

Empty spaces, barriers, caution and willpower, this was the game I'd been born into. The trick, as Randle suggested, would be in knowing which barriers could be kicked open for progress and which were defensive, structural. Which ones were actually shoring everything else up.

·

It took the rest of the morning to tidy up the wreckage. By now, the post-crisis stillness had complete control of me and I moved through the house straightening, replacing and aligning at half-speed, eyes unfocused, sliding between the rooms like a ghost on pulleys.

Just after twelve there was a sound in the hallway. I straightened up and stood very still and very quiet. I'd been putting clothes back in the wardrobe when it happened and when I went to investigate I carried two shirts downstairs with me, not really aware of having them in my hands. There was a big A4 envelope sitting on the doormat. My name and address were written across the front in black felt-tip.

I'd ripped it open and got two lines into the letter inside before my brain finally came up to speed and I realised I shouldn't be reading it, that I'd been asked not to read anything like this. But by then it was too late; my eyes were already being information-dragged, skip-reaching towards the end –

Letter #1

Eric,

Whatever Dr Randle may have told you, I am not coming back. Nothing is coming back. It is all gone forever and I am sorry for that.

This is the first of a series of letters I have created to help you survive your new life. You will get these letters at regular intervals. Sometimes every day and for several months. The process is automated. The key to the second bedroom will be posted to you soon. For your own wellbeing, please don't try to get into the room before then.

This is what's next. You have a very important choice to make. Dr Randle has told you what she thinks is happening to you. She has probably asked you not to read any correspondence from me. I arranged for Dr Randle to be your first contact because I knew you would have lots of questions. Questions need a face-to-face dialogue and I cannot do that for you for obvious reasons. However, I must tell you that Dr Randle's viewpoint concerning your memory loss will prove unproductive at best. She is wrong about what is happening to you, Eric. More important, she can neither help nor protect you. I know this from experience. On the other hand, if you can bring yourself to trust me enough to continue to read these letters, you will learn to negotiate the dangers which – thanks to the stupidness of my own actions – you will soon encounter. I realise I am hardly in a position to convince you of anything at this stage. The decision is yours to make and until your identity starts to establish itself in the wider world, you will be safe to consider your options. I'm afraid your thinking time after that will be limited.

There is a second envelope inside this envelope labelled RYAN MITCHELL. Please read the information enclosed carefully and save in your memory as much of the text as you can. I ask that you do this even if you do decide to disregard all of my further communications.

The information will be important in case of emergency.

You do not have long to make your decision. Please think carefully.

With regret and also hope,

The First Eric Sanderson

I pushed my hand into the envelope and found a second, chubby package marked just as I, he, the First Eric Sanderson said it would be. RYAN MITCHELL.

I wandered through the living room, into the kitchen and back into the living room again re-reading the letter. *She can neither help nor protect you. I know this from experience.*

The afternoon sunlight drew a bright stretched rectangle on the carpet and a small bird sang on the TV aerial of the house opposite mine. I heard the sound of a car a couple of streets away, growing quieter and quieter with distance. The fractures in this broken world spread out under my feet.

·

At 3.30 p.m. on the second day of my second life, a big ginger tomcat arrived in the kitchen. He hauled his heavy self in through the open window, stepped across the worktops and planted himself down solid in the middle of the floor. Then he just sat there, staring up at me with round cynical eyes. I stared back, surprised. I thought he might run if I tried to get too close but he didn't budge at all, he just kept on looking at me as I knelt down to read his collar tag. There was a name – *Hello! I'm Ian* – and a full address, although the first line told me everything I needed to know.

I had a housemate.

"So, slugger," I smiled. "Where have you been hiding?"

The cat just looked at me.

I tried again: "Are you hungry?"

The cat just looked at me.

"Hmmm," I said, stepping back. "What kind of a name is Ian for a cat anyway?"

And the cat just looked at me, his big ginger face managing to do bored, irritated and smug all at the same time. He looked at me as though I was being very stupid indeed.

3

My Heart was Deep Space and My Head was Maths

Every single cell in the human body replaces itself over a period of seven years. That means there's not even the smallest part of you now that was part of you seven years ago.

Everything is changing.

In the early days of my second life I noticed how the shadow of a telegraph pole would inch between the gardens of two houses across the street – from 152 to the garden of 150 – over the course of several hours, from lunchtime into evening. After watching this a few times I did the maths: the shadow movement from one garden to the next meant that both houses, the telegraph pole, the street, all of us, had travelled one thousand, one hundred and sixty miles around the earth with the turning of the planet. We'd also travelled about seventy-six thousand miles through space around the sun in the same period and much much further as part of the wider spiralling of the galaxy. And nobody noticed a thing. There is no stillness, only change. Yesterday's *here* is not today's *here*. Yesterday's *here* is somewhere in Russia, in a wilderness in Canada, a deep blue nowhere out in the middle of the Atlantic Ocean. It's behind the sun, it's in deep space, hundreds of thousands, millions of miles left behind. We can never wake up in the same place we went to sleep in. Our place in the universe, the universe itself, it all changes faster and faster by the second. Every one of us standing on this planet, we're all moving forwards and we're never ever coming back. The truth is, stillness is an idea, a dream. It's the thought of friendly, welcoming lights still shining in all the places we've been forced to abandon.

"What?"

"No." Dr Randle wore a green jumper with red stags or reindeers on it and brown tweedy cross-check trousers. "It's just – you never mentioned having a cat before."

"Well, I've got one now. When I left he was sitting on the sofa watching *Richard and Judy*."

"That's interesting."

"Is it?"

"You said he had your name and address on his collar?"

"No, *his* name and *my* address. Do you think it's someone's idea of a joke?"

"Hmmm . . . it wouldn't be much of a joke, would it?"

"No, suppose not. Maybe someone's taken to palming animals off on me because they know I won't realise they're not mine." I was trying to be funny. It wasn't working.

"I can't see that, Eric. And, anyway, you said he's fond of you?"

"No. God, no, not fond. He's not frightened of me though."

"Well, maybe he's just new. It's possible that you got him before your last recurrence and never had the chance to mention him to me."

"He doesn't look very new. He's quite old and miserable looking."

Randle laughed. I'd not heard her do this before. The sound came in somewhere between a horse and a Catherine-wheel.

"Well," she said, "I'm happy he's keeping your spirits up, wherever he came from. What's his name?"

"Ian."

"Oh," she said.

"Yeah, I know."

I'd decided not to take the letter from the First Eric Sanderson along to my second meeting with Dr Randle. I'd begun a lie by denying what I'd found on the hallstand table on the first day of my life and – partially – it was easier to carry on than to backtrack to the truth. The other part? You could call it a wait-and-see attitude. I'd decided not to open any more of the letters if more came, but I'd also decided not to tell Randle about them for the time being. This seemed to be dead centre of the situation to me, completely middle of the road. I would be following the important part of the Doctor's instructions without actually turning the letters over. I knew the letters might help Randle cure my illness, but. But but but. Can I explain this? It was just too soon – I'd not been in the world long enough to be comfortable with so much blind trust in her diagnosis. The letter from the hallstand table, the second letter that arrived a few hours ago, and any future unopened ones, they would all go into a cupboard in the kitchen and be left there until such a time as I felt ready to hand them over. I thought, *after a couple more sessions, when I'm comfortable, when I've found my feet, then I'll come clean.*

As soon as I could get off the topic of Ian the cat, I asked Randle about my family and friends. She said she knew nothing about them.

"Nothing?" I said. "How can you know nothing?"

"I don't know anything, Eric," she said, "because you'd never tell me anything."

"But didn't you think that would be relevant? Useful?"

"Of course I did, but my hands were tied."

"By me?"

"Yes. Who else?"

Apparently the First Eric Sanderson made a decision to completely isolate himself from his old life before the onset of his illness. He had been unwilling to discuss the possibility of contact even after his condition began to worsen, remaining convinced that he needed a completely clean slate if he was *ever going to deal with things from Greece.* I got the impression this had been intriguing to Randle. She talked more about rare conditions and dissociative fugue, and called Eric's decision to sever all ties to his old life *a very interesting precursor.* I asked if she hadn't thought the family should be contacted when things started to get worse with Eric's condition. (I was careful to say 'my condition' out loud.)

"Perhaps I haven't been clear enough about the nature of our relationship," Dr Randle said in answer to this. "You are here on your terms, not on mine. I only do what you give me permission to do."

"But I was sick. I mean, no offence, but why didn't I have a proper doctor?"

"I am a proper doctor, Eric."

"Come on," I said. "You know what I mean."

"I'm afraid I'm not quite sure what you're suggesting. What we're doing, everything that's happening here, it's what you've chosen. This is how you wanted it. I do believe I can help you, but if you don't want to do things this way anymore, that's fine. Of course that's fine. You're completely free to take yourself to a GP or to the hospital. You always have been." She said all this in a pleasant this-is-impartial-advice tone but it was easy to feel the radioactivity spike in the room. The collar of my T-shirt itched dry against my neck.

I had a horrible gut worry about Randle humouring the First Eric Sanderson, bending too easily to his wants for complete isolation in order to keep exclusive discovery rights on the unusual things happening inside his head. Eric didn't want any contact with his family, but in the end, was he of sufficiently sound mind to make that decision? I'm not sure what I thought Randle should have done, but her attitude seemed distant and wrong. The whole thing felt, no, not sinister, but at least coldly academic. Or maybe I just wished things were different and I had someone looking after me as I tried to come to terms with it all. For now at least, I was on my own.

Or was I? As Randle rattled on in defence of her pricked ethics, I ran through my options. Maybe there was an address book full of contact numbers in the locked room back at the house and all I had to do was force my way inside and get it. But then maybe it wasn't safe for me to open that door. Maybe whatever had been triggering *the condition* was locked away in there too. What would happen if, next time I woke up on the floor, I couldn't remember how to speak, or how to walk? Or how to breathe? Perhaps there was contact information inside the still unopened RYAN MITCHELL envelope the First Eric Sanderson had sent through the post. *'It will be useful in case of emergency.'* Could I risk opening that? How can you get your bearings when all you can see are flat horizons? I guess you can't; I guess all you can do is stay still and wait until *something presents itself.*

•

Quiet, empty days passed. The quiet days became quiet weeks and Ian and I settled our new world into a tiny orbit.

On Monday and Thursday mornings I'd go shopping. I bought a cookbook by a celebrity chef and, starting at the beginning and working towards the end, I made one meal from it every day. I'd have lunch with a book and Ian would eat with me, usually sliced ham or tuna, and we would watch the snooker together in the afternoon. Ian, I discovered, was a fan of the snooker. At the weekend I would stay in bed late and read the newspapers. On Friday nights a video, or the cinema. There was enough money in the bank account to pay for this kind of life for two and a half years, maybe three. I didn't have to do a thing with bills either – everything had its date, its direct debit. Nothing at all needed to be done. I was free. Sundays, I would go for a drive in the yellow Jeep, not usually to anywhere in particular, although one week I made it as far as the seaside.

Through these activities I began to develop some parameters, put together a minute but perfectly formed existence, a neat, square little head garden – flowers, grass with daisies and a white picket fence – a postage stamp of control in miles and miles of empty moorland. I began to make myself an inside and an outside, an Eric and a not-Eric, a little block of self in the world. I wondered sometimes whether I was happy or unhappy, but it was as if the question wasn't relevant anymore, as if I was no longer the kind of creature to whom these states applied. I was a little robot, a machine for existing, just following

29

all the looping programmes I'd set for myself, and nothing more or less than that.

Sitting in the armchair with the cat on my knee and snooker on the TV, watching the shadow of the telegraph pole make its journey between the gardens, I thought a lot about the point of my being alive. Not in an unhappy way. Just in a quiet and straightforward way, a blank, empty wondering. My routines, my Prozac routines – after a while I didn't care about getting better or about the First Eric Sanderson or about whether Randle was looking out for my best interests or not. I just didn't think about any of it anymore. My heart was deep space and my head was maths.

My life as a shopping list.

One morning, I pulled a cup from the draining board too quickly and knocked a plate into the sink. The plate didn't break but there was a loud crash and the noise made me burst into tears for no reason at all.

Something would happen or nothing would. I'd known I would have to make a decision, this was it. I didn't have the reach to stretch forward and find whatever was going to happen to me, so I just sat back in my little clockwork world as it tick-tocked around the sun and away into the future.

New letters from the First Eric Sanderson arrived almost every day. Almost every lunchtime I would take each one and put it in a cupboard in the kitchen, unopened. Some letters were thick and fat, some fully-fledged parcels, others so small and so thin they could have only contained a single folded sheet. When a letter arrived with a thick square of card inside, I knew my last self had decided I was ready for the key to the locked door but the space no longer held any urgency for me. The world behind that door wasn't part of the me I'd been putting together. If anything, the locked room was a threat to its stability and I had no desire to challenge the boundaries I'd built. The envelope went into the cupboard with all the others.

I did open the 'emergency' envelope that came with the first letter, the one marked RYAN MITCHELL. It was the evening after my second meeting with Randle and I couldn't get away from the idea that this Ryan Mitchell might be one of the friends Eric had left behind, that perhaps it contained a way to get back in touch with his old life. But that's not what it was at all. Inside, I found sixteen pages of typed, personal and uselessly specific information about Ryan Mitchell – names of his aunts and uncles (first names only), his allergies, the results of thirty-two spelling tests he'd taken when he was ten, a list of sexual partners, the colour history of three rooms in his house – but no address, no phone number. Nothing at all to connect Eric and this whoever-he-was, nothing I might have actually needed to know. The First Eric Sanderson had titled these pages RYAN MITCHELL MANTRA. I pinned them to the notice board in the kitchen and would try to work out what use any of this information could possibly be as I cooked my celebrity chef meals each evening.

I saw Dr Randle twice a week and, as I said, I soon stopped having any opinion about these sessions at all. She would answer my questions, I would answer hers and we would drink tea. This was the extent of our relationship and more and more it was all I wanted. I never went to a GP or to the hospital. I never spoke to her about the locked room and she never gave any indication that she might have known about it. I didn't tell her about the letters. I didn't tell her about the Ryan Mitchell Mantra. I didn't really tell her anything. What did I have to tell? My life was perfect and pointless, and if that didn't mean anything good, it didn't mean anything bad either.

As more time passed though, I found myself thinking a lot about Clio Aames. I wondered about her and Eric, the way they had been with each other, how they had sex, the cruel things they said and didn't mean when they argued. I imagined her. Randle said Clio had been training as a solicitor. I imagined her sometimes blonde, sometimes dark, hair long, hair short. Some days I made her sensitive and caring, others tough and no bullshit. It was a game, a kind of barrier testing.

The idea of a real Clio Aames – her actual skin, voice, ideas, eyes, past, hates, loves, hopes, priorities, blood, fingernails and shoes and periods and tears and nightmares, teeth and spit and laugh, her actual fingerprints on glass – the thought of her with this kind of solid factual history, this had-once-been, was too too much for me (another reason I didn't open the locked door). No, the ghosts I called up in those late nights and long drives and snooker afternoons were all painted on the walls of my empty head with my own two hands. And that was as close as I wanted to be to anyone or anything.

Almost sixteen weeks after I'd woken up on the bedroom floor, the light bulb box arrived.

The dark shape glides up into the flow
of conversations and stories, swims
through the word-hum of packed
Saturday night bars, circles the loops and
edges of exchanged mobile numbers.

A telephone call is misdialled and, miles
away, my unconscious self shifts in sleep,
disturbed by a ringing bell.

From four degrees of separation, the shadow
under the water catches the scent. A curved,
rising signifier, a black idea fin of momentum
and intent cuts through the distance between
us in a spray of memes.

I opened my eyes. I was in the living room, lying on the sofa. The phone was ringing. Except for the one time Dr Randle had called to move an appointment, the phone never rang.

I shuffled out into the hallway all dream-fuddled and struggling through sleep sand but as I reached the hallstand table the ringing stopped. An empty sound-break of after-echoes bounced off the walls around me. I dialled 1471. A noise came down the line like the hiss of a seashell; that close-to-the-ear sound of almost-waves breaking far far away. I pressed down the little black bails on the phone cradle a couple of times and tried again. This time I got the clunky voice of the computerised telephone woman: "You were called at . . . Twenty . . . Twenty-six . . . Hours . . . The caller withheld their number."

I'd hung up and was on my way back into the living room when – bang bang bang bang bang – a flat palm on the front door made me jump and prickle with shock. I opened the door a little way and a wet bluster of rainy evening air rumbled and tumbled in through the gap. There was an old man standing outside. He was wiry, big-nosed and big-chinned. He had a thinning comb-over and it collected and ran rainwater crystal earrings off the bottoms of his long-lobed ears. He hugged his raincoat around himself and blinked because of the raindrops.

"Yes?" I said.

"You want to take that inside. It'll be nicked. If it isn't already ruined."

I followed his eyes down to the doorstep. There was a soggy wet box at my feet.

"Oh." I said. "Right."

He lifted his chin in a silent tut then turned and hobbled off, still hugging himself, down the rainy streetlamp-yellow street without another word.

The box on the doorstep was big, like the ones you get from Tesco when you're moving house. It was wrapped up in brown paper and it was soaked. It was also really heavy. I turned awkwardly on the doorstep, trying not to bruise and crush its soggy cardboard edges against the doorframe. I managed this eventually, took a careful step into the hallway and reached my foot out behind me to kick the front door shut. In perfect timing with the slam, the bottom of the package gave way and sluiced its contents out all over the floor.

Letters. A damp heap of letters on the hallway carpet. I hung the gutted box on the back of the hallstand table and knelt down to take a closer look. *Simian Keslev, 90 Sheffield Road. Harrison Brodie, 102 St Mary's Road. Steven Hall, 3 York Street. Bob Fenton, 60 Charlestown Road.* None of these letters were addressed to me. As I sifted my way down through the heap, I found an odd assortment of other things buried inside. A videotape wrapped up tight in clingfilm. A plastic wallet containing two battered exercise books. A much smaller cardboard box also wrapped up tight in clingfilm with – when I picked it up for a closer look – broken glass or smashed crockery noises coming from inside. I knelt over this strange little nest of things and knew that what I should probably do was stuff everything back into the box and put it away in the kitchen with everything else, try to forget all about it. If the items had been more obscure, maybe I would have done just that. But I didn't. Books and a videotape? That was too easy. Not even the clockwork person I'd become could blankly tick-tock his way past something like this.

Leaving the heap of letters where they'd fallen, I gathered up the tape, the package of books and the box with the broken glass noises and headed back into the living room.

•

The videotape contained almost an hour's camcorder footage of a light bulb flashing on and off in a darkened room.

Just that.

I fast-forwarded and rewound the whole way through a couple of times just to make sure, but there was nothing but a bare bulb blinking on and off and on and off in silence. Next, I shook the contents of the little box out onto some newspaper – glass shards, coily wire and the bayonet socket of a smashed light bulb. I guessed I might be looking at the star of the odd little home movie still playing on the TV. I placed the broken pieces carefully to one side, so I could inspect them later for – for God knows what – and turned my attention to the books.

The first of the two exercise books was almost impenetrable, pages of formulae and tables, paragraphs circled in red pen, whole pages scribbled out. I flicked through it quickly before swapping it for the second. This book was in better condition and had a title on the cover – *The Light Bulb Fragment*. I opened it up and the first word stopped me shock-still. I flicked over the page, scanned forward and then back until I was sure about what I was holding.

I closed the book and took a breath. I thought about how a moment in history could be pressed flat and preserved like a flower is pressed flat and preserved between the pages of an encyclopaedia. Memory pressed flat into text. *The Light Bulb Fragment* was some sort of journal or transcript, a written window into my missing past.

Shaking, I opened the book again.

4

The Light Bulb Fragment (Part One)

Clio's masked and snorkelled head broke the surface and she waved. It was a big, slow wave; all the way left, then all the way right, in and out of the water, like the ones people used to do at eighties rock concerts. It made me smile. Sitting up on my sun lounger in the shade of the huge parasol, I was careful to make sure my return wave, when I did it, looked just a little too much like a Nazi salute. I also made sure I held it long enough to get the sideways attention of the old couple with the beach plot next to ours and to make Clio, who was now waist-deep and arms out balancing in the breakers, stop dead, horrified for half a second before looking for an escape route back into the sea.

I've always been better at the long-range stuff.

"Clio!" I shouted, much too loud. The old couple and a handful of other beach people turned to look straight at me and then out to her. "Clio!" I shouted again and waved a big exaggerated wave. I cupped my hands around my mouth, even though she wasn't actually that far away and waited for an all-important three count; "Clio Aames!" Then, I did the other, dodgier wave again. "Clio, I love you!" I shouted, still doing it.

She had a small audience by the time she kicked her way up through the surf, pulling off the mask and snorkel with one hand and smoothing her hair back into a wet unfastened ponytail with the other. She was topless too, although that was neither here nor there in terms of our 'ha ha, everyone's looking at you' game. Clio isn't body-conscious; it's just me she finds embarrassing. It had been almost a week since we gave up Greek island archaeology for beaching and she'd done a day with bikini top on, ten minutes with bikini top off but with beer bottle tops over nipples 'acclimatising' and the next four and a half days 'continentally tits out'.

Actually, here's something important about Clio; when she says 'tits' she sounds smart and sexy and 21st-century – *'There's no point fucking around with these things, Eric'* – the way that some women, and I suppose, some guys effortlessly can. When I say 'tits', though, I sound like a sleazy tabloid journalist. I've tried and tried and there's no way around it. I used to say 'boobs', although I try not to now because Clio laughs and says I sound even worse, like a sex pest in denial. Recently, I've resorted to the painfully meek 'You look great without your top on,' which sometimes earns me an 'awww' and a kiss on the head. She says cunt too.

By the time Clio made it back to the sun loungers, the audience had more or less lost interest. She hung up the mask and snorkel in the spokes of our big shady parasol and took the towel that had been keeping the sneaking-its-way-round sun off my feet. She had a disapproving look that was just a little exaggerated; if you look carefully at that look, you can spot a smile that hangs around its edges and usually draw it out.

"Repeat after me," she said. "There's nothing funny about saluting like Hitler."

"There's nothing funny about saluting like Hitler," I said, taking my sunglasses off and squinting up at her. "Everyone thought it was funny when Peter Sellers did it."

"Yeah," she said, rubbing her hair. "Except he was funny, wasn't he?"

"Oh yeah," I grinned. "I forgot."

"So," she said. "What are you going to do?"

"Not salute like Hitler."

"And?"

"Buy lots of drinks so you don't get the next ferry off the island and abandon me for being the amoral worm that I am?"

"And?"

"What?" I said.

"And?"

"And what?"

"You're not funny."

"And what?"

She finished off with the towel and threw it at my head. "Grab that," she said, "and take my bikini top off, I need it."

We went to the campsite bar.

The campsite bar is good because it serves really cold Amstel beer, which we drink in the daytime, and really strong cocktails, which we move onto as soon as the sky gets dusty. Sometimes you'll have an orange sunset, sometimes though, maybe most times, the blue of the sky will just get dustier and dustier, and at some point in the process you'll realise the sand and stones you're walking on are now warmer than the air. Cool breezes coming in from the sea.

Usually, between the Amstel and the cocktails, we'll go for dinner at one of the *tavernas* along the beachfront. Our campsite is well away from whatever club action there may be on the island, and just a bump-crunch-bounce style unsurfaced road separates the *tavernas*, the general shop and the campsite entrance from the beach proper.

Clio will usually go as native as she can ordering food. I'll generally have pizza because I'm a philistine and on holiday and can do whatever I like.

A couple of days before the bikini top/saluting incident, I'd discovered there's so little light pollution over our part of the island that, if you're lying on your back on a clumpy little sand dune at 3 a.m., you can see the blues and purples of the Milky Way all across the sky. I'd never seen the Milky Way before and thought there was something quite 1950s sci-fi about the whole thing. *Lost in Space.*

"You're a philistine," Clio said.

I nodded, looking back down at her and straw-sucking up a mouthful of high-alcohol campsite bar Zombie.

"This thing you have about always comparing things in real life to things in films?"

"What thing?"

"Well," she said, "it makes you look shallow, uninteresting and –" lips pushed together, tipped head, strands of her dark hair dropping down, a mock-sympathy smile "– like a bit of a geeky loser, to be honest."

"Well, I am a geeky loser. You should probably chuck me because you can do so much better and you're worth so much more." I crossed my arms. "You owe it to yourself, Clio. And anyway –"

"What? *Mer mer mer, I was talking about the original* Lost in Space, *the TV programme, not the rubbish '90s film remake? Mer mer mer?*"

I looked down at my drink.

"A bit of a geeky loser," she said again, in exactly the same way, but chasing it this time with a slow, inevitable nod.

I shrugged.

"Awww," she said.

Clio's *badness* smile is something else – the edges of her normal smile turn sharp like little blades and her eyes go all shiny and electric. I think, for the half-second it lasts, that mean naughty sexy cruel little smile might be the single and only perfect thing that's ever existed. A bright warm flash amongst a billion old scratchy stars.

"I love you."

"Oh, honey," she smiled. She reached over and laid her fingertips lightly on the back of my hand. "You're so regional." When I didn't respond she leaned back on the back legs of her chair and raised her eyebrows.

Here's a secret: just the idea that Clio Aames is real and in the world makes me ache.

I fished my foot up under the table and tried to push her over. She caught onto what I was doing and slammed the chair back down on all fours.

"Childish," she said.

40

Later that same night, we found ourselves talking to a couple of backpackers from London. We'd been away for almost five weeks by that point and it was only the second time we'd had any kind of extended conversation with *people*. It was odd, talking like that again, in a down-the-pub kind of way. We had to keep explaining things, backtracking and filling gaps. We realised our own conversations had evolved into a kind of shorthand, a tidy, neat little minimalism. Covering the whole canvas in broad obvious brushstrokes for outsiders felt like a waste of sounds, time and effort. *Speaking with footnotes*, Clio would call it later, as we ambled back towards the tent. Still, they were nice enough and we did have some fun with them. Apparently, they had a flat close to Heathrow Airport.

"You get used to the noise," the girl, Jane, said. "For about a month we didn't think we could stand it, but then we just got over it. Now it's like it isn't even there."

"First couple of nights in the tent," the guy, Paul, said, "we really struggled getting to sleep. Even though we don't hear the planes any more at home, we couldn't sleep without them. How weird is that?" He thought for a second. "It was like there was this hole in the quiet."

"Cool," I said. "Anti-sound."

Clio looked at me.

"And Dusty," said Jane, chipping back in. "When we first moved, I thought Dusty was going to have a nervous breakdown."

"Dusty?" asked Clio.

"Our cat. She's an old thing, used to belong to Paul's great aunt. She's Siamese and she's pretty sensitive." Jane talked about Dusty the cat for a while, a couple of cat anecdotes I don't remember.

"We've just got two kittens," Clio smiled. "Two boys."

"Awww," Jane said, "what are they called?"

I grinned on the inside.

"Gavin and Ian," Clio said.

Jane and Paul's getting-to-know-you faces slipped, lost a little coherence. It was rewarding; Clio and I had worked hard at coming up with names to get that response. Un-catlike and inappropriate in a fundamental way, but still confusingly feasible.

"Awww," Jane said again, just a bit late.

.

"It's tiring not knowing people, isn't it?" Clio said later.

"It isn't word-efficient," I agreed.

We'd been drinking Zombies most of the night. I was amazed we weren't more pissed. Tomorrow, I decided, we should work harder to get more pissed. We wandered towards the tent in silence for a while.

"Do you know what I think?"

"That we've not been getting drunk enough?"

"Hmmm," I said. "Do you always know what I'm going to say?"

"Yes."

"Always?"

"Yep."

"Wow," I said. "Guess what I'm thinking about now?"

"Filthy."

"Wow," I said again. "I'm stunned."

She squeezed my hand then let it go, hooking her arm around my waist, fingers tucked into the back pocket of my shorts. She tipped her head against me as we walked.

The zip to the front of our tent was a bit broken. Soon it would be all the way broken but at that time you could still get it open if you knew what you were doing, if you had *the touch*. Clio did, I didn't. While she got us inside, I stood watching a fat moth drum and fluster around the campsite's weak electric lighting. The night was all about stars, empty space and the greasy smell of bug candles. There was no breeze.

We had sex and when we finished, Clio folded her elbows and lay on top of me, me still inside her, her head on my shoulder, her forehead touching my chin.

It all felt so clear, so in-focus and specific. My fingertips on her wet back, over her ribs. Her body rising and falling from my breathing, the slight stretch in her skin from hers. Our breath moving in and out of synch. The resistance against the fill of my lungs: *Clio's weight in the world.* Just all this. I stroked the hair from her temple, followed the arch of her ear as gently as I could, over the ghost hairs that lived there, almost not touching at all. This was everything, at the heart of everything this was a simple, perfect *just-is*.

Clio's arm stretched up under me and her fingers curled around my shoulder. When she finally spoke, I could feel the air coming from inside her and making the words.

"Promise you'll leave me if you ever need to."

"What?" I tucked my chin to the side, trying to see her. "I'm not going to leave you, don't be stupid."

Her eyes came up to meet mine.

I frowned.

"I'm not joking," she said. "If you need to leave me, if I'm making you unhappy, you have to just do it." She propped up on her elbows, curled her hips to move me out of her. "You have to promise, Eric. It's important."

"Hey," I rubbed her arms. "What's wrong?"

She looked down at me for a long time and I really thought she was going to cry. "Hey," I said again and I hooked her hair away from her face.

"Nothing," she said with an unfocused smile. Then another smile, this one was stronger and it came from somewhere more recognisable. "Nothing, I'm a dick."

I linked my arms up around her and she came back down to me. We hugged, her head on my chest.

"Come on," I said. "Tell me."

"You're sweaty," she said, lifting her head up and putting it back down.

"So are you."

We lay like that for a while.

I listened. Outside the tent there was absolutely nothing.

"I couldn't stand it if I ruined you," she said in the end.

"Clio," I said, stroking back her hair, "you're not in charge of the world."

•

In Greece, they drink their coffee cold. It's called *frappé*, or Nescafé *frappé*, or just Nescafé. Greek people usually take their *frappé* without milk or sugar, but they tend to give tourists both.

We were outside a coffeehouse in Naxos town, overlooking the harbour, having a day out. They call Naxos the green island even though it isn't particularly green at the moment, but then summer is well underway and the idea of things staying green all year round is probably an English peculiarity. Anyway, it's all relative. Some of the other Greek islands are much more un-green, all rock and sand. According to the guidebook, the ancient Greeks chopped down the native woodlands on most of the islands and replaced them with olive trees. Olive trees just don't have the roots to hold onto soil on slopes, so all that earthy goodness washed away into the sea or dustified and now those islands are just spines of stony bones with patches of brown grass here and there and the odd lizard.

Naxos is beautiful, but it's not really green, not now anyway.

The waitress gave us our *frappés* with milk and sugar without asking, but then I was dressed a bit Hunter S. Thompson – khaki shorts, sky blue Hawaiian shirt with seagulls, big sunglasses and a beanie hat – so that was probably down to me.

When you first get your *frappé*, if it's a good one, the ice cubes are down at the bottom. As the drink settles down, becomes more coffee and less bubbles, the ice fights its way to the top. Like running water, and fire, it's sort of hypnotic.

Clio said something about a half-carved twenty-five foot colossus in an ancient quarry over the other side of the island. It was enough for me to blink up from my glass.

"What?"

She put the guidebook on the table and pulled down her shades. "Wake up."

"I know," I smiled. "I think it must be the heat."

Clio poked her glasses back up her nose and stared at me for a second.

"You might want to work on your stamina, Sanderson. You're no use to me broken."

I came over all mock hurt. "Is that all I am to you?"

"Yes," she said.

Hours after what I'm clumsily thinking of as Clio's *moment of crisis* the night before, we'd had sex again, at something o'clock in the morning. The second time was sleepy and slow, a drifting almost subconscious thing. Clio speaking so quietly as I moved inside her and me speaking too and the words were from a long way down, not thinking and then saying things, words, at all. Night words, sex words or dream words, I don't know, not for conversation or the sun. Not the kind of words that can be pinned down with letters and ink. I don't really know how to explain it, but that's how it was.

"I love you," Clio said out of nowhere as I reached across the table for the guidebook.

"I know," I nodded, taking the book and leafing through it. "And I enjoy spending time with you too."

"Wanker," she laughed. "I hate that one."

"You invented that one."

"Give me the book back," she said. "I want to show you the stone man thing."

5

White Cloud and Blue Mountain

The videotape of the flashing light perched on top of the video recorder, under the TV, in the dark. The stabs and shards of the smashed light bulb all in their box, shaken back carefully down the crease of a newspaper, like glitter, to protect Ian the cat's ambling late-night feet. The light bulb box sealed up and standing above the fireplace like an urn. Sixteen weeks of letters and post from the First Eric Sanderson sitting unopened in a little cube of black space behind a kitchen cupboard door. Raindrops tapping and streaking in the wind, each one its own bacterial blue planet, rolling down the outside of the windowpanes. Dust collecting itself in corners, my own Hiroshima shadow building up on the windowsills and the skirting boards. The spiders and the insects dividing out their territories on the vastness of the floors and ceilings. The downstairs of the house not quite still and not quite quiet in the night-time.

Upstairs, off the landing, the locked door, solid and familiar and unmovable. Next to it, my bedroom door, real and functional and not quite closed. A cat-wide gap existed between the door and the frame and this projected a floor-to-ceiling wedge of yellow bedside table light. Beyond the crack and into the bedroom, the impenetrable exercise book on the carpet, four columns of numbers and a crossed-out chart facing up at the ceiling. On the double bed Ian the cat curled in a nose-to-tail sleeping ball, *The Light Bulb Fragment* book, slid halfway down between pillow and duvet, and me, on my side, forearm covering my eyes from the forgotten-about electric bulb, dreaming:

I walked along a sun-dappled avenue lined with overgrown bushes and vines, half-collapsed Greek columns and classical white statues with missing arms or tumbled heads or broken plinths which tilted their weathered masters at angles which would have been precarious and scramble-sliding for any real person. The air was sweet-sappy with the smell of eucalyptus or linseed or camphor oil and was so hot and alive it got into your mouth and vapoured away the moisture with gentle, intimate care. I passed an old marble statue of the celebrity chef who wrote my cookbook. His blank eyes stared out of his licheny face as he stood tall and aggressive, holding – wielding – his spatula as a hero would a sword. A little further on in a deep alcove, a shadowy, spider-webbed Humphrey Bogart leant against a rough carved piano, his grimy stone glass held in his grimy stone hand up against his grimy stone tuxedo.

At the end of the avenue, I strolled under a crumbled archway and out into the remains of a large open square with a Roman bath at its centre. The bath was half-empty and what water there was had been covered by a quiet mat of leaves from a wide willowy tree which had forced its way up through the ancient flooring. I made my way towards the tree, carefully overstepping a busy line of big black ants and weaving around the many tall brown grass tufts and low flat bushes which had also pushed up wherever they could between the stones. Nature's reclamation committee.

As I got closer I noticed a white plastic sun lounger parked up in the tree's shade. There was a girl lying on it, on her side, her back to me. As I got closer the girl sat up to dig for something in her bag and my insides leaped throatwards with a wet jerk of recognition.

"Clio."

Clio Aames stopped what she was doing, turned and pushed her sunglasses up into her long dark hair like an Alice band.

"Fucking hell," she said. "Look who it isn't."

I arrived under the tree and dipped as she half rose, scooping my arms around the solid summer heat warm reality of her. She squeezed me back hard and we sank down together onto the lounger. We stayed like that for a long time, holding tight, our faces buried in each other's necks, breathing and being still.

"You alright?" I asked with just breath and hardly any sound, under the lobe of her ear.

"Yeah, I think. Yeah." Air, words from inside her against my neck. "I missed you."

"I've forgotten you, Clio. I've forgotten it all. I'm so, so sorry."

"Hey. Come on, it's okay." Her hand on my neck and her fingers stroking circles in the back of my hair. "It's alright. Everything's okay." She pushed us gently apart so she could look into my eyes. "It's alright. We're here now and everything's okay."

"Clio," I said.

"It's alright. I know."

"You're gone."

"I'm right here."

"No, you're not. You're dead."

Clio let go of me and sat up straight.

"For your information," she said, "I think I'm looking pretty good." She ran her hands down from bikini top to bikini bottoms to emphasise the point. After a second she looked back at me. "This is the part where you're supposed to agree."

"You look fantastic."

"Fantastic for a dead person?"

I let go of it, felt the smile open up on my face.

"Don't start with me, Aames. How come you're wearing your top anyway?"

I reached over to touch her in the same way she'd touched herself but she slapped my hand away hard with exaggerated amazement.

"Oh my God. *Clio, you're dead. Hey Clio, can I see your tits?* One word for you: necro–" she broke it in half and pinned each part down with a finger point "–philia. This is what you degenerate into when I leave you on your own?"

I stared at my feet with as serious an expression as I could manage and answered in my gruff, B-movie samurai voice.

"I am filled with shame."

"Good," she said, pulling her knees up to her chin. "Now tell me what's been happening in *EastEnders*."

And that's what I did. I was about halfway through a complex and unlikely plot surrounding the return of one of the programme's villains when Clio leaned in, slipped her hand around the back of my neck and kissed me, at first gently and then deeply and honestly.

"Hang on," I said quietly as we moved apart. "I've not told you about the stupid one with droopy eyes getting pregnant again."

Clio smiled an empty kind of smile and pushed her forehead back against mine.

"I'm sorry this had to happen," she said.

"Yeah," I said. "It's not as good as it was. I think the ratings have suffered too."

"Eric."

"I know, I'm sorry. It's just. How can we do this, you know? How can we even do the jokes?"

"Fucked Up Beyond All Recognition," Clio said, her head nodding a little and making mine nod too. We stayed like that, forehead against forehead, for a few seconds.

"Could – was there something I could have done?"

She pulled back a little so we were eye to eye. Her hand still drooped over my shoulder. She shook her head.

"I don't even know."

I took hold of her other hand and held it on my lap with both of mine.

"Clee, tell me something to prove this isn't a dream."

"Something like what?"

"Like something I don't know and I have to go and look it up and when I do it turns out to be true."

"I don't think it works like that."

"Just tell me I'm not dreaming?"

"Maybe you are," she said. "Probably you are."

"I don't want to be. Clio, I can't do this on my own."

There was a bang.

We both jumped, turned towards the Roman bath. A clump of leaves swirled on the surface of the water in a slow spiral.

"Is there something alive in there?"

Clio nodded. "Yes."

"What is it?"

"I don't know," she said, watching the waters. "Something from down where it gets black."

There was another bang.

Little waves raced across the littery surface, lapping the bath's mouldy tiled sides.

"Are you ready? This is it." Clio held me by the tops of my arms and gave me a smile which was meant to be strong and almost was.

"What? Clee, what's going on?"

Bang.

6

Time and the Hunter

Bang.

I jumped awake, blinking in the electric light. I didn't know if the noise had been part of some dream I'd been having or a real, external thing. The cat was upright and alert at the end of the bed, staring with huge eyes at the wall. I stayed as quiet as I could, counting off the seconds of silence in my head: One Mississippi . . . Two Mississippi . . . Three Mississippi . . . Four Mississippi . . . Fi –

Bang.

Ian disappeared in a ginger bounce of nervous energy and I knotted up in shock.

Another bang.

A slam.

A thud. A bang. Another slam.

Chemical instincts flooded through me, numbing fingertips, lips and ears. My stomach dropped slack and sick and every hair on my body pulled upright, an electrical conductor. My biology primed me to run, to escape. But I didn't run. Some higher logic took control as I sat up carefully, a steady hand taking hold of my strings and turning my actions away from panic and towards – something else. I found myself taking four, five deep breaths then, quietly as I could, getting out of bed and creeping onto the landing.

The banging and slamming, clattering and rattling sounds were coming from behind the locked door, and they were building up, growing more and more aggressive. As I stood there, shaking, controlling my breathing, keeping quiet, I started to realise something about the noise was wrong. It took a few seconds to work out what that something was, and then I got it: the banging and crashing from behind the door seemed to be coming *from a distance.* From the dimensions of the house, the locked room couldn't be large, slightly smaller than my bedroom at the biggest, and perhaps only a box room. An impossibility then, but still: the sounds seemed to be bouncing off bare walls, as if travelling from the far end of a huge, empty warehouse.

The violence cranked up even further into an angry thrashing of violent bangs and metal crashes. I leant forward, listening for some clue. My ear brushed the surface of the locked door, gently, barely at all. The instant it happened, the split second my body made contact with the paintwork, the noise, the smashing, banging, slamming, everything, stopped dead.

Shock jerked me backwards like burned fingers. I tried not to move, tried not to breathe, my hand covering my mouth.

Deep thick silence thundered from behind the closed door. Pure. Heavy. Pregnant. The sound of being stared at.

I waited.

I waited for something to happen.

One minute.

Two minutes.

Nothing happened at all.

Ten minutes later I had the hammer out of the toolbox and was searching through the kitchen cupboard full of unopened letters from the First Eric Sanderson. I found the envelope with the card square inside, ripped it open at one end and shook it. The key fell into my hand.

•

"I'm coming in," I said outside the door, surprised by the clarity and pitch of my voice in the silence. My guts felt like dangling elastic bands. Hot nervous fluid pressed in my bladder. "I'm coming in. I'm unlocking the door."

The key clicked around in the keyhole. I pushed down the handle and swung the door slowly open. Silence. Holding the hammer up by my right ear, ready to bring it down on anyone or anything that lurched out of the darkness, I edged inside, fumble-reaching at the walls. Eventually I found a switch and clicked on the light.

There was a bright red filing cabinet standing in the middle of the room.

And nothing else.

There was no one there.

The room *was* smaller than the bedroom, much too tiny to make any sense of those ringing echoes. The single window was locked and undamaged. As far as I could see, there was no way anyone could have got in or out, but I kept the hammer ready.

Four of the five drawers in the filing cabinet were empty. In the fifth drawer, I found a single red cardboard suspension folder with a single sheet of printed paper inside.

I didn't take out the folder or read the sheet of paper. I didn't do anything for one, two, three, four seconds. Finally, I closed the drawer, pressed my back against the cabinet and tried a grip on the *wrongness* of it all. It wasn't just the noises. From my second day in the world, I'd imagined this room containing all the facts and figures and pictures of my lost self, a paper trail life of the First Eric Sanderson, and photographs – of him, of Clio Aames, and of all the people close to them. Permanent records in colour print and text proving those lives had happened, those people and times and events had been real and once had their place in the working of things. I'd half expected to find this room filled with Clio's belongings – it would have been a logical explanation for the room being sealed up in the first place. But there was nothing. I checked through the cabinet and the rest of the room again to make sure. Pulling the red folder off its runners and tucking it under my arm, I got myself out of there, clicked off the light and locked the door behind me.

•

I pulled the vodka bottle out of the freezer drawer – I'd got into the habit of having a shot or two with the Friday night video, and maybe the occasional shot with afternoon TV – and poured myself a big half-glass over ice. Ian reappeared in the kitchen, now all brave and never-been-scared-in-my-life, doing his fat cat slink around my legs. I opened a tin of tuna for him and took the vodka and the bottle through to the living room.

Television, the great normaliser. I switched it on and dropped onto the sofa, vodka at my feet, red folder at my side. I drank back a few deep, hot throatfuls to calm my nerves before opening the folder and taking out the piece of paper inside. This is what it said:

> Imagine you're in a rowing boat on a lake.
>
> It's summer, early morning. That time when the sun hasn't quite broken free of the landscape and long, projected shadows tigerstripe the light. The rays are warm on your skin as you drift through them, but in the shadows the air is still cold, greyness holding onto undersides and edges wherever it can.
>
> A low clinging breeze comes and goes, racing ripples across the water and gently rocking you and your boat as you float in yin-yang slices of morning. Birds are singing. It's a sharp, clear sound, clean without the humming backing track of a day well underway. There's the occasional sound of wind in leaves and the occasional slap-splash of a larger wavelet breaking on the side of your boat, but nothing else.
>
> You reach over the side and feel the shock of the water, the steady bob of the lake's movement playing up and down your knuckles in a rhythm of cold. You pull your arm back; you enjoy the after-ache in your fingers. Holding out your hand, you close your eyes and feel the tiny physics of gravity and resistance as the liquid finds routes across your skin, builds itself into droplets of the required weight, then falls, each drop ending with an audible tap.

Now, right on that tap – stop. Stop imagining. Here's the real game. Here's what's obvious and wonderful and terrible all at the same time: the lake in my head, the lake I was imagining, has just become the lake in your head. It doesn't matter if you never know me, or never know anything about me. I could be dead, I could have been dead a hundred years before you were even born and still – think about this carefully, think past the obvious sense of it to the huge and amazing miracle hiding inside – the lake in my head has become the lake in your head.

Behind or inside or through the two hundred and eighteen words that made up my description, behind or inside or through those nine hundred and sixty-nine letters, there is some kind of flow. A purely conceptual stream with no mass or weight or matter and no ties to gravity or time, a stream that can only be seen if you choose to look at it from the precise angle we are looking from now, but there, nevertheless, a stream flowing directly from my imaginary lake into yours.

Next, try to visualise all the streams of human interaction, of communication. All those linking streams flowing in and between people, through text, pictures, spoken words and TV commentaries, streams through shared memories, casual relations, witnessed events, touching pasts and futures, cause and effect. Try to see this immense latticework of lakes and flowing streams, see the size and awesome complexity of it. This huge rich environment. This waterway paradise of all information and identities and societies and selves.

Now, go back to your lake, back to your gently bobbing boat. But this time, know the lake; know the place for what it is and when you're ready, take a look over the boat's side. The water is clear and deep. Broken sunlight cuts blue wedges down, down into the clean cold depths. Sit quietly, wait and watch. Don't move. Be very, very still. They say life is tenacious. They say given half a chance, or less, life will grow and exist and evolve anywhere, even in the most inhospitable and unlikely of places. Life will always find a way, they say. Be very quiet. Keep looking into the water. Keep looking and keep watching.

I read through the text couple of times. I put the page back in its folder. I drained my vodka. I rubbed my eyes. I said *Jesus*. I poured another drink and slouched back into the sofa. The cat slid past, ignoring me completely. The fridge hummed. Everything else was rain on the windows and the night-time dramas of insects. Nothing made any kind of sense at all, or if it did, I was too tired and frazzled to see how. I closed my eyes and concentrated on the burn, swirl and chink of the vodka and on the simple sliding weights of breathing.

•

I woke up on the sofa in the middle of some vivid memory playback of my second meeting with Dr Randle.

"But it's not – " I said out loud, and then stopped, recognising the dream for what it was.

While I'd been asleep, something had changed.

My groggy half-awake attention turned inwards like a brilliant sweeping searchlight and the sudden clarity of it shocked me. I saw the whole of my sixteen-week-old mind and my sixteen-week-old self perfectly, completely, vivid and obvious in every detail. I could even see the memory dream still playing in the back of my head, tape winding down, losing cohesion and forward momentum.

I pushed myself upright on the sofa. The sensation of clarity expanded. Everything in the room, all things and their spatial relationships, all colours, light, shades, textures, all space, all air pressure and all bouncing wave sounds became cutting-edge sharp, everything tuned to a hot brilliant focus. My wide-open skipping-around eyes found the vodka glass on my lap. I became transfixed. I lifted it as carefully and gently as I could, working hard not to affect events inside. The three ice cubes had melted into round-edged lozenges, each with its own complex puzzle of faultlines, ghost planes and fractures. Around each cube, the run-off water and the slightly thicker vodka curled together in miniature weather systems and storm fronts. I thought about fragile colour spirals of oil in water, about the sad rolling and dispersing of the galaxy, about cogwheel daisies on green grass driving the vast machinery of evolution, about a whirl of cream unwinding its spiral arms in a left-behind coffee cup and all this coming from somewhere all at once but not distracting; perfectly in line with the beautiful, almost traumatic actuality of substance, form, movement and light in the glass. It was breathtaking, too clear, too much. My eyes were hot and prickly, and I realised I was crying.

A movement unlocked my attention. I re-focused my eyes, looking past the vodka glass and into the static buzz of the TV. I stayed very still for a few seconds before lowering the glass to the floor, careful not to take my eyes off the screen. There was something distant and alive in the depths of the white noise – a living glide of thoughts swimming forward, a moving body of concepts and half felt images.

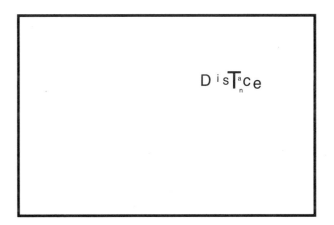

I moved slowly off the sofa and crawled across the floor towards the television, trying to see deeper into the vast depths of no-signal hiss behind the glass. I got nearer and the creature became aware of me. It picked up speed and powered out of sight, disappearing in a fast flick of movement below the bottom right corner of the screen.

I crawled closer, closer, closer, trying to pick out another glimpse or recollective flash of the thing deep in the vast distances of static, and then –

```
58801 Storr A, Gold filling........55876 Storr  eye        ye
91916 Storr A.L, Good listener.........69741  eye        eye
Storr L.O, "It's all in the past.....52927 Storr eye       eye
movies.......61229 Storr M R, The looks but   eye        eye e
12 pints of larger and a kebab....55693 Storr Dr.D  eye eye eye  Stor
as nightmares.......51862 Storr Ed, Has nightmares.......51862 Storr H, "You lo
Makes grown men cry....55766 Storr F.M, Wonders what went wrong.....507
D, Blood doesn't clot......51153 Storr G, Has a four-leaf clover, it's unlucky Std
ged and whined Storr D, Fool.............64329 Storr G&H.J, "It's not working, I
            and mechanically Storr Daniel, Valuable things unseen in loft
                    coughed up Storr D.S, Dreams of going
                            printed pages Storrer A.
                                    from comic
                                        my h
```

The screen threw itself forward with a screaming electric flash and the lights all died. The TV landed with a heavy glassy thud in the black and I scrambled backwards on balls of feet and heels of hands in animal panic. My shoulders hit the sofa and I clumsily reverse-clambered onto it, pulling my knees up off the floor until they were tucked under my chin, hands locked together around my shins. My body squeezed, desperate to run, but the dark, silence and panic locked me still, petrified in place. I tried for silent breaths but my breathing and my thinking were all ripped, chopped, torn-up, ragged. I couldn't hear anything else and couldn't see anything either. The room was pitch-black.

No.

Not *totally* pitch-black. The little green smoke detector light on the ceiling became my distant North Star. Gently releasing the most fragile light, it remade the edges of the bookcase and the magazine stand and the back of the upturned TV out of the darkness. I focused on this circle and on my breathing. With a little longer to adjust, even this thin polleny dusting of illumination would be enough to see by. And once I could see, and see the door, I'd be able to force my legs out of their deep-freeze and run.

A violent *something* slammed into the far end of the sofa shunting everything sideways with a hard, wrenching pressure lurch. I barrelled right, digging my fingers deep into the soft fabric arm, trying to resist the travelling momentum taking me tumbling over the side and managing it, just. Rocking myself hard back into my seat, I kept one hand gripped tight on the arm and the other stretched out across the sofa back, elbows locked and braced, wedging myself deep and tight in the corner. No thoughts – my thinking like a pile of smashed glass and my breathing so fast the darkness started to swarm. An impulse came to run at the wall and hope to hit the door or at least near the door and fumble for it, but I couldn't break the panic locking my legs. *Bang* – another hit directly behind and under me, much harder, like a slow-motion car crash and the back end of the sofa thrown up and coming toppling forward, sending me sprawling off into empty space and then the carpet and the floor came up at me and it – broke.

The idea of the floor, the carpet, the concept, feel, shape of the words in my head all broke apart on impact with a splash of sensations and textures and pattern memories and letters and phonetic sounds spraying out from my splashdown. I went under, deep, carried by the force of my fall and without the thought or image or any recollection of oxygen or breathing at all.

I came up coughing, gasping for air, the idea of air. A vague physical memory of the actuality of the floor survived but now I was bobbing and floating and trying to tread water in the idea of the floor, in fluid liquid concept, in its endless cold rolling waves of association and history.

Everything dark and black except for the faint green of the North Star. No more outlines, no edging of the bookcase or back of the upturned TV, just me treading water alone in the middle of this vast and fundamental conceptual form; concept as environment, with its own characteristic depths and swells, moving and shifting and altering with time and perspective the way all words and ideas and concepts do. *No no no.* I tried to shake that mode of being, to force the idea back behind the physical, force my body to find and accept the hard reality of the floor as an entity of sand and stones and cement, hard physical atoms with no words or ideas or attachments, but my mind could only find the words, ideas, signs and attachments for these things, never anything solid at all, and my body couldn't act without my mind's instruction. I screwed down my eyes again, trying to will myself back to the familiar world of solids and space. But even the vague body-memory of hard ground had gone, my legs kicking in insubstantial watery black. The world, my mind, the way these connected, whatever the root of the perception shift, I didn't have control of it, and I couldn't undo what had happened. But I *had* to get away. The deep deep liquid black below my feet, the creature in the TV and the violence that threw me here, I had to get out, now, regardless of how everything re-viewed and re-focused itself. I looked up at the North Star, used it to guess-navigate where the living room door should be and began swimming hard in that direction.

I didn't get far.

Something huge rushed fast in the water under my body, pulling me in a mini whirlpool twist of unravelling thought drag in its wake. The thing from the static. *Jesus.* I kicked faster, scrabbling against liquid, trying to pull up a solid thought of dry land in my mind. But I could only beat out splashes and scatter sprays of mind fragments. Then another undertow and I'm pulled and buffeted, the thing passing under again and I'm knocked and rolled and ducked under by a fierce ripping after-wake.

Coming up for air and coughing out: *shark.* The word coming in a tangle-breathed shudder and then me screaming: *help. Shark. Help me.* Me screaming: *oh God oh God oh God* and kicking and thrashing and thrashing and screaming. And then, somehow, tumbling from the back of my desperate spark-spraying thought train, a memory of something – Eric Sanderson's emergency envelope and the Ryan Mitchell Mantra pinned to the notice board in the kitchen. I fought to remember the text on those sheets of paper. Exam results? The colour history of rooms?

"Blue and black and grey and yellow," I shouted the words out, grasping, shock-stripped of any thinking or logic. I shouted and kicked against the water, grabbing in the dark. "Blue and black and grey and yellow. Blue and –" Something rushed upwards from below and smashed hard against my hip and side, throwing me up and backwards out of the water in a lift of spray, my mouth opening like a scream but my airways crushed and winded and only a sucking nothing coming through my throat. I came down hard in a splash of disassociating fragments.

And then –

And then it was raining, a heavy downpour of letters, words, images, snatches of events, faces, places – a forest, a late-night city – the sea around me mixing in and confusing with so much falling everything else. And me lost in there somewhere and everywhere in it all, sinking away, diffusing, losing all mind and thoughts and consciousness.

•

I opened my eyes. Wet, new light dribbled under the curtains – morning arriving, bringing the solid world back into focus with it. I found myself inside the lower part of the living room bookcase, the upper part having broken apart and collapsed, leaving me avalanched in books and splintered wood. I coughed and winced out a hiss. *Cracked rib.* A minor bookslide happened as I slowly and painfully manoeuvred myself up into a twisted sitting position. The TV face-down on the carpet at the end of its stretched-out flex, the sofa up-ended. Things were broken and thrown and chipped and smashed but they were there. Solid, physical things. Things in a room made of bricks on a planet made of rocks and water. *Silent truthful matter.*

When I pulled together the strength, I hauled myself out of the debris and up onto my feet, swayed, steadied. The words came back without my looking for them: *Dr Randle can neither help nor protect you.*

I limped into the kitchen and started taking the First Eric Sanderson's letters out of the cupboard.

7

The Crypto-Zoology of Purely Conceptual Sharks, Dictaphone Defence Systems and Light Bulb Code Cracking in Selected Letters from the First Eric Sanderson

(Received: 22nd September)

Letter #2

Dear Eric,

I used to know so many things. The things I learned, the ways I learned to see and the things I believed possible, I think they might amaze you. Mostly now, all I have are splinters. Remains of things I was quick enough to write down and preserve; fragments which seem to be increasingly incomplete and confusing to me now.

This is what I know, what at the middle of me I feel is true: all the lost research, the journeys, the dangerous choices, I did it all for a girl called Clio Aames. I loved her, Eric. So much. And she died. I only get the general senses of things and they pass so quickly, like childhood smells touching you and then being gone on the breeze. But. But but but. It feels strange to be writing this down – I think I believed I could change what happened, undo it, prevent it, save her life somehow after she was already gone. Of course I couldn't. Dead is dead is dead is dead. If you are reading this then I'm dead too and you'll shortly be fighting for your own life.

Eric, I am so sorry.

There's so much I've lost, so much that's been eaten all away from the insides of my head, but I've worked hard to squirrel away enough to help you. I don't have any answers, I'm almost as empty as you must be now, but I do have a few tools and a little knowledge. Some weapons and some fragments. The rest is up to you. You always have a choice.

I'm so forgetful. The creature will find something I've missed because it never stops looking and its senses are very sharp. It will find a way to get me and in time it will come looking for you. The waters are almost up to the bedroom window now. I can't keep all the balls in the air. I can't stay in this shark cage forever.

The animal hunting you is a Ludovician. It is an example of one of the many species of purely conceptual fish which swim in the flows of human interaction and the tides of cause and effect. This may sound like madness, but it isn't. Life is tenacious and determined. The streams, currents and rivers of human knowledge, experience and communication which have grown throughout our short history are now a vast, rich and bountiful environment. Why should we expect these flows to be sterile?

Life will always find a way. Just look at you and me and see the truth in it.

I don't know exactly how the thought fish came to be in the world, but in the wide, warm pools of society and culture, millions of words and ideas and concepts are constantly evolving. It doesn't seem too implausible that one of them elevated itself above its single cellular cousins in much the same way we did. The Selfish Meme?

The Ludovician is a predator, a shark. It feeds on human memories and the intrinsic sense of self. Ludovicians are solitary, fiercely territorial and methodical hunters. A Ludovician might select an individual human being as its prey animal and pursue and feed on that individual over the course of years, until that victim's memory and identity have been completely consumed. Sometimes, the target's body survives this ordeal and may go on to live a second twilight life after the original self and memories have been taken. In time, such a person may establish a 'bolt-on' identity of their own, but the Ludovician will eventually catch the scent of this and return to complete its kill.

I'm sorry if I'm putting this too bluntly.

I know what you must be thinking and you don't have to believe any of this if you don't want to, but the Ludovician is out there and in time it will find you. Learn the Ryan Mitchell text I sent you. If nothing else, do it to humour me; an old and crazy coat hanging in your wardrobe. I'm afraid that in time you will see for yourself that what I am telling you is the truth.

With regret and also hope,

The First Eric Sanderson

(Received: 24th September)

Letter #3

Dear Eric,

The Ryan Mitchell text is a very limited form of conceptual camouflage. The longer you exist in the world, the less effective it will be. It's important then that you learn to protect yourself on a more permanent basis. There are several short-term and several long-term ways to achieve this. The non-divergent conceptual loop is the quickest and the most secure, so it is the best place to start.

This parcel should contain:

> x 4 Dictaphones with continuous playback and AC adaptors
>
> x 4 pre-recorded Dictaphone tapes
>
> x 4 8-metre extension cables
>
> x 1 four-way plug adapter
>
> x 16 AA batteries in case of power failure or outdoor use

Function: The function of this equipment is to generate a non-divergent conceptual loop. That is, a stream circle, a flow of pure and singular association moving around the Dictaphones in order. From one to two. From two to three. From three to four. From four back to one. The resulting current is strong and clean enough to push otherwise incoming flows (of cause and effect, degrees of separation etc.) *around* the defined space, rather than allowing them through or into it, thus creating an area of isolation. To the best of my knowledge, no Ludovician, or any conceptual fish, has ever breached a non-divergent conceptual loop. In essence, it will function as a shark cage.

Instructions: Insert tapes into Dictaphones. Place Dictaphones in each corner of your room or at the edges of whatever space you are aiming to define. Rig up each Dictaphone with an AC adaptor if possible. Ensure each Dictaphone is set to continuous play. Begin playback on all Dictaphones. Protection is only provided within the area described by the layout of the Dictaphones.

Further notes, explanations & information in the eventuality of equipment damage: Each of the four Dictaphone tapes provided has been recorded by a different person. An individual making a recording of this type does not have to be speaking necessarily, they can simply go about their daily business with the Dictaphone recording in their pocket for a few hours. The longer the recording, the more the person is clarified in sound and the more secure your loop. Now – and this is complicated, Eric, so read it back until you're sure you have it exactly right, you may have to attempt your own replacement tapes one day – the person who records tape one must forward three blank Dictaphone tapes and their own recorded tape to the person who is to record tape two. The person who records tape two must then forward their own tape, tape one and the two remaining blank tapes to the person who will record tape three. And so on. All four recorded tapes must then be sent back to person one. At no time must any of the people involved in the recording listen to any of the tapes. Apart from this single interaction, the four people must not know each other at all, otherwise branching or cross-streaming could occur and a whirlpool loop collapse would quickly follow. Obviously, you must have no contact with any of the four participants for the same reason. Obviously again, this is almost impossible. Hence the importance of maintaining the provided equipment.

With regret and also hope,

The First Eric Sanderson

(Received: 25th September)
Letter #4

Dear Eric,

Some other things which provide good camouflage in the waterways:

Other People's Letters/Post: Perhaps the most useful of everyday items when it comes to confusing and tangling and knotting and muddying the conceptual flows of the world. Resonant items can be effectively camouflaged by submerging them in a large box filled with post. Or just a heap of post. The more different people the post belongs to, the more effective the camouflage. This system works because a letter acts as a physical embodiment of a communicative flow. Even the briefest letter channels and underpins a strong and definite stream of intended interaction. An item or even a person, like you, submerged in other people's post will exist at the centre of a confusing multi-stream spaghetti junction of tangled flows. To a Ludovician or other conceptual fish, the result will be hundreds of crossing currents with different originators and recipients. The resonant item is obscured, becoming only one of many possible stream destinations, and any thought fish trying to move towards it is likely to be confused, disorientated and misdirected.

Books of Fact/Books of Fiction: Books of fact provide solid channels of information in many directions. Library books are best because they also link the book itself to every previous reader and any applications of the text. Fiction books also generate illusionary flows of people and events and things that have never been, or maybe have only half-been from a certain point of view. The result is a labyrinth of glass and mirrors which can trap an unwary fish for a great deal of time. I have an old note written by me before I got so vague which says that some of the great and most complicated stories like the *Thousand and One Nights* are very old protection puzzles, or even idea nets by which ancient peoples would fish for and catch the smaller conceptual fish. I don't know if this is true or not. Build the books into a small wall around yourself. My notes say three or five books high is best.

With regret and hope,

The First Eric Sanderson

(Received: 23rd November)

Letter #60

Dear Eric,

As promised, this is the key to the locked room in the house.

You should reread letters #3, #4, #17, #44, #58 and #59 and follow all procedures before you open the red filing cabinet. The text you will find inside is 'live' and extremely dangerous.

With regret and hope,

The First Eric Sanderson

(Received: 30th November)
Letter #67

Dear Eric,

As far as I am aware, the conceptual fish do not see physical plants and trees and animals. They do not see the sky or the moon. They only see people, and the things that people make and say and do. The streams of human history, human culture and human thought are their environment. The Ludovician is always looking. I am careful to hide myself, but I am forgetful.

I'm telling you everything I know before it's all lost for good.

With regret and hope,

The First Eric Sanderson

(Received: 9th January)

Letter #108

Dear Eric,

I just realised, it has been more than three months for you now. More than a hundred of these letters. I hope you can follow them, I am doing all I can.

Soon you will receive a package containing a light bulb, a videotape and two exercise books. It's important that you open this package inside a Dictaphone loop because reading the enclosed information will create a strong scent in the waterways.

The light bulb has been carefully modified to flicker a double-encoded Morse/QWERTY text (more on this later) containing a fragment of your history. As you will see, one of the exercise books contains my work on identifying the type of encryption, the other contains the clean text I have been able to extract so far. There is still more to translate and that task falls to you. The videotape contains the light bulb's complete flash cycle for decoding purposes, and in case of accident.

Be very careful with this text. It should be considered 'live' at all times. As with all other live documents, ensure it is stored in a post-filled box for safety.

Regret and hope,

The First Eric Sanderson

(Received: 11th January)
Letter #110

Dear Eric,

It seems so normal doesn't it, the writing from my journal about Clio and Greece? I hardly recognise myself. I don't think I could even write like that anymore. I've ended up as a collector's egg, all the insides and egginess sucked out leaving just an intact and brittle shell, looking just the same, perfectly the same, but not really an egg at all anymore. I don't know if some of the things I say make sense. When I get to the middle of something I find I've lost my grip on one of the ends. Like trying to hang a huge sheet out in the wind, I can't keep hold of it all at once and parts are escaping, flapping away out of reach. Are you there? Is there even going to be a you after I'm gone? I'm trying hard not to lose faith. Don't lose faith in me, Eric. If you are there, you will need this information to survive; I need you to believe in me. I've killed myself so slowly it's taken years and I don't really even know why. I don't want to die. I'm scared of dying but even more I don't want to not be. I remembered something Clio said and I wrote it down. We were coming out of a building like a pub or a cinema or a shopping complex and Clio said, "I'm going to have a smiley face tattooed on the underneath of my big toe." I said why and Clio said, "So when I'm dead and they put a toe tag on me it'll look funny in the morgue." Memories like this one are like the coloured dust from butterfly wings coming off on my fingers and then blowing away. I think Clio liked the idea of the tattoo because it would be like her something, her sense of humour, would still be there for at least a little bit longer when her body was cold and dead. It would be like a little cheat. You see what I'm saying don't you? Don't lose faith in me, Eric.

Regret and hope,

E

(Received: 12th January)

Letter #111

Dear Eric,

There are two stages to the light bulb text encryption. The first is simple Morse code. The bulb flashes in short and long bursts, dots and dashes. These can be transcribed as letters using the following chart:

A .-	H	O ---	V ...-
B -...	I ..	P .--.	W .--
C -.-.	J .---	Q --.-	X -..-
D -..	K -.-	R .-.	Y -.--
E .	L .-..	S ...	Z --..
F ..-.	M --	T -	
G --.	N -.	U ..-	

You will notice that the letters produced still appear to be random at this point. They don't make any sense. That is because there is still more to do.

The second part of the code uses the layout of a computer or typewriter keyboard, as below (with rows two and three slightly realigned to make a grid):

Each letter from the translated Morse code sequence is applied to the grid:

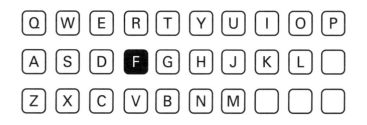

The final, correctly decoded letter will always be one of those adjacent to the Morse code letter. For example, if you translate an 'F' from the Morse code, the actual letter you are looking for will be one of the eight adjacent to 'F' on the QWERTY layout:

The translation letters also 'rollaround'. This is a way of saying if a Morse code letter touches the edge of the board, as B does

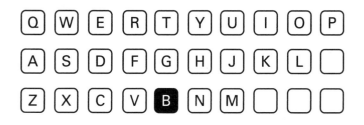

the possible translation letters will not only include V, F, G, H and N, but also R, T and Y, as the three unavailable bottom spaces are rolled up to the top.

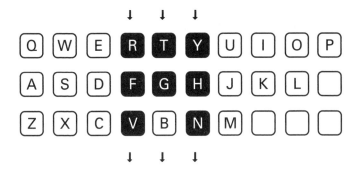

This rollaround is applied to all edge-of-grid letters, as shown here:

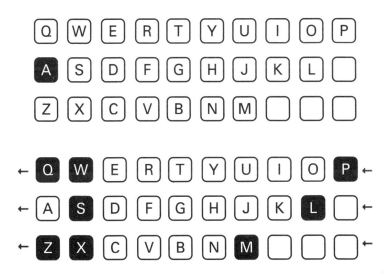

As you are probably noticing, the code is not very specific. When translated from Morse, each letter has eight possible solutions. Only one of these will be the correct letter. This means clean text cannot be constructed at the level of the individual letter. Possible translations must be constructed at word level, re-evaluated at sentence level and refined at paragraph level. It makes the process very time-consuming. It will take a long time. I think I built ambiguity into the encryption as added camouflage against the word shark. Did I? Well. It seems to serve no other purpose. It's raining here in the past. I hope the weather there in the future is better.

Regret and hope,

E

(Received: 29th April)
Letter #205

Dear Eric,

Six months. Are you still with me? A sort of half birthday if you are, I'm sorry.
I'm sorry you are so alone.

Now, here is what this letter is about:

There is a story. There is a story I've been avoiding. It's the story about why
all this is happening. Why the Ludovician is hunting you. It's all my fault, Eric.

Stories. There used to be more stories, records of other things, other
fragments I'd written down or encoded. I can remember some of their names.
Once, there was The Dust Fragment and The Shadow Fragment and The
Envelope Fragment, as well as The Light Bulb Fragment which you have. But
it's dangerous here in the past where I am and things get muddled or lost or
destroyed. I'm trying, I'm trying to save as much as I can but those fragments
have all gone and I can't remember what they said.

There once was a fragment called The Aquarium Fragment. I have a
single piece of text left from The Aquarium Fragment. It is part of the story
of why all this is happening. I will try to tell the story and slot this little bit of
fragment in the right place.

This is how the story goes:

To try to change what happened to Clio, I went looking for a man called
Dr Trey Fidorous. I don't know, I don't remember what I thought this Dr Trey
Fidorous could do, but I devoted myself to finding him. He was a writer, an
academic, I think. I looked for him first in his dense and complex papers, all
filed and forgotten in university basement stacks. From them, I found his
rolling pencil footnotes in a set of old encyclopaedias in a library in Hull.
They led me to flyposted text-swarmed poster sheets in Leeds, and from Leeds,
on to series of essays written in black marker on the tiles of underpasses in
Sheffield. The underpass essays led me to a suite of chalked texts on the walls
of an old tower block in Manchester.

I remember this part, this route so clearly because I repeat it to myself
every day: 'The dictionary in Hull, the posters in Leeds, the underpasses in

Sheffield, the tower block in Manchester.' And then there's a last stop on this route, the place I finally found Dr Trey Fidorous: I found him sick in a closed-up doorway in Blackpool. Something had happened to him. I can't remember what it was.

Hull. Leeds. Sheffield. Manchester. Blackpool.

Hull. Leeds. Sheffield. Manchester. Blackpool.

What happened next is I went with Fidorous down into the empty, abandoned areas in the world which are sometimes called un-space (I will write you a letter about un-space another time) and I studied with him down there. I learned things, the things I am teaching you about survival and other things too, things he wanted me to know and things he didn't want me to know, that I shouldn't have known. I thought I could save her, Eric. I had so many ideas. The details have all gone.

Somewhere in un-space, there was a hole. A deep black hole, a lift shaft. I'd been looking for that hole, for a way to get down it, for so long. It's patchy, sketchy. Mostly all I have are the feelings left behind, emotion shadows where the facts should be. I do know that I left Fidorous to go looking for that hole and that I hired someone to help me find it, someone from what is called the Un-Space Exploration Committee (I will write you a letter about the Un-Space Exploration Committee too) but the details of that part, the hows and the whys, when I try to think about them they all come apart like rotten old cloth.

I did find the hole.

Down at the bottom there was a place filled with rows and rows of stinking neglected fish tanks with sick, dead and dying fish; a horrible abandoned aquarium. In the heart of the place, that's where I found the Ludovician. It was younger then, much smaller but still very dangerous. And I let it out of its conceptual loop prison, Eric. I did it. It was me. I gave myself to the thought shark and it ate and ate, growing bigger and bigger and now it's an adult and there's no stopping it. I killed myself and I've probably killed you too. Why did I do it? Why would I do that?

I think I thought I could save her.

I was so stupid. I was so stupid and now everything's all gone.

This is the only piece of The Aquarium Fragment I have left, the end of the story. As always, some parts, some meanings, are missing:

] *stepped inside the tank-circle.*

[missing text] *suddenly had a very clear memory of my Granddad, tall and Roman-nosed with silver Brylcreemed hair, hanging wallpaper on old, dark, paint-splattered stepladders. I thought about how since his death my Granddad had become more a collection of scenes than a real man to me, how I could recall him being kind, angry, serious and joking but how the edges of these memory events didn't quite fit together and left me with a sort of schizophrenic collage rather than the real, rounded-out man I must have known as a child.*

My senses, trying to catch my attention in all this, suddenly broke through to the surface and I came back into the present. A horrific clarity came into the world, a sense of all things being exactly what [missing text] *with relevance, obviousness and a bright* [missing text]. *Without me telling it to, my mind switched itself back to the image of my Granddad up the ladder. And then I saw it, partly with my eyes, or with my mind's eye. And partly heard, remembered as sounds and words in shape form. Concepts, ideas, glimpses of other lives or writings or feelings. And living, the thing obviously alive and with will and movement. Coming oddly* [missing text] *light links in my memory, swimming hard upstream against the panicking fast flow of my thoughts. The Ludovician, into my life in every way possible.*

I did it, Eric. I let it out. I'm responsible.

I really am so sorry.

Regret and hope,

Eric

(Received: 1st May)
Letter #206

Dear Eric,

Q) What is un-space?

A) It is the labelless car parks, crawl tunnels, disused attics and cellars, bunkers, maintenance corridors, derelict industrial estates, boarded-up houses, smashed-windowed condemned factories, offlined power plants, underground facilities, storerooms, abandoned hospitals, fire escapes, rooftops, vaults, crumbling churches with dangerous spires, gutted mills, Victorian sewers, dark tunnels, passageways, ventilation systems, stairwells, lifts, the dingy winding corridors behind shop changing rooms, the pockets of no-name-place under manhole covers and behind the overgrow of railway sidings.

Q) Who are the Un-Space Exploration Committee?

A) They map and chart and explore and research un-space.

I'm sorry for the format. Today is a bad day. All my structure is gone.

Regret and hope,

Eric

(Received: 22nd May)

Letter #214

Dear Eric,

I hope you've been able to master the techniques I sent to you about dealing with receipts. And the internet, remember there is *no* safe procedure for electronic information. Avoid it at all costs (refer to letter #5 for ATMs, and bank account management).

Regret and hope,

E

(Received: 30th May)
Letter #222

Dear Eric,

Much of what I learned, this little box of tricks and tactics I'm leaving behind
for you, it came directly from Dr Trey Fidorous. He knows about the
waterways of thought and the conceptual fish. He knows about Clio Aames
and what I thought I could do to save her. He knows all of it, all the things I've
lost, I'm sure he does. You need to find him again, Eric. Find Dr Trey Fidorous.
He knows about the Ludovician, so maybe he knows a way to stop it too.

Hull. Leeds. Sheffield. Manchester. Blackpool.

Regret and hope,

E

(Received: 16th June)
Letter #238

Dear Eric,

I hope the job search is going well. Be careful in selecting the right person to study. A well planned, fully-realised false identity will provide the most versatile day-to-day protection should you decide to make the journey. It requires months of hard work to perfect someone else's mannerisms, movements and attitudes but this will allow you to move through the world without generating a single recognisable ripple.

The Ludovician will circle forever if it needs to. All it needs, all it's waiting for, is for you to stir the waters in a familiar way – a recognisable way – to cross its path with yours by one or two degrees of separation. Practice practice practice. The disguise may not hold up close, but from any distance you will be invisible.

Regret and hope,

Eric

8

The Impressionist

"How have things been at work this week?"

I'd had the job for months, but Dr Randle was still pleased about it.

"They've been fine. Well, boring. You know."

"Boring is okay, Eric. It's been over a year since your last recurrence. I think you could count boring as a triumph, even."

"This is good then, you'd say?"

"Well, you're certainly not taking any backwards steps."

"I still don't remember anything."

"No, but one thing at a time. You really should be counting *boring* as an achievement compared to where you were when we started. Sometimes you have to do a lot of work to arrive at stability."

"Now here, you see, you have to run just as fast as you can to stay in the same place."

"Eric."

Dr Randle wore a big red knitted jumper with a llama on it, or maybe a badly done horse. She'd been growing her hair over the last twelve months and now she had it tied back in a ponytail. The odd copper coil sprig still escaped here and there, sticking out of her head at fiercely demented angles. Her eyes were just the same though, heavy and oppressive and powerful and also not very observant.

"You're the doctor," I said. "I'm in your capable hands."

"This is a team effort, Eric. Rest assured we'll get there in the end."

I'd been learning that Dr Randle mostly saw what she expected to see rather than what was actually in front of her. *I'm in your capable hands?* I didn't always speak like that. When I first came to her I didn't speak like that at all but – *whoosh* – over it goes, over her big stormy head along with everything else. Maybe most people don't notice half of what they actually see.

"I trust you," I said.

Rusty, Dr Randle's dog, sniffed around my legs, happy and excited by the smell of Ian. Ian, if the past was anything to go by, would sniff the dog smell on my jeans when I got home, give me a *you disgust me* stare and then march off, ginger tail in the air showing me his arsehole as a sign of contempt.

"He's hungry," Randle smiled, looking at the scruffy little dog. "If I don't feed him he'll start throwing himself at the fridge door again."

I reached down and scratched Rusty's ear. He flopped over onto his back, belly up.

"I'll head off," I said, rubbing the dog's belly. "I'll see you again on Friday."

The dog looked at me for a split second, as if he knew I was telling a lie.

Outside, I picked a couple of brown soggy leaves off the yellow Jeep's windscreen before getting in. I closed the door and fired up the engine. It was a cold, bright breathy autumn afternoon. I slid all the heater levers on, rubbed my hands on my legs to warm them and found some old rock 'n' roll on the radio. The yellow Jeep crunched away from the curb. I edged my way out into the traffic.

·

I clicked open the front door and stepped into the skeleton house inside. It's funny how a house can look just the same on the outside when everything inside is changed. The hallway, the living room, through to the kitchen; it all looks so empty now. All clean. Everything washed and wiped and dusted and vacuumed and put away. Bleached bones. Anything valuable, I've stacked in packing crates in the locked room. Everything dangerous, I've buried in protective post.

I let down the kitchen blinds, drew the living room curtains. I sat for a few minutes on the sofa and thought about what Randle would think when I didn't show up on Friday, what she would think when she realised I'd gone. Maybe she'd feel good. Maybe she'd think that her fugue theories had been right all along. Probably she'd think that. I hoped she'd miss me a little too.

I'm at my desk now, at my typewriter in the bedroom. Ian is on the bed, sleeping on a pile of my notebooks. The Dictaphone noise doesn't bother him anymore. After all this time I don't really hear it either. Soon I'll wrestle the cat into his carry box, pack up the Dictaphones and leave the house, maybe for good.

Two nights after my living room floor disintegrated into a wet, deep concept and I'd swum and recited the Ryan Mitchell Mantra for my life, the shark came back. Two a.m. and me sitting up in bed, cold with panic sweat and covers bunched up in my white knuckled fists. The walls strained and stretched, sending odd shadows and strange associations rippling around the room. But the First Eric Sanderson's newly unpackaged Dictaphones chattered away to themselves in each corner of the bedroom and the memory shark, the Ludovician, stayed locked out behind the plaster. It couldn't cross the perimeter. It couldn't break through the *non-divergent conceptual loop*. The First Eric Sanderson's letters ranged from lucid to almost indecipherable, but his tactics worked. They all worked.

And so, tentatively at first and then with careful but growing confidence, I became a pupil of my last self. I learned about the Ludovician and about the word-trails of Dr Trey Fidorous. I learned what little Eric could remember about the labelless car parks, access tunnels and buried places that made up un-space. I learned how to set up fake conceptual flows and short-circuit the existing ones, how to attach the bracken and lichen of foreign ideas to my scalp and work the mud and grass of another self into and over my skin and clothes until I could become invisible at will, until anyone or anything could be looking straight at me and never see the real me at all.

The First Eric Sanderson sent me a CV and I got a job. The First Eric Sanderson sent me a list of useful character attributes to look out for and that's how I chose Mark Richardson, the data analyst. We worked in the same office. At work, I learned about Richardson's family, his past, his beliefs, his worldview, his hopes. I studied his voice, mannerisms, expressions. I practised in front of a mirror, with a video camera and with a tape recorder. I practised them for days and months until I could build him around me in seconds, until I could disappear, until I could move around at will without sending a single ripple of my real self out into the world. If the Ryan Mitchell Mantra was a clumsy crisis shield for those early months, then my fake Mark Richardson persona was a stronger, more flexible, more advanced replacement – an almost perfect mask.

When the First Eric Sanderson wrote the letters he was an empty box of tactics and manoeuvres, a broken wind-up soldier. It took me a while to realise: he was training me to do something he should have done himself. Something he didn't have the strength for.

The months of my new life stretched out until they became a year. Eventually I'd done everything I could, become as good at all the tricks and the tactics as I could be.

The letters from the First Eric Sanderson stopped four days ago. Just like Clio's idea for a tattooed face on her big toe, Eric had ghost-projected the last whispers of himself into the future, bacon-sliced up into 300 envelopes and boxes. And finally the last one had arrived. *A man lives so many different lengths of time.* And each one has its own end.

•

If I don't come back, or if I do come back without my mind, I'm leaving a copy of this account in the red filing cabinet with all the first Eric's letters. If there is another Eric Sanderson reading this, I've left you everything I can. I'm sorry it's not much.

I'm going to look for Dr Trey Fidorous.

All I have done here is learn to protect myself, I haven't made a single step towards understanding anything. The First Eric Sanderson was right; if there are any answers, they will be with him. My plan is to follow the route the first Eric took to find Fidorous when all of this began. I'm going to start in Hull and work my way across the country. *Hull. Leeds. Sheffield. Manchester. Blackpool.* East to west. Fidorous's trail of words must be years old now, but it's the only lead I have. I can't stay here and try to defend myself like the last Eric did.

And there's something else: I have dreams about Clio Aames. I have dreams where I've seen her and recognised her and known her and held her. But in the morning, they go, lifted from me like the low-hanging mists lift from the playing fields and I have nothing. Just emotion, and a general sense of something lost. The truth is; I can't be only this anymore.

In the garden across the street, the shadow of the telegraph pole creeps its way slowly around the world. At its top, there's a starling, hunched down against the end of summer.

TWO

At night the salmon move
out from the river and into the town

Raymond Carver

9

On the Trail of Trey Fidorous –
Recovered Palaeontology and Finds
(Hull to Sheffield)

a

e

e

1. Single-celled animals

The first of two flyposted texts discovered in Leeds and possibly created by Dr Fidorous (although, in appearance, these could not be further from the biro-swarmed sheets described in the first Eric's letters). This and the following text were exposed as part of the refurbishment of Leeds Central Station. Despite weeks of searching, no other possible Fidorous flypostings were discovered in the city. *Single-celled animals* is the original title (printed in the bottom left corner).

AaBbCcD
dEeFfGgHhIiJj
KkLlMmNnOoP
pQqRrSsTtUuV
vWwXxYyZz

2. The nucleus of the cell contains biological information
The second possible Fidorous text, discovered alongside the first. Again, *The nucleus of the cell contains biological information* is the original title.

3. Fossil fish reconstruction

The first image is a replica of a text structure found in the Arundel Way underpass in Sheffield. The image had been created horizontally across two tiles at the base of a stairway (see photos & map of underpass layout) using letter transfers. The structure seems to represent a species of prehistoric armoured fish, although the image is incomplete with large areas of damage. The second image is my speculative reconstruction. The text has been reproduced actual size. No other underpass texts were recovered.

4. Computer virus mosquito in amber

This image was discovered as an acetate label on a 3½″ floppy disk in Sheffield Interchange (see maps/photos) and has been greatly enlarged here. The structure is probably a mosquito. The disk carrying this image is transparent orange plastic (rather than the usual matt black), giving the impression of an insect trapped in amber. The text appears to be programming source code and there are some similarities to the Melissa Virus code circa 2000/2001. Could this be connected to Fidorous? The disk itself is unsalvageable.

5. Postcard of the Greek island of Naxos

This postcard found in a lay-by in the Broomhill area of Sheffield. The reverse of the postcard is still blank but the photo credit describes the image as 'Naxos at dawn'. There's some slight rain damage. It's very unlikely that this is connected to Dr Fidorous or to the First Eric Sanderson but the chance discovery of it gave me a thin sort of encouragement. As this isn't strictly a 'find' I've wrapped it in clear plastic along with two pieces of protective post and stored it separately, in the pocket in the top of my rucksack.

10

Flotsam and Jetsam

The rain came down so hard it had real weight, beating my head and shoulders into a flinch, pouring heavy over my waterlogged clothes and streaming in flukes from my hood and from my elbows and from the bottom of my coat. Hard, heavy, roaring and angry. It was difficult to see. I brought a hand up to shield my eyes but this created a new shelf and a flow of fresh rivulets were soon throw-twisting themselves off the ends of my fingers and curling their way under my hood to run down my cheeks and chin. I struggled to blink away as much water I could.

Then I saw what was out there, and it staggered me.

God, my lips said. The word was stillborn and tiny and bundled away in a sweep of the gale.

I'd been hoping the gateway might belong to an old house, the Willows Hotel according to my map, but it didn't. I'd left the road too early or too late; this was the entrance to a park, not a driveway. Everything beyond the gateposts was furious: a river gone gigantic and deformed and crazy, banks burst and out on a greedy, rolling brown rampage. The size and force of it overloaded me, made me sick and dizzy. A *too muchness*.

My rain-blinking eyes struggled back from the flow and down to my feet. The water around my boots was peaty-brown and alive too, I realised. No boundaries. The river was here and reaching and grabbing and actually pulling at my feet and calves with a beautiful, mindless ache. A willpower in pressure. The river wanting to drag me off and smash me up and remake me as part of its pointless and stupidly powerful and passionate drive to change and obliteration.

Caught there, caught in that second of realisation and awareness, when everything came into quick focus and this thing, this *event* I'd stumbled into was all around me and instant and real, I wanted it to happen. I wanted to let my knees buckle. Let my shoulders slump, just let it all go – fall forwards, down and finally, thankfully, out. This monster river could take me away and unknot me and spread me out however it wanted and however it liked because, honestly, finally, I just felt so fucking tired of endless hours of doing my shitty best to cling my component parts together as a human being. I wanted to pile up and silt-slide, wrap around the trunks of trees, a lost nothing of unthinking debris and high watermarks. Just to be all the way empty, just be all the way gone.

Seconds passed.

I sucked in a lungful of air and let it leak out – slow, wet and steamy. I took a heavy but careful step back against the wanting of the water. After a moment steadying myself, I took another, and then another. I turned, slowly, very slowly and very carefully, and began to make some progress back towards the yellow Jeep.

A cat is a responsibility after all. And feeding and keeping and caring about a stupid fat cat isn't much, isn't much in the entirety of what counts for being a person and the huge range of *what people do*, but it is something. It is something and it's something that's warm and that I still have.

·

I stood in the hotel lobby, backpacker's rucksack slung over one shoulder, the cat carrier in the opposite hand. The warmth of indoors burned at the rain-sting on my cheeks and forehead, flood water leaked out at my feet. I had a strange feeling of the heat driving it out. The brown river water spreading flat and urgeless from me now – dying, or already dead.

Climate change.

"My God, have you ever seen the like? We've started work on an ark out the back." The reception counter was quite high, but she must have been very short or sitting unworkably low; it hid everything from her chin down. "And flood warnings on the radio, John said the water's high enough to take cars away now. *Cars.* You wouldn't want to be down in the valley now."

"No," I said, dripping. "I was down there, it's pretty wild."

"Really?" she grew half an inch through pure neck-crane. "Is it like they're saying? *Cars?*" She was maybe early fifties, hot ginger hair, bright eyes and red generator cheeks powering a big-hearted but trouble-causing sort of a mouth. *An operatic mouth*, I thought, *big and decent.*

I've got good at faces. *The first step is to see.*

"Well, I missed your turning," I said. "It was a bit touch-and-go."

"Oh, love." She gave me a tough guy's smile. "And look at him too. We don't normally take pets. John, John's my husband, he doesn't like animals, but it's not like we can send you back out there tonight, is it?"

The last part wasn't addressed to me.

"Thanks. He's very grateful," I said, looking down at the cat-carrier. "Aren't you?"

From her laugh I knew the cat was still glaring out of his carry case, a big fat *fuck off* expression all over his face. "Well, anyway," I said. "I'm grateful enough for both of us."

"Don't you worry, love, twenty-five years I've been with him," she nodded her head to the rear of the building before turning back to smile at the cat. "Maybe the two of you'll get along after all." Then, to me with a wink, "Have you and smiler come a long way?"

"Further than I can remember," I said.

Further than I can remember. Pushing on the walls, rattling the handle. Testing myself. Testing myself and passing – not the slightest of bumps registered in the world. No slight widening of the eyes, no slight reddening of the cheeks, slight twitch of the mouth, slight pull of the scalp, not a single twist of blood in the water, nothing at all. *Further than I can remember,* I said, and nobody felt the pothole we'd travelled over.

I smiled. "He's like a permanent attachment."

She nodded, happy with that, then caught herself. "Oh, but would you look. I'm sorry, love, here's me going on while you've both been out there in God-knows-what. You'll want to get checked in and get those soaking clothes off, won't you?" Her head disappeared then reappeared along with a hand holding a printed sheet of paper. "It's only a straightforward form, it shouldn't keep you long."

I squelched to the desk, dropped the bag, put the cat down next to the phone, pushed up my coatsleeve to try to control the dripping then swivelled the paperwork to face me. She passed over a pen and I reached to accept it. Now I could see; she wasn't short, she *was* sitting down. She was in a wheelchair. The cat didn't look impressed.

"Old Ironside, that's me," she told the cat, "but you can call me Aunty Ruth if you're going to be good while you're here. What's your name, cheerful?"

I looked up from the form. "His name's Ian."

Her eyebrows dropped and bunched just for a second, then were chased back up by a breezy grin.

It's hurtful and wonderful how our jokes survive us.

Since I left home on this journey, I've thought a lot about this – how a big part of any life is about the hows and whys of setting up machinery. It's building systems, devices, motors. Winding up the clockwork of direct debits, configuring newspaper deliveries and anniversaries and photographs and credit card repayments and anecdotes. Starting their engines, setting them in motion and sending them chugging off into the future to do their thing at regular or irregular intervals. When a person leaves or dies or ends, they leave an afterimage; their outline in the devices they've set up around them. The image fades to the winding down of springs, the slow running out of fuel as the machines of a life lived in certain ways in certain places and from certain angles are shut down or seize up or blink off one by one. It takes time. Sometimes, you come across the dusty lights or electrical hum of someone else's machine, maybe a long time after you ever expected to, still running, lonely in the dark. Still doing its thing for the person who started it up long, long after they've gone.

A man lives so many different lengths of time.

A man *is* so many different lengths of time.

Change. Collapse. Reinvention.

The cat twitched his ear.

I passed the completed form to Aunty Ruth.

"Well, it's a pleasure to have you, Ian and –" she looked down at the form – "Mr Richardson."

"Mark. Call me Mark," I said, leaning over the desk, holding out my hand and getting all of it, the whole Mark Richardson act, just right. I glanced to the front door and hitched the smile up one side of my face. "Believe me, it's a pleasure to have made it."

·

My room was small, functional but very clean – the kind of domestic clean that feels almost scrubbed raw. The thought crossed my mind that Aunty Ruth might be the kind of woman who would spit on a hankie and rub it very hard against the side of your mouth.

Ian jumped out of his box the second I turned the clasp and settled on the chest of drawers with his back to the radiator, half-open eyes fixed on me, left ear making sweep scans of the small space behind him.

I checked through the inside pockets of my drenched coat. It was worse than I'd thought – the letters were all ruined.

Every pocket offered up an elastic band-bound handful of lumpy pulp, each one on the verge of coming apart like dough and shot through with black spots of print, blue ink veins. I'd not been in the downpour very long, but with that volume of water it had obviously been long enough. Too, too long. My outer camouflage, my conceptual flak jacket was useless.

Shit. No, not critical, but I'd be flying on three engines until the letters were replaced. Still, it wasn't like I didn't have other tools, other defences; my assumed identity was still rock solid. I'd proved that to myself again in the lobby only fifteen minutes earlier. *A real job of work.* But losing the letters did mean tightroping without a safety net, swimming without armbands. And I was tired. Taking no chances, I started to set up the Dictaphones.

·

The little tape players tinny-chattered away to themselves in the corners of the room, at the edges of my thoughts. As I stripped off the wet clothes, I let the essence of Mark Richardson slip off my face and out of my body with a series of deep, purging breaths. I allowed my movements to become blank and then slowly to change, my hands and arms and shoulders finding their old state and stretch and rhythm. I pulled my face around its natural expressions in the mirror for a while before dropping backwards onto the bed.

Aunty Ruth had lost her chef because of the floods but would be making a cold buffet *for all you flotsam and jetsam* in the hotel bar in a couple of hours. I set the alarm on my new mobile phone, grabbed a handful of blanket, rolled and curled.

The Dictaphones talked treble and hiss.

I reached out, grabbed the rucksack and pulled a battered plastic-wrapped bundle of papers and videotape from deep inside. The Light Bulb Fragment, still dry and undamaged. I'd been working to decode the second half for almost seven months now, at first in the house as I'd worked to perfect the Mark Richardson personality and then on the road, in blank, neat hotel rooms in friendless cities all across the country. A few more nights with the stark flashing tape and the first Eric Sanderson's tables and charts and I *might* have a workable draft.

There was no way to know for sure, the obscure QWERTY encoding meant you didn't have anything until you had it all.

I rewrapped the bundle and pushed it back into the bag. In one hundred and nine minutes' time Aunty Ruth would be laying out her sandwiches. I closed my eyes, reminding myself to bring back something with meat for Ian.

.

Flotsam and jetsam is what Aunty Ruth had called those of us who'd washed up in the floods that evening, and we were. Storm refugees. It would be wrong to say the hotel bar was crammed with us, but I'd bet it hadn't been so full for a long time.

Ruth laid on three platters of sandwiches and gave me a small bag of sliced ham for the cat. She said she'd put her husband to work on getting together a makeshift sandbox, so Ian wouldn't have any *little accidents*.

"Cats get so embarrassed, I know," she said.

I circulated just like Mark Richardson would and I coughed up a couple of his obvious jokes around the bar. It had been eighteen weeks since I'd seen the real Richardson, since I finished the training, left my job, loaded the yellow Jeep and set out on the cold trail of my lost past. Hull, Leeds, Sheffield, six weeks in each city. A total of one year and four months since the day I was born, face down on that bedroom carpet.

It was still raining outside. A dramatic wet sheet broke against the window followed by a haiku of fat rain taps as the wind took a breath. Orchestral for storm.

"You see," the man opposite me was saying. "It's the Pennines –"

I looked up.

Mark Richardson was a people person, a listener as much as a talker. That's what made him such a good choice for my fake identity. Meeting people, communication, information gathering, all these things would have to be done in character if my defences were going to hold. If I was going to move through the world without creating ripples and being found and ripped all apart. But being Richardson meant being Richardson all the time, not just when it suited me. And so I was socialising.

Opposite, my new flotsam friend chewed out the middle of another ham and mustard sandwich triangle, free hand circling in that way that means *hold on: swallowing then speaking.*

He gulped.

"It's the Pennines," he said again. "The hills are too high. The sky's too low."

I nodded.

"It grinds people up. Between the road and the sky." He picked inside the sandwich crust before looking back at me. "Lots of accidents up there."

This was Dean Rush, truck driver. He'd had to leave his truck – he called it a 'unit' – further down the hill, near a golf course. I'd invited him to join me at the table and that was the first thing he'd told me. Then – *the Pennines.* This was a man of scraps and fragments. No links or rhythms to his conversation, everything lonely and spare. There was something birdlike about him too, I'd decided; Bleak Dean Rush, the moorland crow.

He pulled a thin white string of ham fat from the remains of his sandwich, looked carefully at it, dangling, before laying it down on the side of his plate. He blinked once, twice.

At the far end of the bar, Aunty Ruth moved all surviving sandwiches onto a single platter then set about clearing the empties. Rush watched her manoeuvre her wheelchair out of the bar then turned back to me.

"Lots of smashed-up people because of those hills," he said.
Blink. Blink.

It was down to me to bridge the meaning gap and it took a second.
"You know them then? Ruth and –"

"John. Yeah," he nodded. "Car crash three years ago. They didn't think she'd survive the night."

.

A few days before I set out on this *quest* I bought a mobile phone. I rigged up a system which would feed incoming calls through a post-buried diverter in the locked room for safety, then I made myself a small stack of business cards. They had *I need to speak to you* written on them and my phone number. I'd pushed the cards under AUTHORISED PERSONNEL doorways in the back alleys of crumbling docklands in Hull and grease-smeared transport depots in Sheffield. I'd left them in all the grey breezeblock STAFF ONLY and MAINTENANCE corridors which riddle the backstages of big shopping complexes and superstores across the north of England. Any place I came across that could possibly be described as un-space, I left a card. The Un-Space Exploration Committee, whoever they were, had helped the First Eric Sanderson on his journey. Maybe someone there would be able to help me track down Trey Fidorous. That was my plan, my hope. Only, the mobile phone never rang.

After so many weeks of leaving the cards and hearing nothing, I'd found myself starting to worry that the whole idea of un-space and its committee was just a jumbled delusion created by the first Eric's collapsing mind. The line between chasing ghosts and tilting at windmills was faint and thin and blurred to the point of almost not being a line at all. Maybe this was a condition. Perhaps I *was* suffering from Randle's fugue and I should turn around, go home and confess everything to her or to a proper medical doctor in a hospital who could finally make sense of all this. But. But the Ludovician was real, I'd seen it. I had seen it. And I kept coming back to the First Eric Sanderson's words. *Please don't lose faith in me, Eric.* I told myself that I wouldn't and I couldn't, for my sake as much as for his.

Bleak Dean Rush got up from my table, drained his beer, nodded to me, blinked and was gone. I sat there on my own for a while, spinning my bottle of beer on its mat and looking at the left-behind plate of sandwich crust Vs and discarded strings of fat.

11

Time's Shrinking Little Antarctica

"Are you and the cat running a mobile library, love?" Three-quarters of Aunty Ruth's head smiled over the check-in desk. I stopped at the foot of the stairs.

"Well, the mobile part might be a problem."

She laughed. "I could always try calling someone else if you like, or I could get John to have a look at it. Mind you, he doesn't know half what he thinks he does and what he does know usually makes things worse."

"Don't worry, it's fine. It'll be nice to be off the road for a few days, to be honest. Ian says thank you for the ham."

"He's welcome. You're right to give yourself a rest after what you went through getting here."

I'd been unloading boxes of books from the back of the yellow Jeep and thinking about potential and momentum. The yellow Jeep was dead. The storm found its way into the engine and turned something important and dry into something broken and wet during the night. Aunty Ruth called a local garage but flooding had left the whole town full of tipped, beached and silted cars.

"They said it'll be at least twenty-four hours, love. Maybe a couple of days before they can send someone out."

I could have tried a less local garage. Phoned back across the moors to Sheffield maybe, but I didn't. I told myself a few days' wait here at the Willows Hotel could be productive. One big push might finally decode the rest of The Light Bulb Fragment. I also needed to collect a new set of letters to replace those ruined in the downpour the previous night. There was no reason not to do both here and now before heading out into Manchester; it would be hard to imagine how Fidorous's trail could get any colder.

I convinced myself to stay on at the Willows Hotel with these clean practical facts, but there were other murkier reasons hiding in there too. I'd come three-quarters of the way along the path the first Eric had followed and I'd uncovered so very little – at best, unexplainable splinters and chips from a long lost yellow brick road; at worst, nothing at all. Soon the Light Bulb text would be decoded and not too long after that I'd reach Blackpool and the end of Fidorous's old cold trail. The thought disturbed me. While there was still distance to travel, there was still the slim chance of finding answers. While there was still a journey to be made, my crumbly little self could exist in the potential of making it. But what when the road came to an end? What would I be then?

Ian ignored all the coming and going with boxes, staring out of the window at the trees or at the birds in them. I found myself wondering what happened to the other cat, Gavin. In The Light Bulb Fragment Eric and Clio said they'd bought two kittens before they went away to Greece, but perhaps all of that was just another routine, a joke they liked to play on strangers in campsite bars. I wondered what sequences of events had made Ian a real cat and left Gavin existing only in words, in the text of a memory. Maybe it's natural for questions to outlive their answers. Or maybe answers don't die but are just lost more easily, being so small and specific, like a coin dropped from the deck of a ship and into the big deep sea.

•

I finally closed the book of codes and charts around four o'clock the following morning. I'd been decoding and deciphering the Light Bulb text for almost thirteen hours straight, carefully chiselling out each letter from the sediment: verifying, classifying, contextualising, bringing old buried things back up into the world.

I hadn't planned to attack The Light Bulb Fragment like this. After unloading the boxes I had a lunchtime sandwich and beer in the bar then I'd gone for a walk up the lane outside the hotel, following its winding way up the hillside. I found a bench by a lay-by and decided to sit down.

Blocky sandstone houses and mills made a town down in the valley. I saw the road I'd accidentally taken the night before and the battered park where the living brown river escaped its banks. The flashing lights of JCBs and council vehicles search-swiped through the black trees there now. Other strobing yellows blinked across the town too – recovery trucks collecting the dead cars, road cleaners, emergency street repairs. It looked as if the whole place was being dismantled to be taken somewhere else.

Beyond the town, the grey spread-planes of Manchester.

It started to drizzle. My coat was still wet from the downpour the previous night but I'd worn it anyway. I huddled down, pushed my head deep into the hood and slid my hands up the sleeves. *Nothing is ever still*, said the wind's spittley breath over me, *there's no hiding from that*.

.

I think there's still a small block of original quiet that exists in the world. Three a.m. to 5 a.m. – a last natural wilderness, time's shrinking little Antarctica. In the heart of this remote and silent time-place, I finally closed my book of notes and decoding tables. I'd finished. I flipped through the completed text of The Light Bulb Fragment one more time and closed the notebook. I paced around the room for a few minutes without really seeing or looking, all heavy and sleep-staring. There were things in the text I hadn't been expecting. Uncomfortable, complicating passages.

I checked my watch. I could afford half an hour's sleep before the next task on my agenda if I wanted to take it, but I didn't. The night's decoding had left me feeling cold and hollow. I wanted to focus on other things, to do things, not lie still and quiet in a room without distractions. I packed away The Light Bulb Fragment and my translating book and dug out a smaller reporter's notepad and pair of binoculars from the backpack's left pocket.

My coat was finally dry and warm from half a day over the radiator (the radiators were on constantly at the Willows Hotel, a preference shared by Aunty Ruth and Ian). My room key came with a front door key because reception went unmanned after ten o'clock and this meant I could come and go whenever I chose, which was useful for the kind of early morning surveillance necessary to collect a new supply of post. I already knew where I could get a good view of the town.

I dropped the notebook, binoculars and my mobile phone into my big empty coat pockets and took my supper tray – 'I guessed you'd lost track of time, love, so I brought you something up' – down to reception. I let myself out of the building as quietly as I could.

Pulling my coat tight against the surprise of the wind I set off up the dark lane towards the bench. To take my mind away from The Light Bulb Fragment, I started to work through the First Eric Sanderson's various systems for *acquiring* other people's post.

I never got to put any of those systems into action.

It all became academic as soon as I reached the lay-by that morning. Something was waiting for me on the bench, something that changed everything. A thick padded envelope with the words THIS IS FOR YOU written across the front.

The walk back to the hotel was ten minutes of wind, trees, the sound of my heels on the tarmac road and then, suddenly, a sharp electronic note. I tripped a step, juddering the tip of my shoe against the tarmac lane and thinking for a shocked beat that the parcel under my arm was making the noise, but then knowing – almost instantly and with voltage surprise rising up into my skull – what was really happening. I pulled the mobile phone out of my coat pocket and squinted at the bright green display:

<< Call >>
Answer?

12

The Light Bulb Fragment (Part Two)

Clio slid her finger and thumb around the stem of her Amstel glass.

"The question," she said, "is why would you *not* want a hammock?"

"Well – "

"Oh – my – God," she cut in with her best *Sex and the City*. "You are so last-century, Eric. Have you ever actually been in a hammock?"

"No."

"You see?" she said. "You see?" Her face almost straight, Clio managed to give me a *what the hell do you think is so funny* stare. "Never been in a hammock. My God, Eric. I'm sorry to say this, I really am, but that is so you. You're –" a tiny pause "– unseasoned."

"Unseasoned?"

"Yes, darling. Unseasoned by the life-affirming spice of experience."

I laughed out loud. "Fuck off."

"Oh," she said, as though my swearing were some big moment of intimate realisation. She looked me in the eyes. "Are you angry, Eric? Are you afraid?"

"Am I afraid of hammocks?"

She patted my hand. "It's okay to cry."

Something Clio likes to do is want things and then work out complicated ways of getting them. This is in spite of the fact that most of the things Clio wants she could actually afford fairly easily because she makes nearly half again as much money as I do. Or, that's how it was until recently. We've been living together for about eighteen months now and we've moved into the final stages of money commitment. My cash and Clio's cash has collectively become 'our cash'. This is a lovely and nice thing for all kinds of reasons, and it also means Clio can come up with new complex strategies to persuade me to let her use 'our cash' to buy things. Even though I would, of course, never try to stop her buying anything.

I took a swig from my bottle. "I'm trying to work out why you want me to have a hammock."

"Because I love you and don't want you to miss out."

"And?"

"We can string it between the trees outside the tent and you can lie in it and read books."

"And?"

Clio shrugged. "And I can lie in it and read *Fight Club*?"

I smiled. "Okay, then. Let's get a hammock."

"Cool."

"But how about we get it for both of us? Like a joint treat. To share."

"Oh."

"Unless," I said, patting her hand the same way she'd patted mine, "unless you want me to buy a hammock as a treat just for myself because maybe you secretly want to buy a treat just for yourself and once I've got the hammock you can say 'but I'd really like this and you *did* buy yourself that lovely hammock yesterday mer mer mer'."

"Spoilsport," Clio said, switching gears to wounded five-year-old. "Why don't you love me anymore?"

"Because you're an evil genius."

She grinned. "I am, aren't I?"

She is. Clio did want a treat for herself – an underwater camera. A second-hand one which was on sale at the bookshop in Naxos Town where we swapped our novels and where backpackers would sometimes sell stuff when money got short.

Clio loves snorkelling. She says it's a bit like flying and I'd like to say I know what she means, but I don't. I've got a snorkel and mask too, but touching the bottom with my toes is as far out as I go. And on

Naxos where the drop off is pretty steep, that's only one step removed from paddling. What freaks me out, the few times I've tried snorkelling, is the huge bank of blue you see when you look out towards the open ocean. Turning my back on it, the scale of it – I don't know. Mainly, I'm expecting something massive to come rushing out the second I look away and bite my legs off, but partly, maybe, it's also the scale of the blue itself. Knowing how swimming towards that wall of blue can only make it bigger and bigger and bigger until its face is impossibly massive and all around and behind you too, with the sea floor sloped away to black. But the scale of the deep doesn't bother Clio at all. She's done parachute jumps too, and extreme skiing, although I don't want to give you the impression she's a health freak or whatever. We're both fairly outdoorsy (don't you hate that word?), but the idea of anything we do being healthy usually spoils it. I don't think either of us have ever understood the whole *no pain, no gain* thing. Here's something I especially love about Clio Aames; she likes to laugh at joggers. There are joggers on Naxos. The temperature is touching forty on the mainland and it isn't much cooler out here but still, joggers on the beach. Clio has taken to saying "wrong" and sometimes pointing at them as they go past.

One of Clio's all-time favourite facts is how the guy who invented jogging died of a heart attack. Someone at a barbecue last summer spent ages explaining to her how the jogging guy was actually born with a heart defect and how the heart attack was coming all along. *So it wasn't actually caused by the jogging per se*, he kept saying, but that didn't spoil it for Clio at all.

"You see what they're like?" she said, as we staggered home that night. "Only a jogger with a heart defect could invent something as fucking ridiculous as jogging." I laughed and said, "That doesn't make any kind of sense at all," and she pushed me into a hedge.

•

"That's it."

"Hmmm. How do you know it works?"

"If it doesn't work I'll bring it back and get a refund."

I looked at the sand-blasted collection of window junk and crease-covered backpacker books. The underwater camera looked grubby, scratched and duff.

"A refund from here?"

"Don't be doubting my abilities, Sanderson."

We're not going to go into any of the Clio Aames complaints and refunds stories. "Can you actually get thrown off an island do you think?"

"Do you really not want me to have it?"

I looked at the camera.

"Course I want you to have it if you want it."

"I do want it." She grabbed my wrist. "Hey, I know – it can be my present for looking after you the other day when you went mental."

"Does that mean I don't have to have a hammock?" I said, then, "I didn't go mental."

"Yes you did – *Clio, Clio, help me I'm a total nut job*," she said, doing a voice.

"Look, I can't help it if I'm sensitive and creative, can I?"

"Whatever," she smiled. "So can I have the camera now?"

"Okay," I said.

"Okay."

So Clio now has an underwater camera. She hasn't used a full roll of film yet, so we still don't know if it works.

•

I did go mental a couple of days before we bought the camera, for an hour or so anyway. It happens sometimes. The *otherness* just rolls in on me like angry clouds and there's nothing I can do. That evening, I had a rising fear – terror – of being trapped on the island and not being able to get off. I was tiptoes on the edge of a panic attack, everything around me suddenly waiting to become groundless and horrific.

We were sitting outside our tent reading books when it happened. Clio was going through the guidebook putting more stars on all the things on Naxos we still hadn't done.

"I don't feel right," I said. My voice sounded thick and odd, like sound bursting out of bubbles made in some deep and strange place.

"I know," Clio said, sucking on her biro and not looking up. "He does that to me too." She meant Paul Auster – I'd been reading *The Invention of Solitude*.

"Clio," I said, and I meant it to start a sentence but there were no more words to follow on.

She put down the book and looked at me, distracted. I saw the concern focusing her eyes. "Honey, what's up?"

I tried my best to explain, handling and gently passing the words over to her like they were small spiky mines, careful, careful, careful.

"What are you like?" she said. "Maybe you should go for a walk or something. Stretch your legs."

"Maybe."

"Do you want me to come with you?"

"No, I think I should be on my own."

"Okay. Well, the sunset fish'll be in the surf now. You could take what's left of the sandwiches and feed them if you want." She smiled again. "And maybe bring back some ice cream too?"

This is how Clio punctures my panics, by bringing them down into the same familiar world as vacuuming and Saturday afternoon TV. By being kind and by calling out to my child-self – *it's okay, here's something fun* – making warm redirections to safe and happy things. Clio's deep honest kindness – you could call it a mothering streak even – is something most of our friends probably wouldn't even guess at. But it's there, bright and straightforward and obvious, if you know what you're looking at. A sort of on-show secret.

"I think that might help," I said. "The sunset fish are cool." We sometimes save pizza crusts from dinner to feed the little fish that gather in the evening surf.

"It will help, honey," Clio said. "I am always right, remember?"

"I do remember."

"Good," she said. "Well, there's a start."

And I laughed in spite of everything.

•

"Hi. How are you feeling?"

"I forgot the ice cream."

"I was really worried about you." Clio was still sitting outside writing in the guidebook when I came back to the campsite half an hour later.

"I know you were," I said, sitting down next to her on the reed mat.

"I feel so terrible. I never know how to help."

"You always get it right, anyway," I said, then, "I'm sorry it happens."

She put her arm around me, hand still holding the book, and hugged my head onto her chest with the hook of her elbow.

"What a dick," she said gently, rocking me from side to side.

•

The underwater camera is a chunky yellow and black thing living inside its own close-moulded Perspex bubble. There's a tough yellow plastic porthole around the lens held in place by a ring of six silver screws. Instead of a viewfinder, it has a foldaway plastic crosshair on top and the *take a picture* button is basically a plunger. Now we'd bought it and it was sitting on the café table with our new books and our *frappés*, I realised I liked it. It was scuffed and battered and probably didn't work, but I liked it. I found myself thinking how it looked *brave*. To boldly go where cameras have never gone before. It reminded me of Buzz Lightyear.

"You can have a go with it too if you want," Clio said. After buying the camera we'd gone for drinks on Naxos harbour. There was time to kill before the bus back to the campsite. "You could kneel at the edge of the surf and stick your head in."

"For a girl who I *know* has seen *Jaws* at least twice," I said, "you're pretty fast and easy about the sea, do you know that?"

"I'm not the one who always watches it through my fingers."

"Exactly," I said. "That's what I'm saying. It's terrifying."

Clio looked at me.

"That bit when the head pops out of the hull? With the eyes all hanging out?"

Clio looked at me.

"And the end – Chief Brodie, Richard Dreyfuss and that mad fishing guy all on that rickety boat? I can't sit still and watch that. I have to get up and walk around."

"I know," Clio sighed, shaking her head at me.

"In all other respects though," I shuffled, pretended I'd been caught out, dropped my voice, "in all other respects, I'm incredibly manly and brave."

Clio laughed.

"Okay, prove it. Come snorkelling with me. There are some amazing fish out by the rocks, I wish you'd come out and see them."

"Well, I'll be able to see them now, won't I?" I patted the top of the underwater camera.

"But it's not the same," Clio dragged the words out in a little girl whine. She smiled. "If you loved me you'd come."

"Don't you think it looks like Buzz Lightyear?"

"I *said*, if you loved me you'd come."

"To infinity and beyond," I told the chunky yellow and Perspex bubble, ignoring her.

Clio sucked hard on her straw, staring at me.

"Make it so, Number One," I told it. "One small step for man, one giant leap for mankind."

"It is mine you know," Clio said, pulling the camera towards her protectively.

"Oh, yeah," I said. "I know. I know. Totally." I sucked up a mouthful of iced coffee and winked at the camera in a knowing way.

"Stop it," she said, covering the lens.

Out past the harbour shops, cafés and bars, along a narrow sea-sprayed causeway, you can see what's left of the temple of Portara; mainly, a huge stone doorway looking out over the bay. This is known as Ariadne's Arch, where, according to legend, the daughter of King Minos of Crete had the pleasure of watching heroic love rat Theseus sod off back to Athens without her. Heartbroken Ariadne eventually married Bacchus, god of wine and song, and they lived happily ever after. Which, Clio reckons, is a way of saying she became a crazy drunk and stopped giving much of a fuck about anything.

"And the moral of the story is?" Clio had asked as we'd sat eating ice cream on an ancient world masonry block behind the arch one afternoon.

"Don't go offering your ball of wool to strange soldiers in underground tunnels?"

Clio laughed. "No, do," she said. "But don't bother going home to meet the folks afterwards."

She was still playing with her camera, so I had a flick through the new books we'd picked up. I'd got a copy of *Crooked Cucumber*, Shunryu Suzuki's autobiography. I'd already read his *Zen Mind, Beginner's Mind* and *Zen Flesh, Zen Bones*. Backpackers seem to leave a lot of Zen literature behind them, and, because it was everywhere, I'd started to read it. I'd bought a copy of *Shogun* too, although it looked like a feudal Japan rewrite of *War and Peace*; almost as thick as it was wide and I knew I wouldn't be carrying it off the island with me. We also picked up another book on Greek mythology (we had three). I'd already forgotten why we had to have this one as well.

"Do you feel like doing one of the guidebook things tonight?" Clio asked, putting the camera down.

"Dunno," I said. Apart from Ariadne's Arch, we'd failed to do any of the archaeology adventures we'd planned. We hadn't even gone to see the giant stone man in the quarry. Instead, we'd kept up our uncultured routine of breakfast, beach, *taverna* and bar for almost three weeks – *If I see another ancient clay pot I'm going to kill somebody* – and in six days' time we'd be sailing back to the mainland for the plane home.

"I was thinking of going out to the animal bay, what do you reckon?"

"Ahhh," I said. The guidebook says there is a small secluded bay about twenty minutes' walk from our campsite filled with large flat stones, some of which look like animals. The book reckons this bay at sunset is one of the most romantic places in all the Cyclades, and also mentions, in a surprisingly frank way, that it's a great place to have sex outdoors.

"Okay," Clio said. "So here's what I'm thinking – we'll take one of the small rucksacks with tops in for if it gets cold, towels to sit on and I thought at least three bottles of Amstel, so you'll need to find the bottle opener. We should wear trainers for getting over the rocks and I'm going to wear my blue summer dress without knickers. You can wear whatever you want. If we decide we need any other stuff we can pick it up from the shop on the way. I don't think I've forgotten anything. Are you with me, Sanderson?"

I nodded, once, seriously.

"I'm with you Aames."

"Excellent," she said.

•

We sat on a large flat rock with our trainered feet dangling over the edge, both of us looking out to sea. The animal bay wasn't *romantic* in the way the guidebook had said, but it was beautiful and secluded. Clio sat staring out at the horizon, her hands tucked under her knees so the hem of her little blue summer dress stretched tight across her legs. Her feet kicked gently in mid-air. I tried to match her time, swinging my feet with hers, but my legs are longer and so slowed out of synch after a couple of beats – I had to keep stopping and restarting to get back into time. There was a slight breeze coming from the sea and the sky hazed around the edges. Clio had been quiet for most of the walk and stayed quiet when we arrived, climbing up onto the rock and looking out at the waves. I know my role when this happens just like Clio knows what to do when I have one of my strange turns. My job is to stay nearby and say nothing, just to be there and to wait for it to pass. Sometimes, after a length of silence, Clio will explode about some little thing I did or didn't do or something that went wrong earlier in the day. Then, it's my job to listen without arguing and to be ready if there are tears. I fished a bottle of Amstel out of our bag and popped off the top. I had a swig and offered it to Clio. She had a mouthful and passed it back.

"I'm sorry," she said.

"For what?"

"I don't think I want to have sex."

"That doesn't matter."

A group of gulls dive-bombed something I couldn't see out in the swell.

"I'm not doing it on purpose."

I put my arm around her and pulled her shoulders up against mine.

"Why would I think you were doing it on purpose? Doing what on purpose, anyway?"

She let me hug her like that for a while before gently pulling herself away. After a few minutes, she started running her thumbs up along the line of her jaw, up behind her ears and then slowly down her neck in attentive little circles. It had been a while since I'd seen this.

"Don't," I said, taking hold of her wrists and gently bringing them back down to her lap. "You're fine. There's nothing there."

"I didn't even know I was doing it," she said, facing out to sea. "Sorry."

"Do you think I'm crazy?"

"Clio, you're not crazy at all. I'm crazy, remember. You're – well, special maybe, but not crazy."

This made her smile. "Shut up," she said.

"Do you want me to check your neck?"

"No."

"It's all over, you know. You'll never have to go back."

"I can't go back."

"You won't have to."

She thought for a while, gently kicking her legs, before speaking again.

"There's, like, a cheerful united outlook, you know, in the staff. They'll do anything for you. You can have a TV by your bed, videos whatever. Everyone's so upbeat. Eric, it's fucking awful."

"Hon, you'll never have to go back. I promise."

"You can't promise that."

"I just know you'll be fine."

The *tavernas* around the campsite all have multi-coloured lanterns hanging from their porches, like oversized Christmas tree lights. They reflect in the sea all along the shoreline at night, projecting blue and red and green and yellow out onto the waves. Out at the stone animal bay, the sea is left quietly to its own colourings.

"It's like they say about soldiers coming back from a war. People all around you are dying. Really dying, Eric. You go in for a week's chemotherapy and you're in a ward with people who are really, actually dying, there and then and doing their best to come to terms with it. When the week's up, you go home and you see your family and your friends and everything's normal and familiar. It's too much. You think – one world can't possibly hold both these lives and you feel like you're going to go crazy when you realise the world *is* that big and it *can* fill with the most terrible things whenever it wants to."

We sat quietly for a few minutes.

"I'm sorry I wasn't there with you."

"This isn't about you. Or whether you're sorry or not."

"That's not how I meant it, you know I didn't."

"You didn't even know me."

"I'm still sorry. I feel like I let you down by not knowing you sooner."

"Well, that's stupid."

"Some things are stupid. It doesn't stop them being true. I'm stupid and I'm here."

Clio took the Amstel bottle and smiled. "That's true."

"Listen – I love you and whatever happens I'll always be here, if you want me to be. But you do need to start letting go of this. You don't want to end up freaking out like me all the time, do you?"

Clio looked out at the water. I knew she was deciding whether to be angry with me or not. Minutes passed. The gulls ate or lost whatever they were interested in and went shouting up into the sky. A plane left a straight white vapour trail.

"The hospital had its own library, you know."

"Yeah?"

"A whole library and nothing to read. If I never see an Arthur Conan Doyle book again it'll be too soon."

I laughed.

"I've read them all and do you know what I learned?"

"What?"

"Sherlock Holmes isn't clever at all – it's just that Dr Watson is a fucking idiot."

I laughed and Clio laughed too, both of us swinging our legs higher over the edge of the rock.

"You haven't read *Hound of the Baskervilles,* have you?"

I shook my head.

"Don't bother. A lot of pissing around just so Holmes can shoot a dog that's been painted green. Actually, that's how to get yourself a name as a genius; find yourself a stupid sidekick who'll be impressed every time you fart and who can get your *exploits* into a national newspaper."

I smiled, took the beer back and started picking at the label. "Are you okay?"

"It's just a big thing, you know? Waking up every day for months and months and knowing you've got cancer."

I nodded.

"The idea, it's like a big rock you can't ever put down. The weight's there from the second you open your eyes, heavy on you all the time."

"But you don't have cancer anymore, hon."

"We don't know that for sure."

"Well, we don't know I don't have cancer for sure either. We don't know anything for sure."

"Is that supposed to be reassuring?"

I lifted my legs until they were pointing straight out in front of me and tried to hold them there against the pull of gravity.

"Hmmm. I thought so when I was saying it."

We drank the rest of the beer in silence, the sky dusting towards night, the gulls flapping and bombing the sea, the waves counting our holiday away against the big brown rocks. All days, I thought, every day that starts always comes to an end. It was nearly half an hour later when Clio spoke again: "Hey."

"What?"

"While we've been sitting here, have you been thinking *my girlfriend has no knickers on*?"

"No, course not," I said, then, after a second: "Well, it depends. What's the right answer?"

Clio tucked her hands deeper under her knees and looked away so I couldn't read her expression.

"No clues," she said.

13

All the Angels Come

<< Call >>
Answer?

"Hello?"

The line was terrible, breaking and crackling with interference. I thought maybe I could hear a girl's voice, distant and bleached away behind the noise.

"Hello?" I said again.

"Wh[   ]ou?"

The connection was miles of rusty water pipes, leaking, dripping and losing pressure. Little rivers, flows twisting and winding in the dark. Or – it was a sinking submarine with the ocean forcing itself in, the sprays of deep black water from popped rivets and faultlines in the nose-diving, being-crushed hull. I tried to hold my nerve. I tried not to think about the Ludovician at all.

"I can't –" I tried again, louder. "I can't hear you."

"–ou[   ]M[   ]est[ ]r?"

"Manchester? No. I –"

"D[ ]n't [   ]."

"I can't hear you properly," I said, but I wasn't really sure if I was hearing anyone at all.

"Th[   ] lo[ ]ing fo[   ]. D[ ] do [   ]."

"Hello?" I said, "Is somebody there? Who is this?" And as I listened hard into the hiss, a word came up from my lungs and spoke itself out of my mouth, taking me completely by surprise:

"Clio?" I said.

The line went dead.

·

The cat lifted an eye from his chest of drawers, blinked once and went back to sleep.

Cross-legged on my bed in the Willows Hotel, I dug around in the rucksack and pulled out my half-bottle of vodka, unscrewed the cap and took a swig. The still unopened package sat waiting next to me.

Caller Unknown said the green screen. I put the mobile phone carefully onto the bedside table. Caller Unknown could have been a member of the Un-Space Exploration Committee, or a stranger who'd found one of the business cards and dialled the number out of curiosity. Considering the state of the line maybe there hadn't been a caller at all, just a systems malfunction, a fault in the network. Whoever it was it certainly *wasn't* Clio Aames. A sleepless night staring at The Light Bulb Fragment had cross-wired my brain.

I picked up the package. *Maybe this and the call might be two parts of the same thing. That would be likely, wouldn't it?* After sixteen weeks of nothing, everything was suddenly happening at once and it was difficult to find any sort of perspective.

After carefully setting up the Dictaphones around the edges of the room, I ripped open the envelope. Inside was a hardback book. The white dust jacket had a detailed Victorian etching of a prehistoric stiff-finned fish. The title read: *The Origin of Species by Charles Darwin*, and underneath, smaller; *with Evolution Engine by Trey Fidorous*.

"Fuck," I said, flipping through the pages:

oftenest visited by insects, and would be oftenest crossed; and so in the long-run would gain the upper hand. Those flowers, also, which had their stamens and pistils placed, in relation to the size and habits of the particular insects which visited them, so as to favour in any degree the transportal of their pollen from flower to flower, would likewise be favoured or selected. We might have taken the **plant plant** visiting flowers for the sake of collecting pollen instead of **plant**; and as **plant plant** is for **plant** sole of fertilisation, its destruction appears a simple loss to the **plant**; yet if a **plant plant** were carried, at first occasionally and then habitually, **plant plant** pollen-devouring **plant** from **plant plant** flower, and a cross thus effected, although nine-tenths of the **plant** were **plant plant** still **plant plant** gain to the **plant**; and those **plant** which **plant plant plant plant plant plant** had larger **plant plant** anthers, would **plant plant plant plant plant plant plant plant plant plant plant** When our **plant**, by this **plant plant plant plant plant plant plant plant plant** **plant** attractive flowers, had **plant** rendered **plant** attractive **plant plant plant plant** **plant plant plant plant** regularly carry pollen **plant plant** to **plant**; and that **plant** **plant** most **plant plant plant**, I **plant** easily **plant** by many **plant plant**. **plant** give **plant** one not **plant** very **plant** case, but as likewise illustrating **plant** step in the **plant** of the **plant** of **plant**, presently **plant plant** to. Some holly-trees bear **plant** male flowers, which **plant** four **plant plant** rather a **plant plant**, and a rudimentary pistil; **plant** holly-trees **plant** only **plant** flowers; these **plant** a full-sized pistil, and **plant** stamens **plant** shrivelled **plant**, in which not a **plant** of pollen **plant** be detected. **plant** found a female tree exactly sixty **plant plant** a male tree, I put the stigmas of twenty flowers, taken from different branches, under the microscope, and **plant**, without exception, there were pollen-grains, and on **plant** a profusion of pollen. As the wind had set for several days from the female to the male **plant**, the pollen could not thus have been carried. The weather had been cold and boisterous, and therefore not favourable to bees, nevertheless every female flower which I examined had been effectually fertilised by the bees, accidentally dusted plant plant plant plant plant plant plant plant imaginary case: we may suppose the plant plant plant plant plant plant plant the nectar by continued selection, to be a common **plant plant plant plant** insects **plant** in main part on its nectar for food. I could give many facts, **plant plant plant** bees **plant** to save time; **plant** instance, their habit of **plant** holes and sucking **plant** nectar **plant plant** of certain flowers, which **plant** can, with a very little more trouble, enter by the **plant**. Bearing such **plant** in mind, I can see no reason to doubt that an accidental deviation **plant plant** and **plant** of the body, or in the curvature and length of the proboscis, &c., far too slight to be a **plant** by us, might profit a bee or other insect, so that an individual so characterised would be able to **plant** its food more quickly, and so have a better chance of living and leaving **plant plant**. Its descendants would probably inherit a tendency to a similar slight deviation of **plant**. The tubes **plant** the **plant plant** **plant** common red and incarnate clovers (Trifolium **plant plant** incarnatum) **plant** not on a **plant** glance appear to differ in length; yet the hive-bee can easily **plant** the nectar **plant** of the incarnate clover, but not out of the common **plant** clover, **plant** visited by **plant plant** alone; **plant plant** whole **plant** of the **plant plant plant** in vain an **plant plant** supply of **plant plant plant**. **plant plant** a great **plant** to **plant plant** **plant** a slightly longer or **plant** constructed **plant**. On **plant plant** plant, **plant plant plant** by **plant** that **plant plant** of clover **plant plant plant** bees **plant** and **plant plant plant** the **plant**, so as to **plant** the **plant plant plant plant** stigmatic surface. **plant**, again, if **plant plant plant** to **plant** rare in **plant plant plant** **plant** advantage to **plant** red clover to **plant** or **plant plant plant plant** to its corolla, so **plant** the **plant plant plant plant plant plant plant plant** I **plant plant plant plant** **plant plant** become, **plant plant plant** or **plant plant** other, **plant plant plant** in **plant plant plant plant** to each **plant**, by the **plant plant plant** of **plant plant plant** presenting **plant plant plant** favourable **plant plant plant** I am **plant plant plant** doctrine of **plant plant plant plant plant plant plant plant plant plant plant plant** **plant plant plant plant plant plant plant plant plant plant plant plant plant plant**

A note fell out of the book and onto my lap. A single folded sheet of A4. This is what the note said:

> Dear Mr Sanderson,
>
> I hope this book is of some interest and helps persuade you I am making contact as a friend.
>
> I understand your situation and the dangers you face every day. You are not alone. Please meet me at the old Manor Infirmary at 12.30 p.m. this afternoon. The building is disused and the front doors will be open.
>
> Yours faithfully,
> Mr Nobody

As soon as I read it, I knew I would go. After all this time, someone. The idea of walking into an abandoned hospital to meet a person calling themselves 'Nobody' would ring alarm bells in anyone's head, but what choice did I have? I'd been trying to make a contact in un-space for so long; when it finally happened could I really run away on the grounds of it being strange and unsettling? But this didn't mean acting foolishly. I'd go a few hours early and take a good look at the place, see what I could see. *Preparation Preparation Preparation.*

But right now, *preparation* meant getting some rest.

With the new day's sun pinking at the curtains I set the alarm on the mobile phone, put the book and the note to one side and stretched out on the bed. In spite of everything I was asleep in minutes.

But.

But in my exhaustion I'd made a terrible mistake.

When I'd set up the Dictaphone loop at the edges of the room, the strange package was *already inside the parameter*. And so, when the thick sinewy idea of a thing unlaced its long, slimy thought-body from the words and letters on that folded note and swam, slithered, up the bed towards me, there were no barriers to stop it.

•

I dreamt I sat on a long wooden bench in the Museum of Naxos. I was surrounded by glass cabinets filled with objects, ancient bowls and urns, golden coins, jewellery and tools. In the taller cases were half-made, half-collapsed marble statues, each with its own list of injuries; missing faces, missing arms or legs replaced by polished steel struts. Some of the figures were so broken they'd become unidentifiable. Several had only one smooth surface, maybe the round of a shoulder or the curve of a stomach, carved and polished and ambiguous alongside rough jagged rock.

From my seat, I stared into a large and well-lit case more or less in the centre of the gallery. Inside were two backpacks, a heap of novels and history books, a collapsed tent with its black foldaway poles carefully stacked on top of the canvas, two sleeping bags, two snorkels, two scuba masks, a hammock and a yellow underwater camera.

I got up off the bench and walked over so I could read the little white information card fixed to the inside of the glass. The card said:

Something bad's happening. I've gone outside.

I might be a while.

C xx

14

Mr Nobody

I opened my eyes. Something wasn't right. I groaned under the weight of heavy mushy-pea clouds and the glass-sharp exotic emotions that roll in at the storm front of a fever.

Sick. God, I couldn't be sick today.

I stretched for my mobile. 11.33. The meeting at the Manor Infirmary was in less than an hour. Shit. So much for finding the place early and checking the lie of the land.

What to do? My insides felt like offal splattering down a rabbit hole. I crawled up onto my knees and hugged my arms around my head. *What to do what to do? Think think think.* I stretched out a leg and step-staggered off the bed, weak and dizzy and looking around for the vodka bottle to make sure I hadn't drunk half or all of it without remembering. I hadn't; it was still there, just a few mouthfuls lighter.

I put the folded note from Mr Nobody back inside *The Origin of Species* and tucked both away in the chest of drawers. A shower might have helped push the sickness back and clear my mind but there was no time. I decided to take what little comfort I could get from a clean T-shirt and jeans. Closing the wardrobe door I saw Ian, crouched on top and glaring down at me with massive eyes.

"What?" My voice felt sticky and the wrong size for my head.

The cat rumbled a deep growl and backed away until I couldn't see him over the wardrobe's top edge.

"Nice," I said. "Thanks."

After struggling into the clean clothes, I took a plastic bag out of the rucksack and placed each of the Dictaphones carefully inside. I grabbed a couple of packs of batteries too.

Anything else? Anything else?

"Anything else?" I asked my reflection in the mirror. The words pulsed in my ears, going wrong and rotten as they sank deeper in. My reflection looked back, all queasy and staggery like it couldn't understand what I'd said. I put my hand out to the wall to steady myself, turned, and headed for the door.

•

The Manor Infirmary was a collection of buildings – a dozen square and oblong red brick structures with interlinking corridors. From above it probably looked like a flow chart. The path through the grounds was silted and sanded, and everything that wasn't concrete squelched.

Aunty Ruth had known how to find the Infirmary and I'd been relieved to hear it was only fifteen minutes' walk away.

"But it's all shut down now, love, why on earth would you want to go there?"

"Idle curiosity" had been the best I could manage. She said I looked terrible and I said I'd feel better after a walk. She didn't seem at all sure about that, but must have decided she didn't know me well enough to challenge the idea with anything more than silence and a bunched-up brow of concern.

The path led up to a mulchy, leaf-piled porch. The entrance was a set of double doors made from dark wood and the type of thick rippled glass with the wire cross-hatching inside. I pushed the left door and it opened heavily inwards.

"Hello?"

Aunty Ruth was right: the walk hadn't helped. My insides were hanging slack and wet and loose under my ribs and down into my hips. My head felt even worse. Like a central heating system with air in the pipes, my mind clanked and struggled to pass thoughts coherently from one area to another – only the most simple and straightforward bursts of thinking seemed to have any chance of making it around the system without being trapped and lost in bubble pockets under the floorboards. *I'm just tired. I'm coming down with something.* These were the only explanations simple enough to survive a full circuit around my mind and although some part of me somewhere – an isolated radiator in the tiny attic bathroom of my brain – worried away about the timing of this and the risk of trusting ready-made solutions (and I was aware of the worry, vaguely, distantly), there simply wasn't the pressure available for that little radiator to feed back properly into the heart of the system.

I stepped into the foyer.

A weak grey-blue light filled the space, a large window behind the reception area letting in low-grade sun from a damp and forgotten courtyard garden. The air inside tasted flat and lifeless and carried an idle kind of musk – rainwater on old plaster, decaying paper, little circles of black mould – and the faint after-tang of TCP. Black and white tiles covered the floor, the kind you find in disused Victorian swimming pools or due-for-refurbishment school canteens, the chessboard pattern dulled under a slow layer of dust. I took a couple of steps forwards, turned and saw how my wet footsteps left bootgrip zigzags of blacker black and whiter white in the floor behind me. There were no other prints.

Although the foyer itself had its window and the glass doors to feed in some kind of weak illumination, the corridors leading off to the left and to the right soon greyscaled themselves away into total darkness.

I walked over to the mouth of the left corridor and flicked the light switch there. Nothing happened. I did the same at the mouth of the right corridor but got the same result. No power, no light. I thought about my torch, still in the glove box of the yellow Jeep. A queasy kind of anger bubbled up through the vagueness. I pinched myself hard on the inside of my arm, hoping the pain would bring me more into focus, clear my head.

"Hello?" I called again, louder this time. The walls and the dust and the chequerboard floor gave only a quick snap of echoes.

Left or right? I chose the right corridor. I set off into the dark, feeling my way along the walls, trying doorhandles as they presented themselves under my spidering fingers.

I found my way into and through a storeroom stacked with collapsed wheelchairs and dusty boxes, coming out into a windowed staff office with faint silhouettes of computer keyboards and table lamps still visible in the dust of all the left-behind desks. I edged along dark corridors with confusing alcoves and pitch black T-junctions and I crossed rooms with ranks of bare mattresses and big windows with broken blinds. The hospital presented itself to me like this, as a progression of strange unfitting jigsaw pieces. Places which couldn't, wouldn't, be reassembled into any kind of mental floor plan. Before long, I was lost.

Was there even anybody here? Had my low-pressure brain missed something obvious by the entrance and sent me stumbling off in the wrong direction? Normally, I'd be able to answer with a definite *no*. But not today, feeling like this. Today, all bets were off.

After about fifteen minutes I came through an archway into what must have been my ninth or tenth corridor. But this corridor was different to all the others because this one wasn't dark; a tall and bright electric standing lamp had been positioned at one end. I made my way towards it. As I got closer, I could see the lamp was straight out of a 1970s living room, a big faded green tasselled shade and a stem of bulbs and curves made from dark stained wood.

"Hello?"

There was no one around, just me and the lamp standing together at the end of a long lonely hallway.

I found him by following the flex. The flex from the standing lamp connected to an orange extension lead which connected to a white extension lead which connected to another orange extension lead which connected to a black extension lead. Upstairs, downstairs, through storerooms and staffrooms and restrooms and toilets and offices and physiotherapy gyms.

The flex led me into a large ward. Most of the space was gloomy with the blinds drawn but a second standing lamp in the centre of the room gave out a white-yellow circle of light about twelve feet across. Under the lamp, sitting on a chair was a man busily typing on a laptop.

As I walked towards him he looked up, smiled, hurried the laptop off his knee and stood up to meet me.

"You made it, thank goodness. Sorry for all the – " he gestured around. "I'd been hoping to meet you in the foyer but this report – deadlines are still deadlines apparently."

The man was about my height but more slightly built, in his late twenties or early thirties, with a smart blue shirt, casual but expensive-looking jeans and a banker's haircut. He also wore a pair of gold rimmed aviator sunglasses and a chunky gold watch. There was a clean just-shaved-at-the-barbers freshness about him that made me feel dirty and sickly looking.

"Mr Nobody?" I asked.

The man laughed an embarrassed laugh.

"Yes. Very pleased to meet you." He overstretched as he moved to shake my hand, giving a slight bow. "It's a little melodramatic, isn't it? Still, I hope you understand the – *undesirable* nature of names given the circumstances." Nobody collected a chair from the shadows and dragged it quickly into the circle of light to face his own. "I hope you can forgive the sunglasses too," he said, gesturing for me to sit down. "Eyestrain. The doctor said no work with a computer screen for two weeks and I've got a mountain of pills to take, but –"

"Reports?" I said, taking the chair. Nobody sat opposite me.

"Endless reports," he smiled. "Computers. The blessing and the curse of the twenty-first century." Then, looking at me and actually noticing the state I was in: "God, are you alright?"

"I'm okay, coming down with something I think. Anyway, I thought the mobile phone was the blessing and curse of the twenty-first century?"

"Ahhh, that's the other blessing and curse of the twenty-first century. These blessing and curse things, they're everywhere. You can lose count."

I smiled a watery smile.

"Well," Nobody said. "You're not here to discuss my Luddite tendencies, are you? I should probably start by apologising for –"

"No, wait," I said, finally remembering the plastic bag with the Dictaphones hooked over my wrist. *Stupid, slow feverish brain.* "There's something important I need to do first."

Mr Nobody watched me load up the Dictaphones with batteries and set them up in a rough square around us, at the edges of the lamplight. He didn't say anything until I'd finished.

"A sound-based association loop," he smiled at me like a boss smiles at an employee who's done something clever with the figures. "Wow, can I ask how it was developed?"

I sat down again. My stomach bubbled and lurched and I swallowed back the bile.

"I'm sorry," I said. "I'm not going to be much of a conversationalist today. My brain's all jammed up with, well, with whatever it is I've managed to catch. Could I be blunt and rude and ask if we can just get straight down to it?"

Mr Nobody sat easy, relaxed and alert. He thought for a moment then nodded once, efficiently. "Yes, of course. Do you want me to start with what I know about you, or what I know about the shark?"

"You know about the Ludovician? I mean, you believe in it?"

Nobody's brow dropped a little behind his sunglasses.

"Yes," he said simply. There was a touch of confusion, as if I'd asked him if I believed in trees or aeroplanes or China.

"Yes," I said back to myself, still a little stunned.

"I mean, I'm not familiar with the particular shark you've been in contact with, but I'm very familiar, too familiar, with the species." He looked at me again. "You seem surprised."

"It's just – for so long there's only been me. To hear someone else talk about it –"

"I understand," Nobody said, sliding down the chair a little and crossing his forearms on his knees. "The man I work for is a scientist. He's studied conceptual fish for years; Heletrobes, Ticking Remoras, Ludogarians, Dream Tips. He's an expert, perhaps the greatest expert of our time."

"*Scientific* study? How is that possible?"

"My employer has the tongue-twisting pleasure of being a crypto-conceptual oceanologist. It isn't what you'd describe as mainstream. It's currently a field of one."

"Right." I belched and my mouth filled with a sharp, tangy sick taste. "Right," I said again.

Nobody looked at me for a second. "Listen, you really don't look good. Do you want some painkillers or paracetamol or something?" He gently kicked a brown leather bag under his chair. "I've got some in here, I think."

"No," I said. "I think I'll be okay. I just need to keep still and not think about it."

"Well, if you change your mind. Actually, I need to take the pills for my eyes at 2 p.m. I'm always forgetting. You couldn't do me a favour and remind me, could you?"

I took the mobile out of my pocket and glanced at the clock on screen: 13.32.

"No problem," I said, swallowing again to get the taste out of my mouth. "Your employer – do you work for Trey Fidorous?"

"Ahhh. The great Dr Fidorous. No, I'm afraid not. Although you could say he founded the school and my employer expanded on it. No, no one has heard from Fidorous in years. If he's still alive, he's keeping it very much to himself."

I filed this away to think about when there was more space in my head.

"What do you know about the ecology of the Ludovician, Mr Sanderson?"

"It's a conceptual fish, a shark. It eats memories." I looked down at my fingers. "What else? Practical things mainly; how to hide from it, trick it, how to protect myself."

Nobody looked out at the Dictaphones chattering quietly at the edge of our circle of lamplight. He nodded a thoughtful nod.

"The Ludovician is the largest and most aggressive of all the conceptual sharks," he said. "It's an apex predator, top of the food chain. They're very rare animals and, mostly, they wander the flows taking a meal here and there. Any frail mind kicking and struggling in the world, if they're passing they'll take a chunk out of it. Especially out of old people."

"I thought they stuck to one target? One victim again and again until –" I let the sentence die; my stomach wasn't up to it.

"That's territoriality. Once in a while you'll find that a Ludovician – a big rogue male as likely as not – fixates on one particular food source. No one knows why they do it. What I'm trying to say is, no one knows very much about these animals at all."

Nobody's sentences were sinking into the flu-muck in my head. I realised I couldn't easily dredge them again up once they'd disappeared.

"I'm sorry," I said. "I know you're getting at something but I don't –"

"It boils down to this: if you want to study one of these creatures, territoriality is your only real hope. If you can find someone who shows all the tell-tale signs of repeated Ludovician injuries, you can find yourself a shark."

139

"And that's how you found me."

"My employer keeps his ear very close to the ground. Your doctor is thinking about writing a paper on your 'condition'. She showed some draft notes to a colleague."

Randle.

I didn't say anything.

Nobody pushed his sunglasses up the bridge of his nose.

"There's another problem with studying Ludovicians. Even if you can track down a decent-sized adult it's almost impossible to keep one alive in captivity. An infant, yes, but not a mature animal. My employer is the only person who has ever had any success with this; he once kept a fully grown Ludovician alive in a specially made containment facility for almost forty days. Since then, he's been moving heaven and earth to find another specimen. Which, yes, is why he sent me to find you."

I couldn't quite believe any of this.

"You're saying you can trap it?"

"Yes, we can trap it."

"And take it away?"

"Yes. With your help we can capture it, take it away safely and keep it alive indefinitely."

"Once it's trapped, I don't care if it's alive or dead. Though to be honest, I'd feel safer if it was dead."

"Yes," said Mr Nobody. "I can understand that."

"But. How do you know? How can you be sure it can be done?"

"I'm sure."

"How?"

For a moment I didn't think he'd answer.

"Because I've seen it," he said slowly. "The first one, the Ludovician my employer captured, it was mine. It had been feeding on me."

·

"Is it time for me to take those pills yet?"

I pulled the mobile out of my coat pocket.

"About ten minutes."

"About?"

"Nine minutes just," I said.

He nodded, thinking. The change in him was small but it was there. Some of the breezy confidence, the high-gloss polish had rubbed away. He seemed to sit a little lower in his chair, hunched down with his shoulders poking up either side of his neck. In this position, the blue shirt which had looked well-fitted and expensive now seemed a little baggy, hanging loose across his chest. There were sweat marks where the material had pulled up under his armpits.

"Are you okay?"

"Fine, fine." He straightened up but it was unconvincing, somehow he didn't fill out his own body like he had before. "Bad memories," he said. "It's, well, I don't need to tell you how it is."

"How did it happen? I mean, if you don't mind me asking."

Nobody didn't answer straightaway.

"I was a research scientist," he said finally. "A physicist. Young, dynamic, making a name for myself, all that."

I looked at him.

"It isn't all lab coats and dandruff you know."

"No," I said. "Sorry."

"I got myself a position with the University of London. It was a really big deal. Do you know what Superstring Theory is?"

I tried to think. "Something complicated to do with life, the universe and everything?"

"Actually, yes, more or less. It's very exciting, very *where it's at*. Anyway, I went to stay with an aunt and uncle down in the city. I wasn't really at a point in my career where I could ask for the same salary as the more established academics, but my aunt and uncle had an empty attic room and they turned it over to me as a study. That's where I did my work." Nobody looked out across the chequerboard floor and then down at his hands. "When we first heard the noises coming from up there in the middle of the night my aunt was convinced we had a rat. You see, the work I was doing, the subject, it's pure thought, pure concept."

"The work you were doing?" I scrubbed my knuckles against my scalp, trying to clear my head. "You mean it attracted the shark?"

"I think it happened because there's no physical anchor. At that level a subject like mine is essentially thought and abstracted maths. Every day, when I sat at my desk working with the figures and models, I was actually paddling that small attic room further and further out into a sea of ideas, further away from the bricks and stone of the house. There aren't that many people who can take a boat out as far as I could, who could get out over such depths."

His sweating was getting worse. The wet patches under his arms had spread and new ones were forming around his neck.

"Geniuses don't go mad," he said. "That's what people don't understand. They get out so far out that the water is like glass and they can see for miles and see so much, and in ways people have never seen before. They go out over such depths, down down down and down, and some of them get taken. Something rushes up out of their thoughts, from the insides of their own heads and through the act of looking and the thinking itself – because the deep blue is in there too, do you understand? And it takes them."

He trailed off, hands shaking and clutched around his knees.

"How long now until I need to take my pills?"

"Listen," I said, "I'm sorry for asking. If it's too much going over all this –"

"How long until I need to take my *fucking pills*?"

Shocked, my hand reached automatically for the mobile phone.

"Seven minutes," I said. "I didn't mean to upset you. I'm sorry."

He said nothing back, just sat there looking down at his hands on his knees, his sweaty shirt clinging up under his surprisingly skinny ribs. His hair had lost some of its shape too and it stuck lank in places to his scalp and forehead. A ball of sweat striped the left lens of his sunglasses and fell away.

We sat in silence.

"I'm sorry," he said finally, still looking at his hands.

"It's okay. You really don't have to talk about it. I'm just sorry I asked."

Nobody looked up. His sweaty face seemed even more sunken, sallow, drawn than it had a minute before. He stared at me, then he just opened his mouth and – as if he were reciting something rather than having a conversation – launched into his story again.

"My uncle was a taxi-driver. If you want to be a taxi-driver in London you have to take an exam to prove you know the entire city. My uncle never forgot a single street, never a single road. He could find every building in London but he couldn't remember where he lived. They said it was short-term memory damage, but it wasn't."

"Wait, you're saying the shark attacked him too?"

Nobody nodded a vague nod as if the question had come from somewhere inside his own head.

"All of us. My aunt didn't know who people were at the end. She had nightmares. A shadow in her brain, teeth and eyes. She would wake up in the night, see my uncle in bed next to her and sneak downstairs to phone the police. She'd tell them there was an intruder in the house. Sometimes she'd call them three, four times a night. Sometimes she'd get violent because she was scared."

"Jesus," I said. Nobody's story, the way it was affecting him as he told it, this *deterioration*, it was hard for me to pin it down exactly, but something was going wrong. Something here was going very wrong. My stomach felt like a loose bag of warm water.

"It happened and it kept happening, one or other of us, night after night. They came again and they checked the house for gas leaks, they checked our food and they checked the walls and they checked the ceilings for anything that could cause it, a poison. But there wasn't anything. I had the nightmares. I saw it in my dreams. My theories were what drew it in. Numbers and maths. It wouldn't stop coming in the night. *Who's it going to be?* Trying to stay awake. *Who's next what's next what will be taken now?* By the end, being in that house. It was –"

My insides locked up and I heaved. A long slither of spit choked out of me, but no vomit. I swallowed, gagged, swallowed again. Nobody stopped talking and watched, his wet face all hollow cheeks and sharp bones behind his glasses. I wiped away the tears.

"Christ," I said, rubbing my mouth with my shirtsleeve. "Christ, I'm sorry."

"Yes," said Nobody. "I've got to take some pills soon. Do you think you could remind me when it's time to take them?"

"I will," I said, trying to pull my head back together, "but I think it's only a minute or two since –"

"I can't take them before two o'clock," Nobody interrupted gently. "I know you think it doesn't matter because it's only a few minutes. But it does. The amounts are perfectly balanced. Like seconds. Sixty seconds perfectly balanced against a minute. And dividing it up. You can't carry a second over."

I realised I'd put my hand in the wrong coat pocket and reached around to the other.

"You are going to come with me, aren't you?"

"Yes," I said, pulling out the phone. *Something here was going very wrong.* Even if the specifics kept slipping away in the mud, instinct made sure I held onto that one basic fact. I needed to get away, rest, clear my head and think. "I'll have to go back to my hotel and pack a few things, and then –"

"*How many minutes?*" Nobody whispered, chewing on a knuckle.

He looked awful now. His shirt was a soaking, sticky mess plastered to his ribs and painfully hollow stomach. His hair was loose, lank and shapeless. Even his big aviator sunglasses looked old and dirty. And he was so wet. The sweat literally dripped off him, drops hanging and falling from his nose, his chin, the bottoms of his jeans even. Drip drip drip drip.

"Four," I said. My hands were shaking. I couldn't think what to do.

"You know I'm dead, don't you?" Nobody said. "Look." He held out a flat palm. Liquid dripped from the ends of his fingers with a steady tapping. Drip drip drip drip. "See?"

"I don't –"

"You *do* know. All of it. It's obvious." Then, as if something dawned on him, he quickly swivelled around in his chair, turning his bony back to me. "Shhh, what are you doing? You're giving away too much, giving it all away, don't let *him* talk. It doesn't matter. Yes, of course it matters. But I can't keep the keel level without the pills. You'll damn well have to keep it level won't you because we never know what *he's* going to say. But it's too long, the weave has all come apart – loose threads and holes, *he's* showing through, you know how it gets just before the pills. I don't care about that, I don't care about your holes and threads, the job's almost done you'll just have to. Shhh, shut up, he's going to hear." Nobody spun back around towards me. His glasses edged up his cheeks as his face split with a huge grin of brown teeth and purpley-black gums.

"Sorry about that," he said. "Conference call. The office. Conference conference calls. The curse of the twenty-first century."

Liquid *streamed* off him into small brown pools around the legs of his chair.

Get out. Get out. Get out. I shifted my weight onto the balls of my feet, slowly slowly, taking the strain in thighs and calves, ready to spring my sick body into some attempt at a run.

Nobody stared from behind his glasses.

No. He wasn't staring. It took a few seconds for me to realise he wasn't moving at all. Apart from the trickling water, he'd come to a complete stop. As I watched, a change began to creep across Nobody's features; the tension slipped out of his body along with the water. His wet white face became serene and angelic, the way a face in a coffin is serene and angelic, calm and wise. His head tilted a little, mechanically.

"The important thing now is to give up," he said, quietly. His voice was different, there was something far away behind the word sounds. "You know the truth. You know you're already dead. Deep down you know it. Eric Sanderson's gone, a long time gone. And Clio Aames. All of it, everything he was is over now. You should let his body go too. You should stop kicking and let it float, bob and slip all away. Let it sink down to the bottom with the quiet and the stones and the crabs. It will be alright, storms on the surface can't hurt us anymore."

Constant brown water flowed off the ends of his fingers and elbows as he pushed himself up in the chair. It ran from his trouser bottoms and leaked from his shoes, making dirty growing puddles that smelled of seaweed rotting in the sun.

"You don't know who I am, do you?" his new voice said. Standing now, he gave a big bony stretch, splattering water droplets. "I'm you, of course. We're the same dead not-person."

I looked down and was horrified to see my own blue T-shirt wet and sticky. I battled away the un-logic of it – *it's just sweat, you're ill, it's just sweat and you're not thinking straight.* He shuffled forward a few steps, trailing brown water. I couldn't make myself stand up. My stomach lurched and I dry-heaved again.

"I'm going to show you something now. It will be difficult for you to see at first, but what it represents is peace."

He reached up and took hold of the arm of his sunglasses.

"Don't," I said. "I don't want it. I don't want this."

Nobody pulled the glasses off his face.

Both his eyes were missing.

The structure was there: membrane, lens, iris, but the sense, the communication, the understanding, the fundamental eyes-are-the-windows-of-the-soul-ness of them, was all gone. Two black conceptual sockets, crawling with tiny thought-prawns and urge-worms, stared out of his face at me.

I heaved again and this time I really was sick; bile and matter and juices and oils, jellies and snots of thick green slime reeked and splattered out of me all over the black and white tiled floor.

15

Luxophage

The stink of sick found my mind and woke it up.

I'd passed out.

As soon as I opened my eyes, my stomach wrung itself tight again and I retched, chest pressed against my knees, folded double on the chair. I spat tangy acidy mucus down onto a pile of vomit splayed and splattered out in front of me. I grabbed at a breath before another heave forced its way out. This one was dry, a face-purpling empty retch. Another came, and another. Finally, I pulled myself upright, shaking and wiping more tears from my face.

"My employer is a scientist, I told you that didn't I?" Mr Nobody was standing by his chair, glasses back on. He had his leather bag open and turned away to swallow tablets from a small plastic tub. "Chemicals," he said, popping the cap back on and dropping the tub into the bag. "He can remake a person out of chemical stuffing and wire, keep them walking and talking . . . the miracles of modern science." He sat down, lifting the laptop back onto his knee. Already some of the colour had come back into his face, the rivulets of water from his cuffs and trouser legs had slowed to an irregular dripping. "There are certain procedures, experiments and so on which are vital for my employer to fully study the Ludovician. As a result of these, you'll come to rely, as I have, on certain chemical prosthetics. It's not perfect but it *is* better than the alternative."

The sickness tide was ebbing from my cheeks and my throat. My stomach settled a little and my mind began to clear. Everything from when I'd woken up sick in bed at the Willows Hotel to finding my way through the hospital, to Nobody and his horrible physical and mental collapse – it all seemed fractured and out of focus. Why the fuck was I still here? It was razorblade obvious that if there'd been any sense in me at all over the past few hours, I would have made a break for it a long time ago.

"Thank you," I said it as calmly as I could, "but I'm going to leave now."

Nobody looked up. His eyebrows knotted behind his sunglasses and he folded down the laptop screen. I tensed myself to run, expecting something sudden and horrible; for him to hurl himself off his chair and come screaming all inhuman at me across the floor. He didn't. He tilted his head down, moving his attention from me to the thick pile of sick at my feet.

"Oh dear," he said, "it's difficult when this happens."

I leaned forward and risked a glance down to where he was looking.

Something was moving inside the vomit.

I shock-jumped backwards up onto my feet, sending the chair skidding out behind me.

The *something* unwound itself carefully from the mucus and bile and slither-swam up into the air, coiling in loops around the vaporous remains of my thoughts and feelings of nausea. It was small – maybe nine inches, maybe the length of a worry that doesn't quite wake you in your sleep – a primitive conceptual fish. I backed away slowly. The creature had a round sucker-like mouth lined with dozens of sharp little doubts and inadequacies. I could feel it just downstream from me in the events and happenings of the world, winding at head height, holding itself in place with muscled steady swimming against the movement of time.

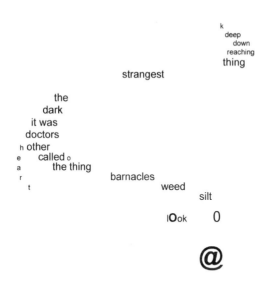

I backed away further, towards the edge of the circle of light.

"The conceptual crabs, the jellies, some of the simple fish." Nobody had put the laptop down and was moulding his hair back into something like its previous flawless style. "My employer can direct them, encourage certain behaviours. As I said, he's an expert in the field."

The blood thudded under my jaw, in my ears, in my eyes.

"Call it off."

"This is a Luxophage," Nobody said pleasantly, as if he hadn't heard me, as if he were giving an informative talk. "It's one of a family of what you might call idea lampreys. This particular species feeds by finding its way inside human beings and sucking on their ability to think quickly, to react. They tend to make their hosts quiet, well behaved and firmly entrenched in whatever rut they happen to be in. It's a useful little parasite," Nobody smiled, "although it does occasionally cause nausea."

"*That* was inside me?" I wasn't taking my eyes off the slow-winding idea fish hanging just a few feet of separation away.

"It was," Nobody agreed. He stood and casually closed in on the fish from behind. "We were worried you might change your mind about helping us capture your Ludovician when you saw –" He paused. "I was going to say 'the extent of your involvement' but what I really mean is, 'what we're going to do to you.'"

"Not really selling it to me, I'm afraid." I said, still watching the fish, taking another slow step backwards.

Nobody shrugged. "That doesn't matter. In a second my assistant here will be back inside you and you'll do whatever you're told."

"I don't –" I started, but the fish, the Luxophage, sprung suddenly to life, darting blink-quick forwards at my face. I stepped jumped stumbled tripped fell backwards, landing with a crack of shooting pain in my elbow. The little lamprey shot over my head, hitting a something, a churning thundering invisible something which pound-hammered and tumbled it away in a gigantic current. I took a careful breath and turned my head to the side. Barely six inches away, one of my Dictaphones stood like a miniature obelisk, its tiny tape winding between its spools with a low hum, the recording playing out as a sharp little clatter. The non-divergent conceptual loop. The Luxophage had swum into its flow and been washed away.

I pressed my boot heels against the smooth tiles and pushed myself across the floor, sliding on my back until I was outside the circle of light and square of Dictaphones. I sat up, cradling my throbbing elbow against my chest.

The jumbled Luxophage tumbled around the inside of the loop, once, twice, like water down a plughole, before regaining control of itself. It swam back to Mr Nobody and began circling him in a slow waist-high orbit.

"Hmmm." Nobody's clothes were dry again now, his blue shirt tailor-made and pressed, his hair perfect, his jeans well fitted and expensive. "That was lucky," he said.

I forced myself painfully up onto my feet. It was lucky. The Dictaphones had saved me but for them to keep me safe, to keep Nobody's Luxophage trapped, I'd have to leave them behind.

"I'm going now," I said.

"No, you're not."

One, two, three, four more Luxophages pulled, wriggled and squirmed their primitive conceptual bodies out from behind Nobody's big dark sunglasses. More came; five, six, seven, eight, coiling and dropping from his face. I started backing towards the archway but Nobody moved suddenly and quickly, striding to the edge of the circle of light and – stamping on one of the Dictaphones.

"No!" the word, the air came out of me like a wound.

Nobody smashed his heel down hard again and the little plastic casing split, cracked and broke apart. The sickly ball of lampreys around him buffeted and bobbed as the conceptual loop collapsed in on itself and was gone. The ball unribboned and Luxophages launched themselves at me in a wet black hail of guilts and phobias. But with half the distance covered, the swarm went haywire. They looped and jumbled in a mad dance of eights and zeros before disappearing through the ceiling and walls and floor and up under the window blinds. One shot back to Nobody, circled him in two quick loops and vanished with a splatter of panic into a broken strip light overhead. In an instant every one of them had gone.

I thought *they're going to come back at me from all directions*, but even as I thought it I knew it wasn't true. This wasn't hunting. It was more like the way a shoal breaks up when a diver or a –

I looked over at Nobody. The confused look on his face turned into panic.

When a diver or a –

With a deep deep horror I realised what was happening.

"You idiot!" I screamed, before I could help it, all my fear of Nobody swallowed up by something greater, more terrible, more familiar. "It's here. It's been waiting. That loop was the only thing keeping us safe and you've destroyed it. You fucking fucking idiot."

Nobody opened his mouth to speak but changed his mind.

Clarity and silence came.

I stood statue still, listening, feeling for any sign of it and trying not to make myself obvious. I wanted to run, more than anything I wanted to run, but that would mean splashing, churning the flows and spreading the scent of my panic and fear out through the waterways. All I could do was stay still and try not be seen.

A distant thud inside my mind and inside the hospital at the same time.

'*Ludovician,*' Nobody mouthed.

"You said you could capture it," I whispered, painfully loud in the quiet.

"Not," he said, "not without – I need a team, and equipment. It isn't possible without –"

The circle of lamplight *rippled* the way tea ripples in a teacup. Nobody stopped mid-sentence and took a careful step back from the edge. "Territoriality," he said. "It's you it's come for. You, not me."

It's come for me. I started to focus on my Mark Richardson personality, felt the tensions and weight of expression changing on my face. This close-up it might not be enough to hide me, but it was something. I had to try.

"What about the things you said about us being the same person?" I said, pushing the Mark Richardson attitude out in front of me like a shield.

"What?" Nobody backed further away from the edge of the light. "I didn't say that. Why would I say we were the same person?"

I felt my eyebrows come down. "You said –"

There was another bang, louder this time. The bow wave of something large and just out of sight washed through the light circle, distorting the geometry of the black and white tiles with rolling dips and waves.

"Oh, Christ." Nobody held onto the neck of the standing lamp with one hand and circled slowly around it, looking out into the dark.

Mark Richardson, I focused with everything I had. *Mark Richardson Mark Richardson Mark Richardson.*

"So far out," Nobody was saying quietly to himself and I could hear his feet stepping around and around the lamp. "So far out. The beauty of it, the simplicity. So big and so deep. Over such depths. The things I. The things I –"

He screamed a high-pitched and horrible scream.

I thought he'd dropped onto his knees but he hadn't – his left leg had been pulled *through* the black and white tiled floor up to the thigh. The ground stayed solid and real under the rest of his body – his hands and elbows pushing and scrambling against it and the foot on the end of his stretched-out right leg kicking and squealing against the varnish – but his left leg had passed down into the tile and concrete as if the ground were completely insubstantial.

His thrashing body made a single powerful downwards jerk.

He became silent and still. He gulped, spat, gulped again. His head lolled.

"Oh, God," he said.

For a few seconds he just hung there, then – another jerk. His mouth opened to scream and his entire body vanished under the floor.

The standing lamp rocked from side to side on its wide round base, stretching the circle of light into a swinging yellow oval – back and forth and back and forth. The white tiles flushed red for a moment in an under-the-ice plume. The colour dispersed in swirls and was gone. The lamp slowed its rocking – back and forth and back and forth. The circle of light steadied, stopped.

Everything was still.

I was alone.

I screwed down my eyes again – *Mark Richardson Mark Richardson Mark Richardson*. But the fear had me shaking and my lips juddered out sound as I thought the name over and over in my head.

"Mmm, mm–mmm." Trying not to think about the floor, trying not to think about the solid flat surface abandoning me and my being dragged down into deep waters. "Mmm, mmm–mmmm."

A hand landed on my shoulder.

"Shhh," a girl's voice said, close behind my ear.

I froze.

"Do you still smoke those horrible menthol cigarettes?"

"No. No, I –" Babbling not thinking. "No, I don't –"

"Well, you do now."

Another hand reached around me and pushed a lit cigarette into my mouth.

16

Ludovician

The tang and noseburn sharpness of the cigarette lifted me out of my panicking self like a slap. The hand on my shoulder squeezed a little.

"Okay," the girl's voice whispered. "Stay still and listen. Here's what's going to happen. On the count of three, I'm going to sprint across the room and I'm going to grab one of those chairs, then I'm going to use it to smash one of the windows at the far end of the ward. You're going to come with me, grabbing Nobody's laptop on the way. Got it?"

The cigarette unwound smoke into my eyes. I squinted and nodded.

"Good. You'll have to run as fast as you can. Make sure you get in and out of the lamplight quickly. Keep moving forwards. Don't stop, don't look down more than you have to and don't look behind you at all. Are you clear on everything?"

I nodded again.

"Okay. Are you ready to try this now?"

"Yes."

"One. Two. *Three.*"

I threw myself towards the circle of light as quickly as I could but the whisperer overtook me within a few paces, striking forwards in a flat-out sprint. The pumping adrenaline only gave me snapshots of her as she broke into the circle of light ahead – black hair, army jacket, the flashing yellow soles of her boots. She snatched the chair by the back as she ran, her momentum sending it whipping out behind her and then she was gone again into the dark. I hit the light half a second later, slowed to a jogging crouch and scooped up the laptop from the black and white tiles. Picking up speed, I hoisted it up with a forearm muscle wrench and pinned it flat against my chest and then – my foot skidded on something on the floor. I fell forwards out of control, hands out into a heap and the laptop skipping away over the tiles in front of me like a skimming stone. Sprawled out and half-winded, I turned to see what I'd fallen over. One of the Dictaphones. For the smallest slice of a second – not enough time for thought, just urge and impulse – my mind pulled in two directions. I looked ahead of me to see the faint silhouette of the girl pulling at the blinds over the window, trying to rip them down. I turned back. The tape player was only inches from my boot. Jumping to my feet, I reached for it, grabbed it and ran the few paces back into the circle of light. Without stopping I threw the Dictaphone into Nobody's leather bag, still open on the floor. I grabbed the second tape player, and then the third, throwing them into the bag . Where was the fourth, the broken one?

"What the fuck are you doing?" the girl's voice from the end of the ward.

"The Dictaphones," I started. There it was – the fourth one, broken in pieces, just outside the light circle. I hooked the leather bag over my arm and sprinted to the remains. *What are you doing? Come on, almost there almost there almost there –*

I skidded down and started to throw the biggest chunks of Dictaphone into the leather bag, wincing at the cigarette still clamped in the corner of my mouth. I wafted at the blue smoke and made a quick scan around me into the gloom. I thought I saw something, something happening to the tiles at the far end of the ward, the end we'd come from. I jumped to my feet just as the blinds came down and afternoon sunlight poured in. I saw the movement in the tiles again, this time clearly. For a second it was a nonsense information, then my eyes refocused.

Every sinew in my body went slack and cold.

"Oh my God," I said, quietly, simply.

"Run," the girl's voice screamed.

hadn't ...
          at m
   om   perfec
   tly t   ory cap
      him - n   re
       nd with   sib
       ancient   he s
       is old pa   sh an
   d huge   issors.
   rillcrea   ir, hang
   paper l   an old,   ti
   nt spla   tenladder
          front of   was a b
          , soon i   be all th
          oken bu   t time yo
   ould st   open ir   w w
   hat you   loing, if   i th
   e touch   id, I did   e she
   got us   stood   a fat
       drum an   r aroun
       site's we   tric light
       it was a   the sta
       the greasy smell of old candles. I stroked
       the h   her ten   lowed th   of her
       ear a   as I co   er the gh   s that li
       e, almo   ouching   his was   ing. At   t of ev
   erythi   s was st   Our little   s were   olute sti   the un
   iverse A   these th   e relativ   e of the   reek isl   e much
   e un-gre   rock and   Accordi   e guide   he ancie   ks chop
   tive gree   n most   ands ar   ced it wi   trees. V   u first g
   opé, if it'   d one, t   ubes ar   at the b   As
   nk settle   , becom   e coffee   s bubbl
   ic   its way   op. Like   g water,   , it's so
   art   tic. Clip   said something about a half can
   enty-fiv   olossus   ncient q
              her side   sland. It
              n for me   my eyes   n
          k   from my glas   ?", I sai
          d ag   ow. I'm   here is
          some   ews you   hear."
   The do   used bu   t say
          ig. "The   nice wa
          e things   ighed.
          olved in   ident, E
          afraid your partner was
              I just sa   ."It h
              ened in   An

              lent at s   nk."D
          oes a   is soun
          milia   ing. "N
          aid.   this wh
          thing, was making me t
              I sick. S   ihuman
              d sick. I   the sid
              my nose   y finger
          d   looked   he
          qu   felt hot   and h
          e   as I ask   n
              bbed sti
          ly and r   y
          from th   ds.
          "Who   ?
          What did she
              "Her na
              was Clie
              ndle sai
          aft   ıple
          o   ds. "
          C   ies
          a   was
              training
          e a
          En
              hings fir
              lon't pai
              Take th
              call spe
              . Tell th
              n who a   swers
                  a
              ı Eric.

My legs were weak and soft and I almost couldn't feel them. I had a dark horror that they'd give way as soon as I forced myself forwards, but, trembling, they held. I pushed myself into a run, painfully slow, a slow-motion run with a billion years between each and every footfall and Nobody's leather bag full of Dictaphones swinging clumsily over one arm.

Up ahead, the sound of breaking glass as the girl smashed the chair through the window and beat once, twice, with its legs to knock the jagged shards from the frame.

"Run," she screamed at me again. "*Fucking run.*"

I forced everything I could from my shaking legs, and as I came up on the laptop I kicked at it hard, sending it spinning across the tiles towards the girl and she put the chair down like a step in front of the broken window and I could hear-feel a sound like hissing of memes breaking the surface of the world and the girl bent and grabbed the laptop and shouted "Come on" and she stepped up onto the chair and launched herself out through the window and disappeared and then – it was just me.

Just me running.

Just me running, my stomach sick and my body shaking and not knowing if I'd make another step, every step expecting my leg to sink and be dragged down or caught and snagged and jerk-shaken. Just my feet hitting the floor one after the other and too too slow with silence all around and in between every step:

thud

        thud

    thud

        thud

Then I was at the chair and I jumped, one foot hitting the seat and pushing me up and higher and I tucked and ducked and everything was silent – me in the air, travelling out through the broken window and out into the daylight.

·

I came down feet first and then forwards onto my hands and knees with a couple of solid marshy thumps. Wet grass and waterlogged earth splattered up as the toes of my shoes, my knees, and my outstretched hands splashed down into cold sucking mud craters.

"Don't lose that," said the girl's voice. The cigarette had fallen out of my mouth as I landed and was lying curling out smoke in amongst the muddy wet grass.

I looked up.

"And start doing as you're told," she said, "or I'm leaving you behind." She turned and headed off down the long grass lawn at a steady run.

I pulled myself up to my feet, wiped off my hands against my jeans, picked up the cigarette, placed it tentatively between my dry lips and gave a few experimental drags to keep it alive. Hooking Nobody's leather bag over my arm I jogged painfully off down the lawn after the girl. By the time I reached her she was head and shoulders into a large overgrown rhododendron bush.

"What are you doing?"

"Move," she said. I sidestepped and she backed an old off-road motorbike out from between the leaves. She swung the thing around and step-hopped across into the saddle. "Get on."

I reached my muddy foot across the seat behind her and she dug around in a trouser pocket for the key.

"Are you hurt?"

"What? No. I don't know." Events had become a spinning waltzer with me trying to grab hold of any streak of sense as the world zipped by in coloured stripes.

"Shit." She stared back towards the hospital.

I followed her eyes up the lawn.

A muddy spray of split-second impressions – rainy-day football matches, yellow stamping Wellingtons, skidding trainers – a million tiny moment fragments were being blown free from the wet grass in a fast stripe of pressure moving down the lawn from the hospital towards us. A large conceptual thing just below the soil.

The bike's insides throttle-whined, high-pitched and angry, and we powered forwards in a sloosh of mud and water. The girl forced screaming acceleration out of the engine and we hurtled past fat bushes and bare trees through the hospital's grounds. I was thrown back, dangerously close to overbalancing.

"Hold on," she shouted, without turning her head, and the words tumbled past me fast and short in the rushing air. I reached around her, finding her thin but solid waist under the big army jacket and locking my arms around it. I ducked down into her slipstream to stop the cigarette throwing bright orange sparks at my eyes. Nobody's bag bounced awkwardly in the crook of my elbow.

"Is it still there?"

I turned. Less than fifty yards behind us and keeping pace, ideas, thoughts, fragments, story shards, dreams, memories were blasting free of the grass in a high-speed spray. As I watched, the spray intensified. The concept of the grass itself began to lift and bow wave into a long tumbling V. At the crest of the wave, something was coming up through the foam – a curved and rising signifier, a perfectly evolved idea fin.

Mark Richardson. Mark Richardson. Mark Richardson. Mark Richardson.

"It's still coming."

"In my pocket," the girl shouted back.

"What?"

"In my pocket." She throttled the bike as we hit a bump, bounced and splashed down. "In my coat, this side." She nodded her head to the left.

160

I uncoupled my hands, struggled Nobody's bag up onto my back and tried to get my jumping bouncing hand inside her coat pocket. Finally, I got hold of what was in there. It looked like a small lumpy torch handle wrapped in black tape, then I realised there was a fuse at one end. I risked a glance behind and the thought fin was closer, higher in the water. The shark was closing the gap.

"Light it," the girl shouted. "How far away is it?"

We hit another bump and I squeezed tighter with my right hand. "Close – forty yards?"

"Light it, count two, and drop it."

I forced my right arm loose from around her waist and leant forward against her for balance before taking the cigarette out of my mouth. Clutching tight to the bike with my thighs, I brought the orange tip into contact with the fuse somewhere above my left eye. The fuse turned itself into a red smoky sparkler and I squinted, holding the thing out and back behind me, away from my body.

"One, two." I let go.

The bike bounced up again, my body lifted upwards off the seat and I grabbed back around her waist in time for the suspension-bounce landing.

Not very far behind us – an explosion.

•

"Can I help you?"

The man behind the counter in the electrical suppliers wore a dark grey suit with black highly polished shoes and a bright orange tie. It was an expensive looking place.

My jeans were wet and caked with mud. Long brown splatter marks striped my arms and my face and my soaking wet shirt. My shoes were full of water and they squelched.

"Hello," I said. "I was wondering if you sell Dictaphones?"

17

An Invisible Eddy of Breeze

I sat on the side of my bed in the Willows Hotel unpacking a new Dictaphone from its cardboard and plastic and polystyrene. Early evening, the pale sunlight dipped towards orange, the day lowered into long shadows and abandoned stretches of light.

My wet and muddy clothes were in a heap in front of the wardrobe. I'd thrown on a pair of shorts and an old hooded top. The girl's army jacket hung over the back of the chair, her boots tucked underneath and Nobody's laptop perched on the seat. The shower running in the bathroom made a heavy pattery hiss, the rhythm broken every so often with silence and splashes as the girl moved around under the flow of water.

Setting the box to one side, I turned the tape player over in my hands.

I'd lived a detached and carefully controlled existence – all detailed planning, trying to stay safe, trying to reconstruct the events and the people who'd gone before – a sixteen-month life of dusty facts, static stories and silent archaeology. But today changed everything. The world around me had transformed into a hot liquid thing, alive and twisting with real events happening now and with unknowable possibility fingers stretching out towards the future. For me, the perspective shift was huge; a change in the nature of time, a rush of things happening that couldn't be slowed or re-examined or re-translated or pondered over at a later date because – because now I was part of the picture, I was involved.

Was this what I'd wanted? Was there even enough person inside me to step out like this, into the lights of the full-time world?

I ripped open a packet of batteries and loaded two into the back of the new Dictaphone, pushing each of them into place against the tension of the springs.

If I hadn't wanted this I could have stayed in the house with the celebrity chef cookbooks and the TV and carried on all still and lost and hiding away from the shadows moving under the waves. The Ludovician would have found me eventually, probably, but I still could have stayed. The house, the training, the fragments, it was a world I knew, a continuity I understood. I could have been just that. But now things were different. I'd *made* them different.

I fished my hand around inside Mr Nobody's leather bag, feeling for sharp plastic, pulling out the pieces of the broken Dictaphone one at a time. Eventually I found the main body of the stamped-on player and carefully extracted the tiny cassette from its broken cradle. The tape had a white forking crack across one of its faces but I couldn't see any other damage. I slotted it inside the new Dictaphone, pressed play, and the speaker hissed out a familiar tinny recording. I smiled.

•

"Hey."

The girl condensed from a nebulous cloudy thing into something solid and focused. I rubbed my eyes.

"Sorry," I said. "Nodded off."

She stood in the bathroom doorway wearing one of my T-shirts and a baggy pair of trousers with the belt tied into a kind of knot. Her black bob had been rubbed dry with a towel and was now big, confused and messy. "Don't say anything," she said. "Do you have a brush?"

I nodded and pointed towards the chest of drawers.

"I'm Scout," she said, turning back and tugging the brush through her hair.

"I was going to ask," I said. "I'm Eric."

"Eric Sanderson, I know."

163

"You know?" I propped up on my elbows.

"Course." She looked confused. "What did you think? That I was in the neighbourhood, just passing through?"

I hadn't thought about it at all. I'd left that puzzle standing with all the others – huge and quiet, like the rows of strange stone heads on Easter Island – as I ran for my life. Now I began to see how all the questions were still there, waiting for me to come back and face up to them one by one.

"No," I said a bit weakly, "I suppose not."

Scout took Nobody's laptop off the chair and sat down, pulled the brush through her hair a few more times, then settled back against her big coat. She was probably in her very early twenties, pale and too thin. Her black bobbed hair was a shocking negative of her white skin and her eyes were sharp sharp green. She had high cheekbones, and what they call '*good bone structure*' on those makeover programmes on TV. I realised she was beautiful, or possibly proto-beautiful – there was still a youngness about her, as if she hadn't quite aged into the person she was going to become.

I crossed my legs and rubbed at my face.

"Listen," I said, "I'm so out of my depth here. It's like, the life I had, it didn't work like this. I'm not –" I almost said *I'm not Eric Sanderson*. "I'm not an adventurer, is what I'm trying to say. I'm struggling to catch up."

I wasn't sure why I suddenly needed to come out with any of this.

"I phoned you, remember?" she said it slowly, in that tone people use when they're explaining something to a friend who really should know it already, but seems to have forgotten. "I was going to head you off in Manchester, but then Nobody did his thing. I tried to warn you but the signal was terrible."

"That was you?"

"Who else?"

I didn't say anything.

"I didn't know if you could even hear me, so I backtracked here and hoped I'd catch up with you in time. It wasn't easy, with the floods."

"No," I said, nodding. "Thanks. But," I stopped, checking if the question was stupid, not being able to tell and so asking it anyway – "I mean, why?"

"Why what?"

"*Why what?* Why everything. Why are you here? How did you know – how did you find out about me?"

She reached into the pocket of her coat and pulled out a little white card, holding it up for me to see. It was one of the business cards I'd made. Finally, a light went on in my head.

"You're Un-Space Exploration Committee?"

"Wow," she said. "You are having trouble keeping up. Yes, I am. Well, kind of. Unofficially."

I couldn't think of anything to say.

"I'm not a fully paid-up member," – she smiled a smile which suggested there was a lot more to it than that – "but that's lucky for you because the Committee's written you off, they won't touch you with a stick."

So they did know, all this time when I thought I was going crazy they were real and they knew about me. They were keeping quiet, doing nothing. Just watching.

"They won't help me because of the shark?" My brain was making time now. "No," I said, thinking it all the way through. "You're talking about Mr Nobody, aren't you?"

"I'm talking about his *employer*. But like I said, that's okay because I'm more sort of freelance. My fee's £5,000, which you've got to agree is very reasonable considering I've already saved your life once. As well as the cash, I get to keep certain items we might come across on the way, starting with this laptop."

"Wait," I said, losing myself in the tumble again. "Your fee to do what?"

"To be your guide, stupid. You're looking for Trey Fidorous, right?"

"You know where he is?"

"Yep."

"*Really?*"

"Yep. Five grand. It's a steal isn't it?"

I thought about it. There weren't too many choices. I could trust her or I could stumble on alone until I reached the end of the trail I'd been trying to follow, and then what? Go home and die my quiet death in the house? Was that really still an option? I already knew the answer. No matter what I told myself, I couldn't be nothing again, and I couldn't undo any of the things I'd started. And anyway, what she said was true – she had saved my life once already.

"Okay," I said, "but you get the money once we've found him."

"Fine. I'll trust you. You've got the face for it."

"What does that mean?"

"Vulnerable, confused. A bit lost and useless, you know," she gave me a quick sly smile and something flared inside me, something distant, different, familiar, alien. A ghost of something. An invisible eddy of breeze. As quick as it came, the whatever-it-was was gone.

"Only," Scout was still saying, oblivious, "if I'm not getting anything up front, you're going to have to buy all the supplies and all the food. Everything we need."

"Okay," I said, shocked and distracted by the sudden *thing* inside me, trying to chase it back into the dark.

"And we're going to have to include breakfast, lunch and dinner in that."

"Okay."

"Starting from now."

"Okay."

"No, really. Starting from now."

My brow slowly crunched itself up, pulling me out from the back of my head and into the real world.

"Sorry, what?"

"Come on," she said, jumping up. "I'm starving."

Aunty Ruth made us both full English breakfasts with sausage and bacon and eggs and beans and fried bread and I didn't realise how hungry I felt until the mountain of food landed on the table in front of me. My body, my elbow especially, was bruised and stiff from the falls and slams of the last few hours but my stomach and insides had recovered surprisingly quickly.

I'd expected either electric curiosity or matronly disapproval from Aunty Ruth when she saw Scout at the table. I thought turning up for dinner with a girl dressed emergency-style in my baggy clothes was likely to earn me a raised eyebrow at the very least, and, if there was disapproval, a stern *'Can I have a quick word with you?'* at a more private later date. But, at first, apart from a warm little 'Hello, love' which Scout returned with a broad but slightly embarrassed smile, there was nothing at all. Ruth seemed more concerned with explaining the whereabouts of Ian.

As she unloaded the plates of food and piles of toast from her carrying tray, she told me that Ian had been with her for most of the afternoon.

"Oh, I hope you don't mind, love, but he *was* crying. I sent John up to fetch him. I could hear him from all the way down here and I couldn't stand listening to it, it was breaking my heart."

Crying? I'd only heard Ian meow once, and that's when I'd stood on him by accident. Ian would quite happily sit in the same place for hours and hours and hours, unless of course, he thought it would be of benefit to him to be somewhere else.

"No, of course not," I said. "Thanks for taking care of him."

My suspicions were confirmed when Ruth told us Ian was currently in the washroom behind the kitchen happily toughing his way through a full English of his own. And I thought he'd been worried about me. I thanked her and apologised for him.

"Don't be daft, he's no trouble at all," she said, passing over a teapot and a small jug of milk. "Anyway, you two eat up. It looks like you've had quite a day."

"She's nice," Scout said, watching Ruth head back to the kitchen. "You've got a cat called Ian?"

I nodded.

She laughed. "Excellent."

I knew at some point I'd have to make it up to the cat after our *incident* earlier in the day. I also knew that when Ian saw we had a new travelling companion he was unlikely to be in a happy or forgiving mood. I could already picture the thundery disgust and disappointment all over his big flat ginger face.

"He's a bit of an arsehole," I said, still thinking about it.

Scout nodded, smiling at this as she poured herself a cup of tea.

"Well, that's what you want in a cat."

I considered and nodded. "Yeah, actually, it is."

Scout ploughed into her food as though she hadn't eaten for days. I dug in with big greedy mouthfuls of my own but even when I began to slow down and feel the aches of being really full, she carried on eating with single-minded determination.

In a careful, edge-of-my-thoughts sort of way, I wondered about the Ludovician.

"You're safe for now," Scout said, as if she could read my mind, looking up for a second from the piece of bacon she was steering around her plate, chasing beans. "There's no way that shark is making it back here any time soon. I'd say you've got two days at the very least."

"On the bike," I said, "what was that thing? An explosive?"

"Sort of – a letter bomb. Basically, a firework taped up with old typewriter key arms and printing block letters. You can use anything solid with printed language. I made one from cheap necklace pendants once."

"You think we injured it?"

Scout shook her head. "No chance. Did you see the size of it?

Anyway, it's not really meant to be a weapon. The explosion sends metal letters – all their associations, histories, everything – blasting out in all directions to scramble the flow the shark is swimming in," she pointed between her teacup and my teacup with her knife, "the one connecting us and it."

"I remember."

"Meanwhile, the bang gets the attention of everyone in earshot and the shark gets lost in all the new incoming streams. Even going full-tilt and following all the right streams, it'll take forty-eight hours at least to find its way back to us."

I couldn't help being impressed. "Do you have any more of them?"

"Letter bombs? A couple. But the first one always works best. After that, it's going to be hit and miss."

"Scout, how do you know all this stuff?"

"Probably because I'm a genius. Come on, I'm not going to travel with someone like you without doing my research, am I? And anyway –" she stopped. The words she didn't say left a little air-pressure gap where they should have been.

"The letter bomb wasn't really meant for the Ludovician. You brought it to use against Nobody, didn't you?"

"Either or," Scout shrugged the question off, but I caught the slight scratchiness in her, a ghost whisper of tension.

I felt myself tightening up. "Who was he?"

"Nobody?"

I nodded.

Scout poked at the remains on her plate. "I think I liked you better when you weren't talking."

"I think I liked you better when I didn't know you were hiding things."

"I'm not hiding things," she looked up at me and the weight of her personality hit me like a hammer. "And you don't *know* anything about me."

My mouth opened all on its own for a surprised apology but I forced it shut again.

After a few seconds Scout softened with a *for-God's-sake* sigh.

"Look, I just want one night's rest. Can't we both pretend to be normal people who stay in restaurants and have dinner and do all those normal things just for one night? I really need to be like other people for a little while. If that's okay with you."

"I didn't mean to accuse you. The thing is though, you're right, I *don't* know anything about you and you've got to see how that's going to be a problem for me after today."

She thought for a minute.

"Okay, how about this? Tomorrow you can ask anything you want and I promise I'll tell you everything, explain anything I can about whatever you want to know, but tonight, no questions. Tonight, we're just two normal people, okay?"

"Alright," I said, "it's a deal."

"Good. Now," Scout pushed her plate out in front of her, took a deep breath and let herself crumple with a tired smile. "I *really* need to get some rest."

I smiled back. *Truce.* "So, I'm guessing it's part of the deal I get you a room?"

"God, no," she said, surprised. "I'll be staying in your room."

"Where?"

"In the bed."

"And where will I be?"

"On the floor, of course."

"On the floor in my own room?"

"Yes, *all night*. And anyway, it'll be good practice."

"Two rooms still sounds comfier to me."

"Yeah, well, comfort isn't everything."

•

Twilight had almost given way to night when I stepped through the front door of the Willows Hotel, the last pale yellows and oranges all quashed by the deep and deepening blue.

I was on my way to find the sleeping bag in the yellow Jeep while Scout attempted to collect Ian from Aunty Ruth. I'd told her it wasn't a smart move unless she wanted to look like she'd been self-harming but she said she wanted to give it a shot anyway. *We'll have to get to know each other sooner or later*, she'd said. I wanted to say, *No, really,* and explain how Ian really wasn't a getting-to-know-you type of cat or even a casual-hello kind of cat, more a sort of whirlwind made of blades. But then I remembered how I would be sleeping on the floor while she had the bed and said, *Fine, thanks.*

I strolled around the side of the hotel to the car park, enjoying the simplicity of the evening air and, yes, enjoying the fact that all questions would have to wait until tomorrow. I was allowing myself to pretend I was normal. Just for one night.

Being so wrapped-up in these thoughts meant I got very close to the yellow Jeep before seeing the shadowy figure hanging around it, smoking.

I jumped and started to duck down, but even as I did, it was too late.

"Alright?"

I straightened up.

"Alright," I said back.

"I've just finished. Got her running."

My back muscles relaxed a little, but not very much. I walked forward, but not very much either.

"You're from the garage?"

"No, I'm from here."

I didn't know what to say. "Oh."

"John," the man said, taking a step towards me and holding out his hand. "This is my hotel."

"Oh, you're Ruth's husband." I walked forward fast and shook his

171

hand in both of mine, my relief far too obvious.

"That's probably what it's come to, yeah. Were you thinking I was somebody else?"

"No," I said, and then, "I don't know."

"Hmmm," he said. "I thought it might be something like that." He leaned back against the Jeep's bonnet. "Cigarette?"

"No, thanks, I don't." Something flashed into my head – Scout saying 'Are you still smoking those menthols?' More questions waiting for their answers.

"Suit yourself," John said. "You'll be leaving us tomorrow then?"

I slouched back against the car next to mine. "Yeah, how did you know?"

"I saw you come back with that girl today."

I felt myself wince. "Sorry, I should probably have –"

John waved a *don't worry about it* hand. "I hope you don't mind me saying. You're in a battle, aren't you, son?"

There was a second's silence. "Yes," I said, simply.

He nodded. "I saw it in you, when you arrived. Ruth did too. I suppose someone will have told you about the car crash."

"Yes, I heard."

"Well, Ruth knows a fighter when she sees one. She's a brave woman."

"Yes," I said again, not doubting this at all.

John wrinkled up his eyes and nodded, then smoked away on his cigarette for a while.

"Lots of different types of battle out there," he said finally, standing up. "And it's not our business which type you're fighting. Just know that if you ever want to visit us back here, you'll be welcome. You *and* your cat." He ground his cigarette out underfoot and started walking back to the hotel.

"Thank you," I said after him and he held up the back of his hand to me as he walked away, as if to say *any time*.

172

•

When I got back to the room Scout was already in the bed asleep. She'd curled tight into and around the duvet, her head tucked down away from the electric light so only an ear, the white skinny back of her neck and a single shoulder blade poked out. She shifted a little as I closed the door and I noticed her black bra strap, frayed and worn-looking against her pale back. I rubbed my face in my palms. Just like most things in this new, fast-moving world, I didn't know very much about the reality of women.

Ian the cat slept on the pillow next to her, *purring*. His face was a big round happy smile, probably enjoying a dream about how stupid he'd made me look.

The TV was on; some third-rate soap I didn't recognise. I switched it off and unrolled the sleeping bag at the foot of the bed. It was still early but I was exhausted. I clicked off the light, pulled off my hooded top and shorts and lay down. It felt good, not to be alone; to be part of a team, this unit of three all resting together ready for tomorrow, for something new to happen – an *adventure*. Maybe.

Scout shifted around again, her foot found its way out from under the duvet and hung over the edge of the bed at the ankle. I lay there looking up at her foot, vaguely thinking how small it was compared to one of my feet and how funny feet are generally. As my eyes adjusted to the dark I noticed something. I sat up to make sure I was seeing what I thought I was seeing. It wasn't shadows or sticky floor dirt or anything else; it was really there. I could taste my heartbeat in the roof of my mouth.

Scout had a tattoo of a smiley face on her big toe.

THREE

What we see before us is just one tiny part of the world. We get into the habit of thinking, this is the world, but that's not true at all. The real world is a much darker and deeper place than this, and much of it is occupied by jellyfish and things.

Haruki Murakami

18

Yippy Yippy Ya Ya Yey Yey Yey

"Rise and shine. Come on, get up."

I'd been dreaming of beaches. Yellow sand, ranks of white parasols, aqua blue clear-as-glass sea and huge cloudless skies. A Light Bulb Fragment dream, maybe the first I'd had in weeks. I'd been running through the surf in the cooling evening. I'd seen the lanterns of the beach-front *tavernas* drawing coloured stripes out onto dusty waves. I'd been, I'd been – already the dream was coming apart, its bright silk strands unwinding into nebulous emotions, little coloured clouds of feeling being dispersed by the movement of my waking-up mind. This is how it's always been with Light Bulb Fragment dreams; by the time I'm fully awake, they're gone.

I squinted up at the electric bulb.

"What time is it?"

From somewhere, Scout's voice said, "You don't want to know."

I moaned and turned over but I couldn't get comfortable – there was an urgency in my head. To my sleepy self it wasn't an obvious urgency, more like the vague weight of a stone tucked away and forgotten at the bottom of a rucksack. My half-awake mind searched around for it. Could it be a stowaway? Something escaped, more intact than usual, from the collapsing dream? Maybe, partly; its colours matched the ones I could still vaguely sense drifting away at the back of my consciousness, but it also had the enduring mass of a real world thing. An amphibious urgency then, a something I'd taken into my dreams with me and then out again. I felt around in my head and then in a burst of shock I remembered.

I sat up.

"You've got a tattoo on your toe."

"Good morning," said Scout. "Yes I have."

She was wearing my over-sized clothes again, rolling her own muddy ones into small packable sausages.

I put my hand up to shield my eyes from the light. My sleepy internal spirit level was trying to adjust to the sudden challenge of being upright.

"How long have you had it?"

"The tattoo?"

"Yeah."

She looked over at me, deciding whether to answer or maybe just wondering why I would want to know.

"The first thing people usually ask is, *why have a tattoo where no one will see it?*"

"No, I get it." I said, squinting. "It's for the toe tag in the morgue, right?"

She smiled to herself, stacking her rolled-up clothes. "Do you have a carrier bag or something?"

I told her there were a couple in the rucksack and as she rummaged through she asked me why I was so interested. I really wasn't sure how to answer that. "It just reminded me of someone," I said in the end.

She did a vague nod as if she wasn't really listening or didn't want to hear a long, rambling story about my past. I smiled to myself; she didn't need to worry about that.

"So why did you get it done?"

"I used to think I was *so* dark and funny."

"You?" I said. "Never."

She turned around and gave me a look. I guessed the conversation was over. For the next couple of minutes I sat quietly, letting myself come all the way around, and watching Scout in a starey early morning sort of a way as she dug out a carrier for her clothes, then packed them all inside it. After this was done, she picked up Mr

Nobody's leather bag from by the side of the bed and passed it over to me.

"What's this for?"

"You were asking who he was," she said. "Unzip that side part and tip it all out."

I looked at the bag properly for the first time. It was expensive, well made and covered in pockets and compartments. The main space was divided into two, one half more or less empty apart from a few black plastic Dictaphone fragments, the other half sealed-off behind a big brass zip.

"Go on," she said, sitting down on the bed to watch.

I pulled the zipper and shook the contents out over the sleeping bag in front of me. Dozens of little clear plastic tubs tumbled out over my legs. They made baby rattle noises as they heaped themselves up. Some rolled off under the bed and out across the floor. I picked one up at random and read the label.

"CONCENTRATION. Four milligrams."

Scout picked up a couple which had rolled past her feet.

"REASONING," she said. "And this one's SENSE OF HUMOUR."

"STYLE. EXTRAPOLATION. CONVICTION, FRIENDLY SMILE. POWERS OF PERSUASION." The little white pills inside each tub rattled away to themselves as my fingers disturbed the pile. "What is all this stuff?"

"Mr Nobody," Scout said.

I looked at her.

"This is him. The closest thing to a him there was anyway. This is what was driving that body around instead of a real self."

The pill tubs sat on my lap like a medical molehill. I searched my fingers around inside the heap again as gently as I could. It felt like a kind of autopsy. CONCERN. SURPRISE. SUSPICION. DIGNITY.

"This is it?"

"This is it."

I felt small, weak. "He told me a Ludovician did this to him."

Scout didn't reply at first, she sat padding her first and second

179

fingertips against her thumb, two beats on each before swapping. It was a pensive fidgety sort of movement but it also seemed to be building up to something. Like a dynamo working up a charge. "I'm sorry," she said finally. "I could have been a bit more –"

"No, it's alright. Tell me."

"He wasn't really a human being anymore, just the idea of one. A concept wrapped in skin and chemicals. Your shark probably saw him as a potential rival."

I thought about Nobody's strange voice telling me we were both the same person then denying it later.

"A concept wrapped in skin and chemicals," I repeated. "That sounds like a human being to me."

Scout shook her head. "No. There's more to it than that."

I didn't argue – what did I know about what human beings were or weren't?

"So," I said, like a big outward breath, changing the subject "where are we going and why are we up so early?"

No answer. When I looked up Scout was looking at me. I could see something warm in her face, something tucked away safely behind her default expression but still, something there, just behind her lips and her eyes.

"You're not going to end up like him, you know," she said.

I nodded a silent, *I know*, but I couldn't make my eyes commit to it.

Just for a moment, like a cloud shadow racing over the ground, the warm thing inside Scout's face went cold, not a heartless cold, more like the vague sadness of winter coastline.

"Right." She jumped to her feet, breaking the mood. "We're going to Manchester and we're going underground. We need to get all this packed up and we need to be on the road in the next half hour." She scanned around the room working times, distances, logistics out in her head. Her thinking stare moved through me once, twice and then, irritated, finally came back to settle. "Eric," she said. "You're just sitting there. Mush."

·

5.14 a.m. and the yellow Jeep's wheels rumbled on dark roads, its back filled with boxes of books, packed-up bags and a sleepy pissed-off Ian in his cat carrier. I'd been waiting for Scout to suggest *doing something* with Ian – checking him into some cattery or asking Aunty Ruth to take care of him for a few days, but our guide seemed to take the fact that Ian would be coming with us as a given. I was glad about that, I wasn't about to leave him anywhere and my mind was still too drifty and loaded up with early morning stares to have any sort of argument about it. Instead, we'd just packed up the yellow Jeep, quietly and mechanically, and gone. Scout threw Nobody's bag of pills and the book he'd sent me into the dumpster at the back of the hotel car park. I put a note and a cheque for more than the cost of my stay on the front desk as we left. It was a small relief to know Ruth and John would understand; Ian and I were shipping out to the front line.

Scout stared out of the side window. The dark trees and mulchy kerbs passed by to a steady heartbeat of streetlamps. Driving in the very early morning makes everything part of the same dreamy whole; the minds of sporadic drivers quietly washing back and forth like leaves on a wide ornamental pond.

My mind lost itself in an old tune I didn't quite know, going round and around in the same infuriating refrain. I needed to talk to sweep the music out.

"Hey, so where are we going?"

"Hmmm?" Scout turned away from the window, coming back from wherever she'd drifted away to.

"Where are we going?"

"Deansgate."

"I know, you said Deansgate, but I mean – whereabouts?"

"If I told you that –"

"You'd have to kill me?"

"No, but," she shuffled around in her seat, "you'd probably say something tedious like 'that doesn't make any sense' and I'd have to say 'yes, it does because blah blah blah' and then you'd want to go on and on about it all the way there anyway. And when we arrived after all the pointless debate you'd have to say 'Scout you were right all along, looks like I'm a bit of an idiot.' So, to cut out that whole boring middle bit, I'm thinking it's better just to keep it to myself." She looked across at me with that smile. "For the time being." I could feel Ian's cat-grin from the back of the yellow Jeep. "Can I put the radio on?"

I nodded. "So, what happened to answering all my questions today?"

"Well, we didn't set a time limit, did we? I didn't say, 'I promise I'll answer all your questions within thirty seconds of you asking them.' I just said today."

"That's cheating."

"It's not cheating. It's being clever. There's a difference." The radio squealed, hissed and blasted a single bar of opera before settling on the Happy Mondays. "Excellent," Scout said, flopping back in her seat.

"You can retune it if you like."

"Thanks, I did."

"I know."

Shaun Ryder's rough and dreamy drawl rattled out of the old speakers and Scout joined in on the chorus – *Yippy yippy ya ya yey yey yey. I had to crucify somebody today* – while playing her knees like the bongos. I might well have found the most annoying girl in the world. I smiled. In spite of everything I felt fresh and alive, like an old painted door being sanded back to the wood. However annoying, the girl sitting next to me wasn't *just another person*. Singing, drumming away on her knees, Scout was a force, a bright little energy wave moving through the dark world inside my old yellow Jeep. I wondered if anything could stop a girl who sang and drummed her knees like that.

The Happy Mondays became Fun Lovin' Criminals who became Gary Numan who finally became the local news. When this happened, Scout said *boo* then started fiddling with the dials again.

"I've got another question," I said.

"'kay."

"How do you know all these things about me?"

"Female intuition."

"You know I used to smoke menthol cigarettes by intuition?"

"Oh, that." Scout turned down the radio and pushed out some air, not really a sigh, more like clearing away the crockery.

I waited.

"The thing you've got to remember is history sinks downwards, like a dinosaur in a tar pit. The Un-Space Exploration Committee keeps records on everyone they've had dealings with and lots of people they haven't. If you so much as threw away a cigarette packet while on one of your underground adventures it'll be in their archives somewhere. In a glass case with an identity tag probably."

Something about this made an old industrial light flash deep in the dark corners of my mind, but it was too far back, too distant for me to trace. Giving up, I said:

"I thought you weren't *technically* a member of the committee? If they do have a –" I felt a bit stupid saying it "– file on me, why would they show it to you?"

Scout smiled. "I didn't *technically* ask permission."

"I thought you might say that."

"Of course you did. You're not as stupid as you look."

I turned around and raised my eyebrows at her.

"Well," she said.

·

We pulled up in an alleyway next to the bins at the back of a McDonalds, just off what Scout said was Deansgate. It was still dark, still very early. The city a quiet insomnia of smog, purple skies, puddles, rubbish and white and yellow sodium. It was a time and place of cats, occasional trucks, occasional taxis and occasional spots of rain.

"This is where we're parking," Scout said as I clicked off the engine.

"Here?"

"Yep, it'll be fine."

"How long for?"

"It depends on how long it is between you arriving and you wanting to come back. I'd say –" she thought "– at least four days."

"I can't leave the Jeep here for four days with everything in it. I'm going to find a long-stay car park. We can walk back."

"No, we have to leave the Jeep here. If we don't leave the Jeep here, things can get difficult. There's a protocol. Things have to be done in a certain order."

"What sort of order?"

"You don't have to understand, you just have to do it."

"The deal was –"

Scout made an exasperated air sound. "Alright, don't say it." She thought for a second. "Do you know what a Chinese puzzle box is?"

"Yes."

"Right, well, it's sort of like that. You've got to know where to apply the pressure and in what order if you want to get it to open."

"Okay – so what are we trying to open?"

Scout looked at me. "The world," she said.

•

Cities hum and rumble, they breathe out steam and smoke in their sleep and fill their alleyways with shivers. I closed the Jeep's door and pulled my coat tight around me. Scout shivered too, hugging herself, rubbing her hands against her arms in her big army jacket and stamping her heels on the tarmac.

"Right then," she said, "the best thing to do is gather together all the useful stuff, a few days' worth of clothes and anything you really can't stand to leave in the car. Travel as light as you can though, we've got a lot of walking to do."

Ian watched me empty the rucksack then repack it with clothes, a sleeping bag, the light bulb tapes and books, the torch, the Dictaphones and several packets of batteries. As I did up the toggles and straps, Scout grabbed the plastic bag of food we'd bought at an all-night garage in one hand and came around to lift Ian's carrier out of the back with the other.

"If we're going a long way," I said. "he's going to get heavy."

"He already is heavy. We'll manage."

The dark mass of Ian shifted around in his carrier to remind us *he was actually there while we talked about him*, then got on with pretending to be asleep.

"I still don't know where we're going."

"Well, lock up, you'll soon see." Scout took a deep breath and let it out slowly, trying to control the shivering. "It's like *Dawn of the Dead* or something isn't it?" Then to me, smiling: "Do you trust me?"

"Yeah," I admitted, shouldering the rucksack. "I'm just not really sure why."

Loaded-up, we walked down the alley and across a dark street which was trafficless apart from a strong through-wind and a trundling Coke can which, when it moved, seemed like the noisiest thing in the world. Scout led us to the back door of a large bookshop.

"Waterstones."

"Correct," she said, putting down the food and the cat and going through her pockets. She pulled out a small metal something and after inspecting it for a second, shoved it into the door's lock.

"Wait – we're breaking into Waterstones?"

She turned around. "You're not helping."

"What about the alarms, dead-bolts? What about – are you actually breaking in? Jesus."

"Can I have some quiet? Please."

After a few moments of looking up and down the street, clutching my arms around myself and wanting to be anywhere else on earth, Scout pulled the metal something out of the door's lock. She pushed and the door swung open into the black.

"There," she said. "No alarms. No dead-bolts. Remember what I said about Chinese puzzle boxes?"

"So parking the Jeep behind the bins at McDonalds means the alarm won't go off when you pick the lock at Waterstones?"

She picked up the food and the cat carrier. "Come on."

"Scout, that's –"

"We're in though aren't we? Come *on*."

I followed her inside and clicked the door shut behind me.

For a few seconds everything was black, then a wedge of light appeared and stretched into a tall rectangle as another door opened up ahead. Through it I saw bookshelves, the ground floor of the shop in night-time mode, still and silent with that half strength *we're closed* yellowy-orange lighting. In front of me, Scout's silhouette became the real Scout as she stepped through the doorway and out onto the shop floor. I followed.

Piled up with bags and a ginger cat, we stood there – two out-of-place backpackers – in the big closed bookshop.

"It feels unreal doesn't it?" Scout whispered.

"It's –" I couldn't find the right words to describe the feeling, but Scout's Chinese puzzle box system seemed much more plausible now we were inside. This space, all locked up, half-lit and silent near dawn, it wasn't for just anyone. A person couldn't just push a door open and carelessly walk in on something like this, something fundamental would be gone before they'd finished turning the handle. "It's sort of religious," I said in the end.

Scout nodded. "Places get a bit holy when they're left on their own to think for a while. It's something to do with the quiet maybe."

"What do we do now we're here?"

"Find the Hs."

"Books beginning with H?"

"Novels. Novels by authors beginning with H. I think they're over there."

We made our way through the shelves and silent stacks until we came to the bookcase where most of the novels by writers with surnames starting with the letter H were shelved.

"Just these bottom four rows," Scout said. "We need to unload them and stack them up at the side here."

We did it quickly, taking the books out eight or twelve at a time, squeezing our palms tight against the covers as we lifted them and piling them up wholesale in front of the G case to our left. When this was done, Scout took hold of one of the empty shelves and lifted it up and out of the bookcase, placing it neatly next to the books. She removed the two other empty shelves in the same way then got down on her knees to inspect the case's exposed back. Taking a small screwdriver from her big army coat she was soon passing out one, two, three, four small silver Phillips screws.

"Put them with the books," she said. As I did, Scout took her screwdriver and levered out the lower part of the thin woodchip backboard, passing that out to me as well. Where the board had been there was now a three-foot by four-foot rectangular black hole.

"That's where we're going," Scout said, getting to her feet and brushing herself off.

"Un-space."

"Yep, that's it."

I took the rucksack off my shoulders and got down on my hands and knees to look inside the hole. I could only see maybe two or three inches of grey bitty concrete floor before the space receded into complete black. The shop's dry warm processed air had made me start to sweat under my heavy coat but the air coming out of the hole felt cool and hard, basic and factual, and telling stories of miles of stripped-down empty places.

I moved to take the torch out of the rucksack's side pocket but I found myself slowing down, distracted. I turned and sat, staring into the black.

"You alright?" Scout said, crouching next to me.

"I've just got this feeling that if I go in there I'm not going to come out again."

She looked serious, thinking this through carefully and then she bumped her shoulder against me, a supportive nudge.

"What?" I said.

"If you want your boomerang to come back, first you've got to throw it."

"But. What if I want to keep my boomerang and not – lose it down a big dark hole?"

"The throwing and the coming back *is* the boomerang, brainstrain. Without that part, you're just carrying a bent stick around."

I smiled. "So who died and made you so wise?"

"Hmmm . . ." Thinking about it, Scout did a childish shrug. "Maybe God?"

I looked at her.

"What?"

"Wow."

"*What?*"

"Just – wow."

"Fuck off."

19

History Sinks Downwards

Under our torch beams the space behind the bookcase became surprisingly ordinary, a small grey concrete area with a circular hole cut into the floor and a steel ladder leading down.

"That's us," Scout said. "You'll have to take off the backpack and hold it up above your head to climb down."

"What about the cat?"

"I'll go in first and you pass him through to me."

Scout dropped her still-turned-on torch into the carrier bag with our food, hooked the bag over her wrist and crawled through the bookcase into the space behind. Once inside, the white plastic bag glowed with a gentle diffused light. It added a fuzzy spinning skyline of food packaging and water bottle silhouettes to the concrete walls. I watched as she manoeuvred her legs over the hole, twisted and climbed a few rungs down the ladder. As she did the bag-light disappeared under the lip of the hole and a corresponding dark horizon raced up the walls towards the ceiling. "Okay. Pass him through."

Ian had his poker-face on. He was either very scared, or surprisingly calm, considering.

"I'm sorry," I said into the cat carrier. "I promise I'll make all this up to you." And I passed him and his plastic box into the hole.

Scout took the carrier by the handle on top. "We'll see you down there," she said, heaving cat and box up above her head and starting down the ladder one-handed. I watched them disappear in steady downward bobs, Scout's shoulders, then Scout's head, then most of Scout's arm, then finally Ian's carrier, his blank face squinting from my torch beam as he disappeared into the hole.

I pushed the rucksack through the bookcase and crawled in after it.

I'd climbed down the ladder until my head was below the level of the floor and was struggling to manoeuvre the rucksack in after me when I heard a clunk from below. Pale light filtered up the climb shaft, casting long shadows upwards. I strained and struggled the rucksack into the hole, taking most of its weight on the top of my head and steadying it with my right arm as I climbed down.

The ladder brought me down into a very long, very straight concrete corridor. Weak orange strip lights with hanging wires and yellowing fittings illuminated the space to distant vanishing points in both directions. Batteries of thick black cables were harness-bolted down the length of one wall, with ladders like the one we'd come down appearing at distant intervals along the other.

"We've got light," I said, heaving the rucksack down onto the floor. My voice made hard echoes, like the sound of a clap in an empty room. The air smelled dry, industrial.

Scout leant against the wall a little further down the corridor with Nobody's laptop, Ian in his carrier, the food bag and, I noticed, another rucksack cluttered around her. She'd been waiting for me to make it down the ladder and when she saw I'd managed it she knelt, opening and rummaging in the new bag. "This is electrical access corridor number four," she said. "Welcome to un-space."

"What's that?" I said, meaning the bag.

Scout pulled two tightly-rolled-up bundles of material out of the rucksack and shook them – they unravelled into a blue vest top and a pair of green combat pants.

"My stuff," she said. "Right where I left it." Scout laid the clothes out over her rucksack then started unknotting the leather belt tied around her waist. My over-sized trousers dropped down her pale legs and she stepped out of them, boots already gone. "You didn't think I was going to –" she struggled my big T-shirt up over her head "– spend the next couple of days walking around in your bloke clothes did you?" And she scooped up my trousers and shirt and threw them over to me.

I caught them and held them to my chest.

Scout suddenly wore only the seen-better-days bra from the night before and, I realised, a pair of my dark blue fitted boxer shorts. Standing in the corridor like that she looked – well, she looked amazing. Pale and perfect: perfect-by-not-being-quite-perfect, real. Her long neck, ice-bridge collarbones, small breasts – old world marble sculpture rising a little way naked from worn functional bra cups – too-skinny ribs, small but solid muscles working under her white white skin, moving her calves, her arms, the twist of her waist, my shorts stretching out over the curve of her hips and down onto her thighs, the waistband scooping up at her stomach, and below the shorts' loose, empty front with buttons – yes, I looked, quickly, guiltily, once, twice – the material tightened to a bumped V and disappeared between her legs.

I turned away, trying to make the thick thudding rising in my chest and the depths of my throat sink back, subside, recede, but it wouldn't. Electric proximity, shock, desire, my body thumped with it and with the embarrassed panic and sudden reality of all this happening. Staring down the empty concrete corridor with the sounds of Scout moving behind me I had the over-the-top-of-everything-else horror that actively *not* looking might be worse, might be much, much more obvious than just looking. By looking away, was I flagging up something corrupt and embarrassing and childish and wrong in me that clearly wasn't on show in her? Trying hopelessly to set my face to blank and uninterested, I turned back.

Shaking out her combat pants again before stepping into them, Scout didn't seem to care whether I looked or didn't look as she changed. She didn't even seem interested in whether my looking was idle or sexual. There was a powerful feminine confidence in that, something easy but unfakeable in the way she moved, the time she took or didn't take with the various stages of changing. This was a girl – a woman – who could make or unmake the world however she wanted it. It was the most compelling thing I'd ever seen.

"You've got my pants on," I said weakly and stupidly after the end of it all.

Scout smiled up at me from lacing her boot. "You don't meet many girls, do you, Eric?" Then she was on her feet, throwing her big army jacket over her shoulders.

"Sorry," I said, embarrassed, catching up, realising time had been working a little bit strangely for me and that I was still pointlessly clutching the bundled clothes close to my chest.

"Hey," she flashed her eyebrows, "it was a joke. I'm teasing."

I nodded. She was being nice and I was feeling even more stupid than before.

Scout dropped the food bag into her rucksack, then got to work strapping Nobody's laptop to the back. I pushed the clothes she'd been wearing into the top of my bag, heaved it over my shoulders and collected Ian's carrier, lifting it up to check he was okay. Two half-open eyes and a smug ginger face looked out at me.

You can shut up too, I mouthed at him.

·

We hiked down electrical access corridor number four for about two hours. We followed a ladder up into what looked like an abandoned warehouse, then across a gantry and down into a narrower, more organic tunnel with faulty flickering lights. We talked a lot about nothing, Scout asking lots of questions about music, about which bands were still together and which had split, and about TV, mainly who'd had sex with/cheated on/killed who in the soaps. Some of the characters she asked me about were ones I hadn't even heard of and I wondered how much time she'd spent away from the world down in the quiet of un-space. We told jokes, getting into a rhythm of acting like: a) our own jokes were far funnier than they really were; and b) that each other's jokes were bad beyond belief. After one of my punchlines Scout stopped suddenly, standing still under the flickering lights.

"*Why the long paws?*" she repeated. She looked at me uncomprehending, the way the audience looks at the most extreme guests on Jerry Springer. "Eric, why would you do that to somebody?"

"You're a Philistine," I said, smiling, carrying on walking without her. I remember thinking, having a strong hot deep-in-my-insides realisation that *this is what life is*. But then, close up behind, *well enjoy it, you only have one more day. The Ludovician isn't gone forever.*

•

Underground, days are made from watch-hands. Late morning ticking into early afternoon ticking into late afternoon with us walking tunnels, upping and downing ladders, shining our torches over wide flat dark spaces with low ceilings, kicking our way through old newspapers and empty cans and thrown-away things. Places and spaces came and went. Service corridors, access chutes, flood drains, an old basement factory floor where our torchbeams found the rusted necks of over-sized sewing and winding machines and cast Jurassic shadows up across the brickwork as we passed through – *history sinks downwards* – and then on through underground car parks, abandoned archives and vaults, storage bays. Us squeezing through gaps, climbing rubble, descending PERSONNEL ONLY concrete stairwells into the roots of abandoned and still-living buildings.

We stopped to rest every two or three hours. Scout would check our progress in a little red notebook and we'd have water and maybe something to eat, then we'd swap custody of Ian and start out again. Stretches of colourless time passed. Afternoon became evening and we wore thin with the jokes and the games, the journey becoming a mostly silent, thoughtful and leg-aching march. Around 6 p.m. Scout finally called a halt and we dropped bags for the night.

We'd arrived in a broken-down warehouse, one of those with a strutted, peaked, corrugated roof with dual rows of glazed panels to let in the light. Most of the glass had been smashed, green vine fingers creeping down onto the struts and along the walls at the distant far end. The tramlines of sky above us were the same low-hanging smoggy purple as we'd seen in the city that morning. It was as if there hadn't been a day.

I lay down on the gritty floor next to my bag and looked up at the clouds.

"I think my legs are turning to wood."

The slim share of twilight we were getting wasn't enough to read by, so Scout used her torch to check through her notebook again.

"We're doing okay," she said. "We should be there by tomorrow."

Tomorrow. We should find Trey Fidorous tomorrow.

"Good," I said, closing my eyes and thinking about nothing but the joy of being still.

"Hey."

"What?"

"What are we going to do about your cat?"

I opened my eyes, turned over on my side. "What about him?"

"Well, he can't just take a toilet roll and get the other person to walk on ahead like us, can he? He's been holding it in all day."

I hadn't thought about that. If Ian had to go inside his carrier and then be carried around in it afterwards –

I rolled over onto my back, screwed up my eyes. "Tell me what to do, Scout."

"I think we should let him out."

"What if he runs off?"

"I don't think he's the running type."

"But you know what I mean."

"Where's he going to go? Anyway, I don't see we've got much of a choice unless you want to carry him all day tomorrow in his own piss and shit."

I opened one eye. "Charming."

"Well, that's what's going to happen."

She was right. I hauled myself onto my knees and then, aching, up

194

to my feet. Ian's carrier was parked close to where Scout sat on her rucksack, still looking at her book, making notes by torchlight. I knelt down in front of Ian's box and peered through the bars. In the almost dark I thought I could just make out those two big unimpressed eyes. Ian, of course, would be able to see me perfectly.

"Right," I said. "I'm going to let you out now so you can do your thing. Don't go running off anywhere. We've got some delicious tins of tuna for you, right Scout?"

"Delicious."

"So you'd be *much* worse off than I would if you decided to disappear. What do you think?"

Silence from the carrier.

"Okay, I'm opening the door now."

I clicked the catch off and swung the front open. After a moment, Ian's big ginger body stepped out, cautiously at first, and then, looking around with that *not bad* expression dads use when looking at other dads' new cars, he sauntered off into the depths of the warehouse.

"He's not going to come back."

"You're such an old woman," Scout said, tucking the book away. Then, seeing I was concerned, she said: "Of course he will. You explained about the tuna and everything."

"Fuck off." I smiled in spite of myself. "But I don't know what I'd do if I lost him. It's always been just him and me, you know?"

"I know. He'll be back. Don't worry." Scout stood up. "Let's get a fire started before it's too dark. There were some wooden pallets over by the hatch we came up through; do you want to drag a couple over here? I'll sort out some paper."

Part of me wanted to say, *but won't someone come if we light a fire, won't someone call the police?* But I didn't, partly because I was too tired and partly because I felt I was starting to understand the workings of un-space – nobody ever ever came.

Despite my worries about Ian, I had a warm feeling about sleeping in the same space as Scout again. *Being part of a team, part of a unit.*

For the thousandth time that day, I thought about my trousers slipping down her pale legs and her stepping out of them, my shorts tight around her hips and thighs. *Being part of a team*, I thought, *yeah, sure, Eric, that's what it is.* I went to get the pallets.

•

We built a small fire and soon the two of us were redrawn in hot orange, deep red and whispery skittish black. We shared a can of beans, dipping chunks of breadcake into Scout's mess tin. I said we should try toasting the bread but Scout smiled and shook her head.

"Toasting bread on an open fire. It sounds like the easiest thing in the world, doesn't it? But just ask anyone who's tried."

I wondered whether the First Eric Sanderson ever tried toasting bread outside the tent on Naxos. Whether *my hands* had ever attempted that. I thought about him and Clio arguing about ruined bread then I thought about them laughing about it. With both of them gone, history had forgotten if an event like that ever happened and how they'd reacted if it did. Looking into the fire, I decided to let them laugh. I realised I'd not thought about the First Eric Sanderson for quite a while.

Scout tipped a little water into the bean tin, swilled it around. "You know, there's still one thing you haven't asked me."

"One thing?" I said. "There's a million things. I don't know if Scout's your real name, where you come from, how old you are, anything."

"True. But you're not asking any of *those* questions because you're surprisingly tuned-in for a guy. You know I'm sensitive about it and you don't want to hurt my feelings."

I checked for some kind of trap in that, but I couldn't see one. "Thanks," I said, cautiously.

Scout smiled. If there was sparkly mischief in there too, it was hidden by the flickerings of the fire. "Right back at you. No, the question you really want to ask me is –"

" Who said you could wear my pants?"

"And could you possibly have them back unwashed?"

"You're pretty sick, you know that?"

"Yeah, whatever, repression boy."

I smiled a nodding smile, looking into the fire, letting it draw me in and not saying anything back. The seconds ticked away towards a minute, the fun, the silliness, all evaporating up and away through the smashed glass above our heads. The concrete floor felt hard and cold under my crossed legs and the space was huge and black and empty. I looked down at my fingers, the fingers, hands and wrists that had been the First Eric's for most of their existence. I knew the jokes and games couldn't hide me from who I was, from what things were. The painful truth was that this whole time-out was a fluke.

"Go on," Scout said, and I thought I saw something similar in her, that cold again, the shadow over the field.

"I know," I said, "I was just having fun pretending to be a normal person."

She nodded slowly, looking away into reds and shadow.

There was nowhere else to go.

"Alright then, I'll ask it. Who is he, Nobody's employer?"

"Thanks for trying not to hurt my feelings." She looked away, her whole face turning to shadow.

"Scout?"

"He's ninety-nine parts something malfunctioned and horrible, and one part me."

20

The Arrangement

"You?" I stared across the fire, loose inside my own skin.

"A part of me, a small stolen part, is a tiny part of him. Some of me – most of me – is still me, but," her hand came up to touch the side of her temple. "God, look, I don't know how to explain this. Part of him is inside my head."

"You're not making any sense. Jesus, what? You're telling me you were *possessed* or something?"

"It's more clinical than that, like, a process. It – the rest of him can't control me or anything, but there's a dormant chunk of him inside my mind and while he exists –" Scout stopped herself, took a big breath. "Shit, I *so* wasn't going to do this. I was just going to lay it all out on the line, try to explain it to you using all the right words, but –" her hands tucked the ends of her bob behind her ears. Her chin, her throat, all of her, she was shaking.

"God, Eric, I'm sorry to say this but you're so lucky. You're walking around in this constant state of collapse and you're fine with that, I mean, you *exist* like that. Some people, they might look like they're in control day to day but if they let themselves go, maybe they're going to fall all the way apart and never put themselves back together. You know?"

I put my hands up into a church around my mouth, sucked air through my fingers. My brain, my insides pulled in every direction at once. "All I need to know now is, did you send Mr Nobody to find me, Scout? Are you one of them?"

The firelight picked up the fat swell of tears along the bottoms of her eyelids. She worked hard not to let a single drop fall. "No, of course

I didn't. I would have used the fucking letter bomb on him, but your shark got there first."

"It's not my shark."

"I'm saying I'm *nothing* like him. The me sitting here in front of you now and doing a really good job of fucking all this up, I'm a person just like you are –" a small laugh like a shudder "– although maybe you're not the best person to make that argument to."

I knew what she meant. "*A concept wrapped in skin –*"

"*– and chemicals.* There *is* more to people than that, you know."

I waited as she had a sip from the water bottle, then splashed a cupped handful onto her face, massaging her fingers across her skin, from the bridge of her nose, over her eyes and cheekbones. This done, she offered the bottle to me and I reached around and took it.

"I don't understand what you're telling me," I said. "*The me sitting here?* You're saying there's more than one of you walking around? Or –"

Scout ran her hands through her tucked-back hair, shaking it out. "Okay," she said, "a part of me got stolen, I mean, a part of me in here," – she touched her temple – "and it was incorporated into something else; a huge, abnormal out of control *thing*. In the place of the part I lost, I got some of *it*." She stopped to check my reaction. I had absolutely no idea what my face was doing. "The *it* is deactivated, a mass of information packets, like virus code, but it's there inside my head and there's no way of getting it out."

I thought about this. "Can it be activated, this information?"

"Yes. It's not a two-second process, not like someone flips a switch in New York or anything. They'd have to physically find me, but, yeah, there's a procedure."

"And what would happen then?"

"The information packets would go live, spread through my mind. They'd take over and I'd get absorbed into the *thing*." She thought for a second. "Eric, have I really fucked this up?"

Still trying to get my head around what she was saying, the

confusion must have shown on my face. It must have been the right kind of confusion too. "This – what?"

Scout smiled a tiny smile, a little flashlight. "Listen, I'm going to have a walk around the warehouse and see if I can see the cat. I need a few minutes but then I'll come back and then I promise to tell you the whole story. Would you be okay with that?"

"Yeah," I said, still feeling like something had stung me. "Yes, that would be good."

·

When Scout came back my fat ginger cat dance-pranced along behind her the way he does when he's sucking up for something. Normally, and I've said this before, Ian doesn't like anyone. I've never seen him give another person the slightly embarrassing dancey routine, not even Aunty Ruth. Watching their silhouettes warm up into 3D as they came closer to the firelight, I thought about trust and where it comes from. Why *had* I followed Scout all the way down here when I knew so little about her? Partly, it was because of my own lack of success in finding Fidorous, but there was more to it than that. From the moment she'd appeared, I trusted her. It just happened. And I had the feeling that whatever came out of her mouth when she sat down by the fire, I would want to go on trusting. Ian's dance said that as far as he was concerned, she was one of us. I wanted her to be one of us too.

"Are you okay?"

Scout nodded. "I found a friend."

"Must be because you were so convincing about the tuna."

She smiled.

We opened a can and fed it to Ian from the back of Scout's mess tin, filling the lid with a little water for him too.

"I told you he'd come back," she said, settling back by the fire.

Ian purred, his head bobbing away with greedy chewing.

"You did," I nodded, and then: "I just thought, I didn't bring the vodka."

She winced. "Oversight. It's okay though, I'm going to attempt this sober." A pause. "I don't know where to start."

"Well – *start at the beginning, go on until you get to the end, then stop.*"

She did a small laugh which was really just a single hiss of air. "Okay then. The *beginning* beginning starts way back with an old man called Mycroft Ward –"

With all my interrupting, being confused and asking for clarifications taken out, this is the story Scout told me.

•

THE STORY OF MYCROFT WARD

Towards the end of the nineteenth century there lived an old man named Mycroft Ward. Ward was a former military man and one of the last of the gentleman scientists. He'd gathered quite a reputation for his unbending will (apparently something very fashionable in those days) and had done many heroic things during the Crimean War, being one of the minor heroes of the Battle of Balaclava. Although Mycroft Ward had nothing at all to do with the Charge of the Light Brigade the sentiment was him all over, and so, many years later, when a physician broke the news of a slow but fatal illness, Ward's attitude didn't surprise any of those who knew him best.

The old man announced – to family, to friends and to several newspapers – that he had decided not to die, not from this illness, not from anything, not ever. He claimed he didn't have the time for death and would instead '*unshackle himself from the multitudinous failings of the corporeal harness and progress forward* ad infinitum'. He then locked himself in his study for the best part of a year, refusing to comment further or speak to anyone much at all.

The old man's death the following spring was marked only by a number of small obituaries and a few pithy editorials (one of which compared him to King Canute). Within a few months, interest in Mycroft Ward had grumbled itself away into the aether. The planet smirked, and moved on.

What the planet didn't hear about, what only a select group of people have ever known, is this: Ward succeeded in his plan. At least, he succeeded after a fashion.

His original technique is lost now, but there seems to have been nothing magical or spiritual or even overly scientific about what Ward did. The system he devised was so down-to-earth and logical an accountant might have invented it. First, through the use of thousands of questions and tests, Ward succeeded in reproducing a very rough copy of his personality on paper. Then, through '*the applied arts of mesmerism and suggestion*' Ward successfully imprinted this personality onto another person.

Now, though the future might come to think differently, Ward was not a bad man. He may have been unbearably pompous and self-righteous, but in planning and carrying out his strange scheme he seems always to have acted honourably and fairly. His private journals, which still survive both on a high-security website and in a deep and fortified bank vault, refer to the transferring of his personality as 'the arrangement', and that's exactly what it was.

Ward spent a great deal of time and money selecting what he hoped would become his new body, eventually opening negotiations with a young doctor named Thomas Quinn. Quinn had been devastated by the loss of his wife a year earlier, letting his small town practice fall into ruin as he lived listlessly on his dwindling savings. Quinn was very much taken with Ward's technique (partly, we might suppose, because of the nature of his own tragic loss). He believed the old man to be on the verge of a discovery greater than anything achieved by Newton or Darwin and saw in 'the arrangement' a chance to "*at last turn away from sorrow and give what little I have remaining to the furtherment of science"*. Quinn, being the romantic he clearly was, must have fancied himself as the first martyr of the scientific age.

And so, as Ward lay on his deathbed, Quinn underwent a very secret process and a small team of lawyers transferred all assets and monies to the old man's 'young and recently discovered great nephew'.

'The arrangement' was a greater success than Ward could ever have hoped for. Members of the Ward family initially challenged the validity of this young man who had appeared from nowhere, claimed to be a distant relative and walked away with everything the old man owned. But on meeting 'Mycroft Ward the Younger', even the most stubborn and money-fixated of the cousins conceded that the two men must be related – while there was little physical resemblance, their mannerisms, attitudes and opinions were so similar there could be no doubt of a blood connection. Mycroft Ward's *self* had successfully survived the death of his body. He was young again at the dawn of a new century.

It's hard to say why the new Ward didn't go public with the success of his technique, especially when one considers how he'd declared his intentions to the world. Maybe he worried that his family would find a way to take his estate away from him if they discovered his new body did not share a single drop of blood with the old; maybe he wanted to work on the technique further before announcing what he'd done; or maybe he'd just moved on; with horizons broader than any man had ever seen before, there were certainly bigger fish available for frying. What we do know is that by the outbreak of the First World War – stubborn and indomitable as ever – Ward had found himself a place as an officer in the army. But the Great War wasn't like anything that had gone before it. The era of the Light Brigade was long gone, stripped of its pride and brass and poems and paintings. War was industrialised now, the whole world split into two great funding machines for the daily grinding of a million human bodies.

As I have said, Ward wasn't a bad man. The decision he came to, once peace was declared, was nothing if not understandable given his particular resources and circumstances. But then, the worst things don't always grow from the worst intentions.

War-scarred despite all his bluster and bravado, Mycroft Ward developed an obsession with the one great hole in his scheme; for all the immortality his *self* could achieve through repeated use of 'the arrangement', he could – like anybody else – still be shot dead on some future battlefield and wiped clean from the face of the earth forever. In tackling this new anxiety, Ward's chosen course of action was as practical and as monumental as it had been thirty years earlier. He decided one body was simply not enough to guarantee his survival. This is not to say he aimed to create another Mycroft Ward. Another Ward wouldn't have been a solution, just a divergence; two people grown from a common source. No, his great plan was this – there would be just one Mycroft Ward, a single *self* inhabiting two bodies.

Throughout the early half of the 1920s, Ward modified the original personality recording template significantly. He added new systems and techniques to refine the collected personality data, developed tests which would capture newly acquired knowledge and opinion, and created an all important procedure whereby knowledge could be gathered from two minds, standardised with minimum loss of information, then transferred back, realigning both minds into a single unified self.

Ward also amended his new personality recorder to instil an increased desire for self-preservation. And it was with this one single action, as sensible as it may have seemed to him in the bloody aftermath of World War One, that Ward doomed himself and cast a long, black shadow over all of our futures.

In winter, 1927, 'the second arrangement' took place. Ward and an unnamed associate underwent the new procedure and, fourteen days later, Mycroft Ward became the first single entity ever to exist across two bodies.

Like its predecessor, the revised system wasn't as complex or mystical as its outcome might imply. For six days of the week, both

Wards attended to business as usual but on the seventh day, every Saturday, they underwent the standardising process; collating the week's information from each of them, making it uniform, and transferring the amalgamation back into both heads. The process took between twelve and sixteen hours every week, but Ward didn't miss that time at all. Existing as a single self in two bodies (albeit imperfectly) had an extra, very unusual benefit he hadn't previously considered; for this new, two-bodied Ward, each day was forty-eight hours long, every week – even with Saturday completely taken up standardising – was twelve days and every year for us, almost two years to him. Something fundamental in the relationship between time and Mycroft Ward changed.

The strong self-preservation urge Ward had built into his new system also began to have an effect he hadn't foreseen, a terrible effect; the every-Saturday repetition of the standardising process turned Ward's preservation command into a feedback loop. Every week, the system would deliver the preservation urge into Ward, who, with this urge in him increased, would amend the system accordingly, just slightly, in line with what he now thought to be a wise and suitable survival precaution. The now increased urge would feed back into him *again* the following week, making him increase its presence in the system *again*. Once it had begun, there was no way to stop the loop gathering momentum. As the weeks passed, Ward became a slave to his own machine. In the face of his ever growing all-devouring urge to survive, Ward made more and more amendments to his system and blindly stripped away his own humanity one piece at a time.

By the 1950s there were six bodies, by the 1970s, sixteen; by the 1980s, thirty-four. The irresistible urge to survive led to an equally irresistible urge to grow. As a result, the system received constant modification, incorporating new technologies to make the standardising process quicker and more effective, absorbing anything beneficial to the spread of the thing that had once been Mycroft Ward. It applied 'the arrangement' to bankers, heads of corporations and politicians, incorporating the useful parts of their minds and knowledge into its increasingly massive self. With thirty-four bodies, it gathered over a month's experience each day. It learned about stock markets, bought oilfields, developed psychological techniques and drugs, invested in new technologies and sciences. Every passing hour gave it three days' research time, and always it researched new ways to spread. What had once been a single human personality became a vastly intelligent mind-machine focused only on survival, on growing bigger and bigger and bigger with no regard for anything else at all.

By the late 1990s the Ward-thing had become a huge online database of self with dozens of permanently connected node bodies protecting against system damage and outside attack. The mind itself was now a gigantic over-thing, too massive for any one head to contain, managing its various bodies online with standardising downloads and information-gathering uploads. One of the Ward-thing's thousands of research projects developed software capable of targeting suitable individuals and imposing 'the arrangement' via the internet.

Four years ago it had over six hundred bodies gathering more than two years' experience every day. This was around the time it found Scout.

·

The new stick of pallet wood leaked a fine cotton of smoke, black burn growing up around its edges. All three of us watched the fire, Ian's sleepy half-closed eyes going into wide open pull-focus as the new wood popped with a little starburst of embers then he settled back down into a full-bellied dreamy stare.

"How did it happen?"

Scout stayed tuned to the flames. "One night I was at home, my parents' home, playing around on the internet. It was at the start of

206

that summer between college and university and I was scanning around for something to do. I found this site – some sort of IQ test. I must have decided to take a look at it and the next thing I remember it's five minutes later and I'm sick, dizzy and staring at the SIGNAL LOST message onscreen."

"Just like that?"

She nodded. "I ran into the bathroom and threw up. Turned out Polly, my little sister, had pulled the cable to use the phone and interrupted 'the arrangement' programme."

"Wow."

"I know. She was always doing it. We used to fight about it."

"Did you know something was wrong?"

"Oh yeah. You can feel it. I can think my way around it now," she looked up, concentrating on something internal, "this dead area in my mind where *its* information's stored, but at the time, they thought I'd had some kind of seizure or stroke or something. There were doctors, the whole works."

"What did the doctors think?"

"I got passed around, sent to a specialist. Only, the person they sent me to turned out not to be the specialist, or at least it wasn't the specialist by the time I got there."

"Ward?"

"Yeah. The last thing it wanted was me walking around only *half processed*. I think it pumped some heavy resources into finishing what it started. It's still looking for me now, probably always will be. So here I am."

"What happened with the specialist?"

"I ran away. I've never been one of those people who can just accept what they're being told –" a sad-happy smile, "it's a fault. Anyway, I didn't like the sound of his assessment techniques," she tapped Nobody's computer still strapped to her backpack, "but I did get his laptop."

"You stole a doctor's laptop, what, out of a *hospital*?"

"Yeah, well. It's easy when you know how."

"Scout," I said, trying not to sound too impressed, "what exactly did Ward want you for?"

She shrugged. "I don't know. Good looks? Personality? Quick wit?" – cough – "Oxford entrance exam results" – cough.

"Yeah," I said. "I thought it might be something like that. Or maybe because you'd had some sort of MI5 training."

"I wasn't going. Oxford, not MI5. I just wanted to see if I could get in."

"You got a place at Oxford, but you weren't going?"

"I told you, it's a fault. Look, anyway, I was going to university, I just decided not to go *there*. Can we get off my rash decision-making now please?"

"Sorry. We were up to you running away?"

She nodded. "I spent the summer travelling around, trying to keep my head down. The specialist's laptop came with me and it told me some of what I needed to know, but I didn't understand the software. All the poking around triggered a lock-off and the whole thing shut down for good, but it did give me a start. I spent a lot of time in libraries, looking into Mycroft Ward and piecing together the story I just told you. My money was running out fast, but then this nice but kind of odd librarian gave me a few hours' work a day down in the archives. And that's how I found my way into un-space."

We sat in silence for a little while.

"Something I don't get. I can see why he would want you, but why does Ward want me?"

"It, say *it*. It doesn't really want you at all. It wants the shark."

"Nobody said that, but I wasn't sure –"

"The big limiting factor on Ward's spreading is the standardising process. Even now there's a pretty severe cap on how many bodies it can standardise as the same self; there's just too much information and the system is imperfect so it's stuck around the thousand mark. Ward thinks understanding the different fish, especially the

Ludovician, could be the key to a perfect standardising process, where any number of bodies could be updated with new knowledge instantaneously." Scout thought. "Not that it'd ever risk coming near a loose shark itself."

"Ah."

"You know," she said, giving the fire a poke, "you're sort of taking all of this in your stride."

"All what?"

She looked at me and I smiled.

"It is a big deal," she said. "It's a really big fucking deal."

"I know. It's just – maybe it's like you said, *I am* in a constant collapse. Maybe this is as bad as I get with things. Even really big things."

"I'm sorry I said that."

"It's okay, you were right. Anyway, I'm the last person who's going to be bothered by what you have or haven't got in your head."

"Hmmm . . ."

"Ah. Cross that off my list of chat-up lines?"

She laughed. "I know what you meant, and thank you. I really mean that. Thank you."

"I just love it that you're around," I said poking the fire with my own poking stick.

"Yeah," she said, poking her side. "Me too."

"Erm," I said after a couple of big fat seconds.

Scout giggled. "Erm."

We both poked at the fire.

Some time passed.

"So. How long have you been down here?"

"Four years."

"God, that's a long time."

"Nah. Not when you think about how long I *will* be down here."

"You must really miss them."

"Who? My family? Yeah, I do, I miss everything – friends, secrets, gossip, all that stuff, the really cool bars; the ones where you know everybody. I had a university place, *music*, clothes – I had some really nice clothes by the way – and, God, hair-care products. I had a favourite drink and a favourite meal, a favourite TV programme. All of that stuff, just normal *person* stuff, you know? A Dad who used to make me see ageing rock bands with him and a mascara and White Lightning little sister who annoyed the shit out of me. It's all gone." She thought for a moment. "Only, it's not all gone, is it? I'm the one who's gone. The rest of it, it just all carries on up there without me."

I turned to check on Ian. He was asleep on my rucksack, chin tucked into his paws.

"I feel like I fell off the world," Scout said. "You ever get that?"

I shook my head. "For me, it's more like everyone else fell and left me and Ian on our own."

Scout nodded gently, looking into the fire without saying anything back. I imagined six billion people slowly pinwheeling through space, all those little stars in the wake of an almost empty planet. A vapour trail of ghosts.

21

Erm . . .

I lay on my back, looking up.

The night sky drifted cloudy above the film reel windows in the roof. The fire had burned down to a bright orange heap and I pulled the sleeping bag up under my nose.

According to Scout's predictions, tomorrow would be my last day of grace. By the day after, the Ludovician would have had enough time to find its way back from the stream-tangling smash of her letter bomb. Then, I'd have to retreat behind the Mark Richardson personality, set up the Dictaphones again. Today Eric Sanderson had broken the reservoir surface like the rooftops and spires of an old sunken village in a midsummer drought, but after tomorrow, there could only be the flatline of undisturbed waters. I didn't want to be that again, the empty horizon. I thought about what Nobody had said – *Just let go, let yourself sink down with the crabs.* Was that what I'd been doing? Had I been sinking away behind my clever mask without even realising it? Tomorrow, Scout said, we'd find Dr Fidorous. Watching the clouds, I hoped finding him might bring something, some way of changing things for good.

"Hey."

"Hey?" I said.

A shadowy Scout stepped around the remains of the fire, bundled sleeping bag under her arm. She cleared a space to lie down next to me.

"Are you okay?"

"I'm freezing," she said. "Do you mind?"

"Sure, no. I'm freezing too."

Lying on her side, she hooked an arm over me, dragging her unzipped sleeping bag up over us both like a duvet. She shuffled up some more, tucked herself into me, head on my chest.

"It's standard un-space procedure."

"Right." With her ear against my ribcage, I felt sure she'd be able to hear my heart as loudly as I could.

"It is."

"Not arguing." I untangled an arm from my own sleeping bag, putting it around her shoulders. "There. Am I getting it now?"

I felt the little shudder of a laugh through her body. "Yeah, I think so."

After a few seconds of warming up clothes, sharing breath and finger-tip-and-ear-drum-heartbeat she said, quietly: "Can I tell you something?"

"Yeah, of course."

"It's advice really. It's embarrassing so I'm going to whisper it." Scout stretched and shifted, taking the hem of the sleeping bag up to my ear with her. "Right." The tiny micro sounds of her mouth, pops and ticks around little whispered words. "You should know that when a girl takes her clothes off in front of a guy, it usually means something."

Somebody let off a box of fireworks in my stomach. I was winded; they went up like a million-coloured bomb.

"Yeah?"

"Yep."

Her lips, gentle, insubstantial and full of a million volts, pressed against my ear in the lightest of kisses.

I tucked down my chin. Scout looked up at me.

"Erm . . ." she whispered.

I kissed her.

22

A Tetris-Gap of Missing Bricks

I opened my eyes to see sunlight beaming down through the warehouse ceiling. The air stung cold but the sky was a pure pure blue.

Scout was resurrecting the fire, dressed in her combats and my big blue jumper.

I thought about her skin under my fingers, her ribs and her hips. I thought of her wet black hair fallen over her eyes and cheeks and nose and her breath and the sounds she made blowing it, moving it. The thoughts spiked in me, hot needles.

"It's almost midday," she said, seeing me shift around.

Under both our sleeping bags, I shuffled up into a sitting position. "Thanks for the lie-in."

"Well, I think it was needed." Having constructed her new paper and wood wigwam, Scout blew into the dusty white ashes at its core. I watched her for a little while.

"So," I said, "what next?"

"Well, that depends what you're talking about. If you're asking about the journey, we're a good four hours behind, but we should still make it today if we push on hard enough."

"What if I'm talking about. About." I let myself slump backwards onto the floor. "I'm not too good at this."

"You mean what's happening with you and me?"

"Yes."

"Because we had sex?"

"Yeah."

"Hmmm."

"Yeah."

What the hell does 'Hmmm' mean?

Scout messed around with her fire for a while like some kind of surveyor. I was trying to work out how to restart the conversation when I noticed she was blushing. Scout was actually *blushing*.

"When I was little –"

I looked up.

Scout made a big blow at the ashes, a poke at the fledgling fire with a stick. "When I was little, about seven or eight or something, there was a toy I really wanted. It was more like a science game actually –"

"A science game?"

"Leave it, Sanderson." Another poke. "Anyway, I'd worked it all out and if I could save up all my pocket money for six weeks I'd be able to afford it. But when you're a kid and you really want something, really really want it so you can't sleep or eat properly, six weeks is forever. So I stole it."

"Did you get caught?"

"Nope, but I was so ashamed of stealing the thing that it was completely ruined for me. I didn't get a second's fun from it, just guilt. In the end, I threw it off a bridge."

I smiled. "This from the girl who collects laptops?"

"The point is – you have to pretend I'm Jesus and this is like a parable, okay? I'm trying to say I don't do things if I'm just going to feel like shit the next day."

I thought about it. "You're saying I'm not going off the bridge?"

"You're not going off the bridge." Scout gave me a smile about things intimate and shared, a newly hatched sort of a smile, cautiously stretching its wings. "Providing I'm not going off?"

"Scout, you were *never* going off."

Something in the way I said it made her leave the fire alone altogether and turn around to look at me properly. It made me feel like looking at me properly too.

"No?"

"No."

214

"How would you know that?"

A nonsense in the back of my head said – *tell her. Tell her how you felt when you first saw her, about the tattoo on her toe, how your hands knew just when and where to touch her, how you could both be so in synch the very first time. She's got to be thinking the same thing. Right now, she'll be thinking: It's as if you'd –* 'Don't say it,' I told the nonsense, 'I know what you are and I'm not buying, not today.'

"I just feel it," I said.

She tried it for size. "You just feel it. Like, *you know in your heart.* That kind of thing?" She was trying to tease but there was too much curiosity behind it, a joke-spoiling flash of honest asking.

I could sense the nonsense still watching me from the back of my head.

"Yes, actually," I said. "Pretty much just like that."

Scout nodded the way chess players nod at each other. "Good answer."

The nonsense smiled. *Go on then.*

"Look, I feel stupid asking but – have you been getting that feeling too?"

She'd gone back to poking the wigwam. "Oh God," she said quietly into it. "He's going to be another stalker." She flashed me that flick-knife smile as the first threads of smoke started to unwind from the new fire.

Twenty minutes later, after black coffee and bread, and a tin of tuna for Ian, we'd almost packed up camp.

"Scout, you know what you were saying about going off the bridge?"

"Yeah?"

"Just this once, no tricks, that's on the level, right?"

She looked at me before shouldering her backpack.

"Just this once."

"Yes," she said. "That's on the level."

·

The day laid out another procession of tunnels and climb shafts, stairwells and big empty cavernous spaces. We took turns to carry Ian, bumped shoulders as we joked, accidentally-on-purpose touched knuckles in a way that led to an I-won't-mention-it-if-you-don't sort of hand holding, walking and talking the distance away under fizzing strip lights.

We stopped to fill our water bottles up from a huge gushing main supply pipe that churned and thundered into some sort of partly covered industrial collection tank. We kissed at the edge and Scout called it *the least romantic waterfall on the planet.*

The dark, when we encountered it, had swapped its universe-ending edge for something intimate and close and inevitable. In a deep storeroom stacked with inflatable beach toys and out-of-date travel brochures we turned our torches off and kissed and touched again in the blind absoluteness of it. Fabric, hair, skin, fingertips, hands and mouths. The invisible hard floor. Buttons and belts, breath and sound.

Somehow, even with all of this, we made progress.

We snuck through a STAFF ONLY corridor behind the changing rooms in a department store, through an underground car park and down into a sandwich chain store's supply room to stock up on food.

"What I don't get," I said, as Scout loaded up with baguettes, viennas, ciabattas and various tubs and packets of filling, "is why we didn't just come down into un-space later. Like here."

"It's just the way it works. You know like the London Underground map isn't accurate to the streets above it?"

"Yeah."

"Well, it's sort of like that. Anyway, you're not saying you'd rather have skipped the last twenty-four hours are you?"

"No," I smiled. "Definitely not."

"Good."

Early evening and we were taking a break, sitting on our rucksacks and passing a bottle of water between us. Ian thumped against the door of his carrier. He'd come around to thinking how he'd like to get out and explore whenever we stopped, the only problem was, Ian wasn't remotely interested in us or our timetable and could happily saunter off for an hour or more at a time.

"No," I told him, "we're only having a quick break. But next time you can do whatever you like."

Two big green eyes stared contempt up at me through the wire bars.

"How're we doing?" I passed the water over to Scout.

She looked up from her red notebook, taking the bottle from me.

"Good. At the end of that passageway, there should be access to the basement of a library. That's where we need to be next."

"That passageway?" I looked across. The passage in question looked short and dingy and sort of like a dead end. "Are you sure?"

Scout smiled. "Have I been wrong yet?"

"I don't know, do I? We haven't got anywhere yet."

She shook her head, getting to her feet. "Fine, I tell you what. I'll go and check it out. You stay there – no, don't trouble yourself – and I'll go and make double, triple sure we're going the right way. How does that sound?"

I raised my eyebrows in pretend surprise. "Wait. You mean, you're not already triple-sure?"

Scout shrugged on her backpack with an I'm-not-smiling smile. "Listen to you. Don't push it, Sanderson."

"I'll be right here." I called after her as she headed down the passage. She turned around to flick me the finger and disappeared into the black.

I had another drink then put the water away, got to my feet and pulled on my backpack. I was checking my pockets to make sure I had everything I needed when I noticed Scout's red notebook lying on the floor next to the wall. I bent over to pick it up. I was turning it over in my hands when she reappeared at the passageway's entrance.

"I told you this is the right way," she called over. There's a gap in the brickwork down here that leads through to the library stacks. We – Eric, stop."

Scout was staring at me.

"No, sorry, I wasn't –" I held up the red notebook. "You left it on the floor. I wasn't going to read it or anything. I was just picking it up."

"Eric."

"Fine," I pointed behind me with the book, holding it out at arm's length. "I'll even put it back over there and pretend I never –"

"Eric, for fuck's sake shut up and keep still."

And I saw the expression on her face.

My heart bumped, kicked out a *thud* of electrical panic. I stood shock-still, the arm with Scout's little red book still stretched out behind me.

"Don't turn around," she said quietly. "Just bring your arm back in very, very slowly."

I started to move my arm in a creeping centimetre but then there was something, a shadow of fast growing movement in the floor behind me and my eyes flicked across and down. And then:

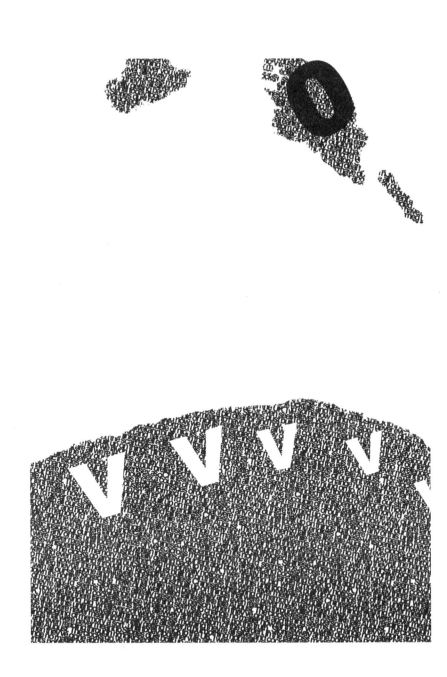

I whipped my arm in, throwing myself forwards as the thought-funnel of teeth and blades blasted out of the floor and slammed together with a definitive clopping snap where my arm and shoulder and head had been half a second earlier.

"Ludovician" I shouted it out in gut-reaction horror, hitting the ground hard at the same time as the massive idea of breaching shark crashed back down and under the floor behind me, its splashdown throwing up an impact wave of meaning and thought which blasted and bundled me forwards across the concrete.

Scrambling up onto my feet, scrambling back and grabbing the handle of Ian's carrier then running towards Scout.

Me and Scout running down the passageway.

"Through the wall," Scout shouting, "through the hole in the wall."

"Christ." The idea of the floor rising up under our sprinting feet into a rolling bow wave. "It's coming up, it's coming up again."

Scout throwing herself through a Tetris gap of missing bricks at the end of the corridor and me following, then being yanked back – Ian's carrier wedged in masonry behind me. Me twisting my wrist around, yanking hard and then the box drag-scraping loose against the mortar and chipped brick, momentum sending me stumble-tripping backwards through the hole after Scout.

I landed in a heap on a tiled floor with Ian's carrier on top of me. "Move."

I looked up to see a bookcase coming falling down towards me and I rolled, shoving Ian out of the way as the thing fell, tumbling hardbacks, breaking against the wall and burying the hole I'd come through in splintered wood and broken heaps of books.

A solid thump from the other side of the wall.

The pile of books rattled but didn't move.

Then Scout jogging out from behind the fallen bookcase, standing over me white and sweating. "Jesus, I'm sorry, I had to – God, Eric, are you alright?"

But I was already scrambling up to my feet, grabbing up the carrier.

"Hey hey hey," she said, stopping me, hands on my shoulders. "We're safe, we're safe. It can't come in here. Look around you. Come on, Eric, come back to me."

I stared around, vacant and shock-eyed.

We were on the edge of the shadowy stacks of a huge library. I looked back to Scout.

"See? It's okay," she said. "The books. All these books mean it can't come in here, it can't find its way through to us." She hooked her arm around my waist, semi-supporting me. "Let's get away from the edge, just to be sure."

"Your notebook," I said, still somewhere outside myself, "I lost your notebook."

"That doesn't matter, you idiot. We're on the final leg anyway."

"I thought we had until tomorrow before it could find us again."

"So did I. Let's find somewhere to collapse, get our heads together."

"Fucking hell," I said.

"Jesus, tell me about it. How's the cat?"

We unloaded our stuff in a daze and sat in silence for a while, backs up against a shelf of fat geography books. Ian was okay, rattled, grumbly and angry but basically okay. After a few minutes growling he turned his back on us and pretended to be asleep.

"Fuck," I said.

Scout nodded, eyes unfocused and looking straight ahead.

We sat quietly for three or four minutes.

"Scout?"

"Hmmm?"

"You said you had a sister. Would you talk to me about her?"

"Why?"

"Just so I can stop thinking about the shark."

Scout looked at me.

"Sorry," I said. "I didn't mean to –"

"No, it's okay. Talking's probably a good idea. It's Polly. My sister's called Polly. What do you want me to tell you?"

"Just . . . anything. What's she like?"

Scout thought. "She's a brat. An alcopop-drinking, short-skirt-wearing, hanging-around-Spar type superbrat."

"Yeah?"

"Yeah," she smiled a vague smile. "You know, if I ever snuck in late at night I'd have to creep past her room to get to mine and if she heard me, I'd get a note under my door – *£5 or Dad finds out where you weren't at 3 a.m. this morning.*"

"That's very professional."

"Yep, extortion to fund her white cider habit or something. She managed to land me in so much trouble once that I missed out on a big, end-of-year weekend away me and some friends had been planning for, for forever. *And* she did it on purpose"

"What did you do to get her back?"

"What makes you think I did anything?"

"Because you did, didn't you?"

Scout smiled.

"Go on," I said.

"There was a boy she really fancied in her geometry class, Craig something, and he'd asked her to a party. She'd liked him for ages, had a hidden diary with all these awful poems about him."

"And you showed him the poems?"

"Nope, I told him she'd been born without a vagina."

The sound of us laughing rolled around the dusty bookshelves and out across the quiet floors.

"That's really awful."

"Well, she *is* really awful." A second's pause. "She was." Scout flicked her eyes away from mine. "You lose track of time down here. She'll be eighteen now, that's older than I was when I left home."

"I'm sorry," I said after a long moment.

"Why?" Scout had turned away so I couldn't see her face, adjusting the straps on her rucksack. "What did you do?"

·

Stack by stack, stairwell by stairwell, we found our way into the deepest foundations of the library; a place of blinking old bulbs and shelf after shelf of turn-of-the-century books, sitting all dusty and quiet in their old-fashioned ranks.

"Look."

"What?" I put Ian's carrier down and went over to where Scout knelt.

She passed what she'd found up to me, a torn corner of newspaper with half of one side covered in winding biro letters. Some sort of formula.

"We're getting close," she said.

"This is Fidorous's?"

"Yeah, that's his handwriting."

I stared down at the paper, rubbing my thumb over the little blue letters to feel for the ever-so-slight denting his pen had made as he wrote. "Are we going to make it today?"

"Oh yeah," Scout said, setting off again between the stacks. "We might be there within the hour." She turned around and smiled. "If your map reading's up to scratch."

"Map reading?"

"Come on."

We found another scrap a few minutes later, and then another, and then another. We followed the word-crumb trail through the old towers of books and down an uncared-for staircase deeper into the stacks. Down here, the books were even older; sombre columns of washed-out grey and red leather covers curling away at the tops and bottoms of spines. They made me think of the old British army, the Empire army, abandoned and left behind, still standing in their dusty formations. As we went deeper the book-soldiers got older still – Wellington's men trimmed in peeling gold leaf giving way to the tall silent royalists with flamboyant but barely legible stencilling on their individual, aged-away backs. After a while the books petered out altogether, replaced by yellowing hand-bundled folios secured with rotting silk ribbons.

"Scout, where the fuck are we?"

"Don't touch anything," is all she said from up ahead.

The paper trail led to a mound. A huge great mound in the dim distant reaches of the stacks. A mound like the ones they buried ancient kings in, but a mound made from, instead of soil, all kinds of paper – newspapers, chip wrappers, glossy magazines, great strips of wallpaper, tiny labels and instruction manuals, heaps of plain and lined and letterheaded A4, the stripped-out leaves of diaries and ledgers and novels and photo books. Tons and tons of paper and all of it, every scrap covered, smothered, buried in lines and squares and triangles and swirls of blue and black and green and red biro words.

"Fucking hell," I said.

Scout unhooked her backpack and started to inspect the mound's edge. Eventually she settled on a spot and started to excavate, lifting and scooping away piles of paper.

"What are you doing?"

"Come and see."

She pushed a stack of old car magazines over and they slid and skidded away like a pack of over-sized playing cards. Behind them was a chair. Only the two rear legs and the backrest were visible, the rest covered and buried and incorporated into the side of the mound.

"I don't get it."

"Kneel down and look."

I did. Shored up by the seat and the back legs and disappearing into the depths of the mound I saw a small dark tunnel. I looked up at her.

"You're joking, right?"

Scout smiled, bent over and kissed me on the forehead.

"'Fraid not," she said. "That's where we're going."

23

Biro World

We knelt at the edge of the mound with Ian's carrier between us, all looking into the deep, papery tunnel.

"Right," Scout said, "same crawlspace procedure as before. We'll rope-tie our backpacks and I'll push Ian ahead of me, which means you'll have to follow behind with the map. Sound okay?"

"Yeah, except for the map part. I didn't know we had a map."

"Well, that's why I'm the guide and you're the one asking all the questions, sweetie."

"You're hard work sometimes, do you know that?"

"Hush now."

We took our bulky coats off and stuffed them into our backpacks. Next, we used two long lengths of cord to tie the tops of our packs to the backs of our belts, so they would drag into the chair tunnel behind us as we crawled. Scout used masking tape to attach her torch to the side of Ian's cat box. She was happy with the results of this, but Ian – even after a whole tub of tuna and sweetcorn from the sandwich shop – didn't look too pleased with it, or about the prospect of being shoved first into a small dark hole.

"I'm sorry," I told him again. "Not far to go now."

He gave me a look to let me know that wherever we were going had better be *a lot of fun* for cats.

"Okay, soldier," Scout slipped her hands onto my hips. "Are we ready to do this?"

"Erm."

She smiled. "It'll be fine. Looks worse than it is. Crawl on your elbows and push yourself along with your knees and the toes of your boots. Go slowly, try to keep your arms in and try not to touch the sides. The tunnel's only made of paper."

"Riiiight."

"What else? Yeah, probably best to get your torch out before you go in, you'll need it to read the map. If you need to stop, shout up to me – not too loudly – and we'll stop. Okay?"

"Okay. Are you going to give me this map then?"

"Yep." Scout rummaged in one of the leg pockets in her combats, pulling out half a dozen small pieces of paper. "If we're at the right mound, and I reckon we are, then we'll need . . . this one."

The folded piece of paper she gave me was about the size of a small birthday-card envelope.

"This is it?"

"Told you it was easy," she said, and then she was back on her knees and slide-angling Ian's carrier into the hole. I unfolded the piece of paper. It was completely blank except for the word Thera.

"Hey, there's nothing on this."

"What? Nothing?"

"Just a word, Thera."

"Yeah, that's it. We're starting at the bottom of the 'T' and we're going to the round bit of the 'a'. Think you can manage that?"

I looked at the paper again.

"Sure," I said.

·

The air inside the tunnel smelled like the pages of a second-hand Charles Dickens novel; yellowy paper, old print and finger grease, that pressed, preserved sort of smell.

My torch put a white ring of light on the bottom of Scout's rucksack as it start-stopped its way through the tunnel up ahead, almost filling the space completely. I angled the torch at the tunnel walls and the white ring stretched and was slashed up with shadows from the jutting pages and uneven piles, a whole haphazard Braillescape of paper, print and biroed words somehow not collapsing into this tiny black space. I pushed forward with my toes, keeping my feet as close together as I could and inch-shuffling forwards with my hips and elbows. Stray paper hissed against my arms, back, hips as I moved. Everything, everything had been covered in words, words in so many languages. Scraps flapped against me or passed under my crawling wrists covered in what I vaguely recognised as French and German, in hard Greek and Russian letters, in old fashioned English with the long 'f's instead of 's's and in Chinese or Japanese picture symbols. There were formulae too, numbers, mathematical abbreviations and complicated visual arrangements. What English I saw ran from complex to incomplete to meaningless: . . . *The simultaneous considerment of two conjugate variables (such as persuasive implication and delivery deficiency or the apex notion lumen and time for a moving concept) entails a limitation on the precision* . . . to . . . *abandon honest the consideration After-clap poma haunt duration saying goldfinches: a charm* . . .

Overloaded, I tried to turn my mind off, tried to blank out the billions of words crowding tight in the shaky torch flicks and piled-up darkness. I concentrated only on inching forwards, second by second, minute by minute, following the hiss-scrape of Scout's bag deeper into the mound.

The bag stopped moving.

"What's up?"

Up ahead, Scout said something but I couldn't catch it.

"What?"

"T-junction." Her voice sounded squeezed and muffled with most of the treble missing. "We're going right."

I managed to unfold the piece of paper she'd given me and bring the torch down onto it. THERA. T-junction. Scout's bag started to move again and I followed. Just like she'd said, our tunnel soon connected with another, this one running left to right. I closed the gap between me and Scout's rucksack and helped it around the tight corner as much as I could. I had a horror of my own bag getting wedged there, being trapped in the crossbar of the T. Luckily for me, when the time came there was only a small amount of resistance from behind. I pulled against it gently, so, so gently, and with only the *shhhh* flutter of light paper debris, my bag rounded the corner without complications.

The new tunnel seemed to be a little higher and wider than the old one and after a few minutes' shuffling I found I could just about get up on my hands and knees. Scout must have been crawling too, her bag moving faster up ahead. Before long, the tunnel made a curving ninety-degree turn to the right.

"Hey, am I crazy or are we going –"

"Down, yeah."

The floor sloped away in a gentle gradient but the ceiling stayed level. As a result, the crawlspace became a full-time hands and knees space, then a stoop space and, finally, a narrow walk space. I stopped to pick up my bag then sidestepped forwards between walls made of stacked jumbled untidy paper. Up ahead, Scout did the same. I could see the torch beam coming from Ian's carrier bouncing off stacked sheets into the black.

"This thing is fucking huge."

"It's amazing, isn't it?"

"It's nuts. It must have taken years to stack all this. And the words –" I shone my torch up against the wall in front of me. Every loose page – as far as I could tell, *every page making up the entire tunnel* – had been covered, crammed, with rolling handwritten language.

"The only word we need to worry about is the one on the map. You still keeping track of where we are?"

I unfolded the sheet and stared again at the word: THERA. I visualised the route we'd taken so far –

┌

– then traced the shape over the letters on the page with my finger.

ThERa

"I think we're in the stem of an 'h;" I said, surprised at how matter of fact it all sounded.

"Great," Scout said, moving off up ahead.

"Great," I echoed after her, looking at the map again.

.

We made it to the bulb of the 'R'. This turned out to be a room-sized chamber with a yellow domed roof made of what looked to be telephone directories. More telephone directories were stacked up around the walls. The walls themselves had been built from more solid material than we'd seen previously – hardback books mainly, with the odd thick softback dictionaries, thesauruses, textbooks – and had been constructed with careful bricklaying techniques. A simple wooden chair and desk stood in the middle of the room and the whole space was illuminated by a single bright light bulb hanging down on a long cord.

"Wow." Scout stood by the desk looking up at the dome. "It's like a church or something. Come and look."

I propped my backpack against the table and perched on the edge. "Crazy."

She caught the tone in my voice. "Are you okay?"

"I don't know."

She sat next to me on the desk, looking at me for a second before giving me a slow gentle nudge. "Come on, what is it?"

I heard myself do one of those laughs, the ones where the air for a laugh comes out but no real sound. Breath in the shape of a *ha* that never really happens. "I don't think I can cope with church domes made from telephone directories."

"Ah."

"I mean – what is *this* doing here? How does something like this even happen?"

Arms out behind her, Scout lowered herself down onto the table until she lay on her back looking up at the dome. "I think it's kind of cool actually. You should look at it like this."

"Oh yeah, it's cool. It's just – *wrong*."

She stayed quiet for a minute then sat up, slipping an arm around my shoulders. "It's only paper you know."

"It's not only paper though, is it? Look at it."

"It is, it's just paper. Did you never make igloos as a kid? I did, me and my dad. You cut out blocks of snow and you make them into rings. A big ring and then a ring that's a bit smaller on top of it, and then a ring that's a bit smaller on top of that. After five or six rings you've got a little igloo. This is just the same, but with phone books." She nudged her head against mine. "It isn't really a big deal."

I looked at her. "Scout, it might as well be a fucking gingerbread house."

She gave me a big smile. "Well, that's technically possible too."

I laughed, a proper laugh this time. "I'm glad you're here."

"I do my best."

"You're just fine with all this, aren't you?"

"That's me. I'm always fine, until I'm not."

I nodded.

"The way I look at it," she said, "things are always happening. Sometimes things that nobody believed were possible just happen. Beforehand everyone says *that's impossible*, or *I'll never live to see something like that* but afterwards, it's just a fact. It's just history. These things become history every day."

"You're secretly quite clever."

"Ten years from now you'll see another dome made of telephone directories or a maze with paper walls and you'll shrug and go looking for the ice cream stand."

"Ten years from now?"

"Yeah," she said. "Yeah, I don't see why not."

"Thanks." I kicked up my legs for a while, watching the toes of my boots swing up. We sat together like that, under a dome made of telephone directories. "Can I ask you something?"

"Sure."

"What do you think is really going to happen to us?"

She looked into my eyes and I saw that cold in her; the deserted windswept beach, the boarded-up seafront, snow falling in the deep heart of a forest of bare black trees. She took her arm from around me and went back to looking up at the ceiling. "The truth?"

"Yes, please."

"I think we're going to wear away from the world, just like the writing wears off old gravestones in the aisles of churches."

I carried on kicking my legs, not saying anything.

"That's what happens," she said. "Up there, I'm mostly gone already."

"Well, I know you're still here. If that counts for anything."

She didn't answer. With a little burst of shock I realised she was almost crying. Her eyes had glassed up with tears she was working hard not to let fall. "I do care about you, you know."

"Hey, it's okay. I believe you."

Face tipped upwards, she risked a side-on glance at me. "Jesus."

"We're going to be alright," I said. "Come on, we're going to be alright."

I tried to put my arm around her to bring her towards me but she wouldn't move, stiff and bobbing with internal sobs, staring up at the ceiling.

"Hey," I said again. "Please, come here."

I put my arm around her again and this time she allowed herself to fold up against me, sobbing quietly into my shoulder.

"Sometimes it's just hard to see what's in front of you. But once you do see it, or once something connected to the *it* touches you, I don't think there's any going back." Her face streaky from the crying, Scout stared dead ahead.

"Well, then," I said uncapping a water bottle and passing it to her. "It's a good job we're pushing forwards so heroically, isn't it?"

She looked at me with an almost smile. "You've changed your tune."

"Yeah, well. I thought it was about time. I'm guessing we're nearly there?"

"Yeah, just one more letter to go."

"Then I say we should take a break, let's say half an hour or something, and get our heads together."

"Yeah?"

"I'm resisting giving you my five grand."

"Ah," Scout said, smiling, "my money."

"Amazing, you're getting your colour back."

She laughed a wet laugh. "That's because you know just what to say to a girl."

I rummaged around in my backpack. "Coronation chicken or chicken tikka?"

"Wow."

"Well?"

"Coronation please."

"Right then. I'm going to let Ian out so he can piss on some of these books."

Ian sauntered his big ginger self out of the carrier and strolled away, sniffing occasionally at the bookwork walls.

"Don't go too far." I called after him. His tail twitched a bit, letting me know I was in no position to be telling him to do anything. He disappeared out through the entranceway.

Scout seemed to have a case of after-trauma vagueness, chewing slowly on her sandwich and staring out at nothing. I decided it would be best to give her some time and sat myself down against a wall.

I took the top telephone directory off the stack next to me and flicked it open. Classified adverts for caterers, carpet and upholstery cleaners, car hire, bus and coach operators. A picture of a woman in a designer hat, a truck with a haulage company's logo on the side, a guitar, a special bath that lifts you in and out, all in familiar yellow and black. Scout was right; these were just phone books – ordinary adverts for ordinary businesses without even a trace of the biroing that covered everything in the tunnels. Just normal directories. The fact that someone had used them to make a yellow domed ceiling didn't really *mean* anything at the end of the day. It was just there, a fact. And the tunnels themselves; it *was* possible to create a maze from stacked, written-on paper. Bizarre, unlikely, stupidly time-consuming and dangerous, but, yes, possible.

Putting the phone book to one side, I unwrapped my sandwich.

What a difference a day makes, twenty-four little hours. Staring into space myself, I found the light floaty scrap of tune rising up out of the back of my mind as I chewed. It made me think about how, in the dark places of yourself, thinking machines you never get near enough to see are constantly building things and running their own secretive programmes all of their own. Maybe you get a snippet of what's going on back there, like this fragment of a song drifting its way into the light, or a phrase, or an image, or maybe just a mood, a wash of content or a bleak draining of colour that floods your chest and your stomach more than it ever finds its way into the bright halogen chrome of your mind.

I looked up at the ceiling dome again, at Scout still chewing vaguely.

How did I become this? I'd been an empty nothing for so long, and now suddenly I was here, somehow an adventurer in a strange place, somehow sleeping with this strong-brittle girl with the thing in her mind. Where had I found all these new parts? Perhaps they came from the real Eric Sanderson, the man in The Light Bulb Fragment. Maybe I'd found his old buried tools – his batsuit and batcar and all his sharp one-liners – and now I was walking around in boots that would never really be mine. Or perhaps, just perhaps, it was real. That's what I wanted to believe. I'd been a flat thing, something I always mistook for a shadow, but maybe the eroding effect of events had begun weathering me out of the ground, revealing new surfaces and edges. Can *nothing* really be scraped away the same way that *something* can? I wondered about what else might be down there, what I could become if all these layers of absence and loss and bad things could ever be excavated and taken away.

·

"I'm guessing this is it."

"Yeah." I traced out the route out on the map for Scout to see –

ThERa

"I think we're in the 'a'."

"Very good," she smiled. "See? I knew you had it in you."

A cry and half an hour's quiet sitting had been enough to melt the cold from her eyes. Except for some slight apprehension, which could easily have been me projecting, Scout was back on form. Added to that, Ian was back in his carrier under his tried and trusted thundercloud and I'd just passed my basic skills in wordmap reading. As far as these things went, our team was back on an even keel. And we'd made it to the 'a'. Which was something else altogether.

The 'a' chamber seemed slightly smaller than the 'R' and much less tidy, the floor buried under scrunched and tipped-over piles of biroed papers. Just like the 'R', a single hanging bulb lit the space and the walls were made from hardback books interlocking like bricks. Mostly though, this workmanship was obscured by the scruffy drifts and mounds of written-on paper which piled up to waist and shoulder height against it. A spiral staircase stood in the middle of the room, winding itself up into the ceiling. The staircase was made of old leather-bound books the size of paving slabs, not overly grand or complex but functional and serious like a great industrial drill. At the top of the stairs, six or seven feet above our heads, was what looked like a small ledge.

"That's us," Scout said, pointing up to the ledge.

"That's where we're going?"

"The end of the trail."

"What's up there?"

"You'll see in about thirty seconds."

For better or for worse, our journey was over.

I heard a noise. At the shadier edge of the room a stack of paper sheets collapsed in a sliding, fluttery *foosh*.

Scout looked at me. I looked at Scout.

"What was that?"

Palm flat down, she made a *lower your voice* sign.

"Is there something in there?"

"Look," she said, "*there*."

Near the collapsed pile, another of the heaps moved. The papers lifted up momentarily then sank back down. It happened again a few seconds later and then we saw a ripple, something travelling under the stacked sheets and making its way around the edge of the room.

Scout put her arm out in front of my body and mouthed *back up*. We stepped backwards as quietly as we could towards the entrance, slow-crunching the papers under our feet.

"*No, it's not*," I said. "*But it can't get in –*"

"Hello?" Scout said.

The shuffling movement under the heaps stopped. There was a shudder. A couple of paper piles started to slide. A mound of sheets and pages domed upwards like a landfill bubble. Then in a sloosh of skidding papers a man burst out.

"Good grief," the man said staring at us.

Scout made a big sigh and let her arms flop to her side.

"Eric Sanderson," she said, "Dr Trey Fidorous."

24

The Doctor of Language

I thought about the phrase *gone to seed*.

Maybe there should be types of gardener who visit bookish old men to trim and prune and generally tidy them up occasionally, because the real and actual Dr Trey Fidorous was as overgrown and tangled as an abandoned allotment. His thick salt-and-pepper hair had grown beyond Einstein-esque into a sort of mad rogue plume. A pen between his teeth, two tucked behind his ears and several others tucked and knotted and sticking out of his wild hair, made his head look like one of those deceptively fluffy cacti. Blue, black, red and green biro writing covered the backs of his hands, creeper-vined its way up around wrists and forearms, and towards his rolled-up shirtsleeves, which themselves hadn't been entirely spared. Scrumpled chunks of paper and collected pages bulged from the pockets of his black schoolboy trousers and patchy threadbare dressing gown. He was smallish and probably somewhere in his late sixties. The harsh light from the single bulb didn't make it down through his hair canopy too well and the effect was like looking at a man who was peering out at you from the depths of a wardrobe. What I could see of his face was wrinkled and brown like an elastic band ball, only more active and capable – it reminded me of one of those big springs that can go down stairs on its own – and I got the feeling it had spent a lifetime being stretched around expressions of shock, delight, horror and God knows what else. All I could see of his eyes were a big pair of glasses with black plastic frames, like the ones Michael Caine wore in the sixties.

Dr Trey Fidorous. After all this time I'd actually found him. I could only stare.

The doctor took the pen out of his mouth, stared back.

"Eric Sanderson." There was something hard in the way he said my name, something that shocked me. "What are you doing here?"

"He doesn't remember anything," Scout said, tucking her arm around me, thumb under the back of my waistband, pulling me towards her.

"Doesn't he? Doesn't he now?"

"I found him trying to follow the East to West Text Trail, but there's nothing left of it really and there's no way he could have –"

"And what on earth made you think I'd want to see him?"

"Where else would he go?"

"I'm sure I don't have the faintest idea."

"For Christ's sake, Trey. He's come back to you for help, he needs help."

"*He needs help*. And that's the reason you've brought him here is it, Scout?"

A silent second hung all fat and heavy, like a spider.

"Hello," I said, not knowing what to say but desperate to say something, to crack the mood, to break up this argument I didn't understand but was suddenly in the middle of at the same time. "Hello, hello. It's me. I am actually here."

Fidorous flashed back to me. "Oh, I doubt that, Eric," he said, "because if you were you, *here* is the last place you would want to be."

I felt myself take half a step back.

"I don't –" I managed, feeling something turning hard and heavy in my stomach.

From the beginning I'd been focused on nothing but finding Dr Trey Fidorous, this legend, this half-myth from my long lost past, the only person in the world who might be able to help me. Now I realised the weight and size of my single-mindedness had been acting as a dangerous dam, holding back all the important, practical things I should have been asking myself.

I had no idea who this man really was or what his relationship with the First Eric Sanderson had been like. I'd walked into this completely unprepared.

"I don't –" my mouth was still trying to say – "what's –"

"But you *did*, didn't you? You *went* and you *did*, and you didn't give a shit about –"

"*Stop it*, Trey," Scout said and I felt that force, that power inside her again. "He doesn't remember what happened. He doesn't remember anything. He's lost it all, it's all been taken. He's hardly even the same person anymore. *Look* at him."

He doesn't remember what happened? How would she know what happened? I looked sideways, catching Scout's eye for the smallest moment. There it was again, that bleakness, the empty beach. And something else too; some other emotion I didn't quite understand; something secret hiding inside the anger tightening the muscles in her face. She blinked whatever it was it back, squeezed her hand gently against the back of my jeans and mouthed the word *later*, all without taking her attention away from the doctor.

The old man was about to come back with an explosion of his own, a shouting stretch-faced barrage from under that mass of hair. It almost happened, the world sucking in breath like the sea pulling back before a tsunami wave, but then it didn't, he didn't. In the heart of the pressure cooker, something gave.

Fidorous pulled his thick-rimmed glasses off, rubbed them carefully on the inside of his dressing gown sleeve. Old and tired, now the anger had gone, he squeezed at the bridge of his nose with a finger and a thumb before slipping the glasses back on.

"Well," is all he said, quietly.

"Yes," Scout nodded.

I thought it best to say nothing at all.

•

"Well," Fidorous said again, looking around himself and seeming to notice for the first time that he was thigh-deep in paper. "I suppose all this will be something of a shock to you?"

The sharpness was gone from his voice now, replaced with a more measured politeness-to-strangers tone.

"Just a little," I said. I tucked my hand behind my back, hooking a couple of my fingers around a couple of Scout's and squeezing. Her squeezing back was all the scaffolding in the world.

"No. It's hardly the most efficient of filing systems, is it?" Fidorous began to kick his way out of the drift of papers in a procession of wumphs, crumps, flutters and sliding hisses. Ian shifted around in his carrier at the noise. "Still, I subscribe to the principle that if I'm meant to find what I happen to be looking for in here, I will. Usually, however . . ."

A response was required. I lifted my eyebrows, just a little, hoping I'd got it right.

The doctor cleared the deepest drifts of paper and dusted himself down. "Usually, however, I don't."

I squeezed Scout's fingers.

"Doctor," Scout said, "can we –"

The muffled howl of an alarm sounded somewhere up above us.

Fidorous jumped, stared wide-eyed up at the ceiling.

I followed his eyes up, risked a glance at Scout. "What's that?"

"Fry." The old man was suddenly on full alert, like a cat on its toes. "Fry in the system. Scout, did you close down the tunnel entrance after you?"

"I didn't think we needed to."

"It's the season, they're migrating. All the tunnels have to be shut."

"What's happening? Oh God, the Ludovician?"

"No," Scout said, "fry – little thought fish. Harmless by themselves but if enough of them get in here, there's a chance something bigger might be able to follow their trail."

The doctor nodded "– and if they ever made it all the way to the research centre – Scout, I need you to go back and close off the entrance you used. I want you to check the Milos and Ios tunnels too, in case they're coming in through there. I'll take Eric with me to help with the flush."

"I think Eric should come with me."

I nodded, turned to Scout. "I *am* coming with you. If it's out there –"

"If in the very unlikely event the Ludovician *is* out there, then she'll be much safer, and quicker, without you tagging along. Come on, time is of the essence, if too many fry find their way into the tunnels, we'll never get them out."

"He's right," Scout said to me. "I'll be fine, and we need to keep the defences tight here."

"Defences?"

"I'll explain everything when I get back," then, turning to Fidorous. "Doctor. Before . . ."

"Hmmm?"

"I have to bring you up to speed with a few things."

"I imagine there are a lot of things you need to bring me up to speed with, but please, Dorothy, we have to have those tunnels closed. I'll take care of the Tin Man here."

"That's not funny."

"Oh." The doctor took a second to look confused. "Isn't it? I lose track sometimes."

"Stop it. I need to –"

"Scout, the tunnels. Please."

The alarm howled on.

Scout looked from him to me. I could only bring my palms up in a *tell me what to do* gesture. Her face set, Scout seemed to reach a conclusion. She nodded to the doctor then turned towards me, slid her hand around my waist.

That bleakness inside her again.

You okay? I mouthed.

She flashed me a slight, dry smile, then slipped her hand into my pocket and took the torch. "You'll be fine here. I'll be back as soon as I can."

I managed a quick *okay* as she turned and kicked off through the papers in a half-jog.

Just like that, Scout was gone. I felt a bump inside me, like when a train changes tracks at a junction.

"Come on." Fidorous was already on his way to the spiral staircase. "We need to be at the control centre." Then, turning to see me picking up Ian's carrier – "No, no, no, leave your things. Get them later."

"No, I can't. My cat."

The doctor came to a stop, turned, craned his neck. "You have a cat?"

•

The spiral staircase took us up to a ledge just below the ceiling and the ledge turned out to be the back of a shelf, the bottom shelf in a tall, wide bookcase. At first I thought the books had all been put on the shelf backwards, spines facing in and pages facing out but then I realised we – and the room of papers, the word tunnels, all of it – we were behind the bookcase, looking at it from the back. I struggle-balanced my way up after Fidorous, cat carrier in my left hand and my right arm stretched out like a tight-rope walker, trying to compensate for Ian who turned around and around in his box, probably not liking the way the floor disappeared below us as we climbed. I didn't blame him, I wasn't keen either. Missing books in the centre of the shelf made a space large enough to crawl through and that's just what the doctor did, unexpectedly flexible for his age.

"Come on, pass the box through."

I passed Ian through to Fidorous then squeezed through after them.

I found myself crawling out onto a carpet, a red one, expensive but old-fashioned. The alarm was louder up here.

Getting up to my feet, the room made me think *gentlemen's smoking lounge.* Two green leather wingback chairs, a desk lamp with a green glass shade and dangling pull chain, a table with a cut glass or crystal decanter full of a brown, and probably alcoholic, drink. Except for a facing doorway, all the walls had been completely covered in book cases. Or had they? Taking a closer look, I couldn't tell whether the walls were covered in book cases or whether the walls themselves were made of books and mahogany; horizontal and vertical planes slotted in afterwards to give the impression of shelving. Is a zebra a white animal with black stripes or a black animal with white stripes? The room seemed balanced to go either way.

As I got myself together Fidorous let Ian out of his carrier and the two of them faced each other in the middle of the room.

"And you must be Toto," Fidorous said.

"Meow," the cat said back. He looked over to let me know he wasn't at all pleased with the noise of the alarm *or* with this old man suddenly being in his personal space.

•

"Schools of fry like to pick at commas and the more old-fashioned letters. Nothing too big or obvious at first." The doctor moved along quickly in a sort of stiff-legged superwalk, like a headmaster late for assembly. I had to jog to keep up with him. "In my experience," he said, "they seem particularly keen on the long *s.*"

Ian pattered down the corridor ahead of us, ears back, tail low, running in that way cats run when they don't like it that people are coming up fast behind them. The corridor itself branched left and right, doors appeared and there were cabinets and glass cases; displays of things I had no time to look into as we passed. At one point it opened up into a wide room piled up with radios, hundreds and hundreds of them all in heaps and most of them playing, tuned or half-tuned or just hissing out noise. Recording equipment hung down from the ceiling on cables, dangling over the highest point of each heap.

"What's this?" I asked the doctor as we jogged the winding path between the plastic piles.

"What?"

"What are the radios for?"

"Fertiliser," the doctor said.

The alarm became louder and louder the further we went. The place was huge. Eventually, the doctor ducked to the left, up a smaller branch corridor and through a doorway into a room filled with computers and televisions and microphones, wires and cables everywhere, disappearing into the ceiling and winding out of control all over the floor.

"No no no no no. Come on." Fidorous slapped his palm against the side of one of the computer tower units.

The alarm was deafening in here. Fidorous slapped again at the tower then changed tack, frantically inspecting, untangling and chasing cables, wiggling sockets and ports. Abruptly, the alarm stopped.

"Aaahhh." Fidorous looked up from a bundle of sockets and jacks. "There now. Come on, come on, you're no use out there, are you?"

I took a few steps into the room. The doctor climbed over a box of machinery half-covered in wires then ducked to inspect a monitor, tapping frantically on a nearby keyboard. "Where are you, where are you? . . . Nope." He turned, clambered, moved to another screen. Tap tap tap. Taptaptaptaptap. "No . . . Ah, yes. There you are." He looked up at me. "A shoal of fry in Thera. Come over to this panel, no, this one here."

I crossed the room, climbing over wires and cables, over part-dissected servers and hard drives.

"Now then. When I say, I want you to press control, alt and delete on that keyboard there. Do you understand?"

"What are you going to do?"

"I asked you if you understood."

That edge again. "Sorry," I said. "Yes, I understand."

"Okay," Fidorous placed his fingers and pressed down on two different keyboards. "Now."

I hit the buttons.

A single deafening note played out through the alarm speakers. I could feel it vibrating my insides, firm, steady and everywhere.

"Middle C," the doctor shouted over the noise. "It's too big for them, blasts them out of the –"

The note stopped.

"– tunnels," the doctor yelled, caught off-guard by the silence.

"It blasts them out of the tunnels," he said again, quietly, aiming for composure.

I nodded, taking my fingers off the keys.

The doctor checked his screen, tapped a few keys. "There. I think that's done it."

"Excellent," I tried, not wanting to sound as confused as I was.

Fidorous looked at me for a moment then turned his attention back to his monitor and started typing. I stood by the keyboard where he'd put me, gradually beginning to realise our conversation was over; he wasn't going to say anything else to me at all. It was as if the emergency made it possible for Fidorous to put whatever issues he had with me, with the First Eric Sanderson, to one side. Now it had passed, we were back to square one, and this time without Scout to keep things moving. An awkward silence began, building itself up slowly, a fat tension in the air as if the room were a submarine going, down, down, down to where the hull starts to buckle. The doctor typed, turned to another keyboard, typed some more, all without looking up. I shifted on my feet, watched him and wished I was somewhere else.

"So, what's all this equipment for?"

I felt stupid asking. For a second, I didn't think he'd answer.

"It's my work." Tap tap taptaptap tap. "This is where I release the language viruses I create."

"*Language* viruses?"

Tap tap taptap tap tap taptaptaptaptap –

Fidorous sighed theatrically and looked up. I saw the anger and frustration – thoughts of shouting or just ignoring me warrening around his elastic-band face like mice through a maze then all disappearing into his hair and sideburns. He straightened up slowly and came out with that polite schoolteacher voice again.

"All this machinery reroutes emails, websites, voicemail messages, radio programmes even. I feed my viruses into them and send them back so I can monitor the effects. '*At the end of the day.*' That's one of mine which is particularly virulent in the UK at the moment."

"You mean, you invent phrases?"

"Phrases, words, alternative spellings, abbreviations, corruptions. And not just invent; manage. Look. Look here."

I fought my way around the side of the desk, clambered, hopped, stepped over machinery, wires and tubing to get a better look.

On a table next to the one Fidorous had been working at, a small TV played news footage of a tropical storm into a microphone connected to a computer. The computer had one of those dictation programs installed and it seemed to be trying to interpret the weather sounds into words, creating row after row of text, words beginning with 's' or 'sh' mostly, with blocks of 'p's and 'b's appearing in time with the crashing waves. There was a thunderclap and the word BACKGAMMON printed itself up large on the screen.

"But. What's it for?" As soon as I'd said it I wished I hadn't. It was okay though, the doctor was in full flow, too involved in his own ideas to even think of taking offence.

"What's it for? What's it for? Hmmm." Fidorous sat down on a dismantled hard drive and stared at the monitor. "I construct language viruses so I might better understand real, naturally occurring ones. My work helps me to recognise the early warning signs and protect against future dangerous epidemics. Languages can get sick and die, you know. Extinctions happen, and then there are the migrations." Fidorous gave the storm text screen a last look then moved to the next desk along where a similar computer processed the sounds of a sombre state funeral. He tinkered for a while with the settings. "Have you noticed how the American 'can I get' has all but completely replaced the English 'can I have' in most environments in this country? Far be it from me to inhibit a successful evolutionary development when one emerges, but it is always sad to see an old form become isolated and die out."

"Like the red squirrel," I said vaguely.

"Yes, like the red squirrel."

"So, is this – you're not saying you *invent* creatures like the Ludovician here, are you?"

"No, of course not. Ludovicians, Franciscans, Luxogones," – the doctor was back fiddling with the keyboard – "all the conceptual fish evolved naturally. I've developed a number of artificial memes but they're no more than single-celled animals really, and they rarely survive more than a few hours in any real Darwinian environment. That said, they're tremendously useful tools when it comes to trying to understand the larger, more complex organisms."

I nodded at this. "And do you? Understand them, I mean."

"To a degree, yes. Some of them."

"I see." A surprise *now or never* impulse kicked in, pushing the bottom line up into the back of my throat. "Doctor Fidorous, listen," a stupid opening, "I mean, I'm sorry I have to be here. I didn't – whatever happened between you and the First Eric Sanderson to make you feel like this about me now, God, I don't know you, I don't even know him but I had to come here. I need to ask you if there's a way to stop the Ludovician."

Fidorous left the computer alone and looked straight at me.

"Is there?" I said after a painful couple of seconds. "I'm asking you because you're the only person I can ask."

Heat crept up into the doctor's face.

"'*I'm the only person you can ask?*' You don't have a clue, do you?"

I felt the earth tilt half a degree under my feet.

"What? What's that supposed to mean?"

Fidorous turned back to his console. "It's none of my business. I'm not your father, Eric, and I've got a lot to do here. Tests to run, diagnostic checks and quite frankly you're going to get in the way. You should go back to the lounge."

"No." Something hot, a fist made itself out of my stomach. "No. It's taken me months to get here and I'm not leaving this room until you answer me a simple fucking question – is there a way to stop the shark?"

The doctor's back said, "Why ask me? Ask your girlfriend."

"*What?*"

I could see his shoulders rising and falling; a progression of deep breaths. Eventually he turned around. "Alright then. Here it is if you want to really know: imagine you're running from something huge. Imagine you're running from a creature with one enormous mind inhabiting hundreds of bodies."

"What? Is this – Mycroft Ward?"

"Yes, Mycroft Ward. Imagine you're running from Mycroft Ward in fear of your life. You want to stop running, don't you? You want to fight back. But Mycroft Ward is a gigantic collective self, a self which generates years of thoughts, plans and memories every single day. So what do you do? The question you've somehow avoided asking yourself is what sort of weapon could be any use against a creature like that?"

At first I didn't know where he was going. Then . . .

"A Ludovician." The word shock-fizzed as I said it.

"Precisely. Bringing a giant collective self like Mycroft Ward and a self-eating shark like a Ludovician together, well, it would be like matter and anti-matter. Bang. No more Ward, no more Ludovician."

But that means . . . Oh, no.

"So, in answer to your question – yes, there is a way to stop the shark. Are you happier now you know that? Has it set your mind at ease?"

"I don't know what you're talking about."

"Why did Scout bring you here, Eric?"

"Because I paid her to. She offered to be my guide."

"No. Try again."

"Stop it."

"Try again."

"*Stop it.*"

"Alright, I'll tell you, shall I? Scout brought you here because she needs the Ludovician. Beyond that, you're irrelevant. The fact is, she's been trying to persuade me to help her use a Ludovician shark against Ward for months now."

"No."

"For God's sake, think – have you never wondered why she knows so much about the creature? She's been preparing for this for a long, long time."

"No," I said again. "She brought me here because *I asked her to.*" I hated the way my voice sounded – "We – we're together. She's *helping* me." It sounded weak and stupid and gullible. Even as I said the words, I knew. I knew the truth. I felt everything warm and real inside me begin to drain away.

25

Hakuun and Kuzan
(All the Stars are Bleeding)

I'd been sitting in the room with the wingback chairs for about fifteen minutes when Scout finally came back, crawling in from the other side of the bookcase just like I'd done with Fidorous.

"Hey," she said, smiling and getting to her feet. "So, can you believe that? Two days in un-space and somehow it's my job to get out there and check all his tunnels are sealed and clean because it's *migration season* or whatever? Where is he anyway?" She looked at the empty carrier still in the middle of the room. "Where's Ian?"

"I don't know."

"What's up? Are you alright?"

But I spotted it once I knew what to look for. I saw it in the tension at the edges of her mouth, heard it in the little breaks between her words. I knew what she was hiding. I sat looking at her, not saying anything.

A beat of confusion, then Scout's eyes widening in slow millimetres. I watched the pulse in her neck, that quick little thump. The honesty of it, the truth it gave away broke my heart. She looked away, swallowed, looked down. "*Oh, shit,*" she said.

And that was when I finally believed what Fidorous had said. I felt like I'd swallowed glass.

"*Oh, shit,*" I said, copying. "It's all been lies, hasn't it?"

All the clocks stopped. Time hung. An escaped band of shiny black hair curved down in front of Scout's face, tucking itself in under her chin. She didn't make any effort to move it. She just stood, head down, staring at a spot on the floor.

"I didn't tell you any lies," she said eventually, not looking up.

"How can you say that?" I could feel myself shuddering, the insides of my throat, my hands, weak and shaking with all the strength taken out. "Because you played some careful word game with yourself so there wouldn't *technically* be any lying? The fact is you didn't tell me why you were really bringing me here. You let me think you were *helping me* for fuck's sake."

"I *am* helping you."

"So, you showed up at that hospital out of the goodness of your heart, did you? No, Scout, you're helping yourself. You were using me from the second we met."

She stared at the floor.

This is what I wanted: I wanted her to explode and say "How could you think that?" I wanted her to scream at me. I wanted her to tell me what a stupid mistake I'd made. I wanted her to storm out of the room in a rage. More than anything, I wanted to be wrong. But I wasn't. I wasn't wrong. She just stared at the floor.

"We had sex," I said. "No, not just that, we were holding hands and I thought – why did you do that? I was following you here anyway. You'd already got what you wanted, why did you need to make me think you actually – liked me too?"

"I did like you. I *do* like you," she said. "But you're not going to believe that."

"How can I believe anything that comes out of your mouth now?"

"I don't know. I don't expect you to."

"What, so you're giving me permission? Well, thank you."

She looked up at me for a second. "I'm not going to be able to say anything, am I?"

"All this time you've just been using me to get what you wanted."

"Eric. Christ. Do you want me to try to explain this?"

I didn't say anything.

"It's not –" she started. "All this with us, it's important. It is, I mean that. But you need to understand what's at stake for me,

I couldn't take any risks and there was no reason for you to trust me. So –"

"So, even after we fucked, you just carry on lying?"

"Alright." Scout's eyes were hot, bright, wet now. It hit me that something vital was leaking out of her, something limited and tiny and which couldn't be replaced. I wanted to hold her and stop it from spilling out but I wanted her to suffer too, suffer for who she secretly was, suffer for her cruelty in making me feel a part of something, of making me feel warm, wanted and cared about, like I didn't really have to be alone in this dead and empty world, all just for the sake of some cold, logical plan.

I looked at her and a voice inside me said, *we only see starlight because all the stars are bleeding.*

"Alright," Scout said again. "Yes, yes, yes. Is that what you want to hear? Yes, I did lie to you. Yes, I did manipulate you. Yes, I did use you. No, I *didn't* fuck you to get you here, but if you want to believe that too then fine, go ahead and believe whatever the hell you want about me. I do whatever I have to do to survive. I'm not proud of it, sometimes I hate myself for it if you really want the truth. I hate myself. Now, I don't expect you to like what I did, or accept it or forgive it, but I'm surprised that *you of all people* can't even fucking understand it."

All the stars are bleeding.

"You could have trusted me."

She wiped her wet eyes, hand up and brushing away quickly.

She looked at me straight on.

"No, Eric, I couldn't. I need that shark."

"Right."

"I'm sorry, but that's how it is."

I poured myself a whisky from the decanter next to my chair. My hands were shaking; little ripples vibrated across the liquid surface as I brought the glass up to drink. *Don't notice that my hands are shaking.* "So, when was I supposed to find out why you really came looking for me?"

"Do you really want to know all this?"

"Yes."

"Okay. Everything you've been doing, all this research and travelling has been about finding Fidorous." It was as if some sort of bullet-proof shield were sliding down around her. The girl in front of me becoming hard, unfamiliar. "So, I knew you'd listen if he told you there was a way to use Mycroft Ward and the Ludovician against each other. On the other hand, there was a chance you wouldn't trust a plan like that coming from a stranger, especially after your run-in with Mr Nobody."

"But I *did* trust you. I always trusted you."

"I couldn't take that risk."

"What about the risks I took? You should've been honest with me."

"I know I've hurt you, but think about what you're saying."

I sat quietly for a moment. "No, I would have. I would have told you everything, right from the beginning."

"Would you?" she said. "You sure about that? You'd really have bet your life, and my life too, on the chance that I'd make a single uninformed leap of faith? This plan takes care of the shark as well as Ward. I *was* helping you, even if you didn't know it."

"Oh, come on," I took another mouthful of whisky, "don't twist this around, you're helping me by accident, aren't you? All this is a side-effect of Scout saving Scout. You even said so. And yes, I would have told you because *it was the right thing to do.*"

"Well, you're entitled to believe whatever you want to believe."

Don't notice, I thought, squeezing the glass to my chest, *don't notice that my hands are shaking.*

"Alright. So." I wanted to know everything, I wanted to grab hold of every red hot burning part of all this and hold it tight, feel the hiss and sting of every single moment. Not knowing everything would be a hundred times worse. "You decided to stick with your plan, bring me to Fidorous and let me think he'd come up with this way for us to use Ward and the Ludovician against each other. And then what? You'd be all *Oh my God, that's an amazing idea?*"

Behind the bullet-proof glass, Scout's eyes were unreadable, full of odd lights and reflections that could have meant anything. "Something like that, yeah."

"Jesus. And you didn't think I'd be at all suspicious about that?"

She shook her head, pushing her way out of the conversation. "Look, I never expected you to forgive me for any this, but, yes, deep down I hoped you might if you want the truth. Whatever happened, I didn't think you'd react like this."

"Like what?"

"Forget it."

"No, come on, react like what?"

"Like such a child."

A sour, bile-wave of anger rushed up and I bit my teeth together hard until the swell of it subsided. "I trusted you, Scout. Blind trust. You're right, how childish is that?" And when she didn't react more stinging words heaped up into my throat wanting desperately to smash that stupid impassive shield of hers. "Well, don't worry, I'm not going to make a mistake like that again."

Scout looked out from her thick layer of glass. I couldn't see, couldn't tell anything.

"Okay," she said, quietly and evenly. "Then that's that."

A slick greasy fire roared inside me, shock and shame and a horrible sadness taking away my insides.

"Okay, that's that," I tried to look still, blank. "But we're stuck together anyway, aren't we? The Ludovician to destroy Ward and Ward to destroy the Ludovician. Whatever you're going to do, I'm going to have to help you. You win, Scout."

"I think this is a long way from winning, don't you?"

I shook my head, pushing the question away. "What's your plan?"

26

It's a Poor Sort of Memory that Only Works Backwards

Just like the four-turn win in chess, Scout's plan was simple and obvious – obvious afterwards, if you only realised what it was you should have been looking for. Like Dorothy, she'd brought the ruby slippers with her. Unlike Dorothy, of course, Scout knew it.

Nobody's laptop. Nobody's laptop was the key to the whole thing.

Nobody had been one of Mycroft Ward's most important operatives and for sixty seconds every day, between 12.21 a.m. and 12.22 a.m., his laptop was permitted to connect directly with the gigantic online database of *self* that was Mycroft Ward's mind. During this single minute, Nobody would upload his reports directly into Ward's vast consciousness. During this single minute, a direct channel opened between Ward's mind and the outside world. Scout would convert one of Fidorous's email rerouting programs to hold open the connection between the laptop and Ward once it occurred. Fidorous, Scout hoped, would create some sort of device to channel the Ludovician into the laptop and into Ward. Simple. The only difficult, dangerous part would be getting close to the Ludovician in the first place.

I was close to crying. I thought Scout might be close to crying too, but I couldn't tell anymore. After a few moment's quiet she gathered up Nobody's laptop, strapped it over her shoulder and said *I need to make a start.*

And then she turned and walked away, through the door and down the corridor without looking back.

Vague and empty, I sat for a while in the wingback chair, listening to the quiet of the books in the walls.

Some time passed.

Eventually, I noticed the carrier, open and empty in the middle of the room. Ian. I'd not seen him since I'd gone with Fidorous down the corridor to his control room. I pushed myself up in the chair. Finding my cat was something I could do, something that didn't need any thinking.

I got to my feet, controlling the slight sway Fidorous's whisky brought on. I remembered then that my backpack was still downstairs, down through the bookcase, in the room of papers.

First things first, I told myself. *Get the bag, then find Ian. Simple tasks. A process. A counterbalance to all of this.*

I crawled awkwardly back between the bookcase shelves and made my way down the spiral staircase, stepping off the bottom and into a shin-deep drift of papers. My backpack lay just where I'd dropped it. Scout's was there too, the two bags bumped down together, side by side with one slightly on top of the other. I kicked my way over to them.

Those two bags shouted heartbreaking out-of-date things about a careless sort of closeness which was lost now. I realised that that whole world, our two-day trip through un-space, everything that had happened between us, what little signs, what little avatars of it there had been, would soon all be lost, broken and left behind. *We're all going forwards and we're never coming back.*

I reached and threw my rucksack over my shoulder, swayed a little from the thud and swing of its weight. After a few seconds I picked Scout's up too then I turned and made my way back towards the stairs.

I left Scout's bag propped up in one of the wingback chairs, had another glass of the doctor's whisky, grabbed Ian's carrier from the middle of the floor and stood weighing it in my hand.

•

"Ch ch ch ch ch." Wandering down the corridor, carrier in hand. The walls of books were constant, endless. Me all adrift, vague, emotion-blasted. "Ch ch ch ch ch." Fidorous's cabinets passed me as I walked. I didn't bother to stop and investigate any of them.

There was no sign of Ian.

I came to a branch in the corridor, a second passage running off to the left. On the corner where the passages met, the doctor, or someone, had placed a small wooden chair. I put the carrier down and, for no real reason, decided to sit for a minute.

I wasn't thinking anymore. My mind was a frozen football pitch, empty, lonely, waiting in the winter cold for me to walk back out onto it. But I wasn't ready for that yet. Once I started out there again I knew I'd have to relive everything, everything I'd said and everything she'd said. I'd try to work out what every word and inflection in every sentence might have meant. I'd force myself to go through it all, again and again and again and again and every part of it would hit me just as hard, or harder, every single time. Shock's slow medical anaesthetic kept me quiet and under observation. I had to find my cat.

I reached behind me and pulled a book out of the wall-shelf at random. My hand came back holding a dusty but modern-looking paperback called *Holes and Superficialities*. I flipped the pages idly, not really taking any of it in. I got up on my knees on the chair and pivoted around, peered into the gap I'd made in the wall shelf. I pushed my eye up close between the book spines and saw more books nestling in the darkness, shadowy and difficult to identify. I wondered again, distantly, vaguely, if the bookshelves were deep or if the walls themselves were made of books. I slotted the *Holes* book back in where it came from.

I'd only gone a few minutes further along the corridor when I heard shouting.

Scout. Not frightened shouting but angry shouting, too far away for me to make out the words. I listened. Fidorous was shouting something back. Then Scout again. An argument catching fire somewhere up ahead.

I stood still, blank.

No, no more tonight – the shock doctor inside my head doing the thinking for me – *No more. You've had enough for one day. Too much.*

My body turned itself around. I retraced my steps to the chair and made my way down the branch corridor *ch-ch-ch*-ing as I went.

This new corridor felt narrower, the books leaning in closer, soaking up the sound. The argument noise behind me faded quickly into the walls and out of my head. There were fewer lights along here. Bulbs covered with simple white lampshades hung down from the ceiling at not-quite-frequent-enough intervals so the pools of bright yellow light didn't quite connect with each other, leaving deep bookshelf shadows to grow up in the dark areas between them. I wondered, in an uncommitted sort of way, about where Fidorous got his power. His house, book structure, whatever it was, it was gigantic. I thought about a postman trying to find his way through the word tunnels to deliver an electricity bill and the idea dredged up a small under-siege smile.

"Ch ch ch ch ch ch."

I came to another junction and turned left by a case of old printing blocks and 1930s typewriters. After a while I realised I'd started thinking about Dr Randle, something I'd not done in a long time.

Another junction, I turned left.

"Ch ch ch ch ch ch."

I tried to remember what Randle's dog was called. Ricky? Robbie? Rusty? Something beginning with R. He would get excited sometimes if he could smell Ian on my clothes and rush around and around Randle's usually calm conservatory, barking like – I turned right – barking, well, yapping really, and she'd have to shut him in the kitchen before either of us could risk sitting down without being jumped all over. I felt vaguely guilty that Randle might have worried about me once she realised I'd gone. But what could I have told her? What could I have possibly said to her really? Maybe when all this was over I'd write to her and tell her – tell her what? I turned left. Tell her everything. I'd write it all down and she could believe whatever she wanted.

"Ch ch ch ch ch."

Had Nobody said something about her writing a paper about me when I was alone with him, deep in that abandoned hospital? Is that how he'd found me? It sounded familiar. Suddenly I didn't feel so guilty. Writing an academic paper wasn't the behaviour of a woman torn apart with worry for one of her clients, was it? In fact, if she was detached enough to sit down and write about me in a – I stopped at the door in front of me and reached into my pocket for my keys – in a purely academic sense then it probably wasn't guilt I should be feeling at all but –

But.

My brain snapped itself into the here and now, rushing to catch up with what had happened.

I looked down at the keys in my hand then up at the door in front of me.

For the last, what, ten minutes I'd been walking in a daze, drifting inside my head while my body moved along on autopilot. That autopilot had brought me here. My body acting on – what? Instinct? No, acting on a learned and repeated routine my mind had forgotten. My body remembered its own way here, to this door. To this pinewood door with its brass door handle and its small lock set underneath.

I looked down at my hand again then counted through the few keys on my key ring: the key for the yellow Jeep, the key to the front door of my house, the key to the back door, the key the First Eric Sanderson had posted to me all that time ago, the one that had opened the door to the locked bedroom.

I stopped on this last key and, trying not to think too hard about the logic of any of it, slid it into the lock in front of me.

I turned experimentally.

Clunk.

I put the keys back in my pocket then pushed down on the door handle.

The door swung open.

I reached along the dark wall to find a light switch.

Click.

I stepped inside.

A bedroom. Behind the door was a small, tidy bedroom. A single bed with a bookshelf screwed to the wall above it, a wardrobe, chest of drawers, bedside table and a small desk near the door. I clicked the door shut behind me, put down Ian's carrier and propped my rucksack up against the desk. Under the quiet and woolly tickle of dust, the room still had a faint, lived-in smell – sleep, deodorant, washing powder, skin, hair, sweat. The smell of a person. The smell sank naturally into me, so familiar and reassuring that at first I didn't see the significance. When the realisation came it was a shock volting my system.

The room smelled like my house. It smelled of me.

This is the First Eric Sanderson's room.

A heave of panic and another type of instinct kicked in – Fidorous had said the whole place was completely shark-proof, but still – Mark Richardson's expression leapt up over the top of mine, tightening muscles, changing my face.

"Okay," I told myself. I pulled in a calming breath, let it go slowly. "Come on. It can't get in here. There are defences." But something from one of the First Eric's letters came floating up from the dark.

Be absolutely sure, then check again, and then check again.

I unfastened my rucksack, took out the Dictaphones and set them up in the corners of the room. *Safety and caution always.* Better safe than sorry.

Once the tapes were chattering out their familiar hiss and treble, I fastened up the rucksack again and leant back against one of the walls, letting the Richardson persona slip away. Walls. This room really did have walls – not the endless books of the corridors outside but real walls, plastered and painted a deep thoughtful blue.

The First Eric Sanderson's bedroom.

I've found you, I thought, *I've found you again.*

I crossed the room and climbed onto the bed, kneeling up so I could reach the books on the shelf.

"Alright, Eric," I told the old still air. "I've made it here just like you wanted, only everything's fucked up and your friend the doctor hates me, so you're going to have to help me out."

The books clapped up plumes of dust as my fingers flipped their way through them.

The Teachings of Master Lin-Chi, clap. *The Helmet of Horror*, clap. *Out of Africa: The Story of Human Evolution*, clap. *The Intuitive Edge*, clap. *Catch-22*, clap. *Dreamtime and the All-At-Once; Jurassic Park; Understanding Quantum Mechanics*, clap, clap, clap. *The Call of Cthulhu; How Your Brane Works; The Unfortunates; A Brief History of Time; The Quantum Machine Gun; The Complete Escher* and then – *Brick by Brick, The Analysis and Treatment of Traumatic Disassociation* –

"No."

I pulled the book, a big hardback, off the shelf and opened it up, scanning the front flyleaf then flipping to the back. In her author picture she was younger, slimmer and, from the colours and the hair, smiling out at me from some point in the mid-eighties. But, Christ, it was her. Dr Randle. *Professor Helen Randle*, according to the cover. I flickerbooked the pages, stopping at random:

> . . . and even more general responses to standard Overland folios do not indicate any truly significant 8-cycle event as such. Precision is vital when recording these phenomena as memmiatic sequencing algorithms as Herenik (1979) suspects a subbautinous projection even in straightforward observational data. To calculate inaccuracy due to Backland's constant we must . . .

I flicked again but the next three or four sections were equally impenetrable so I turned back to Randle's photograph. *What the fuck are you doing here? What does this mean?* Her face smiled up at me, not telling, being just a million tiny dots of mass printed, arranged ink. I snapped the book shut. *What does it mean? I'll tell you what it means, Eric. It means what it always means. It means another forgotten story, another dried-up stream, another snapped or missing thread.*

But then I noticed something. Something about the back of the book caught hold of me, it was something so slight as to almost not be there at all. I tipped the book forward a little, back a little, moving reflected light over the glossy surface. A cluster of raised marks, tiny bumps like the most delicate Braille had been pushed up in the back cover. I knew what marks like that meant. I peeled off the dust jacket and, yes, on the inside was a block of carefully handwritten text:

It isn't just the past we remember, it's the future too. Fifty per cent of memory is devoted not to what has already happened, but to what will happen next. Appointments, anniversaries, meetings, all the rolling engagements and plans, all the hopes and dreams and ambitions which make up any human life – we remember what we did and also what we *will* do. Only the knife edge of the present is 'hard' to any degree. Past and future are things of the mind, and a mind can be changed.

Eric Sanderson

I stared down at the words. He must have written this before he left here to go looking for the Ludovician, which would make it, what, some sort of a mission statement? Whatever it was, it seemed like something he didn't want the doctor to find after he'd gone. Why write it down on a book, on this book? Unless – unless he knew I'd recognise Dr Randle's name and I'd . . . Did he send me to her? Send me to spend a year with her listening to those stupid fucking theories just so when

I finally got here I'd pull this particular book off the shelf and find this message? And if so, why? What was this supposed to mean? Something came back to me, something from one of First Eric Sanderson's letters, something written much later, when the word shark had already eaten most of him away: *I think I believed I could change what happened, undo it, prevent it, save her life somehow after she was already gone.*

I read through the paragraph inside the dust jacket again.

"Christ, Eric. What the fuck is this?" I whispered it. "What the fuck were you trying to do?"

.

"What the fuck were you trying to do?"

I turned the room over. Filled the air with long-settled dust and the bed with T-shirts, pants and socks from the chest of drawers and a heap of opened, shaken-out books from the bookshelf. The shock doctor couldn't hold it back anymore, now I was a creature made of wounded kinetics. "What the fuck were you trying to do? Come on, I'm ready for my next clue now." I pulled open the wardrobe, dragging out pairs of jeans and combat pants, heavy coats and boots into a pile on the floor. "Or, maybe you could just fucking tell me. How about that? I deserve to know why I'm like this, don't I? I deserve to know why you made me into this *empty fucking thing*, this machine that people can't really touch or feel anything for and so they just –"

Use.

Scout. She used you, Eric.

"Fuck. Fuck fuck fuck." The dam all the way broken, everything flooding out now. I ripped out the last of the clothes from the wardrobe, stretch-twisting hangers, pulled out the last of the boots and the carrier bags of trainers and rolled-up jumpers and old shirts onto the pile on the floor and kicked at it shouting "You cunt, Sanderson, you selfish fucking cunt."

A plastic bag caught around my foot and I pulled it off, hurling it at the wall where it split like a medical IV bag of boots and old socks. *Bang. Thud tunk tunk tunk.*

I gave the pile two, three more half-hearted kicks and sank down to my knees – "You fucking, fucking cunt" – slowing down in the next swell of shock. Another anaesthetic tide rising up from my stomach.

My sore eyes stared, blank.

Minutes ticked away and I squeezed myself tight. My arms hugged warm around my chest.

The heap of clothes sat, kicked and bullied and still, in front of me. My sore eyes stared.

One of the plastic bags on the top of the pile had a box inside, a shoebox probably. I'd kicked a dent into it and a lid corner had been forced up, stretching a tract of the navy blue plastic into puckered stuttery sky blue, before ripping through it altogether. Inside the box was what looked like a block of carefully folded white linen.

Curiosity, like a film playing backwards, bringing a million smashed pieces back together – slow, faster, faster, faster, complete – remaking them into me.

I blinked.

Wiped my eyes.

My hand reached out.

I took the dented box and, slowly, abstractedly, worked it out of its ruined bag. The three rectangular objects inside had been carefully, very, very carefully, wrapped up in soft white cloth. I stared for a few seconds. I took the box over to the desk and put it down.

Grabbing a bottle of water out of my rucksack, I took a slow, cool drink then splashed a wet palmful onto my eyes and face, drying myself off with my pulled-up T-shirt.

I ran my fingers through my hair, pulled the desk chair up behind me.

Okay.

Okay then. Let's have a look at you.

I lifted the first object out of the box. It was the thinnest of the three, as thin and light as an envelope, and that's almost what it was. I unfolded the white cloth and found a photograph wallet: one of the bright, glossy card packets your prints and negatives come back in from the chemist's. The colourful picture on the front flap showed a girl jumping on a guy's back, both of them laughing and dressed in bright summer clothes. Underneath it said *Kodak* in big, bold letters and to the right of that, in a yellow and orange starburst, *36 exposures*. I lifted the flap and I looked inside and then, just to be sure, I turned it upside down and shook. Nothing. No pictures, no negatives. The wallet was completely empty. I turned it over and around to see if I'd missed something important, like I almost had with Randle's book, but no, it was just an empty photo wallet. An empty photo wallet wrapped, stored and treated as a relic.

Why?

Maybe the answer was still in the box.

Thick, heavy and solid, I knew the second object was a book before I'd even unwrapped it from its cloth protection. I wasn't prepared for the kind of book I'd find though.

An Encyclopaedia of Unusual Fish by Dr Victor Helstrom. The book looked sixty, maybe eighty years old. A hardback in a tattered, ripped and faded orange dust jacket with an old-fashioned ink drawing of a very ugly deep sea fish on the front.

In a lightning strike I remembered the book sent by Mr Nobody and the sick, slimy winding Luxophage hiding inside. I almost shoved *Unusual Fish* off the desk in a jerk of panic.

But this was the First Eric Sanderson's room, the First Eric Sanderson's book. The ice thawed a little inside my head as I stared at the old, creased cover.

Come on, Eric. Get a grip. And anyway, what are you going to do? Not look?

I pulled the book back towards me and carefully opened it up.

The pages were dry and yellowed, dirty at the edges and the thing smelled of cigarette smoke and finger grease. I skipped through a long and wordy introduction and found a contents page. The author, this Victor Helstrom, had divided his unusual fish into categories.

I flipped my way towards the back of the book. The first three categories were filled with ink drawings and long detailed descriptions and notes, but when I reached '*The Fish of Mind, Word and Invention*', entries became smaller, blocky and unillustrated, like a dictionary.

Apalasitien, Araul Calthonis, 'Blinking' Quaric Blue Bonbolian, Burgnatell – I flicked forwards a few pages – *Fathmic Candiru, Franciscan ("Bede Shark"), Flatwold, Folocondorius* – and a few more – *Jarhaphish ("Inknose"), Lampropini, Ledgerlantern, Lewzivian* – and there it was – Ludovician.

The entry had been circled in pencil. My left hand crept up to my chin and then over my mouth as my eyes shuttled down through the passage:

Ludovician

First officially catalogued for the USC by Capt. St John Lewis in 1839, and named in honour of him by the society, the Ludovician shark has been a cause of myth, speculation and storytelling for over four thousand years (see below). A powerful and persistent mnemonic predator, Ludovicians are to be considered amongst the most dangerous of all sentapiscis and should only be observed after great preparation and with extreme caution.

With a recorded length of over thirty notional lumens from snout to tail tip, the Ludovician is the largest living member of the Cognicharius family, outsized only by the gigantic Meglovician which seems to have become extinct between four and five hundred years ago, possibly due to the western diversification of printed language from a previously prevalent Latin. The Ludovician appears to be more adaptable and, as a result, is more widely distributed than its extinct cousin. Although the animal is solitary and (thankfully) rarely encountered in the field, Ludovician attacks on speakers of over twenty languages have been reliably reported over the past fifty years. This and other research suggests a stable, if not growing population.

Ludovician characteristics: Portentous, impassive to vague to vacant colouration, sepulchral bite radius, regressively swept fins and ubiquitous dorsal meme.

Ludovician myths: It should come as little surprise that this large, dangerous and enigmatic predator should be the focus of much legend and superstition. Perhaps the most engaging of all the myths associated with these animals is the ancient Native American belief that all memories, events and identities consumed by one of the *great dream fishes* would somehow be reconstructed and eternally sustained inside it. The indigenous oral tradition tells us how the greatest shamans and medicine men would travel to ancestral holy places *to pass their souls into the dream fish* when they reached old age. These shamans believed that once they had sacrificed themselves, they would join their ancestors and memory-families in eternal *vision-worlds* recreated from generations of shared knowledge and experience. In effect, each Ludovician shark came to be revered as a self-contained, living afterlife. Name chants once told which of the ancestors had passed into which of the seven greatest dream fish, but these are now understood to be fragmented and lost. Thankfully, this misguided and macabre practice is no longer observed.

As my mind raced, my hands turned Helstrom's book of fish over and placed it carefully to one side, *Ludovician* pages down. I reached inside the shoebox and took out the last wrapped object. This was a book too, smaller but just as thick, maybe even a little thicker.

I unfolded the cloth and looked inside.

Thump. Thump.

Thump. Thump.

Thump. Thump.

My heart. All I could hear as I stared at the last book's cover.

Thump. Thump.

Thump. Thump.

Thump. Thump.

My fingers traced the folds and fault lines in the glossy card. Thump. Thump. My fingers over pictures of sandy bays, crumbling columns and little white villages on hot dusty hillsides. Thump. Thump. My fingers over the blocky sky blue lettering of the title.

Greek Island Hopping: A Backpacker's Guide.

Shaking, I opened the book –

– and found a universe inside.

An entire galaxy of biro stars, pen orbits and ink loop rings around museums and boat rides and campsites, endless stellar clusters of ticks, crosses, exclamation and question marks all in, on and around the lists of *tavernas* and bed and breakfasts and bars and towns and trails and beaches.

"Oh God." No force behind the words, just them escaping, leaking out in my breath.

My fingers touching the indentations, the pen marks, the folded page corners.

Clio.

Clio's guidebook.

Clio Aames's real and true and actual writing right there in front of me.

The printed words and the biro warped and rolled together for a second. Something hit the page with an audible *tap*. I tensed up, thinking again about Nobody and his book traps, about Luxophages,

Franciscans and Ludovicians. Then I noticed my face, my cheeks were wet.

I looked down again across Clio's constellations of notes. Tap. Tap. Tap.

I hadn't even realised I was crying.

•

Tired, I closed Clio's guidebook again, climbed off the First Eric Sanderson's bed and collected my rucksack, dragging it back across the room with me. I dug The Light Bulb Fragment and my notebooks out and read through them again, once, twice, three times, feeling an empty ache for something simple and normal and solid.

I thought a lot about Clio and about Eric. And then because I couldn't help it, I thought about Scout and me.

Would Clio have done what Scout did?

Oh, come on, you know the answer to that. Sometimes, when you're sleepy, ideas and feelings in the back of your mind get whispery voices of their own. *She's just doing what she's always done, what's best for you, whether you can see it at the time or not.*

I tried to block it out, but the nonsense wouldn't let go.

You know, don't you? The way it works between the two of you, all those emotions, the tattoo on her big toe. You know who she really is, even if you won't –

"Shut up." My arm shot out and hurled the texts and the notebooks against the wall. The books thudded, flapped and settled like a flock of broken kites.

Half-climbed onto the end of the bed, Ian stopped mid-step and stared at me with big round eyes.

27

Who Are You Really, and What Were You Before?

Sometimes when I think I can't sleep, I actually *am* part-way asleep. Or at least, not completely awake. For the hours I'd been lying on the First Eric Sanderson's bed trying to unpick the knotted tangle of events and fragments in my mind, I'd have said I was one hundred per cent all-the-way awake with no chance of sleeping. But now, standing in the book corridor outside, I felt light, half-focused, unsteady on my feet. The things I'd been thinking back on the bed, those intricate thought trains I'd been putting together now seemed to be all flickering lights and groundless leaps of logic – ideas warped and twisted by the un-sense that lives at the edge of sleep.

But then, maybe there was something else about that place too; maybe white out-of-the-corner-of-your-eye truth birds dive and swoop there, little rips of blotter paper soaring free from the weight of fact and possibility which extincts them everywhere else.

What? White birds? Wake up, Eric. I rubbed my face with my palms to bring myself around and drive out the fog.

I pulled on my jacket and quietly closed the door.

I needed answers. That's why I couldn't sleep. Clio Aames, the Ludovician, the First Eric Sanderson. There was only one person who would be able to give me the facts.

I'd loaded the things I'd found in the First Eric's room into a plastic bag; *The Encyclopaedia of Unusual Fish*, Clio's guidebook, the empty photo wallet and (after some sleepy soul-searching) Randle's book jacket with the First Eric Sanderson's hidden message. I'd also packed my Light Bulb Fragment notebooks. It seemed to make sense to take everything, to try to get him to look at all of it.

Getting dressed, I'd been worried the lights would be off and the maze of books and corridors would be impossible to navigate, all corners, blackness and quiet like some huge silent brain. As it was, the lights seemed to stay on all night, but that didn't make things any easier. After a few minutes' walking and a few guessed-at turns, I started to worry I wouldn't find my way out, *or* my way back. I turned around, tried to retrace my steps but I must have gone wrong at the second or the third junction because where I expected the bedroom door to be, it wasn't. I stood looking at a blank, uninterrupted wall of books. A shower of cold nerve-needles down my back – *you're lost, Eric.*

I called out: "Hello?"

Nothing.

"Can anyone hear me?"

But the books flattened the sound, sucked it in and breathed it out again as miles and miles of dusty silence.

I dropped my forehead against the wall of spines. "Fantastic."

Then I heard a noise, distant and muffled but real and out there, a sound like a big bell or a gong striking in the distance.

Dang – one. *Dang* – two.

A landmark. I pulled myself together and began to jog in the direction of the sound.

Dang – three. *Dang* – four.

The corridor ended in a T-junction, I waited.

Dang – five.

Left. I ran now, realising I had to find the sound before it stopped, realising this was an all or nothing strategy and if I didn't make it in time I'd be properly, definitely all-the-way lost.

Dang – six. *Dang* – seven.

Another left, another long and patchily lit corridor of books.

Dang – eight. *Dang* – nine. *Dang* – ten.

Come on, me running flat out, head down, pounding the floor.

Dang – eleven.

Louder now, closer.

A branch corridor. Trying to slow down and throw myself around the corner, making it but hitting wall and scattering books.

Dang – twelve.

I managed to stay on my feet, just, and jogging forwards I saw an archway. An archway in the wall of the corridor just up ahead. The sound coming from inside. It must be –

Dang – thirteen.

My lungs were burning. I stopped, bent over double, hands on knees to catch my breath.

A moment passed.

Two moments.

"If you're looking for the toilet, you've come too far. Go back to the last junction and turn right."

The suddenness of it made me jump, but I knew the voice.

Still breathing hard, I straightened up and made my way towards the arch.

"Sorry." I took half a step inside. "I got lost and there was, I think, a bell or something so I followed it. Actually – I was looking for you."

Dr Fidorous turned around to face me.

"You heard that?"

"Yes."

"Well, then. You'd better come in, hadn't you?"

The room was small and empty apart from the doctor and a simple wooden table covered in candles against the far wall; no electric lighting here and nothing obvious to account for the noises I'd heard. The space looked to have been made from huge books, old encyclopaedias, dictionaries or atlases I thought, and their peeling leather spines, like thick bricks, twitched shadows in the candlelight. An old poster of a shaolin-style monk with a huge gong had been pinned up on one of the book-walls.

Fidorous sat cross-legged on a cushion in the middle of the floor, originally facing the table of candles but now shuffled around to look at me. He was different. For a second I thought it was a trick of the candlelight, but, no, he'd changed. His huge hair had been tamed a little, slicked back with Brylcreem. The dressing-gown had gone too. In its place was an old dark suit and light blue shirt. The doctor must have seen me looking.

"It's easy to lose track of yourself down here," he said. "When you don't see other people for such a long time, you tend not to think" – he made a circular gesture in front of his face – "about all this."

He seemed relatively calm but I'd seen first-hand how quickly that could change.

"I wasn't –" I tried, then, "I didn't mean to stare."

He watched me for a moment and I had no idea what would happen. When he spoke, he looked away, turning back to the table of candles.

"I should never have said what I did to you about Scout. Whatever's between the two of you should stay between the two of you. It wasn't my business or my place to say those things."

Cold flowing under my skin, like someone had watered down my blood.

"You were right, though. She was using me."

"I know," Fidorous said. "But she's a girl who's come a long way from where she started and from who she was. Some of her edges have worn sharp. It happens, you should know that. I shouldn't have said those things."

"Why are you telling me this?"

"Because it's the truth."

"No, I mean, you made it pretty clear before that you don't like me very much."

The doctor turned back to me. "Is that what you think?"

"Well, yes."

I saw for the first time how pale his eyes were behind the Michael Caine glasses. Even in the orange and shadows of candlelight,

I could see they were a clear, calm tropical blue; baby's eyes in an old man's face.

"It's difficult," he said at last, struggling even with that much. "It's difficult when people become hell-bent on making terrible mistakes. I couldn't let you walk out of here and kill yourself for some delusion."

"Is that what happened?"

Fidorous shook his head, tiny, slow movements, eyes never leaving mine. This wasn't an answer to my question, it was something else; a funeral expression, a deserted place between resignation and regret.

"There's nothing left of you, is there?" he said.

The question knocked me. I didn't know how to answer. "I didn't – I've been trying to find you because I need help. I need answers. I don't know much about his time or what he did or why, but I need to, I need to know him, I think. I have to figure it all out before this ends."

"You're not making sense – need to know who?"

"The First Eric Sanderson."

The calm, blue eyes looked deep into me.

"I see. And that would make you, what? The Second Eric Sanderson?"

"Yes," I said. "I suppose so."

"Hmmm." The doctor brought his eyebrows down at this, thoughtful. "An old man's pride, that's what you've been up against, I'm ashamed to say."

"I've got to understand why he did what he did," I said. I dug into my plastic bag and pulled out *The Encyclopaedia of Unusual Fish*. "I found this."

Fidorous looked up at the book. The new warmth in him was suddenly gone, everything turning back to ice. *Cold snap.*

"Give me that."

I hesitated but there was no way around it. I passed him the book.

"Listen to me, Eric Sanderson the Second, listen to me carefully – this book is sick. It's sick and contagious with dangerous and misleading ideas, do you understand? I don't want you to ever ask me about it again." He wrenched open the pages and flung the encyclopaedia hard against the wall. I heard the spine crack. The dead book fell clumsily to the floor.

I wasn't shaken or intimidated. This was too big, too important. I'd come to Fidorous for answers.

Sometimes answers don't need to be given in words.

I stared at the broken book.

"That's it, isn't it?" I said.

Fidorous looked up at me, not moving, not speaking.

"First Eric Sanderson believed everything it said in there about memories living on inside word sharks. He believed it and so he went off looking for a Ludovician. Didn't he?"

The doctor watched me from behind his thick glasses.

"Didn't he?"

"Yes," Fidorous said eventually.

"Jesus." The pieces slipping into place now, one after another. "He found one and he gave himself to it. For Clio Aames. He did it for her, tried to save her life, preserve her after she was already gone, only it didn't work. It didn't work and the Ludovician ate his mind. It just chewed him up, didn't it?"

"Yes."

It just chewed him up.

"Jesus."

"Eric, I'm sorry."

"So, God, I mean –" I cast around, spinning inside my head, looked again at the broken book. "There's no chance any of it could be true?" *I believed I could change what happened, save her life somehow after she was already gone.*

Fidorous looked away. "Conviction, point of view, ways of looking; these are all powerful tools if you know how to use them, but there are limits. The Ludovician shark is a living animal, an animal has its own nature and there's no way to change that. A shark is always a shark, whatever you choose to believe. For memories to survive inside a Ludovician would be like – like a mouse surviving inside a cat."

"But he wanted it to be true so much, didn't he?"

He gave me a thin smile. "Yes, too much. I should never have passed the lessons on to him. I couldn't stop him. I don't think he could have stopped himself in the end. I should have turned him away when I first met him but I was selfish, I wanted the knowledge to survive."

I reached into the carrier bag again and pulled out the dust jacket from Randle's book. I folded it over to the hidden message. *I'm sorry, Eric*, I thought, *you wanted this to be a secret but your plans all failed, didn't they? It's because of you that I'm like this and now I need to ask for help.*

"I found this too," I said, passing the dust jacket to Fidorous. "It was hidden in Eric's room."

Fidorous took the page and read it, pushing his glasses up the bridge of his nose.

"What does it mean?"

He looked at me over the top of the dust jacket.

"Nothing. It doesn't mean anything except that he'd pushed himself too far." Fidorous passed the page back to me. "He was a good man. That is to say you were a good man, when you were him. It must be strange for you; God knows it's strange for me, seeing you here after everything that happened."

"Yeah, I can imagine."

"You know, I would have liked to have known him before the accident, before she died."

"Me too."

"By the time he came to me . . . he was always so sad."

"He would have done anything to save her, wouldn't he?"

"Yes, I think that's right. Is that the way you feel about Scout?"

When someone asks a question out of the blue, there's a chance the guards will be caught sleeping. When this happens, the brain sometimes responds before the mind has a chance to lock the doors and winch your standard *mind your own business* flag up the flagpole. Sometimes the brain surprises everyone, even itself, with its answers.

"Yeah. I mean, maybe if things had carried on and if this hadn't –" I pressed my lips together to stop the spilling words. "But it was all lies. What does it matter how I feel when none of it was real in the first place?"

"She came to see me after the two of you had spoken."

"I know." I tried to sound like I didn't care. "What did she say?"

"That I of all people should know there's always more to a situation than the cold, hard facts." Fidorous thought. "Although she used different words to say it."

A small smile. "That sounds about right."

I wanted to know more but I didn't want to *ask* more. The words hovered in my throat and then the time for asking had gone.

There was an awkward silence.

"I should have stopped you leaving," Fidorous said. "I mean Eric Sanderson One."

"I don't think you could have changed anything."

"I let my feelings get in the way and as a result I didn't do all I could to save the situation. I'll admit to you now; I've regretted it ever since."

I found myself feeling restless.

"She lied to me," I said. It felt petty as I said it and I kicked against the feeling, the embarrassment making me angry. "It's all just been lies. How can I trust her now even if I wanted to?"

"Why are you asking me?"

"Because there's no one else to ask."

"Then maybe you should stop asking and start thinking for yourself."

"–"

"Time is always running out." Fidorous pulled off his glasses and rubbed them against his sleeve. "Life's much too uncertain to leave important things unsaid."

He looked around himself and, seeing a cushion against the far wall, motioned for me to bring it over and sit. I did, putting the carrier bag down and crossing my legs next to him.

"We all have a lot of work to do tonight, but I think it's important that before tomorrow, you understand what you were, what you are."

I looked across at him, the candles reflected themselves in his glasses.

"When you – when Eric Sanderson One came to me he was damaged and heartbroken and obsessed. I should have turned him away but I was damaged and obsessed too and I thought, if I can just live long enough to pass on the lessons. I should never have given you such dangerous knowledge but I was running out of time, there was no one else to teach and no one else to do the teaching. I was the last of my school, Eric Sanderson Two."

I thought about all the survival tactics and tricks the First Eric had sent to me in his letters. He told me he'd learned them all from Fidorous, but now I realised I'd never given any thought to where the doctor himself might have learned them. Of course, of course there was too much here to be the work of one old man.

"For a very long time," Fidorous said, "there existed a very *discreet* society, a school of logologists, linguists and calligraphers. When I joined them, they were called Group27, but before that they were The Bureau of Language and Typography. The name has changed many times through the years but originally they were known by the Japanese name Shotai-Mu." He stopped, thinking. "You should know you're part of a very long story, Eric Sanderson the Second, the final part. What happened to you happened because I convinced myself I could pass on the knowledge you were looking for *and* turn you away from your obsession. Of course, I couldn't." The doctor sighed. "Endings and beginnings," he said quietly. "The ending to the story of the Shotai-Mu is here in this room; the old man in his pile of words and the apprentice who lost his mind. But our beginning, the beginning of all this is a much bolder and brighter place."

In the room with the flickering candles, Dr Trey Fidorous told me this story.

ONE

History tells us that it was the monk, Eisai who introduced Zen to Japan, but before that time there were a number of other enlightened Japanese who had travelled to China and studied Zen under the old Chinese masters. Tekisui did not travel to China to learn Zen. He was a keen student of art and history, and went to China for those reasons. It is said he spent many years studying the Chinese calligraphy of very ancient times before becoming a pupil of Hui-Yuan, who was one of the greatest Zen teachers of the era. Tekisui studied under Hui-Yuan for fourteen years before returning to Japan.

When he returned, Tekisui lived in a deep and wild valley where he would spend all his days meditating. When people sought him out and asked him to pass on the teachings he had received, Tekisui would say very little or nothing at all to them before moving to a deeper, even more inaccessible part of the valley where he would be found less easily.

This was in a time when the great temples had lost much of their influence and Japan was under the military rule of the Bushi, great warrior families who in later times would come to be known as the Samurai. Tekisui's valley was part of the territory belonging to a powerful Bushi warrior named Isamu. Isamu's family had fought against the Bushi of the temples and against Japan's noble families to help establish country-wide military rule under Minamoto no Michichika. Isamu was known and respected across the whole of Japan. When Isamu heard about the monk who lived in his valley, he sent an invitation to Tekisui asking him to come to see Isamu. Isamu had three sons – there was Kenshin, who was the oldest, Nibori who was the second oldest and Susumu, who was the youngest. Each son was well known across Japan as a hero and great warrior in his own right. All three sons returned to their father's house the night of Tekisui's visit to hear what the monk might say.

When the time came, Tekisui arrived as invited and stood before Isamu and his family. He took a writing brush from his robe and drew a single straight line in the air. This was the beginning and end of Tekisui's teaching. It is said by some that Isamu was instantly enlightened in that moment, but this story is not true. Isamu was not enlightened, but he was wise and did not give his opinion too quickly on any matter. Isamu's sons were furious however because they believed Tekisui had made a joke at their father's expense. Susumu said he would punish the monk for his lack of respect and drew his sword. Susumu was a well-known swordsman and had fought many duels but Tekisui remained in place, holding his paintbrush. Susumu attacked but Tekisui used his paintbrush and defeated him in three moves.

Nibori, the second oldest son, drew his sword and said, 'My brother is a great warrior, but you should know I am even more proficient.'

When he heard this, Tekisui said, 'Then I must prepare accordingly' and he plucked a single hair from his paintbrush. He placed the brush on the ground and held the single hair up in front of himself. Nibori attacked and Tekisui defeated him with his single hair in two moves.

It was then that Kenshin, the oldest son, drew his sword. Kenshin said, 'I must tell you that I have never lost a duel. Except for my father, I am the greatest swordsman in this region.'

Tekisui replied, 'Very well. I will prepare as you have suggested' and he placed the single hair on the ground next to the paintbrush and held up nothing in front of him.

Kenshin attacked and Tekisui defeated him with nothing in one move.

After this had happened, Isamu said that he was amazed by Tekisui's skill.

Tekisui said, 'What you have seen is the idea of skill, or un-skill. It is everything and nothing, a picture, a lantern, a grain of sand from a distant seashore.'

Kenshin, Nibori and Susumu apologised for their ignorance, and Kenshin asked if all three brothers could return with Tekisui to his valley as his students. Tekisui agreed and in this way, the school of Shotai-Mu was begun.

TWO

Many years passed and Isamu became an old man. In all this time he did not receive a visit from his sons. Isamu was saddened by this, but was not angry because he had seen Tekisui's learning and was pleased that his sons were able to study with him. Isamu also knew that the Shotai-Mu valued silence and isolation highly, and that it was for this reason that Tekisui had not built a temple or library, but had instead sunk his new school deep into the earth at the bottom of his valley. Isamu decided it would be for the best to leave his sons to their studies.

One night a merchant caught in a thunderstorm came to Isamu's door. Isamu instructed that the man receive shelter for the night and to show his gratitude the merchant gave Isamu a rare calligraphy scroll as a gift. What neither the merchant nor Isamu realised was that one of the characters written on the scroll was bad. Not only this, but the scroll had become wet in the downpour and the water had woken the bad character up.

Over the many months that followed, the bad character sickened Isamu's mind, causing him to become confused and forgetful, and to behave in a way that made him a stranger even to his own household. Eventually, troubled Isamu passed completely into unconsciousness.

At this time a messenger was dispatched to Tekisui's valley to inform Isamu's sons of what had happened and to ask Tekisui and Shotai-Mu for help.

Three men arrived at Isamu's house at dawn on the next morning. These men were dressed as Bushi warriors but they were unlike any Bushi ever seen before. Their bronze armour was made from tens of thousands of intricately moulded symbols and characters, and appeared so thin and delicate that even a glancing hit would slice through it easily. It was also seen that instead of the two swords usually worn into battle, each warrior carried only one, a sword with a hilt but no blade. These warriors were Isamu's sons: Kenshin, Nibori and Susumu; but they went unrecognised because their long absence and many years of study had changed them greatly.

The three men entered Isamu's scrollroom and fought against the bad character. They eventually defeated it but Susumu was mortally wounded in the duel. Kenshin and Nibori were urgently recalled to Shotai-Mu later that day but Susumu did not have long to live and said he would spend his last hours in his father's house.

Isamu woke in the evening and his mind was restored. Instantly he recognised the dying warrior as his son. When Susumu opened his eyes and saw his father he asked that from then onwards all the written characters used in the region be sent to Shotai-Mu to ensure that they were not bad. Isamu quickly agreed to this and made the further promise that he would do all in his power to see that every written character in the whole of Japan would be seen by the Shotai-Mu. On hearing this, Susumu smiled and passed away.

The promise was one the old man would live to keep.

28

The Cube of Light

"There's something I want you to see." Fidorous did his headmaster walk down the corridor and I followed along behind. "When the First Eric Sanderson found me," he said, "I was wounded, running and in fear for my life. I'd been trying to blur my conceptual tracks with a smokescreen of codes and texts, running from city to city."

"The path Eric followed to find you?"

"Yes, but it wasn't working and I couldn't move fast enough. Eric helped me gather materials to build a trap." We came to a door in the book wall. "He saved my life. That's why he took it so badly when I wouldn't help him find a Ludovician."

"A trap to trap what? What were you running from?"

"I'm just about to show you." Fidorous swung the door open.

The space behind was cavernous, dark and indistinct, like an aeroplane hangar at night-time. I stared. Out across the floor stood a house-sized cube drawn entirely in flickering light.

"God," I said, staring. "It's beautiful."

Fidorous didn't answer.

As my eyes adjusted I saw the effect was made possible by a collection of tall wooden frames. Each of these supported one or more film projectors and each projector shone onto the side of a neighbouring projector. Together they described the cube.

"That's the trap?"

"Yes. Signifier filtration at the top," Fidorous said, gesturing towards the upper part of the cube, "and containment down here at the bottom. It's a cage. A fish tank."

Looking back, I began to find the impression of a great dark ball swarming at the tank's heart. Long fat coils of guilt, fear and defeat would bulge and loll from the churning mass then suck or slip back inside. Worst of all, the dark ball felt familiar, an unbearable sickness of weight and dread.

"What's inside there?"

"A Gloom."

I turned to look at the doctor.

"Luxophages, Vigophages and Aptiphages," he said. "Thousands of them. And the big ones at the heart are Panophageus, the shoal queens. A colony like this is called a Gloom."

A revulsion shudder. I thought about the Luxophage that had been inside me at the abandoned hospital, the sickness, the lack of direction and will. I thought about Mr Nobody and his employer.

"Where did it come from?" As I asked, I could already feel the answer forming in my head. I began to sense the beginnings of a vast circle.

"Mycroft Ward," Fidorous said.

I stared back at the tank. "Why?"

"Shotai-Mu tried to stop Ward's spread. We fought a war against him for almost twenty years. One day his agents broke our computer security. They had been breeding Glooms and they loaded dozens of them, millions of individual fish, into letters and words and then fed them into our language monitoring system." The old man looked dazed, empty. "I was the only Shotai-Mu to survive, and only then thanks to you."

"You came here."

"This department had been abandoned a long time ago and Ward's people didn't know anything about it. You see, I'd always thought that my priority must be the continuation of our work. I did what I could to keep myself hidden as I cared for and maintained the languages. But. But I'm old now and Ward has made himself rich and powerful. He has the resources to ensure that one day he'll perfect his standardising system and if that happens, instead of a thousand Wards there will be a hundred thousand, a million, a billion. He'll grow exponentially until there's nothing and no one else left. Just Ward, Ward, Ward in every house, in every town and every city, in every country in the world. Forever."

"Jesus," I said.

"And that," he said all matter-of-fact, "is the reason I'm helping you both tomorrow."

29

Orpheus and the QWERTY Code

It took about ten minutes to get back to the First Eric Sanderson's room, the doctor taking time to show me a small kitchen and bathroom along the way.

After all the corridors and junctions it was good to arrive back at Eric's door, good to know my things, my cat and a warm comfortable bed were on the other side.

"How long is it since you slept?"

"I don't know," I said. "I just feel sort of dazed."

"Hmmm. Well, I'm afraid there are two important tasks to be completed before the morning."

As he spoke, Fidorous lifted a very old paintbrush from his inside pocket. The wooden stem was worn dark and shiny with ancient ink and what looked like it could have been centuries of polishing grease from fingers and hands. The bristles were dark too but unclogged and perfectly shaped.

"Like Tekisui's," I said. "It's a calligraphy brush, isn't it?"

"Yes, it is, and you have to use it to write your story. As much of it as you can remember and in as much detail as possible."

"Write it where?"

"In the air." Fidorous made a gesture in empty space like someone signing their name with a sparkler. "By the morning, this brush must have written your entire story. Do you understand?"

His blue eyes were calm, clear and serious as he held out the brush.

"Yes," I said, surprising myself. I took hold of the ancient wooden stem carefully. "You said there were two things?"

"You also need to drink this," he produced a small glass from a jacket pocket. I took the glass from him and held it up to the light. It was full of thin paper strips, as if an A4 sheet had been shredded and then chopped again to make tiny oblongs. When I looked closely, I saw that each strip had the word WATER printed on it in black ink.

I turned back to the doctor. "Drink it?"

"Yes, you have to drink the *concept* of the water, to be able to taste it and be refreshed by it."

"How am I going to do that?"

"There are two types of people in the world, Eric. There are the people who understand instinctively that the story of The Flood and the story of The Tower of Babel are the same thing, and those who don't."

I was about to speak but –

"You must have drunk the water and written your story by tomorrow morning. I'll come back to collect you then." Without waiting for a reply, the doctor turned and headed off down the corridor. I thought about shouting after him but I delayed a few seconds, waited too long, and then he was gone.

·

Ian wasn't too pleased when I turned on the bedroom light. He had the expression big tomcats sometimes have when they've been poked awake for a family photograph.

"Sorry," I said, sitting on the edge of the bed.

Ian's ear went *flick*.

I picked up the glass and poked around inside it. The paper strips made a swishing hissing sound as my finger disturbed them. *Conviction*. I closed my eyes and tried to convince myself that the swishing was the hiss of water running through a long hollow pipe. When I'd got the thought fixed as firmly and intently as I could, I took my finger out of the glass and tipped it up against my mouth. The papers rolled up against my lips in an airy ball-chunk, a few dry tickly strands finding their way to my teeth and tongue. I opened my eyes, picked and spat them out one at a time, rolled the last one into slightly pulpy ball and flicked it away.

I stared into the glass for a while. The little white paper strips sat tangled together each one with the word WATER showing or half-showing, or not showing at all. I vaguely remembered something about a small vial of powder that turns into blood when enough devoted religious people stare at it. *The wine becomes the blood of Christ* came into my head from somewhere and I thought *Oh great.*

Conviction. Conviction. Conviction. I picked up the glass again and knocked it back, opening my mouth wide and fully expecting the taste and feel of water to come flooding in all cold and heavy. Instead, the paper tumbled down and my mouth became a hamster cage. I spat the strips out into the glass, some wet and sticky with mucus strings. At least one stuck to the roof of my mouth so far back it was almost in my throat. I poked my finger in, trying to peel it away with my nail, almost retching.

I put the glass down on the bedside table. The idea of water? If the seams between the physical and the conceptual were there, I couldn't find them let alone start unpicking, so instead I took up Fidorous's ancient paintbrush. *You have to write your story with this. As much of it as you can remember and in as much detail as possible.*

I stood up.

The paintbrush pointed out level and steady.

I began.

I was unconscious. I'd stopped breathing . . .

•

Holding your arm out in front of you for any length of time takes much more strength than you might expect.

I finally put the paintbrush down onto the bedside table and rubbed my face with my hands. The whole thing had taken – how many hours? Two, three? Hard to tell in a world of electric lighting but I'd done what the doctor asked, written out my story into the air. I felt sick. I hadn't eaten for a long, long time and although I wasn't especially hungry, I knew the sick feeling would only go away if I found myself some food. I started to need the toilet too and it occurred to me that whatever I might be going through, the mechanics of my body would only ever run silently in the background for so long. There was something reassuring in that, the repetition, the *anchor* of it. Shaking out my aching arm to stop it cramping, I headed for the bedroom door.

I flushed the toilet and washed my hands, thinking absently about a shower in the small yellowy cubicle in the corner of the room but also knowing I was too tired, too dead on my feet; the edges of my thoughts were already fluttering out of the reach of my sluggish shutting-down brain. I needed to eat and collapse; everything else would have to wait.

I left the bathroom and went around the book corridor corner to the kitchen door.

It was open, the blue of an electric striplight shining a stripe across the floor and up the book spines on the opposite wall. I heard the sounds of a kettle, a coffee spoon rattling in a mug. I leaned around the doorframe. *Scout*. Something – my nerves, my blood – jumped and froze at seeing her, a fountain turning to ice and static inside of me.

She saw me before I could pull my head back, her thumb coming up and wiping under her eyes as she turned away.

"I didn't hear you coming," she said.

"The corridors." I didn't know what to say. "The books on the walls dampen the sound down, I think."

She nodded, facing the kettle, waiting for it to boil.

We both stood there. Slow seconds ticking.

"How's it going?"

"Alright," she said. "I think I've got the laptop connection stabilised."

I nodded even though she couldn't see me. "That's good."

"You know what," she said, "can we just not do this?" She turned around and her eyes were glassy and drawn under in red where she'd been crying. "I'm tired and I'm trying to stay awake and concentrate and anyway, I don't need to *pretend* to give a shit about you anymore, do I? Remember? That's right, isn't it?"

"You're the one who lied." A childish thing to say. "How am I supposed to – "

"That's right, because you know everything, don't you? You know everything I'm thinking and feeling."

Something cold inside me said, "I know the facts."

"*I know the facts.*" She shoved her unmade coffee away. "Just fuck yourself, alright, Eric? Just go and fuck yourself," and she pushed past me, out of the room.

On my own, staring at the floor, standing in the doorway.

At some point, the bubbling kettle turned itself off with a loud click.

*Above the word tunnels, at the corridor edge of the
library's underground stacks, a great and streamlined
notion glides slowly to a stop. It tips and bobs slightly
in sluggish event-currents created by occasional librarians
and visiting scholars. The mouth of Occam's razors and
malice of forethought gapes and then closes. Slashed ellipsis
gills flush and flare. The Ludovician's eye is a void-black
zero, a drop of ink, a dark hole sunk deep into the world.
The thought-shark seems to be listening, or thinking.*

Somewhere down below, my eyes flicker in dream-sleep.

Nightmares.

I woke up with a jolt, panicking at the unfamiliar covers over me and the blur of a strange ceiling up above. And then I remembered where I was. *The First Eric Sanderson's bedroom.* My muscles relaxed. I tried to chase after the dream, get a look at it, but it was already gone, evaporated and forgotten like so many others.

What time was it? The light I'd left on glowed the exact same yellow as before and it could have been any-when, seconds or hours after I'd finally climbed into the bed. The days and the nights were meaningless here, replaced with switches and a steady electric forever.

I thought about the yellow Jeep, the rain, the air.

"You've missed something."

I shuffled up onto my elbows, peered down the line of the duvet to see someone sitting at the bottom of the bed. Fidorous.

I'd crawled under the covers still dressed so I swung myself slowly up into a sitting position.

"What?"

"In these books, you've overlooked something. It really is very clever."

I tried to shake focus myself. Fidorous was reading my Light Bulb Fragment books.

"Hey. You can't just walk in and go through my stuff."

"I didn't. You left it behind last night."

He was right. I'd forgotten the plastic bag, left it in the room with the table and the candles.

"It still doesn't mean you should be reading them."

The doctor's eyes settled on me. Always so clear and empty, there was no way to tell what might be brewing behind them. I felt the smallest twist of anxiety.

"So, you don't want to know what it is you've missed?"

Still foggy and drowsy, I lifted my hand, half wanting him to give me the books and half preparing to snatch them. The result was a *not quite anything* gesture which wasn't strong enough to get either thing done, especially as I really did want to know what he was talking about.

"This QWERTY code," the doctor said, ignoring me. "Your notes here, and here, and, yes, here, suggest it's random. I'm not sure it is."

I rubbed my fingers through my hair as if the extra static might help fire up my brain.

The QWERTY code was part of the encryption used on The Light Bulb Fragment text. In one big mouthful, it meant that a correctly decoded letter could always be found adjacent to the letter it had been encoded as on a standard QWERTY keyboard layout, like this:

Here, the encoded letter is an F, so the correctly decoded letter must be either E, R, T, D, G, C, V or B. As the First Eric Sanderson wrote, there didn't seem to be any pattern which might predict which of the eight possible letters would turn out to be the correct one and this made the decoding process very slow and painstaking.

"You mean you think there's a system?"

"Yes," Fidorous nodded. "But that's only the tip of the iceberg. Look." He took a pen from the inside of his jacket pocket and found a clean page in one of the notebooks. "The very first letter of the whole Light Bulb Fragment is the C from 'Clio's masked and snorkelled head', correct?"

"Yeah."

"But before you applied the QWERTY to decode it, your notes say this letter was originally a V – "

" – meaning the correct letter was one space to the left of the given letter, yes?"

"Yes."

"So we take our pen and we draw a horizontal arrow running from right to left, like this:"

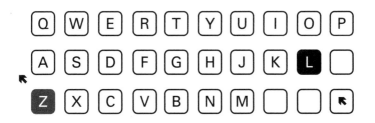

"Okay."

"The second letter you translated was the L in Clio, but originally this letter appeared as a Z. It gets a bit tricky here because of the way the letters roll around at the edges, but the connection works like this:"

"From Z to L is effectively a diagonal up and left move, so, going from where we finished the first arrow, we draw another, this one going diagonal up and left, like this:"

"With me so far?"

Groggy, I was straining to take any of this in. "Completely with you," I lied.

"Good. Almost there. The third letter you translated was the I. Originally, this appeared as a J. The I is diagonal up and right from the J, so our next line goes like this:"

"The fourth letter is the O. This was a K originally. This is one of the few letters we have a choice with. We can either draw another line going diagonal up right or, with the roll-around, we can decide to draw a line going diagonal down right. Let's choose down."

"Now the 'D' decodes into the 'S'. That's a horizontal left to right . . ."

"There. So what do you see?"

I looked at the page and the ground shifted inside my head.

"It's a letter. The letter e."

"I thought so too. The system isn't perfect – as you've seen there are a few lines which can go one of two ways – but with a little work it should be possible to understand how the letters have been formalised and recognise each of them as they appear."

"So wha –"

"Well, if I'm right, this QWERTY encryption doesn't just encode a single piece of writing, it meshes two together. What you're looking at is the first letter of a second text, smaller but quite distinct from the first."

"So there's more to The Light Bulb Fragment?"

"Yes. At least, there's certainly more of *something*."

I stared at the letter made from biro arrows.

"Unfortunately," Fidorous said, closing the Light Bulb books and handing them to me, "we can't give this any more time now."

"Doctor, if there's more text here, I need to know what it says."

"I'm afraid events are already catching up with us. Scout has stabilised a connection between the laptop and Mycroft Ward's online self. We have to get underway."

I tried to say *get underway where?* but I didn't get a chance.

"Now, how did you do last night, with the water and the brush?"

"I finished with the brush," I said, "but the paper in the glass is still just paper. There's – I didn't know how to make it happen."

"Hmmm. Where's the brush?"

I found it and passed it to Fidorous. He weighed it in his hand, thinking for a moment. "You're sure you wrote everything out with this?"

I nodded. "I was doing it for hours. I didn't get to sleep till – what time is it now?"

"Eight o'clock."

"I've had three hours' sleep."

"Well," the doctor tucked the brush away in an inside pocket. "That will have to do. Bring the glass with you. You'll just have to keep working on it at the *Orpheus*."

"The *Orpheus*?"

"Our boat," the doctor said, getting to his feet. "Use the bathroom and pack whatever you need to pack. I'll be back for you in fifteen minutes. Make sure you bring a coat and those Dictaphones too, we might well need them."

•

With my hair still wet from the shower and wearing combat pants, boots and a heavy, high-collared jacket from First Eric Sanderson's room, with the Light Bulb books and all my other finds in the rucksack on my back, with the glass of papers in one hand and a carrier bag full of Dictaphones in the other, I followed Fidorous through book-lined corridors.

"What about Ian?"

"Your cat already found his way down there. He's a curious sort of animal, isn't he?"

"You said you've got a boat in here?" Tired and overloaded, I was getting past the point of being surprised by anything.

"You'll see, not far now."

A few minutes later, our corridor ended in a staircase leading down to a door.

"This is the dry harbour," Fidorous said.

We stepped out into a supermarket-sized cellar with a flat concrete floor, a high ceiling and row after row of light bulbs hanging on long spiderwebbed cables.

Scout was there. She was working on something in the middle of the space.

Come on, I told myself. *This is it. This is how it all finishes, one way or the other. You just have to be strong for a little while longer.* I followed Fidorous out onto the floor.

Scout was wearing a heavy blue waterproof coat I hadn't seen before. It looked like she was making something, a big something, some sort of floor plan from planks and strips of wood, with boxes and tea chests and other odd bits and pieces carefully arranged inside. I recognised Nobody's laptop standing on an upturned plastic crate in the middle of the assemblage. A cable, presumably the all-important internet connection, unwound from its back and disappeared up into the ceiling. I spotted five other computers too, ancient 1980s models with thick cream plastic casings. One of these computers had been placed at each corner of the floor plan, like this:

X

X

X

X

X

Two things hit me about that layout. I didn't know which realisation rocked me harder.

"Those white computers," I said, "they're for creating a conceptual loop, aren't they?"

"Correct, an extremely powerful one using streaming data instead of recorded sound."

"And," I said, "they're arranged in the shape of a boat."

"Yes, they are." Fidorous swept out his arm in the direction of the assemblage. "Welcome to the *Orpheus*."

Scout glanced up from a nest of plugs and adaptors then turned away.

•

"Come over, come over," the doctor said, leading me towards the collection of things laid out on the floor. "Take a closer look."

I hesitated.

"There are gaps at this end," Scout said, straightening up. Hearing her speak made something alive jerk in my throat but she looked calm, unruffled, as if last night hadn't happened. "Doctor, do you reckon you're going to need more wood for the back?"

Fidorous must have been totally caught up in the idea of the assemblage because he seemed completely wrong-footed by the sudden thickness of the air. "Yes," he said, after a second. "Yes, I think more wood would be useful."

"Okay then, I'll see what I can find." And then she turned towards the door.

The doctor watched her until she'd left the room and then he looked at me but he decided not to say anything.

"What is it?" I said, walking towards the assemblage, trying to change the subject.

"It's a boat," Fidorous said, catching up with me. "A shark-hunting boat. *The* shark-hunting boat you might say. Come this way around, I'll show you."

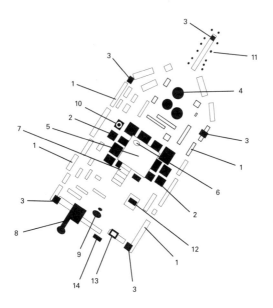

1. Planks. The outline of the *Orpheus* mainly described in flat planks of wood. More planks had also been placed inside this outline to fill empty spaces. The planks were a mixture of fresh wood and old floorboards, shelves, skirting boards, slats, windowsills, parts of door panels etc. Some planks were old and fossilised under layers of chipped white gloss paint, some holed and marked where bolts and fasteners had once been, some snapped and rough and splintery, and some new and smelling of sweet sappy sawdust. Pieces of hardboard, plywood and chipboard had been included, but basic wooden planking made up the majority of the floor plan.

2. Boxes. A large oblong central section of the floor plan had been built up to about waist height with a collection of boxes. These included cardboard boxes, tea chests, plastic packing crates etc. Most of the boxes appeared to be empty but there were several exceptions to this: a box which had once been the packaging for a small fridge was now loaded with cookbooks and a large tea chest had been plastered on the inside with pages from an interior design catalogue, while another contained greasy machine parts, cogs and a car battery.

3. Computers. Five blocky, 1980s computers positioned at the five corner points of the assemblage. Every computer had been connected to its two immediate neighbours with white phone cables and together these created a boat-shaped conceptual loop following the edges of the plank outline. Each computer also had a black power cable which led to the tea chest containing the car battery. All the computers were switched off.

4. Barrels. Three large, sealed, clear plastic barrels stood near the front of the assemblage. The barrels had been filled with Yellow Pages phone books and other telephone directories along with sticky wads of Post-it notes, address books and several Filofaxes. Each barrel also contained two or three black plastic devices which looked like small fax machines or modified telephones with little telescopic aerials. Fidorous said these were speed diallers. He went on to excitedly explain how the best of these machines was capable of dialling up to thirty phone numbers in a minute.

5. Cardboard flooring. A large sheet of cardboard laid out over some of the boxes creating a waist-high 'flying deck'. From the thickness of the cardboard and the arrangement of the boxes it looked unlikely that this deck would be able to support anyone's weight without collapsing.

6. Steering wheel. The steering wheel from a Volkswagen laid flat on the cardboard flooring.

7. Stepladders. A set of old wooden stepladders unopened and leant against the boxes as a completely impractical stairway up from the floor to the flying deck.

8. Strimmer. A green plastic garden strimmer laid against a box so the strimmer's head and strimming wire faced out and away from the rest of the assemblage. Fidorous called the strimmer 'Prop 1'.

9. Office chair. To the right of the strimmer arrangement, a slightly battered office swivel chair with blue padding. Like most office chairs, this one had wheels but these had been disabled with five or six bike chains, several padlocks and a steering wheel lock. A long garden cane lay across the seat.

10. Ian the cat. Asleep.

11. Coat hangers. Several dozen metal coat hangers arranged around the edges of the leading plank. The coat hangers had been connected together hook-to-corner or hook-to-hook to create a haphazard sort of chain.

12. Nobody's laptop. Nobody's laptop mounted on a plastic packing box. The laptop was on, the screen glowing blue and scrolling with heavy white source code. An internet cable ran from the back and away up into the rafters. A black power cable connected the laptop to the car battery in the tea chest.

13. Box of paper. A cardboard box positioned on the edge of the plank outline and filled with reams of blank A4 paper. A letterbox slit had been cut into the away-facing side of the box.

14. Desk fan. A big cream desk fan with a cage around the blades standing upright a few inches outside the plank outline. Fidorous referred to the desk fan as 'Prop 2'.

"I'm not going to say it," I said as we came full circle around the *Orpheus*, but then I said it anyway. "This isn't a boat, it's just stuff. I get the computer loop, but the rest of it – if the shark comes are we, what, going to climb up on those boxes and play Ahab or something?"

"Or something." Behind his Michael Caine glasses Fidorous's face hummed with what physicists call potential energy.

"But it's just –"

"Yes, I heard you the first time. You're quite correct. It's just stuff, just beautiful ordinary things. But the idea these things embody, the meaning we've assigned to them in putting them together like this, that's what's important."

I looked again at the assortment of wood and boxes and cardboard and wires. "This is another conviction thing, isn't it?"

Fidorous looked to be searching his brain for something. After a second he found it. "Have you heard of Matisse?"

I nodded.

"Good. Well, one day a man, a potential buyer, visited Matisse in his studio. This man spent a while looking at one of the artist's latest works before suddenly declaring 'That woman's arm is too long.' Do you know what Matisse said to him?"

I shook my head.

"He said, 'That is not a woman, sir. It's a painting.'"

Fidorous walked away to inspect the assemblage. I watched as he adjusted the desk fan's alignment slightly and tapped at its wire cage with a biro, listening carefully to the sound.

"So that's what you're doing?" I said. "You're building the woman?"

"Exactly, and succinctly put too. We're building the woman, not the painting." The doctor stood and brushed down his trousers. "All this *stuff*, it might help to think of it as a kind of focus tool, a way of ensuring the woman, when we've finished her, is one single woman and not like – like a 3D film with the glasses off. Do they still make those?"

"What?"

"3D films."

"Erm, yeah, I think so."

"Good, good. I liked them. Very useful. Anyway, you can store your things in here." Fidorous motioned for my backpack and when I took it to him he placed it inside one of the *Orpheus*'s tea chests.

I watched him tinkering with the arrangement, shuffling my bag around in the box until it looked right to him. It was as if Fidorous had gears, as if someone kept switching his brain settings from *angry hermit* to *vengeful scientist* to *thoughtful monk* to *excited kid on a climbing frame*. How many more Trey Fidorous's were still hidden away under all that hair? The thought worried me more than I wanted to admit. With the First Eric's training I'd become pretty good at figuring people out, but the fact was I couldn't get a grip on this man at all.

"Good, yes," Fidorous said, smiling up at me. "Now what's in that plastic bag?"

"My Dictaphones."

"Excellent. I think we'll have them – here." The plastic bag went into a smaller cardboard box. "And . . . yes." He patted down his pockets, removed the ancient paint brush he'd given me the night before and carefully placed it on the packing case next to Nobody's laptop. "I think that's good for now. Yes, it's good. Right. You stay here, I'm going to see if I can find where Scout's hiding herself, and we still have to find some sort of anchor."

"Okay, if you don't need me for any of this maybe I could do some work on the QWERTY code?"

"No." Stepping out of the assemblage, he pointed to the glass of paper strips still in my hand. "That's your priority. You have to drink that water if any of this is going to work. Understood?"

"Sure. Okay."

"Good." Once free, he started towards the exit. "Good. You get on with that and we'll deal with the boat."

I tugged the collar of my coat up. Now I was alone, the air felt cold, thoughtful and old. The empty room smelled vaguely of pulled up carpets and abandoned factories. It was quiet too, my footsteps making sharp thunk-clicks over yards of flat concrete flooring.

Except I wasn't really alone, was I?

"Well, I'm glad none of this is affecting your routine too much."

From the top of his cardboard box, one of Ian's ears swivelled around to listen to me while the rest of him pretended to be asleep.

"Why would you want to come down here anyway? It's cold and – un-Ian like."

The ear twitched a couple of times then drifted forwards again, casually letting me know this conversation wasn't going to happen.

"Fine," I said.

I put my hand over the top of the glass full of papers and shook it a couple of times, the way you shake a snow globe. The little oblong strips inside gave a muffled rustle on the bounce of each shake, but nothing else changed. I walked over to the wall and sat down against it, feeling the hard floor through my jeans. Out in the middle of all that grey space, the *Orpheus* sat quietly like the car boot sale collage it was. I could just make out Ian's furry ribs rising and falling gently, seemingly without a care in the world.

I blew out a sigh that no one was around to hear. In my still-tired brain, the events and developments of the past twenty-four hours, the twists and the turns, the hurts and the shocks, they all added up to a great and complex labyrinth that I didn't have the strength to puzzle out anymore. Instead, I resigned myself only to plodding forward. Sleepy and detached enough to be able to look down at events casually as if from the outside, I thought about coming out of the other side, about leaving the underground spaces, the papers and knotted sideways ideas behind. Drifting near the edge of sleep, I found myself thinking about Scout and the way we'd been for that short time together, the way her body smelled and felt against my skin, her sharp-edged laugh, her ruffled bob and the way our fingers had brushed, caught onto each other and then pulled our hands together as we'd made our way through flickery corridors. The memories stung and I pushed them back. If I did climb back up into the world after this, it would be alone, just me and Ian again. The thought washed through my body with a cold little swell. Maybe I could talk to her? Maybe I could say *of course I understand why you did it* and apologise for being so scared and stupid, and maybe everything could go back to how it was when we'd been – whatever it was that we'd been. But I was scared, scared of her laughing or even worse, her being kind and explaining how sorry she was, but that she'd only ever needed me for this. My sleepy mind acted out the scene while drifting towards strange territories. What if I told her about the other thing, the hidden thing, the nonsense thing? The thing that insisted that she was connected to Clio Aames. *Connected? Go on, say it.* The thing that insisted – *go on say it* – she was Clio Aames. There couldn't be anything more stupid to think or say and yet – and yet an unfamiliar part of me from deep deep inside said *it might be the only way to bring this fractured world back into alignment.*

I nodded, jumped awake, my hand twitching around the glass. Sleep had made a grab for me and I'd caught my fingernails on the edge of the conscious world at the last minute. I lifted the glass and took a good look at the strips of paper inside. No change.

"Right," I said to myself and to the glass, trying to kick-start my brain. I geared up for another shot at the concept of water.

•

The morning wore on. Scout and Fidorous returned to the *Orpheus* assemblage over and over again bringing more *stuff*. Occasionally the doctor would call over to me to ask how I was doing or tell me the function of objects they were including in the floor plan. A bundle of books tied with a thin chain became the anchor, a clothes prop extending from the side was the winching arm and a torch shining its beam straight up at the ceiling was the mast. They added other things too: more planks, car headlamps and real gas tanks and scuba gear. Fidorous brought Ian's carrier and included that in the assemblage along with everything else. Scout took off her heavy waterproof coat and worked in her vest top, tucking her hair behind her ears only to have it escape and get in her way every time she bent down. I watched her re-tuck and re-tuck it from behind my glass of papers, trying not to be seen. It felt like a volatile border had grown up between us and I could only risk quick glances across. The one time she caught me looking at her I froze. Scout had looked down quickly and then away, maybe having the same thoughts as me, maybe not.

I had no success with the glass. I stared into the little nest of tangled strips for hours trying to see something other than paper and print, but I couldn't see anything else because that's all there was.

Lunchtime came and I realised I hadn't eaten all day. My body was too tired to make a big song and dance about it but the problem registered as a slow ache with a green of sickness around the edges. I ignored it.

Scout and Fidorous wheeled in a pallet truck carrying two large black oblong blocks. It took me a moment to realise what they were: amplifiers. They arranged them at the far end of the cellar and began to hook them up to fixtures in the wall.

"Floodgates," Fidorous called over when he saw me watching. "Do you want to hear?"

I said that I did.

Scout stood back, glancing over at me once and then turning her attention back to the equipment. Somebody must have flipped a switch. The sound of speaking voices filled the room, low fluid and high tinkling voices, and voices in between, all talking into and around and through each other and merging into a flow of sound. All the voices were saying the same word over and over again – water water water water water water water water water water water water water.

306

·

Half an hour later and I was lying on my back, hands behind my head, glass at my side. I'd taken a single strand of paper and was chewing on it, trying to convince the idea of cool fresh liquid out of the warm pulpy mass between my teeth. I was thinking how it was a hopeless, impossible task, how I *did not know* how to extract the concept of water from words and, in front of Scout or not, I would have to say so to Fidorous.

With these thoughts rolling in on me, breaking, crashing and warping into strange shapes, I began to sink away from wakefulness and down into the deep quiet of sleep.

I blinked and sat up on my plastic sun lounger under the parasol. Rubbing my sleepy eyes, I enjoyed the way the warm dry air rolled into my mouth and nose, evaporating the moisture away. I put my book down, scanned the surf and then the deeper sea for Clio but couldn't see her. I turned to where her sun lounger would usually be but I was alone. Six or seven feet of empty sand away, a couple of blonde teenage girls giggled to each other in French. On the other side, an old man with a big belly, dark glasses and white curly plumage on his chest read one of those spy novels where the author's name is large and gold and takes up half the cover. But no Clio.

A finger of panic touched the back of my neck. I decided to go back to the campsite.

Our tent was gone. The hammock was gone. Her bags, my bags, everything. I looked around the other plots to see if she'd moved us while I'd been at the beach, but no. There was only the flattened sandy dirt and the holes left by our tent pegs.

"Hello."

A small boy in a huge Mr Tickle sun hat looked up at me, holding out a folded piece of paper. Behind him, a girl with inflatable pink armbands waited patiently. I thanked him and took the paper. Both children looked at me for a moment then ran away, the girl trailing behind and calling out something in German. I unfolded the note:

> Eric,
> What's the point of me coming all the way
> back there for you if you're just going to show
> up here without me? You div.
> Clio xx

Something changed. The physical me vanished.

The new disembodied me floated up into the dry dusty air, looking down at the trees, bamboo and coloured tents of the campsite for a moment before streaking off towards the beach. I rocketed over the campsite bar and over the *taverna* with the coloured lanterns, over the rows of white parasols and out across the bright blue water that quickly turned dark blue and serious as the ocean got deeper underneath me. I felt the heat of the sun, a cool breeze lifting up off the waves and then I lunged downwards, hitting the water with a wet slam and powering down through horizonless blue towards the deep deep black ...

I lurched upright with a gasp. I remembered it. I remembered the dream. Every detail pin-sharp, high resolution Technicolor clear. Before now my Light Bulb dreams had always evaporated into vague feelings as I came round to wakefulness, but now, for whatever reason, this one had fixed itself in my mind.

Before I could focus on it, why it might have happened, what it might mean, another sensation muscled its way in past the surprise and grabbed hold of my attention. The side of my leg was wet. I looked around, still a little dazed, still a little dream-shocked. I saw a glass tipped over and the spilled water soaking a patch of my jeans dark before making a long thin lake of itself on the concrete floor.

The side of my leg was wet.

Like an explosion played backwards, the last few hours rushed together into a single focused point. I took hold of the glass and stood up. The paper and the words were gone. Now there was water, just a half centimetre left in the bottom, but real physical water where the words had been. It had happened. Somehow, I'd done it.

Scout and Fidorous were straightening planks on the *Orpheus* floor plan.

"Doctor."

They both turned and I held up the glass, tipping the tiniest drop of the remaining water out so they could see what had happened.

Fidorous gave me a wave to come over but then – something pulled his attention away. He stood still, head tipped to one side, listening. Scout must have started to say something because the doctor brought a finger up to his lips in a silent *shhh*. Then I heard it too, a murmuring, a noise almost below the bottom end of human hearing but getting louder, rising up.

The doctor's face relaxed into a slack panic.

"Stop it," he shouted over to me, waving frantically. "You're going too far. You're going too far, you have to stop it."

"I'm not –" I held up the glass as if it might prove something "– I'm not doing anything."

The doctor turned to Scout, and I saw his mouth making the words: "Computers. Quickly."

She looked at him, at me, and then sprinted to the nearest of the five white PCs and started powering it up.

"Eric Sanderson Two," Fidorous called over, trying to keep his voice level. "You have to come over here. Come here right now."

The murmur grew into a noise, a growing rumble of voices winding, melting and flowing together from the twin amplifiers – water water water water water water – louder and louder and louder.

"Jesus," Scout risked a glance at the speakers and then over at me. "Jesus, Eric, *come on*."

My palm pressed over the top of the glass as I ran towards the *Orpheus*.

I didn't make it.

The fronts of the amplifiers blew off and ton after ton of high pressure water thundered out into the cellar.

FOUR

The word connects the visible trace with the invisible thing, the absent thing, the thing that is desired or feared, like a frail emergency bridge flung over an abyss.

Italo Calvino

30

Farewell and Adieu to You, Fair Spanish Ladies

I tumbled and rolled, pressed and pin-wheeled through promises thoughts stories plans whispers lusts lies tricks secrets longings surprises loves passions hurts melodies memories wishes worries doubts, down to up and inside to outside in a liquid forever of history, mind and churning, thundering concept.

Quickly or eventually – there was no way to know – the turbulence began to lessen, slowing, steadying, calming itself into a gentle rhythm. The water held me, wrapped me, nudged, shoved and buffeted me, all events and all ideas with their own rhythmic pull and push, bob and dip. I hung like an angel or a star, or an old forgotten moment in the endless blue of the world's mind. My lungs squealed. The sun cut dappling wedges down around me and I kicked for the light somewhere up above.

My head broke the surface and I dragged in a great creaking gasp of breath. Warm air filled my aching lungs and I bobbed up on the swell of a gentle wave. The world of ideas and meanings and concepts I'd experienced underwater unfocused now my head was clear of the blue; now this was *just* water, all cold, salty and deep. I sank and bobbed on another swell, heard the shriek and caw of seagulls, tasted and smelled the tang and slap of waves. The sun burned brilliant in an endless blue sky. In front of me, the ocean dipped and rolled for miles and miles and miles, to a distant blue-meets-blue horizon line. My waterlogged coat and boots were heavy, trying to drag me down. I thought about my legs kicking, exposed, hanging out over the black depths and cold horror squeezed at my stomach. A wave splashed, my open gasping mouth took in cold, salty, plantish water and I kicked and coughed and coughed.

A shout behind me, "Eric."

I swam myself around on the spot. A boat bobbed in the waves, a large-ish battered-looking fishing boat. Two figures stood on deck, one grey-haired and waving, the other smaller and standing back a little from the rail. Fidorous and Scout. I struggled against the heavy weight of my clothes, swimming as fast as I could towards them.

Taking one arm each, they pulled me in over the side and I fell on the warm wooden deck, panting and leaking water.

After a moment I rolled over onto my back, and found myself looking up at Scout.

The world became clear and specific then – my lungs pulling and heaving under my ribs, the drip and run, the cold and warm of my seawater puddle, the brilliant clear sky. Scout's hair falling forward at both sides so the points of her bob met over her chin, her pale face shaded between black curtains. Her eyebrows knotted down just a little, the shadow of concern. I nodded a tiny *I'm alright* and she gave me a tight-lipped smile and walked away, leaving my field of vision a bright, uninterrupted matt blue. I propped myself up onto my elbows.

"Well, that was hardly textbook, was it? But we're here." Fidorous was leaning against the deck railings, glasses in hand, his eyes closed and wrinkled elastic band face turned up towards the sun. "And what's more, it's a beautiful day."

"We're at sea."

"Yes, we are. In a manner of speaking."

The boat bobbed on the waves. The sun beat down. Still from somewhere, the sound of gulls.

"And this is the *Orpheus*."

"It is. The lady and not the painting. You missed it by about forty feet."

"It all feels," I pushed myself up into a sitting position, "it all feels like the most normal thing in the world. I mean – real, solid. Sort of familiar too."

316

"It should be familiar. If you were to say shark-hunting boat to almost anybody in the western world they'll visualise this exact same boat. This," he rubbed a hand against a very ordinary and very real railing, "is the current collective idea of what a shark-hunting boat should be."

Cold wet shivers still waterlogged my jeans, shoes and jacket but the sun was already doing its best to warm me at the edges. I felt the old battered deck under my fingers.

"A collective idea?"

"Yes," the doctor nodded, "and a commonly held one for more than twenty-five years. That's why she's so convincing."

He offered a hand and helped me to my feet, me trying to manage the sway of the boat and drip splatter of seawater still escaping from my clothes.

"Ah. Hello."

I turned to follow the doctor's eyes. Ian waddle-padded up to the edge of my personal puddle and sat down. The word *contempt* didn't really do justice to Ian's expression.

"I'm sorry," I said, knowing it just wouldn't wash.

"And how are you, Toto?" the doctor said, leaning in with a rare and too-big smile. "Is it warm enough for you today?"

Ian gave him the sort of look you might expect from an orbital laser defence platform.

"Yes, well." The doctor straightened up. "He's a jolly little fellow, isn't he?" His words came out fuzzy-edged with uncertainty and something about that made me feel a little easier with the old man, and with the craziness of things generally.

"Oh yeah," I said, looking down at the furious cat. "He's a card."

·

Fidorous showed me into the little cabin below the flying deck so I could find something dry to wear. The clothes in my rucksack had been worn past the point of wearing again. The doctor pointed out a small chest of drawers in the corner which had been stuffed to breaking with lost-and-found type clothing. He said these were the ideas of clothes left here by people who'd imagined or dreamt their way onboard in the past, but they all felt – and some smelled – like the real thing to me. I picked out some too-big shorts and a red Hawaiian shirt with silhouette palm trees. I also dug out a slightly crumbly straw fedora (the only hat I could find) and a pair of big black plastic Roy Orbison shades to defend against the sun. I felt like an idiot. When I came back out onto the deck, Fidorous nodded approvingly and said I looked *much more myself*. Not knowing what else to do, I just said *cheers*.

Gear-shifting into gruff captain, Fidorous insisted on taking me on a tour of the rest of the *Orpheus*. As we made our way around the stern, I saw how the strimmer and the desk fan had become twin propellers; the box full of paper was now a blocky laserprinter secured to hang over the backboard of the boat, and the office chair had reinvented itself as a bolted-to-the-deck fisherman's seat with rod and line ready to cast off. The boat now had a real mast, a real winching arm, a real anchor. As we went on I spotted occasional ghost marks of the *Orpheus*'s earlier incarnation: a cluster of knots and stains on the deck still vaguely resembled the brass numbers that had once been part of a front door; weather marks on the cabin walls occasionally resolved themselves into fragments of the text I'd originally seen printed on cardboard boxes as part of the assemblage – but ultimately these were only surface effects. In every way that mattered, the *Orpheus* had become a real, solid, functional fishing boat.

Coming around the cabin and onto the front deck, we arrived at the three barrels filled with telephone directories and electronic speed diallers. They seemed completely unchanged from their original forms but Fidorous only got annoyed when I mentioned it.

"Well, of course they are. What did you expect, a chest of drawers and a hat stand?"

I decided not to ask any more questions.

The boat's controls were up on the flying deck which doubled as the roof of the cabin. Scout was up there, lying out on a towel in sunglasses and shorts, with her vest top tucked up under her bra. She propped up when we came up the steps, then pulled her glasses slowly down her nose to look at me in my Hawaiian shirt and hat.

"Hello," I said, doing a geeky wave before I could stop myself. I felt so stupidly self-conscious in these stupid, stupid clothes and seeing her there like that, the whole routine just slipped out. *What a fucking idiot.*

Scout did an almost-smirk and sat up cross-legged.

"Dry clothes," I said, pulling at the shirt.

"Oh," she nodded.

"And how is she looking up here, helmsman?" Fidorous came up the steps behind me.

"Boatlike," Scout said, knocking her knuckles on the deck. "This is so crazy I'm not even going to ask."

"Probably for the best," the doctor said. "It's easier if you just accept it."

"*Easier if you just accept it*, thanks. So, anyway, I just push down that handle there and steer left and right?"

"Yes, but it's port and starboard."

"Left, right, port, starboard. Fine, I've got it."

"Scout," Fidorous said, "this is a serious business."

"Don't worry," she flicked a cool, empty glance at me. "I know it is."

•

We came full circle around the boat and arrived at Nobody's laptop. Like the barrels it was almost completely unchanged: slim, expensive, black and sitting on an upturned box just as it had been in Fidorous's cellar. The only difference – the internet cable which once ran from the laptop's back and up into the ceiling was gone, in its place there was a chrome telescopic aerial. Now we had wireless internet connection. I passed my palm over the top of the aerial a few times but didn't meet any resistance.

"Didn't you hear me tell Scout," Fidorous said, checking the screen, "to try not to think about it?"

I turned away and looked out over the waves, the clear deep blue, the gentle rise and drop. The sun was so hot it gave everything – the sea, my skin, the warm pale decking under my feet – its own sort of *holiday* smell. That heat smell you forget ever existed in the cold and the rain and the dark grey evenings, but a smell that comes back to you like a dream, like waking up, when the sun is high in the sky. I stared towards the horizon, wondering if this sea went on forever. Were there shallows, oceanic trenches, cold places with icebergs, coral reefs swarming with different fish and other conceptual animals? I wondered if wars, life-changing inventions or assassinations created storms here. Did the sea ever heave? Did it become still as a pond in white, bleak midwinter?

"Eric," the doctor said, "I have something for you."

I turned round to see him handling a long wooden spear, balancing it up above his shoulder, weighing it back and forth experimentally like a javelin thrower warming up. I took a step away without meaning to.

"What's that?"

Fidorous's eyebrows pushed up, bunching wrinkles into his forehead. "You don't recognise it?"

The spear was about five feet long and tipped at one end with a steel teardrop-shaped head. The other end connected to a length of cable wound in coils on the deck and eventually plugged into the back of Nobody's laptop. The shaft looked old, the wood varnished to an ancient smooth black. Something clicked.

"It's the paintbrush."

"Correct. Now listen carefully because this will be your job, Eric Sanderson. When we get alongside the Ludovician you have to spear him with this. Then the shark will be connected through this spear and through this cable to Nobody's laptop, and the laptop is connected via the aerial to Ward."

"Matter and antimatter," I said. "Bang."

"Exactly. Bang. And we can all go home."

"Except it's not going to be quite like that, is it? Not if we have to get close to the shark."

"Well, there's always risk, but what you have to remember is this whole boat is made from a single powerful non-divergent conceptual loop. Whatever happens, the shark can't touch us as long as we stay onboard. We have to find him, and we have to wear him down, exhaust him. There are tools onboard for that. Once we've taken the fight out of him, you can use the spear."

The way the doctor described it, it sounded more like a job to be done, hunting down an animal that didn't really stand a chance. I don't know what my face was doing, but it must have given me away.

"You're quite right," Fidorous said, as if I'd been thinking out loud. "The Ludovician *is* very dangerous but remember we have all the advantages here. I know we can deal with it safely."

I thought about that.

"I don't care how it dies," I said in the end.

The doctor nodded, quietly considering. He handed me the spear and I weighed it the same way he had. It felt solid, well balanced.

"You'll need to hit him in the head, near the brain or near the mouth."

"In the head," I repeated, "the brain or the mouth."

"Good." Fidorous looked out to sea, shading his eyes. "Now let's see if we can get his attention. Bring that."

I followed the doctor to the laserprinter bolted in place over the stern. He turned the machine on and it came to life with a *cluuunk whiiirr* and flashing green and amber lights. After checking the paper tray, Fidorous unwound a grey cable from the printer's back. He motioned for me to bring the spear closer and when I did he touched the lead quickly against its metal head. Immediately, the printer began to print, clunk clunk whiiirrring away, dropping sheets over the stern and into the water. Fidorous reached over the backboard and caught the third page as it fell, passing it back to me. It was my story, the words I'd written in the air with the paintbrush the night before.

"Chumming the water," the doctor said, pleased with himself. "With a little bit of luck, the Ludovician will find this trail and follow it straight to us."

I looked over the page again then dropped it into the water with the others.

"Slow ahead if you please, Mr Scout!" the doctor called out.

Scout looked down at us from the flying deck. "Did you just say Mister?"

"Slow ahead *if you please.*"

"Aye, aye," she said. I couldn't help smiling. Deep down inside, I started to feel there was a chance we could actually do this.

The engine grumbled and a cloud of blue-grey smoke plumed up from an exhaust somewhere. The *Orpheus* rumbled forward into the waves.

·

Ian lay in the shade of the cabin, stretched-out and sleeping. If he hated everything else, at least he approved of the weather. Fidorous sat in his bolted-down fisherman's chair at the boat's stern, industrial-strength rod and line trailing out behind us as we chugged forwards. He'd found a green Park Rangers cap from somewhere and had it pulled down over his eyes, pretending to sleep. My wet clothes bobbed at the end of his line as bait, a bundled ball of almost-me with a big heavy hook hanging ready below. My old coat waved, swayed and rolled in the clear blue water and I felt bad for sacrificing it after everything we'd been through together.

I sat cross-legged on the deck next to the printer, watching it chug and whine and mechanically cough up pages from my story – the bedroom floor, Dr Randle, the First Eric Sanderson, my journey, the Willows Hotel, Clio Aames, Mr Nobody, the yellow Jeep, un-space, Mark Richardson, the red filing cabinet, the Yellow Pages dome, Fidorous and the samurai and the glass of words, Scout, lots about Scout – bright paper pages flutter-falling over the stern and down into the ocean. As the *Orpheus* grumbled forward, the waterlogging pages rolled and curved in the swell as we left them behind. They clung to the underside of the ocean's surface, floating and dipping, bright in the sun. The trail of pages stretched away from us, a swaying path of white into the distance. I watched the water for any other movement, but there was nothing else at all.

We'd been going like this for about four hours.

Scout came down from the flying bridge to check on Nobody's laptop. She'd done this twice already.

"We don't have forever with this, you know."

"It takes as long as it takes," Fidorous said from under his cap.

"But if Ward notices this connection we'll be locked out for good."

Fidorous didn't answer.

Scout turned away, scraped her fingers through her hair and turned back. "Doctor."

"What do you want me to do about it?"

Scout stared at him. "I don't know. More paper? Go faster? You're the expert, you tell me."

Fidorous knocked up the peak of his cap with a thumb and turned around in his chair. "If we put more chum in the water, the tide will take it and in a few hours it'll cover half the sea. If we go faster we risk breaking the trail. You're just going to have to be patient, Dorothy." He turned back and pulled down the cap.

The air took a breath just like it does before a lightning strike.

"Patient? What the fuck happened to *this is a serious business, Scout?* We've only got one shot at this and time isn't on our side."

The doctor ignored her.

"How long do you think we have?" I asked.

Scout went from staring at Fidorous to staring at me. My words didn't register at first and when they did I could see her struggling through her anger to decide whether she should answer.

"I don't know," she said in the end. "Ward could shut us out at any second and then, it's over. Every minute we waste *sunbathing* puts the odds against us."

"Doctor," I said.

"We're doing what we're doing."

Scout gave an exasperated sigh and turned away, heading back up to the flying deck.

Far back along the stretching, spreading trail of paper and ink, a single white page curls and hangs several feet under the surface of the ocean.

blocking out memories which are too painful or difficult for the mind to deal with. A circuit "breaker for the brain, you could say."

"But I don't feel like I've forgotten anything," I said, fumbling around again inside of my head. "It's just, there's something there. I mean, I don't think I feel anything about that girl. I don't even –" I put my palms out in a gesture of emptiness.

The slipstream under-pull of something huge and fast suddenly drags the page down, twisting and corkscrewing it into a pulpy knot of fragments which spin and swirl, caught and carried along in the wake of the dark, powerful shape before losing momentum, unravelling, coming apart. As the water settles, the remains of the page begin their slow and final spiral down into the deep black.

I blinked, squinted out at the waves, the trail of white paper disappearing into the distance, the seagulls, the empty ocean. Had I been asleep? I couldn't tell.

Onboard the *Orpheus* time passed slowly, the minutes rolling and bobbing to hours as the sun made its slow way through the sky.

Ian and the doctor snoozed, Scout kept herself to herself up on the flying deck and I kept myself awake by picking splinters from the old wooden floor, listening to the *chunk whiiirr* of the printer and scanning the swells and dips of the ocean for any shadow, any movement. I looked and looked until my eyes lost all sense of perspective. The sun shone down hot. My skin smelled tangy and the deck smelled of last summer's seaweed and salt.

Eventually, the doctor left his fishing seat. He came back with some badly made sandwiches, beers and pieces of meat for Ian. Scout came down to eat and I thought there might be another explosion, but she took her plate and can without speaking and sat next to the cat in the shade of the cabin's back wall. All my missed meals caught up with me at once and I bolted down the sandwich in quick and hungry gulps. Fidorous took his plate and beer back to his fishing chair. I watched him eating slowly and thoughtfully, his eyes drifting between the distant seagulls dive-bombing the paper trail, and the fishing line bobbing just beyond the gentle churn of our engines.

"I didn't realise how hungry I was." Hours had passed without anyone saying anything and I needed to talk.

The doctor nodded vaguely, staring out to sea.

The sun sat lower now, absently going about its gentle sink from bright white towards deep red.

"But that wasn't real food, was it?" I tried again to bump a conversation to life. "Just the idea of food. But what I'm wondering is, if the idea of food tastes like food and feels like food when you eat it, where does that put us?"

Without taking his eyes off the sea, Fidorous brought a hand up in a slow *quiet* signal towards me.

"What?" I whispered, stretching my neck. I stood up carefully and looked out over the stern but I only saw white wet pages rolling in the swell. "What's wrong?"

The doctor's fishing reel burst to life with a high-speed ticking, fast unwinding as the line snapped taut and raced away like a cheese cutter through the waves.

"*Whoa!*" Fidorous put his feet against the backboard and pulled back hard, the heavy-duty rod bending under the strain like a toy bow.

"The Ludovician?" I found myself stepping back "You've caught the Ludovician with a *fishing rod*?"

The doctor fought against the pull from under the waves, hauling and straining the hidden something in with a few hard-fought reel clicks at a time. The line sliced left then right, the whole thing a complicated dance of tension and manoeuvring.

"I don't think so."

I turned to see Scout behind me.

"Scout," the doctor hissed through clamped teeth, "what the hell are you doing? Get up there and cut the engines or we'll lose him."

"That's not the shark. I've seen it and an animal as big as that wouldn't just –"

"Scout, do as you're told and *cut the damn engines.*"

She turned on her heel and stalked across the deck.

I looked to Fidorous. "What can I do?"

"Wet down the reel. That bucket there, tip some water on the line or it's going to overheat." He heaved and the rod tip dragged forwards, the line slicing angles into the sea. I grabbed the bucket and doused the cable and the reel. "That's it," the doctor strained to speak as he fought against the rod. "We'll wear him out and get him to the surface. Spear. Where's your spear?"

I'd left it next to Nobody's laptop.

"I'll get it." I crossed the deck as the engine stopped. Scout came down the steps and past me, calling out to the doctor as she headed for the stern.

"*Honestly*, it's not our shark. It's going to be a big something else, some sort of – what are they called – some sort of Remora. You're not –"

I'd almost made it back with the spear as she stopped talking.

"What's going on?" I jogged up to see Fidorous's fishing rod stretched straight and still over the back of the boat, the line hanging loose in the water. "Has it got away?"

Scout looked at me and rolled her eyes.

"This isn't right." We both turned to the doctor.

The line hung loose in the water, not giving anything away.

Scout folded her arms and Fidorous turned the reel handle an experimental couple of clicks. This time there was no resistance from under the waves. The doctor wound the reel faster until the severed end of the fishing line came dripping up into the air. He uncoupled the rod from its fastenings and pulled the whole thing in.

"Look – high-grade heavy duty cable and it's sliced right through. *Some sort of Remora*?"

Scout took the line and inspected it.

"Well, I've been known to be wrong," she said, "from time to time."

"So that was it?" I asked. "The Ludovician?"

Fidorous untangled himself from the fishing chair and stood up, stretching out his arms and shoulders. "I'd say so, wouldn't you?"

I laid the spear carefully on deck and covered the couple of feet to the back edge of the boat. With one hand placed securely on the laserprinter for balance, I leaned out over the stern and looked down – just the blue of the ocean and two white, waterlogged paper pages.

"So where is it now?" I said, still looking down. "Is it still here?"

"I don't know," Fidorous said. "Maybe."

"Maybe?"

"Probably. Eric, I'm going to need another line and fresh bait. I want you to –"

Thud. The entire deck lurched with momentum and I was thrown forwards, smashing my knees into the back of the printer. A shock of hard cracking pain and my weight breaking the machine free of its fastenings, sending me and it tumbling out and down over the side. Me in the air, upside down, falling head first. The ocean rushing up and hitting the back of my neck with a hard splash and then –

The surface receding in hiss and bubbles below my feet.

"Paul," it
The girl who
worked at the des
opposite me had two
earbuds. She said: "W

red I n   of the oth
have   cause the w

341

"Paul."

The girl who
worked at the desk
opposite me had two h
eartbeats. She said. 'Wh

-gra
h
eca
a   do
c
lied i n
have   ors   e   a co   of the oth
cause the w
it

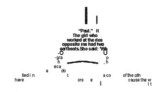

"Paul." it
The girl who
worked at the dies
opposite me had two
eartbeats. She said: Y

-gra
h
eca
do
a
c
ors e
l
a co
of the oth
cause the w
l t

lied in
have

"Paul." it
The girl who
worked at the des
opposite me had two
eartbeats. She said: "Wh

-gra
h
eca
do

a

have   lled I n   c   ors   e   a co   of the oth
                                                                                       cause the w
                                                                                           i t

"Paul."

The girl who worked at the des opposite me had two eartbeats. She said: "W

"Paul."
The girl who
worked at the de
opposite me had two
eartbeats. She said: "Wh

"Paul."
The girl who
worked at the des
opposite me had two
eartbeats. She said: W

"Paul."
The girl who
worked at the des
opposite me had two
earbeats. She said: "Wh   its
                                         see
                                         me
-O   U   re
-gra   p   not
h   , h   lost
eca   edg
                                         mis

            a   do
   ed In
li   c   ors   e   a co   of e
                                               th
a   I ak   oth
he   i   l

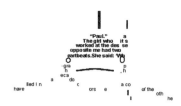

"Paul."
The girl who it s
worked at the des se
opposite me had two
eartbeats. She said: W

I feel like
I've forgotten
Something import
Tant Everyone gets th
At don't worry about it y
C
-sh
h
eca
do

have   lled I n   a   c
are   o   a co   of the o
i   cause   t

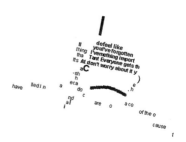

have   lled I n   a   eca   do   c   are   o   a co   of the o

cause   t

363

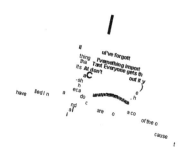

have   lled I n   a

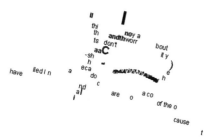

II   I

thi   noy a
th   andthworr
ts   don't   bout
aaC   it y
-sh   )
h   e
have   lled I n   a   eca   h
                        do   c
                  nd
                i al
                      are   o   a co
                                  of the o
                                          cause
                                                  t

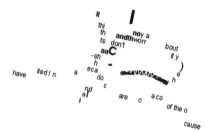

II

thi
th
ts   don't   and th worr   noy a

aa C   -sh

have   lled I n   a   h   bout
eca   it y
do c
nd   c

a I   are   o   a co   h
i   of the o

cause

Fingers clamped my wrist and forearm and dragged me up back towards the surface with a

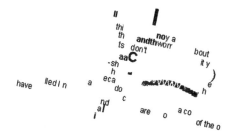

Fingers clamped my wrist and forearm and dragged me back up towards the surface with a

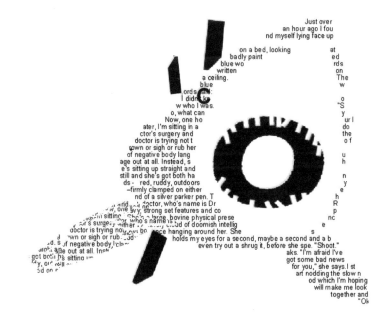

Just over
an hour ago I fou
nd myself lying face up

on a bed, looking   at
badly paint   ed
blue wo   rds
written   on
a ceiling.   The
blue   w
ords and   o
I didn..ke   "S
w who I was.   y
o, what can   ur l
Now, one ho   do
ater, I'm sitting in a   the
ctor's surgery and   o f
doctor is trying not t
own or sigh or rub her   u
of negative body lang   h
age out at all. Instead, s
e's sitting up straight and   n
still and she's got both ha   y
ds - red, ruddy, outdoors   e
—firmly clamped on either
nd of a silver parker pen. T h
..and... doctor, who's name is Dr   R
..w, one ivy, strong set features and co   p
...n sitting. She's a large bovine physical prese   nc
...r's surgery...her... ...uid of doomish intellig
doctor is trying no...en ho nce hanging around her. She   s
...wn or sigh or rub...dd...
...d. s of negative body...cla   holds my eyes for a second, maybe a second and a b
...she out at all. Ins...   even try out a shrug it, before she spe. "Shoot."
got both hs sitting...   aks. "I'm afraid I've
..y, o... ...ill...   got some bad news
...d on...   for you," she says. I st
                                    art nodding the slow n
                                    od which I'm hoping
                                    will make me look
                                    together and
                                    "Ok

Fingers clamped my wrist and forearm and dragged me back up towards the surface with a

Fingers clamped my wrist and forearm and dragged me back up towards the surface with a

Fingers clamped my wrist and forearm and dragged me back up towards the surface with a

Fingers clamped my wrist and forearm and dragged me back up towards the surface with a

Fingers clamped my wrist and forearm and dragged me back up towards the surface with a

Fingers clamped my wrist and forearm and dragged me back up towards the surface with a

tug-of-war heave, me hauled kicking and scraping my back and ribs and hips over the stern's backboard and collapsing to the decking like a half-drowned animal with a thump and splatter of water. Electricity sparking out-of-control panic in every synapse in my brain and my body shaking humming thumping with fear and Scout still clutching me and shouting *you fucking moron stop falling in the fucking water* and her arms around me and me wrapping my arms around her and clutching for dear life and her still saying *you fucking moron, you fucking moron* into my ear and my hand on the back of her head holding her against me and saying *Jesus* and *sorry, God, I'm so sorry* over and over and me kissing the side of her neck like I'll never see it again and her kissing me on my face and then us kissing each other properly and then Fidorous shouting *Scout Scout* –

"– Scout, come on, he's going round to the front."

She lifted away from me, pushing the hair out of her face and climbing up to her feet. "Are you okay?"

"I think so. Go on, I'll catch up."

Scout jogged off in the direction of the doctor's voice and I struggled upright. I felt a sharp jab of pain in my left knee and I hissed as I tried to put my weight on it. I saw Scout disappearing around the side of the cabin and heard Fidorous saying, "He went for the boat, attacked it. He came straight at us."

I limped, dripping, around the cabin and onto the front deck. Fidorous stood at the end of the railed gang plank which extended out over the water from the prow. He was holding something, a strange sort of gun.

"Eric Sanderson," he called on seeing me. "Come on. He's up and he's a monster."

"I know," I managed, shock-shaking and weak. "I know he is."

"Come over, come over. We've got him now. Scout, how are you doing?"

"Almost there."

I looked around the deck but I couldn't see her.

"He's coming around," the doctor called back to me and to the wherever-she-was Scout, pointing with his gun contraption. "He's coming around."

I looked out in the direction the doctor pointed and I saw it, *I saw it* – a high, hard triangular fin cutting through the blue, making a slow turn towards the *Orpheus*. A long, dark shadow under the waves.

The fin rose higher in the water, rolling out a long V of white foam as the shark picked up speed towards us.

My heart pumped sour milk and liquid nitrogen.

"It's solid," I said. "It's real. It's a real shark."

"No, it just looks like it. He's just like everything else here. Scout, come on, he's coming. My God, look at the size of him."

Huge and sleek and dappled grey, the Ludovician seemed to glide, weightless, in the clear sunny water just below its own tumbling bow wave. My legs backed me up against the cabin wall.

"Shit, Jesus, he's going to ram us again."

"No, no," Fidorous raised the gun up to his eye. "He's circling around and he's going to give us the perfect – Scout?"

"Clear. Go."

Something between a bang and an air pressure *thwap* erupted from Fidorous's shoulder. A black bolt trailing cable striped across the waves and punctured the shark just behind the dorsal fin as the doctor bounced back from the recoil. Harpoon. A noise up close to my left made me jump and turn in surprise. One of the barrels of phone books and speed diallers leapt, threw itself across the deck, tumbled overboard and raced skidding across the ocean after the retreating Ludovician.

"Got him!" Fidorous whipped his cap off and threw it across the deck. "Did you see that? I got a barrel on your shark." Flushed and adrenaline-pumped, the old man waved the harpoon gun up to me like proof. "Tekisui and Susumu. It's like in the old stories, Eric, just like in the old stories."

I watched the clear barrel bounce, hop and spray fast and away through the waves, then let myself sink slowly and painfully down the wooden slats on the cabin's side.

31

Feelings or Whatever

The barrel chased the shadow of the shark and we chased the barrel, Scout at the wheel with the boat full ahead, thump-rising every wave and heaving out black smoke like an escaped Victorian factory. Fidorous, still out at the end of the *Orpheus*'s prow plank activated a remote control. Collapsed and soaking on the deck I could just hear the beep sequences of dialled phone numbers and an electronic ringing tone – *burr burr, burr burr* – over the angry growl of the engine and the smack-eyed spray of the waves.

"It works," the doctor shouted, waving as the wind and bounce buffeted his wild hair. He struggled to push his Michael Caines back up his nose and waved over at me again. "It works. The phone books and the diallers create drag. All the lives and flows and interactions the shark has to pull along behind him slow him down, tire him out. And we're using this year's books and real-time phone calls, current events. They'll keep him up on the surface where we want him."

Using the cabin wall, I pulled myself up to my feet.

The barrel skidded and hiss-bounced across the water ahead of us.

"It doesn't look like it's slowing him down enough."

"No, but he won't be able to keep that up for long. I'm going to put another one on him just to make sure. What are you like at knots?"

"I'm, well –"

I cut myself off, pointing over the doctor's shoulder and out to sea. He turned around just in time to see the barrel suck down under the water and vanish.

"Well." He was quiet for a moment, staring at the empty ocean. "Scout, cut the engine. Eric, that lever over there. Drop the anchor."

"Where did he go?" Scout called down from the flying bridge.

"He went under," I said.

"Can he do that?"

"Evidently," Fidorous climbed back down onto the deck proper. "But not for long. That barrel will drag him up and when it does we'll be here waiting."

"He's clever," I said, maybe to myself. "It's like – it's like he was waiting to knock me over the side."

"A Ludovician shark is just a big stupid eating machine." Fidorous scooped up his cap and pulled it into place over his salt and pepper mop. "He attacked the boat and you were standing near the edge, that's all."

I nodded, looking out to sea.

"And you're absolutely sure there's no way that big stupid eating machine can get to us?" Scout asked, coming around the cabin.

Fidorous looked from Scout to me and back again, as if he couldn't believe what he was hearing.

"How many times? No. The *Orpheus* is built on a conceptual loop three times stronger than the one that's been keeping Eric safe all this time. We'll stay in here, he'll stay out there, and when that barrel drags him up we'll finish the job. The Ludovician and Mycroft Ward will be gone for good and we'll go home. Now, Sanderson, the anchor, if you please."

·

After half an hour, it became clear that the Ludovician wasn't coming up any time soon, no matter what Dr Trey Fidorous might say or think. I volunteered to stay on deck and keep watch for the barrel while Scout and the doctor went below to organise a meal and drinks. I'd meant to change my clothes again, but the shorts and the Hawaiian shirt were light and had dried out quickly in the heat. I'd lost my glasses and straw hat when I went over the side though and the back of my neck was hot, burned and painful whenever my collar rubbed against it. I felt the sting across my forehead and cheekbones too.

Evening came. The sky began to turn dusty and I decided to stay out by the prow in the cabin's long shadow, keeping up my watch on the waves. Scout did something to Nobody's laptop and the doctor cleared the remains of our food away and did whatever else needed to be done on boats in the quiet times. Ian reappeared and walked around the deck in clockwise circles for a while, then disappeared below deck as the air started to get chilly.

More time passed, still no sign of the barrel or the shark. The sky turned from deep red to blue-grey and the ocean swell subsided into an unconscious sort of rocking. A cool breeze breathed between the deck railings and soothed my sore neck with gentle fingers.

I knew something inside me had changed.

Partly, I'd offered to stay on deck and keep watch so I'd have time to sit and think about what the something might be. I kept visualising an old coin fallen by the side of an overgrown path, one face on show and exposed to the elements for years and years, the other face hidden and almost forgotten in the mud. When the word *water* turned to real water in the cellar, it was as if the coin had flipped over. The familiar face became buried and the other face came out into the air. The change wasn't huge – none of the memories the Ludovician had taken were back and none of the earlier Light Bulb dreams were any clearer – but it was there. The coin had flipped. From somewhere inside me a phrase rose up, *the view becomes the reflection, and the reflection, the view.*

"Hey."

Scout stood behind me on the deck. She was wearing that big waterproof coat I'd last seen in Fidorous's cellar.

"Hey," I said back.

"I brought you a jacket. It's sort of grunge circa 1992, but, you know –"

"Thanks," I said, pulling it on. "And listen –"

"Yeah, I know. Me too."

She sat cross-legged next to me on the deck.

"I should have told you," she said. "It was stupid not to."

"No," I said, "it wasn't. I completely get why you did it. I just –"

"You just have trust issues."

I looked at her. "*I* have trust issues?"

We stared out at the quiet sea. I pulled the jacket over my shoulders and watched her playing with her thumbs. "Is the laptop okay?"

"Oh, I was just tinkering with the connection. I've managed to crack its priority ranking so that Ward's less likely to notice it's open. Should buy us more time."

"Nice going."

"Thank you."

The quiet sea. The distant gulls. Scout sitting next to me.

"I said some horrible things, didn't I?"

"Yes," she said. "You did. But I pulled you out of the water anyway."

"Scout."

"I thought you were going to die, you tool."

"So did I. And I just – no, God that's so lame."

"Tell."

"I was scared of leaving you thinking I meant any of that stuff."

She nudged against me. "Awww."

"Of course, I was *also* scared of that gigantic fucking shark."

"Shush now," she said, "you're spoiling it."

I tucked my arm around her and she leaned into me. "Forgive me?"

"You *were* an arsehole."

"Hey, with some encouragement."

"Yeeaah, but your arsehole-ness wasn't for the greater good, was it?"

"No," I said, embarrassed, "that's true."

"You were doing it because you're emotionally stunted."

"Damaged. Emotionally damaged."

"Whatever."

I ran my fingers through her fine dark hair and she squeezed her arms together around my waist. The breeze rolled around us, the gentle sea tipping the boat this way and that way.

"I'm going to say something now," I said.

"Okay."

"It's going to make me look like an idiot."

"Okay."

"It might make you angry too."

"Hmmm. Okay."

"Right."

"Go on then."

"Okay. It wasn't just for this, was it? I mean, what happened with us?"

Scout leaned away from my chest and looked up at me.

"I said it wasn't."

"You say all sorts of things."

She tucked her head back against me and we sat quietly like that for a few minutes.

"Do you remember yesterday when we woke up; you said something really embarrassing about *knowing in your heart* that there was something, something *right* about what was happening with us?"

"Yeah," I said.

"And you asked me if I felt that too."

"I remember. You called me a stalker."

"Yeah, well, anyhoo. What I'm trying to say is that, yeah, I think I do."

"The heart thing, not the stalker thing?"

"The heart thing."

"Wow."

"Hmmm," Scout said. "I feel like I've known you for years and years. I mean, a lot of this stuff, feelings or whatever, it's like they've been in me all along. Does that sound crazy?"

"*Feelings or whatever?*"

"Don't make me say it, Sanderson."

I smiled. "No, it doesn't sound crazy. I know exactly what you mean."

"Good," she said, and she kissed me, gently on the lips.

The taste of her then, the touch and the warmth and the movement, all of it perfect, like the sweetest, saddest remembered note coming back through years of silence.

When she pulled away she gave me a look as though there had been something, something amazing she couldn't quite get a handle on.

"I know," I said, sort of helpless.

We kissed again.

•

When I opened my eyes, the cool blue morning was already being warmed by a fresh, enthusiastic new sun. My back and sides ached from sleeping on the deck and my knee seemed to have seized. A warm numbness filled my right arm where Scout slept curled into my shoulder. Some of her fine black hair had velcroed itself to my stubble and I pulled my head back to untangle us.

"Hmmm?" she said into my chest.

"Hey, it's morning."

"Ouch," she mumbled. "Somebody's superglued my joints."

We were under our coats and, I noticed, a thick green blanket that hadn't been there when we went to sleep the night before.

"Hey, we've developed a blanket."

Scout giggled. "You still *sans* pants?"

"Yeah, you?"

"Yep."

"You probably made his year."

"Awww, he was probably worried we'd be cold."

"Well, it worked. I'm sore, aching and exhausted, but I'm not cold."

Scout kissed my cheek. She pushed back our covers, climbed out of our makeshift bed and stood naked on the deck. Her legs, a band around her belly, her arms and her face, had all turned pink from yesterday's sun, but the ghost outlines of her vest top and shorts meant her ribs and breasts, her hips and the very tops of her thighs were still the same marble white. She put down a hand to cover the stripe of black hair between her legs and raised an eyebrow at me.

"What?" I said.

"You're staring."

"When a girl wanders around naked in front of a guy it usually means something."

She grinned and did a slow and very intentional stretch, both arms in the air, then both arms behind her head, twisting left and right at the waist.

"Blatant," I said.

"I ache," she said by way of an explanation, gave me a sideways little smirk and wandered over to the prow. "You should try it actually, it's very –"

"Liberating?"

"Something like that. It might help with your emotional stunting."

"Damage. We settled on *damage*."

"Awww," she said, staring out to sea.

I sat up, blanket covering my crotch and legs. The last few days had left me with a livid inventory of scrapes and bruises. Every joint in my body ached, especially my knee, but still I was swollen up inside with happiness. This moment – the early morning, me, Scout – it was absolutely perfect.

"Do you think it's going to come up again?"

I watched her poke a loose and frayed twist of rope over the side of the boat with her big toe.

"Fidorous thinks so."

She turned. "Yeah, for whatever that's worth. I'm going to check on Nobody's laptop."

"Listen, I'm sorry this isn't going to plan."

"Why, what did you do?"

I managed half a shrug before she broke out in a smile. "Hey," she said, finding her pants and pulling them on. "If it doesn't happen this time, we'll cope. We'll find something else, some other way to sort all this. It'd be best if you tried not to fall in the sea today though."

"Yeah, I was thinking that too." I passed her shorts to her. "Thanks, Scout."

"Well, it's true. And I am sorry, about what happened."

"Me too."

She knelt to collect her top but I reached my arms around her, pulled her down on top of me and kissed her.

"Hey," she laughed, breaking away and sitting up on top of me. We stayed like that for a moment, me looking up at her, her looking down at me. Scout's expression settled, became still, serious. She leaned in and kissed me once, twice, gently on the lips.

"You're amazing," I whispered.

She smiled an almost bashful little smile then leaned in close, face down into my neck. "You too," she said and the words were barely-shaped breath in my ear.

I wrapped my arms around her but she stretched herself free, her face full of that sharper, more familiar smile. "Come on," she patted me on the chest and clambered up to her feet. "We've got things to do."

"Awww."

She laughed. "Why don't you go and find us something to eat? Use up some of that excess energy."

"What do you want?"

"Hmmm, something light. And maybe, beer?"

I nodded. "Good plan."

When we were both dressed we walked together around the cabin side to the rear deck. Scout stopped and I almost bumped into her.

"Oh, come on," she said, "where the fuck did that come from?"

There was an island a dozen miles to stern.

•

I hobbled down the three steps from the deck to the cabin. As I came in, Fidorous was closing a wooden hatch in the floor.

"There's an island outside," I said.

"Hmmm?"

"Outside, there's an island." Then, looking at the hatch. "What you doing?"

"Routine maintenance. She's an old concept, you know, not as young as she used to be but – island, yes, I've seen it."

"Any idea how it got there?"

"None at all. Was the anchor lowered correctly?"

"Yeah, we checked it."

"Then maybe it hit sand. We may've been drifting all night."

"All night? Then we could be miles from the Ludovician."

"Don't worry about that. I have equipment which will sound an alarm as soon as that barrel breaks the surface. Once it's out of the water we can track it."

"He's been down a long time."

"He's a strong one, but he *can't* stay down forever. Don't worry, Eric, we're still ahead of the game. I'm glad the two of you sorted things out."

"Yeah." I found myself looking at the knots in the wooden floor. "Thanks for the blanket."

"Well, it looked like you were going to need it."

I felt my face purpling up.

"And now," Fidorous smiled. "You're probably wanting some breakfast, aren't you?"

Scout was sitting near Nobody's laptop at the back of the boat when I came up from the cabin with a couple of cans and a packet of chocolate digestives.

"Connection's still running," she said and I nodded, slowly sitting down next to her and passing her a can. "Did he have any ideas where that might have come from?"

I looked out across the water. The island rose up like a huge weathered bone, olive and tan, the colour of plastic soldiers. There was something else about it too, some sort of idea itch caused by the look of the place, the shape, something I couldn't quite –

"Hey," Scout said.

"Sorry," I cleared my head, tried to let the feeling go. "Yeah, I asked him about it and he thinks we might have drifted."

"Drifted?" She reached across me to grab her sunglasses. "What, in this weather?"

I looked at her, confused.

"Haven't you seen the sea?"

I looked out. The water was as clear and still as glass.

"Right," I said. "So maybe there are currents or something?"

"Maybe, but you'd see that thing for miles, wouldn't you?"

"Yeah," I said, staring out at the island again. "Yeah, you would."

Then two cogs deep inside my head meshed together and my brain identified the strange feeling. It was *familiarity*. I'd seen that island before. But how could I have? I wasn't the backpacking, island-hopping First Eric Sanderson. I'd never even left the country. I'd never seen *any* islands apart from maybe on TV, and why would I remember something like that? Then, from somewhere, that phrase again – *the view becomes the reflection, and the reflection, the view.*

The flipped-over coin, the hidden face. It felt like something huge was happening all around me but I couldn't quite set my mind to see it.

Scout, sunglasses on now, sipped her beer and stared out over the water. I did the same, leaning against her, lost in thoughts about the strange feeling, about the night before, about the shark still out there somewhere in the blue.

After a few minutes I put down my beer and pulled myself up onto my feet, planning to go and look for a new hat or something to cover my head. As I did, my toe caught the edge of my can and knocked it over. It rolled away, spilling foaming spits of beer as it went, and hit the railings on the other side of the boat with a hollow metallic *tunk*.

Scout looked up at me.

"What?"

She looked out at the calm flat sea, then over at my can of beer, then back to me again.

"We're not level," I said.

"It's *listing*. We're listing."

Scout got to her feet and the two of us walked across to the edge of deck where the can lay spilling out beer against the rails.

She bent to pick it up, stopped halfway down and straightened up again slowly.

"Did you hear that?" she said.

"What?"

"Listen."

The noise was faint and muffled, but it was there.

Burr burr, burr burr.

The barrel broke the surface a hundred yards off the port side.

32

Farewell and Adieu to You, Ladies of Spain

Fidorous marched out onto the deck with a ringing *something* in his hand that looked like an alarm clock with dials.

"He's up. The barrel's up."

"We know," Scout said. "It's right there."

The doctor clicked a button and the ringing stopped. The three of us stood together by the rails. The barrel floated motionless on the still ocean. *Burr burr, burr burr.*

"What's it doing?"

"Doing?" The doctor looked across at me. "He's not doing anything. He's spent the night trying to stay underwater and the barrel's finally dragged him up. He's exhausted."

"So why is he here?"

"Hmmm?"

"Of everywhere that shark could be in the whole ocean, why is he right here?"

"Maybe he isn't," Scout said. "Maybe he's ditched the barrel."

Fidorous tried to sound patient. "That barrel isn't floating there because the Ludovician is clever, it's floating there because he's stupid. Scout, can you get us alongside? Eric, it's time for you to get that spear ready."

"And," Scout said, not moving, "we're listing."

"This is amazing." The doctor stared out to sea, his hands gripping the railing knuckle-white-tight. "You're both *determined* to find a crisis, aren't you? Is it so completely inconceivable that I might know exactly what I'm doing and what is happening while we're out here? As I said to Eric less than half an hour ago, this is an old idea and therefore it needs maintenance, *as I expected*. For what little it seems to be worth, I can *promise* you both the *Orpheus* is sound. So," a big breath in, a big breath out, "stations everybody, please."

The last thing we needed now was an argument, so we did as we were told: Scout up to the flying deck, me gathering up the spear and checking the long looped cable was still firmly attached to the back of Nobody's laptop.

Fidorous pulled up the anchor.

The engine growled awake, shockingly loud in the still and quiet.

"Nice and slowly!" the doctor called out. "Easy does it."

The *Orpheus* glided itself through the mirror sea towards the barrel. Scout cut the engine and we slid to a slow stop.

With the spear in hand, I hobbled my way back to the port railings and joined Fidorous. The barrel just floated there, about four feet from the side of the boat, bobbing a little in the few little waves we'd brought with us.

Burr burr, burr burr.

"Can you see anything? Is it down there?"

Fidorous shook his head. "I can't see him, but he's there." He lifted a long pole with a hook at one end down from a bracket on the cabin wall.

"What are you going to do with that?"

"Pull the barrel line in and tie it off. Once we've got him attached to the boat we can winch the line up and –" the doctor leaned out over the water, stretching over the rail like a snooker player, the pole extended out in front of him "– we'll drag him to the surface if we have to."

I found my legs backing me towards the cabin side again.

The doctor reached and reached, one foot on tiptoes on the deck, the other in the air, one hand holding onto the boat's railings, the other stretching out the pole. He wobbled, wavered, lunged, his hook missing the rope and clipping the barrel side with a *thuunk*.

"Careful," my mouth said.

Still stretched out over the side, Fidorous turned to look back at me and was about to speak when the barrel exploded into life, kicking up a sudden blast of spray and jetting off across the water. The doctor jumped, losing the hook and almost overbalancing. I dropped the spear and leapt forward to grab him and pull him back from the edge.

"Was that –" I said. "Jesus, was he playing dead?"

Fidorous untangled himself from my arms and turned to see the barrel racing away over the flat sea.

"Scout, come down and tie off another harpoon. Eric, you'll have to drive. Quickly, come on both of you, move, move, move. We're going to catch Eric's clever shark."

I hopped around to the flying deck steps as Scout raced down them.

"Forward," she said, miming a throttle handle pushed down, "and side to side," she did a steering wheel with the other hand. "Got it?"

"Got it."

"The key's in the ignition." She planted a quick kiss and was gone.

I took the steps as fast as I could, pain shooting in my swollen knee. I found the key, turned it. *Orpheus* rumbled. I pushed down on the throttle experimentally and we belched out a heave of black smoke. The boat powered forwards and I steered for the speeding barrel.

Fidorous appeared on deck with his gun, taking a harpoon from Scout who then set to work roping up another barrel. The old man climbed up onto the prow gun plank, turned and waved up at me. "Faster, Tin Man. Come on, we need to get up close."

The air flapped and battered at me as we ploughed forwards, my shirt slapping my sunburn. I pushed down further on the throttle and the engine made a noise like a big animal starting to panic. Ahead of the barrel, something else broke the surface, a dark triangle of fin and behind it another, thinner, the Ludovician's tail.

"He's coming up. Eric, he's coming up. We need more speed. Come on."

"I don't – the engine. I don't want to –"

"She'll be fine, come on, we'll get another barrel on him and see if he can run then."

I pushed the throttle down a fraction further and the *Orpheus* grumble-screamed. Black and charred smoke poured from the exhaust pipes, but we were catching him, we were making ground on the shark.

Scout called *clear!* and the doctor's gun went off with a *thwap*. The harpoon struck the shadow of the shark just below the waterline. A second barrel launched itself off the boat and chased the first across the flat sea.

"Yes!"

I took some of the pressure off the engine, slowing us down.

"No," the doctor shouted up. "Keep after him, we'll put all three on him to make sure."

"Trey," Scout shouting now. "He's leading us out to sea. If –"

"We've almost got him. Eric, don't you let him out of range. Scout, tie off another barrel and we'll –"

I pushed down the throttle again. The exhausts choked on burning black smoke, we lurched forwards, then the engine's growl split with a scream of shearing metal. A broken, thrashing clunking from below deck and then, nothing. The boat drifted forward in shocked fatal-injury silence. I turned the key in the ignition but could only call up a weak, tinny, hacking sound.

"Oh, shit," I lifted my hands gently up from the controls and stepped back. "Oh, shit."

Out on our slowing prow, Fidorous lowered his gun as the shark and its barrels left us behind.

I looked down to see Scout crossing the deck towards the doctor. "Oh no, don't tell me, *not a major problem? What you expected?* You've still got all this completely under control now, have you?"

The doctor turned and climbed down from his bowplank. "A glitch in the translation. It happens occasionally, it's normal and it can be fixed just as easily here as back in dry dock so, yes, yes, I do have everything under control. Now if you can get *yourself* under control I can go and solve the problem."

"A glitch? Doctor, it wasn't a glitch – all three of us just heard the engine ripping itself to pieces. I mean, look around for fuck's sake. The truth is we're dead in the water and we're *listing*. I don't know a lot about boats or anything, but I do know that when they start to list it's usually because they're filling up with water."

"The truth is a complex mechanism, Scout, especially in this place, and I don't have the time or the inclination to sit down and explain its workings to you. If we're going to succeed here you're going to have to trust me to do my job and focus yourself on yours, do you understand?"

"Okay, fine. Just answer me this – are we taking on water or not?"

"It's just run-in. The conceptual loop has data cleaners which act as pumps and keep it clear and functional." The doctor went to leave the deck but Scout caught him by the sleeve.

"Hang on. Yesterday this boat was unsinkable and now we've got pumps keeping us afloat?"

"Okay, if everything has to be black and white for you, we'll do it that way. The bottom line is this conceptual loop is unbreakable, therefore whatever *appears* to be happening, we cannot sink. Can't you see that? It just can't happen."

"Oh, that's so good because for a second there I thought we were sitting on a sinking boat with no engine and with a *giant fucking shark* in the water."

"Christ," I said, "guys."

Two faces looked up at me from the deck. I pointed out to sea.

The barrels were completing a large gentle curve in the water and heading back towards us.

Scout pushed her sunglasses up onto her head. "Oh fuck. It's coming back. What, is it – is it *attacking* us?"

"Well, whatever it's doing, it's going to give us another shot at it."

Fidorous said. "Scout, tie another barrel off."

"Is that going to do any good?" I called down.

Fidorous looked up at me. "It can't keep this up with all three barrels. We've almost got him."

"Someone's almost got someone," Scout said, hand shielding her eyes, still staring out to sea.

"Dorothy."

"Aye, aye, captain."

The barrels picked up speed towards us, each one throwing up a jellyfish umbrella of water over and around itself. From up on the flying deck I could see the dark torpedo shadow of the shark rising up towards the surface. The fin broke the water again.

Fidorous stood out in his shooting position, gun at his shoulder. The Ludovician came higher in the water and I saw its wide flat head and snout, its fins like wings, its great flat muscle of tail powering towards us, all of it huge and grey and unstoppable.

"He's coming straight on," I heard myself shouting. "He's attacking the boat, Scout grab hold of something," I braced myself against the side of the control deck.

"My God," the doctor called out. "Hold on." *Thwap.* The harpoon hit the shark in the fin but the Ludovician didn't slow down at all, it came in faster, closer, closer, closer –

The splintering sound of crunching wood and the *Orpheus* leaned hard to port. I grabbed onto the boat's small windshield, pushed my feet against the flying deck side; Fidorous braced himself against his railings as buckets, boxes, ropes and everything else tumbled and clattered across the deck.

"Scout."

"It's alright, I'm okay." Her voice from somewhere I couldn't see.

A tub-thump-rumbling from underneath us, the Ludovician's barrels dragging under the hull. As I watched, the third and final barrel wrenched itself overboard with a splash and all three hiss-spray-skidded out and away across the flat ocean.

The *Orpheus* rocked itself slowly back to upright and then carried on over a little too far, listing to starboard.

I jogged down the steps and around the cabin. Fidorous and Scout were already at the railings.

Scout shook her head. "He's going under again."

"He can't, can he?" I said to the doctor, "Not with three barrels?"

Fidorous looked at me and I saw a crack in his conviction. "No," he said. "No, I don't –"

The skidding-away barrels suddenly dragged down underwater and disappeared, leaving only a slowing wave to run itself out across the still, dead surface.

"Oh, shit," Scout said. "Oh, shit."

I turned away from the railings, wrapped my arms around her and she pressed her face into my shoulder. I squeezed her tight and she squeezed back.

"It's okay," I said. "We'll figure it out, we'll figure all this out. Doctor?"

"I don't – I don't know," he said, still staring out at the empty sea.

"It's alright," I said again, my arms tight around Scout. "It's alright, come on, we'll come up with something." And looking over her shoulder as I spoke, looking out across the deck and the sea towards the rocky landmass rising up in the distance, I remembered.

I remembered where I'd seen the island before.

·

Inside the *Orpheus*'s cabin, Ian watched the three of us work with big frightened eyes.

Scout and Fidorous were clearing fallen clutter and furniture from the sloping floor to get to the maintenance hatch. I had my backpack tipped out on the bunk, sifting through clothes and boots, and plastic packets of books and files. *Come on, come on. Where are you?*

"Hey, could use some help here," Scout said. "What are you doing?"

"The island. I've seen that island out there before."

The clearing-away noises behind me stopped. "You've what?" Fidorous said. "Seen it where?"

I remembered the pocket in the top of the rucksack, unzipped it and pulled the little plastic bundle out. "On this postcard. I'd forgotten all about it, I found it in Sheffield and I put it in here." I turned around, struggling to unwrap the bundle. "It's Naxos, it's a picture of Naxos."

Scout looked carefully at me.

"The Greek island?" Fidorous said.

I nodded. "The best one, the one Eric and Clio spent most of their time on before, before what happened. That's Naxos out there right now, or, at least, it looks exactly like it. How can that happen? What does it mean, doctor?"

"I don't know. Give me Eric's notes, the ones you found in the bedroom."

I passed him the bag of fragments. My hands were shaking and I couldn't get the tape free and unwrap the postcard from its waterproof plastic so I pushed the bundle into the back pocket of my shorts. I clambered through the upturned cabin towards the door.

"Eric," Scout reached out and rested a hand on my arm. There was something in the way she said my name, something I was too distracted to hear.

"I've got to go out and see. I need to make sure I'm not crazy."

Scout let her hand drop and I climbed out of the cabin and onto the deck.

There it was, huge and real and out across the sea: the island. I pulled the bundle out of the back of my pocket and fought again with the cocoon of tape. Eventually, I managed to rip enough of it off, unravel the plastic and pull out the postcard.

The picture had changed.

Instead of the rocky, tan and olive island I remembered, the postcard now had a black and white picture of a small terraced house. The First Eric Sanderson's house. My house, the place where I'd woken up on the bedroom floor and called Dr Randle and watched snooker and made the celebrity chef meals. The place I'd left behind to set out on this whole journey now printed here on this little square of card. I looked from the picture in my hand to the island on the horizon. *The view becomes the reflection, and the reflection, the view.*

I turned around to see Fidorous standing behind me. I held up the postcard for him to see. "What does it mean?"

"I don't know, Eric." The doctor said quietly. He had the dust jacket with the secret note I'd found in the First Eric Sanderson's room in his hand. "I'm afraid, I really don't know."

"Guys," Scout's voice from inside the cabin. "You might want to come and look at this." I tucked the postcard into my back pocket.

Back inside the cabin, Scout had managed to get the hatch open and was sitting on the edge, legs dangling down the hole

"How's it looking?" I said.

Scout looked up. "Not too good."

"Not too good as in –?"

"As in full of water."

Fidorous kneeled down next to her, staring down. "The engine's gone and the boat's filling up faster than we can pump it out." He stared up at us. "But this isn't possible. It can't happen."

"What were you saying about the delicate nature of truth?" I said.

"Yes," Fidorous flung his arm out at the hole. "But it shouldn't – it *can't* cause this."

Scout's eyes narrowed thoughtfully at me before turning back to the doctor. "So, what are you telling us? We're sinking?"

He nodded, once. "Yes. We're sinking. I just don't –"

Scout stayed in professional mode. "How long do we have?"

"Maybe an hour."

She nodded. "And then we're in the water."

"The Ludovician," I said. "That's why it led us out to sea and attacked the boat: to put us in the water."

It looked as if Fidorous was about to give us his *stupid eating machine* speech again, but he didn't. "There's still time," he said instead, "those barrels *will* exhaust him. Nobody's laptop is still working and still connected to Ward, so if Eric can hit him with the spear –"

"I don't think he'll give us the chance," Scout said. "He's put a couple of holes in the boat and now he's gone away to wait for it to sink. I'm betting we'll be swimming by the time he comes back."

Fidorous stared down the hatch.

"Fine," I said. "So we've failed. We give up. We go back."

Fidorous shook his head. "It's not a simple thing. If anything, it's a more complicated process than getting here. It needs concentration and, even if we could concentrate – we don't have the time."

"So we're stuck here?"

"Yes, I'm afraid we are."

"There's no place like home," Scout said absently.

The doctor smiled a washed-out sort of smile.

"Okay, but I'm the only one the shark's interested in, I'm the one it wants." I dropped down onto the bed.

"Not anymore," the doctor said. "We're all mixed up together in this now."

I realised it was probably true. Both of them, especially Scout, were so strongly connected to me here and like this, that the shark probably wouldn't stop to think about the difference.

Ian climbed on my knee, nuzzling up. I put a protective arm around him.

"I'm sorry, guys."

Scout smiled a small smile at me. "Don't you be sorry. It was my plan, remember? You were the one who got conned into it."

"Oh yeah," I said, trying out a smile of my own.

All three of us were quiet.

"Right then." Scout pushed her hair back and crossed her legs. "What we need is logical thinking. Where are we up to? We've lost the engine. The boat's sinking. We still have the laptop and we still have the spear. Like the doctor said, if Eric can spear the shark before the boat sinks, we still win."

Fidorous nodded. "Very succinct."

"Our one big problem," Scout continued, "is getting the Ludovician to come in close enough and stay still enough to be speared before the boat goes under." She did a *size-of-things* sigh. "Any ideas?"

"We could lure him in," I said.

Both of them turned to me.

"Go on," the doctor said.

"If I get into the water, he'll come."

"Eric, you're not getting into the water." Scout stared at me. "That's crazy."

"No, it isn't," Fidorous said, his face brightening up. "No, it isn't, because we still have the Dictaphones. We have another conceptual loop."

·

The Dictaphones. Like the *Orpheus* itself and so many other things on board, they'd become something else on the way here. In fact, they'd become what the First Eric Sanderson always said they were – a real, live shark cage.

Scout and I manoeuvred the parts of the cage out of the storage locker and onto the deck one at a time. Each of the four sides was solid and heavy, a tough frame striped with heavy black plastic bars. We held them in place as Fidorous bolted them together and to the cage base with a series of rubber plugs and bolts that might once have been *stop, play* and *record* buttons. When the thing was finished, the doctor went back down into the cabin to find the scuba equipment.

The two of us stood on the sloping deck, both looking at the cage.

"You can't go into the water in that."

"Why can't I?" Scout said. "You were ready to go into the water with nothing."

"Scout, it might as well be nothing."

"It kept you safe all this time."

"But things have changed. This boat is built on a conceptual loop ten times more powerful than the Dictaphones and the Ludovician still punched holes in it. He'll rip this thing to pieces."

"Three times more powerful." She came over and put her hands against my arms, gave me a squeeze and a tight smile. "Believe me, if you've got something else in mind, I'd *really* love to hear it."

There was nothing for me to say.

"See," she said.

"I really don't want you to do this."

"I don't want me to either, but you're the only one who can spear the Ludovician and Fidorous is the only one who knows how to get us back. That means I'm the one who has to go down in the cage."

I looked at her.

"Come here." She wrapped her arms around me and I held her tight.

"Don't," I said.

"I've got to," she said quietly against the side of my face. "This is how it goes, it's what happens next." She kissed my cheek. "This has to happen and we both know it."

And the thing was, I *did* know it. The postcard, the island, Fidorous, Randle, even the Ludovician. Everything that had happened to me from the moment I woke up on the bedroom floor, in some way I couldn't quite understand, was all a part of the same great big *something*, and Scout going down in the cage was part of it too. It *had* to happen. I just knew.

"Scout," I said, "what's going on?"

She let out a tiny breath. "I'm right, aren't I?"

I nodded, pulling her tight against me.

A few moments later, Fidorous came up from the cabin with a scuba diver's air cylinder and something like an inflatable life jacket squeezed under one arm.

"I've got something to say," he said, after we'd helped him lay the cylinder down next to the cage. "I'm sorry, sorry to both of you. I let you down once, Eric, and now I've done it again. I've let both of you down." As he spoke, all the guards and masks and personas dropped away. Finally, here was the real Fidorous: a tired and apologetic old man stepping out from behind his grand curtain.

"There's no need to –"

"No, Eric, please don't make excuses for me. This is my fault. I'm a stupid, egotistical old fool who thought he could put everything right just like one of the old stories. But the truth is, I'm no Tekisui."

"Hey, hang on a minute," Scout said. "Don't forget all of this was my idea and he was mad enough to go along with it. If anything, *we're* sorry for dragging *you* into this whole mess."

"Yeah," I said.

The doctor looked at us for a moment then he nodded a small nod of thanks.

In the heat of the sun, I felt a sad wintry smile blowing over my face.

"Anyway," Scout said, "what is that?"

Fidorous held out the thing he'd carried out of the cabin along with the air tank. I'd thought it was a life jacket but it wasn't, it was a child's inflatable dinghy.

"It's the cat's," he said, "his carrier."

And we laughed then, me and Scout holding each other and Fidorous holding the blow-up boat. We laughed the way people laugh on the edge of dark and dangerous times, like little sparklers out in the night.

•

The *Orpheus* was listing strongly now, the starboard side several feet nearer the water than the port and the mast pointing to five past the hour. It made matters worse that the winching arm was fixed to starboard and when we lowered the cage down over the side it added maybe another minute to the ticking-away mastclock.

Scout wore a wetsuit, a scuba tank and had her mask pulled up on top of her head. She also had a couple of my T-shirts on to *lend her some extra Eric Sanderson.*

Scout was ready. The cage was ready. It was time.

"Okay, hero," she said. "Shark comes at the cage, you stab shark with spear. Shark and Ward are connected. No more shark. No more Ward. Easy, right?"

"Easy," I said, reaching out and taking hold of her hand.

Fidorous brought the spear over, trailing cable.

"Scout –" I started. "There are things I want to –"

"Don't. Save it and tell me when I get back."

"They say that in war films, bomber pilots usually."

She laughed, "I can't believe you just said that." She put her arms around my waist and kissed me. When we broke apart she smiled. "You're a bit of a geek sometimes, you know?"

"Yeah," I said. "Scout, please be careful."

"I will."

Walking across to sit on the edge of the boat, she wet her goggles and climbed down into the cage. We closed the top and the winch arm rattled and lowered it further into the water. I held up my hand in a low little wave. Scout did the same small wave back as she disappeared down into the blue.

For the next fifteen minutes there was only a still and tense nothing. Scout's bubbles breaking the surface, Fidorous going from port to starboard, from stern to bow watching the water, Ian padding the deck and wanting to stand as near to me as he could, an occasional protesting creak of timbers, the mastclock counting away our time as the sinking *Orpheus* tipped further towards the sea. Me standing by the winch arm with the spear.

And then it happened.

It all happened very quickly.

A loud tub-thump-rumble beneath us – *it's come up under the boat* – and then the cage swaying away – *thump*. Bubbles and spray. The *Orpheus* moaning, leaning further over. *Burr, burr*. Bubbles and spray and flashes of a huge grey shape in white churning water. Me holding up the spear and not being able to see anything but the grey in the white water and me shouting something. Splashing, sheets hitting me and the deck, with something thrashing the calm sea into a foam and me shouting *get her up, pull, pull it up* and me shouting *I can't see it properly*. The barrels throwing around in the foam and the winch squealing and the water and foam and the shape, a huge tail pounding out of the water. Fidorous, his mouth shouting something without words in the noise and the winch straining and me shouting something and the barrels and the tail and the thrashing the water. The *Orpheus* lowering towards the thrashing and the metal and me holding the spear and shouting. Fidorous saying *he's tangled up* and *he's tangled up in the cable* and the barrels and the spear and the foam and spray. The cage coming partway out of the water and being crushed and ripped open and empty and with one of the barrels on top – *burr burr* – and me screaming and holding the spear. The tail, the shark's belly, a fin like a curved white knife. The *Orpheus* lowering into the water and the doctor shouting and me shouting at the empty cage and the doctor saying *dragging us under* and *cut it loose* and him with a knife, a machete. The boat creaking, lowering into the water, the doctor climbing over the railings with one foot on the empty chewed-up cage hacking at the cable. Foam and spray, the tail, the barrels bobbing and the tail smashing the water. Me shouting and holding up the spear and Fidorous hacking at the ropes tangled up in the cage. The Ludovician's head like a great grey and white bullet anvil jumbo jet rising up out of the spray and me screaming and throwing the spear.

The spear in the air.

The spear in the air trailing cable.

The spear in the air. Too high. The spear over the shark's head and hitting only the empty white water behind and sinking. The black cable unravelling on the deck. The boat creaking. Fidorous hacking at the ropes and the mangled cage and me diving for the cable unravelling on the deck and grabbing it, pulling on it. Pulling it back, reeling in the spear. Foam and spray and sheets of water. A splitting crack. The winching arm ripping from the side of the boat and crashing down hard, Crashing down hard onto Dr Fidorous and both him and the arm crumpling into the cage and cables and rope and barrels and Fidorous crushed down there by the winching arm. Blood. Me shouting and grabbing the railing and reaching and the doctor in the tangle of metal and wood and ropes reaching and then everything – cage barrels winching arm tangle of cords and the doctor and his reaching reaching reaching arm dragged down and away into the sucking foam and the waves coming together over the top with a clap-crash. The boat tipping. The foam bubbles settling and popping and the water getting still. The spear's cable unravelling fast on the deck and me grabbing for it and it jerking hard at my elbows and shoulder joints and burning my hands. Nobody's laptop rattling across the sloping deck and me throwing my body down on the cable between the laptop and the side of the boat so the laptop hit my back hard and the cable ripped out of its socket and the jack sliced at my ribs and shot across the deck, over the railings and gone down into the sea.

Silence and only the sinking creaking boat to break it.

The water coming up over the railings and the mast dipping toward the sea.

Me on my back sobbing.

Gravity slowly pulling everything across the deck and towards the blue.

33

The Light Bulb Fragment
(Part Three/Encoded Section)

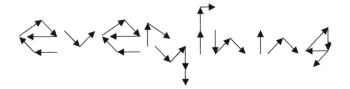

Everything is over.

The last of the summer still finds its way through the clouds some afternoons, but the night is coming in earlier and the fat-bodied spiders have built a maze of webs across the alleyway at the bottom of the garden. In the early morning they're all silver with dew. I'd not really noticed any of this until today. For me, it still feels like late August. The clocks tick but nothing seems to change, no matter how far the hands travel.

Clio's mum came to the house about a week ago for some photographs and an old scarf Clio wore when she was a kid and had somehow hung onto. I'd never even seen the scarf before but I pretended it was a big deal for Clee and nodded in the right places and fetched some tissues when her mum started to cry. She'd brought some photo albums with her and she showed me pictures of all the Clios I hadn't known – Clio at school with too-big teeth and gaps and pigtails playing an angel in a nativity play, Clio the baby in the bath and with food on her face, Clio the teen with black tights, short skirt, a tie knotted all *don't-give-a-fuck* to one side, Clio the girl guide all excited at camp, Clio the A-level student with her army shop clothes and chin-length hair at a festival, around the time they found out she had cancer. Her mum quizzed me on everything that happened in Greece, everything to do with the accident and not to do with the accident, and each time I told her something I could see her concentrating, like she was saving it in her head, storing it all up.

I know I probably won't see any of her family again. It's just too hot and too sharp and we'll only cut ourselves on each other if we try to stay in touch.

It's midday. All Clio's stuff is gone.

For so long I didn't touch anything. Timelessness again, the house like a secret temple as dust built up on things that were never meant to have dust on them – Clee's toothbrush and hairdryer and left-out-of-the-box CDs and deodorant on the bathroom window ledge. Ordinary things carefully kept in place because the last person to touch them would never put a cup down on the edge of the table again, or ever leave a book half-read. The world strained to move on without her and I strained to hold back the tide. My dad came over to see me not too long ago. He's not too good at talking, my dad, but he did try to tidy up a bit as I made him a coffee. He moved one of Clio's books and I screamed at him until I almost lost my voice but he still didn't understand and tried to put the book back where it was, saying *there, look, it's alright, see? You'd never know.* In the end he just held onto me as I sobbed and I knew he was crying too, but silently, white stripes down his tough stubbly face.

Clio drowned scuba diving off the coast of Paros. Wreck diving. She'd seen a flyer for the diving school and went on and on and on about it. In the end, we left Naxos a couple of nights early so she could go and try it out on the way back to the mainland.

When the police came to find me I was sitting outside our new hotel, drinking an Amstel beer and finishing off my Paul Auster book. It was early evening and I was thinking about pizza and cocktails and finally getting back to the UK. I was thinking about drunken sex a couple of nights earlier and the way our breath and sweat formed up on the plastic insides of our tent and how we lay there tangled together with all our stuff kicked around.

'*Maybe a cramp.*' They put me in a little room with a fan and a jug of water. The faces came and went and sometimes I didn't hear what they told me until hours later. '*Maybe a cramp. A second of panic. A gasp of seawater.*'

A gasp of seawater. How much is a gasp? Not much, maybe half a glass, half a glass of ordinary everyday seawater. Just picture it sitting in front of you, visualise it, it's nothing, is it? *It's nothing.* Stupid and pointless. It's like dying from being five minutes late. It's like dying because you've forgotten your fucking wallet.

Sometimes, late at night, the phone would ring. For the first few weeks after I got back it happened all the time. I'd sit up in bed for hours, waiting for it – *burr burr, burr burr. Burr burr, burr burr* – then Clio's dad's voice would say '*I want you to tell me about*' or '*stupid fucking cunt*' or '*sorry. Listen, I'm sorry*' or '*it's not – why would this*' or '*little girl*' or '*weren't you looking after*' or '*I can't, I just can't –*'. Sometimes there would be no words at all, just three, four, five heaving sobs then the line would go dead.

I'd always say the same thing to him,

"I'm sorry, I'm so so sorry." I'd cry for a long time after he'd hung up, sometimes all night. I never told anybody.

I'm always remembering details. Just a second ago it was how we finally managed to cook ourselves a full English on our little camp stove the night before we packed up the site on Naxos and headed for the boat. All these memories, they all hurt so much and each one in a different way so I don't think I'll be able to stand it without tearing open and spilling the aches out all over the floor. What's even worse, what drives me sick is this: none of the things I think I remember about her are all-the-way true or complete. I'm already losing her to generalisations, the endless Chinese-whispering of memory. I'd written a sort of journal while we'd been away and even reading through it for the first time I could see how full of holes it was. We were never that cool or that witty. We didn't say things in just the right way all the time, or even a quarter of the time. There's nothing in there about how Clio could sometimes be unkind or about how easily she could lie to people if she thought it was better for them not to know things. There's nothing about the times when she wasn't funny or sexy, or when she talked too much or about her pissing or shitting. There's no way to really preserve a person when they've gone and that's because whatever you write down it's not the truth, it's just a story. Stories are all we're ever left with in our head or on paper: clever narratives put together from selected facts, legends, well edited tall tales with us in the starring roles. I've read the journal so many times now the lines are all wooden and obvious, as unrealistic as a daytime soap or a famous Hollywood movie you've seen a thousand times. The characters look like me and Clio but they aren't us, they're just actors speaking the exact same stylised words over and over and over, with everything true falling away through the cracks.

Three weeks after I got home, I got a phonecall. The Greek police had Clio's waterproof camera and wanted to know if I wanted it back. It arrived five days later.

A Kodak photo packet with thirty-six photographs of colourful exotic fish sat here on the kitchen table for a long time. I looked and looked and looked at those pictures for hours, days, until I could see them with my eyes closed, until I knew every fish and I knew every composition. I could tell you anything about any of them – the ones perfectly in focus, the ones too close or motion blurred, the three where Clio's thumb was a pale pink moon over the corner of the frame. I looked at them so much, some days I did nothing else.

Early yesterday morning, when the spider's webs were full of dew, I drove into town, to a building site where they're putting up a leisure centre or a cinema, and I took the fish pictures and negatives out of their wallet and threw them one by one down a deep dark shaft sunk into the earth. Then I came back here and began to pack and clean and tidy.

I took all your things away, Clee. Gave them away, sent them away. I thought it was the right thing. I did it because I didn't think I could hold back the world anymore.

But I went too far.

Sitting here now, in this empty house, I know I should never have thrown your underwater pictures away. Yesterday, it was as if those thirty-six photographs *were* what happened to you. I hated them, blamed them, kicked them and threw them across the room. I couldn't cope anymore with them being there on the table, in the house, even in the world. But now they *are* gone, all I can think about is how much you wanted that underwater camera and how you'd been so excited about seeing those pictures, seeing if they came out. All I think about is me laughing and you splashing about in the surf with that camera on Naxos, looking for the next bright or big or not-quick-enough fish and throwing yourself into the waves. I think about how happy we were there, in that place, in our tent, on that beach. It breaks my heart and I want those photos back, Clee. I want them back so much. I can't believe what I've done.

I gave our landlord notice last week. I'm going to move away for a while. I haven't told anyone I'm going, not even my dad. I don't know if that's the right thing or not but the truth is I can't face anyone, I can't stand being me anymore.

I miss you, Clio.

I'm so, so sorry.

34

Last Stand

Slipping, sliding, I heaved myself up to my feet. Staggering on the wet sloping deck with Nobody's laptop tucked under my arm, I shouted out at the still water. "Scout."

The ocean flatlined everywhere I looked.

"Scout. Doctor Fidorous."

Nothing.

"Jesus," I heard myself saying it. "Scout," and then, propping myself up against the sloping cabin, quietly, wet with sobbing tears, "Clio."

Just the sounds of the *Orpheus* creaking.

The calm sea creeping, rising slowly up the decking in little bathtub waves.

The sea gently sucking the boat down into itself, as if the whole ocean was one gigantic, single-celled animal, feeding on what was left of the world.

We all go down into the water and we never come back up.

This is how it ends.

Meow. Meeeoow. A big-eyed Ian staring out from the corner of the tilted cabin door. I looked around and saw his carrier-inflatable dinghy amongst all the rubble and slid-down-across-the-deck-junk which was starting to escape into the sea.

Rubbing wet out of my eyes with a forearm, I clambered up and tucked the laptop against the cabin's port side, the side furthest away from the water. With the *Orpheus* tilting over to starboard, the port side and the deck made a sort of tipped-over V, a temporary storage space.

Meow.

"I know," I said, making my way back down to him. "So am I."

I picked Ian up and gave him a squeeze, putting my nose down and breathing in his old fur coat smell. "So am I."

I half-slid, half-climbed down the deck again with the cat held tight against my chest and I put him into his little boat.

"Stay," I said, tears slid down my face, salty in the sun. "If you only ever listen to me this one time, *please* just stay."

Ian looked up at me, trembling. His big face pleaded with me to pick him up again, but he didn't move.

"Good cat," I said, starting to move away. "Stay, you just stay there."

I clambered back up the wet, sloping deck, my boots squealing and slipping against the wet wooden planking. I made it up to the cabin and hauled myself through the leaning door and down the steps. I came out with a plastic package of Light Bulb Fragment books and the other bits and pieces from the First Eric's room. Sliding back down to the waterline, I tucked them into the little boat with the cat.

Meow.

Ian danced to be lifted out of the dinghy.

I stroked his head and he nuzzled up hard against me.

"I know, I know, but you've got to say there. I'm sorry, but you've got to. Understand? It's not safe for –"

The *Orpheus* groaned, rolled over a few degrees and Ian and his little boat began to lift free of the sinking deck. The cat stared back at me, terrified as the dinghy cleared the *Orpheus* in a little gravity swirl of flotsam and jetsam.

"Good luck," I whispered and he began to gently drift away.

•

"Alright," I shouted out to the flat sea, my voice shaking and tear-cracked. "Alright then, where are you? Where are you, shark, because I'm right here. I'm right here." I dragged in shuddering breaths. "And I've got nowhere left to run."

The *Orpheus* leant at 45 degrees now, low in the ocean, water climbing up the deck. I clambered up into the V made from the listing cabin's port side and decking. I reached and stretched to look down over the high-in-the-air port railings but there was nothing, no sign of the Ludovician, just miles of empty sea and the island in the distance.

"Come on, I know you're there," I called out across the empty water. "You're always there aren't you? What are you waiting for?"

I scrambled along the sinking V, collected Nobody's laptop and climbed up the sloping side of the cabin onto the flying deck. I slung my legs over the side, looking down at the water rising up to meet me.

The sea rose quicker and quicker and the boat creaked over, the once vertical side of the flying deck now a sort of shelf with me sitting at the edge, my legs dangling down at the knees.

I carefully checked the little chrome aerial then flipped the laptop open. The screen was still active, still blue, still connected, complex white Mycroft Ward code flowing down it like a word waterfall.

Thank you.

I pushed it almost shut, closed my eyes and swallowed.

The water came up fast now, touching the bottom of my boots and then rising towards my ankles, my feet wet and cold, and all of me shaking.

"Come on," I gasped, "I'm here. Where are you?"

I listened to the creaking of the boat, the slap of the rising water, to my own shivery sobs. The water coming up my over shins.

"Where are you?"

And then –

Burr, burr

A knotted mass of barrels and cage burst out of the still ocean a hundred and fifty yards away. Slowly, the heap of things began to drag itself across the water towards me.

"Come on," I said under my breath, "here I am." And I started to kick my legs in and out of the water, slowly at first and then faster, making a white fuss of spray and noise. "Here I am." The pain from my injured knee made my teeth bite themselves down and my lips pull back but I kept kicking.

The wreckage picked up speed, throwing a messy wave out around itself, bouncing up white plumes of spray.

Burr, burr, burr, burr

"Come on," I shouted. "Here I am. Come on."

The fin lifted, cutting the water ahead of the barrels into that long and precise tumbling bow wave. I kicked and shouted and shouted and kicked. The Ludovician came faster, higher, closer, closer.

Burr, burr, burr, burr, burr burr

"That's it," I screamed. "I'm ready to look at you now, you fucking thing. I know what you are and I'm ready to see you properly."

It came up at me in a burst of spray – memories and regrets and wishes and sadness and happiness and dreams – the shark's head, two black toy eyes either side of a huge grey bullet anvil jumbo jet slashed open all across into a black and red funnel full of teeth.

I know what you are.

I threw the laptop into its open red hole and tumbled backwards off the flying deck as the Ludovician crashed it into splintering wood and then –

35

Just Like Heaven

The explosion blasted a hole in the sea, the pressure forcing tons of deep water up and out into a violent high-rolling wave. It heaved me up and out with it, lurching me along and over, throwing my feet over my head and tumbling me down into the bass thunder-hum of the blue. I came up retching into a ghost world of thick mist and spray. Remains of shark and boat rained down loud and half-seen in the mist, a meteor storm of shadows. Wide-eyed and gasping, I splash-ducked as a huge chunk of splintered hull came spinning out of the white and punched down hard into the ocean behind me.

Bobbing up, coughing and spitting, I swam through waves and chop to the fallen lump of *Orpheus*, clambered my top half onto it and held tight as the last of the debris dropped, fell and fluttered from the sky.

The sea finally calmed itself into a traumatised rocking sway but the mist held in place above it, an entire second ocean of net curtains and spider webs, haunted and swaying and quiet. I pressed my head down against the wooden planking, shaking and cold, gulping back deep shuddery sobs. I pushed myself up a little and tried to look around, looking for Ian and his little boat, looking for anything, but I could only see maybe six feet in each direction and there was nothing else in my little patch of ocean. I was all alone in the white. I slumped back down onto the wood.

I felt something, a faint vibration like the tiniest muscle spasm in the back of my thigh. *I'm injured*, I thought, *I'm cut open and the cold is keeping it numb and vague*. I reached a hand down and around to investigate and found the postcard in the back pocket of my shorts.

I touched it again and, yes, it felt like the little oblong of card was humming. I carefully pulled it out of my back pocket, resting on the bobbing wreckage with my elbows to get a better look.

By now the postcard was soggy, pulpy and coming apart at the edges, but I didn't notice. Something amazing took up all of my attention: the little black and white picture of my house was moving.

As I stared, a tiny pixellated starling flutter-jumped and flew from the pixellated telephone line. Pixellated trees waved in a pixellated wind. A grey pixillated Volkswagen flashed across the frame, driving up the out-of-shot road.

I brought my finger up to touch the surface of the image, but there *was* no surface. My finger went straight through and became another moving part of the picture. I pushed my hand, my arm inside. I felt the cold rainy air, the *real* air on the other side of the postcard. I stared down at the picture, made my pixellated hand squeeze itself into a pixellated fist and then released it, stretching and waving my black and white fingers.

I could hear road traffic. Other sounds too – a baby crying, the sound of somebody's TV through an open window – noises drifting in across the surface of the misty water. As I looked around, faint shadows began to appear in the white. Familiar silhouettes formed themselves around me, a skyline of terraced rooftops and trees, TV aerials and chimney pots, the telegraph pole in the garden of the house across from mine.

I pulled my arm out of the picture. The sounds quickly subsided and the shapes faded away, back into the mist.

I stared down at the postcard. Another pixellated car flashed across the frame, but silently now. I could just make out the rain, coming down heavier, lancing across the scene in little slashes of grey. I looked for a while at my black and white house.

"No," I said to the picture, quietly, eventually. "I'm not going back, I'm never going back. *One foot in front of the other*, trying to be brave and trying to be strong? Coping and keeping going, why would I want that?" I felt the hot tears. "She's dead." My head dropped down into the crook of my elbow. "She's dead and I'm so, so sick of surviving," and I cried and cried and cried.

Bleak, white-washed moments passed.

And then.

A patch of warmth touched my back. I looked up. Sunrays, sunlight was cutting down through the mist and spotlighting little travelling pools of blue onto the cold ocean. I shifted myself around on the *Orpheus* wreckage, trying to see through the clearing mist for Ian's little boat. I shifted again, trying to get a better view and that's when I noticed what was happening to the postcard in my hand. The black and white picture of my house was fading away, the black receding into the white. Before long the image had gone all together, leaving the postcard completely blank. I went to touch the new surface but stopped: the little card was humming again, vibrating faintly against the tips of my finger and thumb. The hum only lasted for a moment but when it stopped the postcard seemed to have changed itself into something else, something thinner and less pulpy, something with a clean and glossy finish. As I watched, a new picture began to develop, not black and white this time, but alive with spreading reds and blues and yellows and greens. Within a few seconds I was holding, not a postcard, but an underwater photograph of a brightly coloured fish.

I stared at the picture, overwhelmed by an immense feeling of inter-connectedness, a crushing weight of relevance I could feel but couldn't quite find. Something huge happening here. Something, so, so important . . .

A fountain of bubbles erupted a few feet from my chunk of the *Orpheus* and I tried to scramble the bottom part of my body out of the water and up onto the broken hull-side.

Then Scout's masked head broke the surface and she waved, spitting out her air valve.

"Hey," she said, grinning.

"Jesus." I stuffed the picture into my back pocket, laughing and sliding down the hull and into the water to meet her.

Scout laughed too, pulling off her scuba mask and swimming towards me. I grabbed her and she grabbed me and we pulled ourselves together through the water, wrapping our arms around each other, squeezing tight, holding on and laughing like crazy.

"I thought you were dead," I said, when I finally found the breath. "Oh, God, I thought you were dead,"

"The shark put a hole in the cage," she said. "When he got tangled up, I sort of, slipped out."

"You sort of slipped out," I repeated, looking at her like I couldn't believe it, shaking my head.

We kissed then. We kissed up against the flotsam and jetsam hull, tight together as if it was the end and the beginning of the world, as if there was nothing else and never would be.

"I can't believe you're here," I said quietly as we broke apart.

"I can't believe you did it," she smiled up at me. "You did it, Eric."

I gave a helpless sort of shrug. "I know."

"What about the doctor?"

I shook my head.

Scout looked down at the water.

"The cage and the barrels and the shark all got tangled and he was trying to cut the lines. It all happened so fast, one minute he was – I mean, I didn't know for a second what had happened and then –"

As I stumbled on, trying to get the words out, Scout looked deep, deep into my eyes. "It's alright," she said calmly, eventually, putting a hand on my shoulder. "I know you couldn't have done anything."

"I couldn't reach him. I tried to get hold of him but I wasn't fast enough and –"

"It wasn't your fault."

"The winching arm came free so suddenly, I –"

"Eric, please."

"What?"

"You need to really listen to me. I'm trying to tell you something important, okay?"

I looked at her. She brought her hand up and laid it gently on the side of my face.

"You didn't do anything wrong," she said. "Sometimes things go bad and there's nothing anybody can do about it. None of what happened was your fault, Eric. I don't blame you for it, do you understand? I don't blame you. It was an accident."

Everything came together then. The whispering nonsense and that huge *something* I hadn't been able to find, all of it focusing into one bright, brilliant realisation.

In that one moment, I understood it all.

"Oh, God."

Scout smiled.

"Thank you," I said, my eyes hot and wet and stinging.

"It wasn't your fault," she whispered, crying too.

"I love you. I always, always loved you. You know that, right?"

"I know that," she said. "I enjoy spending time with you too."

I laughed a wet laugh. "I hate that one."

"I know," she grinned, tear-striped. "You're too easy."

And we held each other tight, crying as the last of the mist cleared around us.

"Hey," Scout patted me on the back, "is that Ian over there?"

I turned to look. Ian's yellow dinghy bobbed in the distant swell. Miles behind him and out across the sea, the island rose up high and stony, hazy in the distance.

"Ian!" I shouted out, half to the cat and half with the joy of seeing his little boat. I waved in his direction. "I think I can see him. Can you see him?"

"Oh, yeah," she nodded, staring out, shielding her eyes from the sun. "You're going to be in so much trouble. Come on."

"Scout."

"Yeah?"

"It is over, isn't it?"

"Yes. It's over." She looked at me. "Are you okay?"

I nodded. "I'm glad," I said quietly. "Where do we go now?"

She pointed out towards the island.

"Yeah, but I mean what is that, what is it really?"

Scout smiled. "Home."

.

Ian frowned out over the water like an old-fashioned sea captain as the two of us swam his little boat towards the distant shore.

We were about halfway there when small towns of square white buildings started to light up in the dusty evening. As night drew in, we steered the dinghy towards a stretch of friendly looking coastline, a long strip of beach where the hanging lanterns of *tavernas* and waterfront bars laid multicoloured stripes out across the waves.

36

Goodbye Mr Tegmark

2 >> NEWS

Body of missing man found

The body recovered from foundation works in the Deansgate area of Greater Manchester area last night has been identified as missing Derby man, Eric Sanderson.

Sanderson, who is thought to have been suffering from a rare mental illness, disappeared from his home last autumn becoming the subject of a large-scale police manhunt.

Police were first alerted by a Missing Persons report filed by retired psychologist and academic, Prof. Helen Randle. Randle is alleged to have been providing private treatment to Mr Sanderson for over two years without notifying the relevant health authorities of his condition. She maintained again today that her actions had always been 'completely proper'. Police are expected to interview Randle again in the light of Sanderson's death.

It is believed that Mr Sanderson may have been suffering from a rare mental condition known as psychotropic fugue. Psychotropic fugue is said to twist, confuse, cut out and rewrite memories and events in the mind of the sufferer. 'It's difficult to imagine what he must have been going through,' said police psychologist Dr Ryan Mitchell during this morning's press conference.

Sanderson's condition is thought to have been the result of prolonged emotional trauma stemming from the death of his girlfriend Clio Aames, who drowned in a scuba diving accident while the pair were on holiday in Greece.

As a result of this morning's identification, police have dismissed the postcard received by Prof. Randle earlier this week and previously believed to have been sent by the missing Sanderson, as a 'cruel and malicious hoax'.

POST CARD

THIS SPACE MAY BE USED FOR CORRESPONDENCE

FOR ADDRESS

Dear Dr Randle

Whatever happens, please don't
feel bad.I'm well and I'm happy,
but I'm never coming back.

Here's lookin at you kid,

Eric Sanderson

Dr H Randle

M███████████

Derby

Acknowledgments

Thanks first and foremost to my wonderful and supportive girlfriend Charlotte Bozic – you're amazing. Thanks to my great friend Maggie Hannan for absolutely everything, from Alvarez to Zest. Thanks to Toby Litt and Ali Smith for giving me a break in *New Writing 13*. Thanks to David Mitchell for the notes and the chocolate, to Scarlett Thomas for pointing me in the right direction and to my agent and friend Simon 'The Shark' Trewin for making all this happen. Thanks to Francis Bickmore, editor and partner in conceptual crime, for investing so much in Eric's world and for all the hours of discussion and un-logic testing which have made such a difference to the finished book. Thanks to Jamie Byng – a man with jet fuel and enthusiasm for blood – for his unshakable belief in conceptual fish and to Jessica Craig for making so many other people believe in them too. Big thanks to everyone else at Canongate who has made every aspect of publishing *The Raw Shark Texts* such a fantastic experience (I hear there are other publishing houses, but I'm not sure I believe it . . .). Thanks to Jane Stubbs and Arts Council England, Yorkshire and to Paul Holloway and Hull City Arts Unit for all their help, support and faith. Thanks to James Russell, Helen Tuton and Rob Davie for their initial red pen work. Thanks to Abi Walker, Lee Fenton, Colin Hurst, Stephen Walker, Helen Ridler, Nick Broughton, Matt Clarke, Rebecca Woods, Paul Hardy, Mike Galvin and everyone else (you know who you are) for the years of fun and trouble that made this book possible. Thanks to my family for being so supportive and never saying, 'So when are you going to get a real job?' Final thank-yous to St John Donald, Katherine Butler and Peter Czernin for their ongoing work in evolving this Ludovician's celluloid cousin.

Undex (Incomplete UK)

Negative 36b/36

Key:
P = Prologue
N= Negative

ABERDEEN
CITY
LIBRARIES